BLAZING PASSIONS...
SCORCHING SINS...

Dominique de Lasqueront—a handsome French aristocrat caught in the grip of a treacherous double life. Tormented by Christina's beauty, he would stop at nothing—neither violence nor betrayal—to unveil the secrets of her innocence.

Carlotta DeCorba—as dark and sultry as Christina was blond and high-spirited. A woman of violent temper and smouldering lusts, she was determined that Kade Renault would belong to her and her alone.

Blaise Evrion—a woman whose passionate Creole blood had longed for freedom until, in a moment of truth, she understood the meaning of love—and left a mysterious legacy that would one day guide Christina to an enduring gift of love.

THEIR DESTINIES WERE FOREVER
BOUND BY THE FLAMES OF...
THE DEVIL'S LOVE

THE DEVIL'S LOVE

Lane Harris

A DELL BOOK

Published by
Dell Publishing Co., Inc.
1 Dag Hammarskjold Plaza
New York, New York 10017

Dell ® TM 681510, Dell Publishing Co., Inc.

ISBN: 0-440-11915-4

Printed in the United States of America

First printing—March 1981
Third printing—May 1982

ACKNOWLEDGMENTS

This book is dedicated . . .

to Arnett Harris, an actor and poet of exceptional genius . . .

to Martha Harris, a beautiful person whose laughter and good spirits have never waned . . .

to Vanessa Futrell for her diligent work and suggestions, Andrea Cirillo for editorial advice, and Ellen Edwards who took over the helm . . .

And to Rhonda Ferguson, Yvette Hutchinson, Karen White, and Dianne Holloway—in fond remembrance of good times past.

THE DEVIL'S LOVE

PROLOGUE: July 16, 1768

Tall, handsome Kade Renault stood on the beach surveying the horizon as his men loaded a cargo of rum and sugar cane aboard the *Falcon*. His ship was the finest privateer in the Caribbean. Watching her rise and fall gently with the tide, mast proud and straight against the brilliant blue morning, he felt the surge of pride that a captain knows when gazing at his ship. The salt smell of the sea mixed with the pungent scent of tropical plants as seagulls dipped and flew in the distance. Renault decided to explore the interior of the island while his men loaded the cargo.

The surf crashed against the beach in foaming swells, filling the air with sea mist. The island was so beautiful that Renault walked far longer than he intended and found himself deep in the interior before he knew it. He was about to turn back when he heard the faint bubbling ripple of a young girl's laughter. It was muted and barely audible, but Renault's ears were sharp after months at sea, and there was no mistaking the sound. He listened intently, trying to pinpoint its location. For several minutes nothing broke the silence but the occasional cry of a bird. Then he heard a soft giggle drift from somewhere to the right, deep within the rain forest.

He followed a small path that led through a dense growth of palms and ferns. The foliage was so thick that sunlight filtered through overhanging branches and leaves, casting a hazy green glow over everything

beneath. It was easy to hear the laughter now and he
stopped. Peering through the trees, Renault could see
a deep pool twenty yards away, as blue and still as a
sapphire pillowed on green velvet. A very young maid
in a short white shift sat on a rock at the edge of the
lagoon. She was a mulatto with smooth brown skin
and shiny dark hair that appeared damp from swimming.

She laughed and said something Renault couldn't
hear. The girl was staring straight up over the tops of
the trees to a point in the open sky. Kade shifted his
position slightly to get a better view. Suddenly his
eyes opened wide and his body went rigid. There,
perched impossibly high above the hidden pool on a
rocky cliff was another young maid—completely nude.
She had the most beautiful form he had ever seen—
golden from the sun and lightly tanned. Long waves
of dark honey hair spilled over her shoulders and
down her back. The maid on the rock called out to
her again. Incredibly, she seemed about to dive from
the cliff into the pool below—but that would be madness. The ragged rock ledge was hundreds of feet
above the lagoon; he doubted she could even see the
pool clearly. She was so far away he couldn't make
out the features of her face, yet from where he stood
she appeared very young. He could almost feel the
tension in her body as she prepared to spring out. Renault held his breath. She was crazy to dive from that
cliff!

He watched in stunned silence as the slender form
arched up and out from the rocks, sailing through the
air for what seemed an eternity. She cleaved the water
cleanly, barely disturbing the crystal blue surface.
The maid on the rock applauded, laughing—and said

something to the girl that Renault strained to hear, but could not.

A sharp, clanging bell pealed in the distance. He cursed silently to himself. It was a signal from the *Falcon* that the loading was done. Very reluctantly, he turned to go back to his ship. There was no hope for it; he couldn't delay leaving any longer. The cargo had to go out this morning. But even as he walked back to the beach, he knew he would return to the island. Indeed, nothing could keep him away.

CHAPTER ONE

Sitting in the bedroom before a white dressing table, Christina Evrion absently brushed the butterscotch curls that framed her temples. The mirror reflected the oval face of a girl in the first bloom of womanhood—with creamy skin, high cheekbones radiant with color, and a short straight nose with nostrils that flared slightly, promising passion to the eye of an experienced man. Aquamarine eyes the color of the blue sea at midday glowed intelligently against a luxuriant fringe of dark lashes. Her mouth, lovely and provocatively curved, had caused many a young man to lose his head and heart.

Christina was beautiful. It was not an unusual sight to see her shopping in the fashionable, palm-lined streets of Lawrence with a group of young men trailing discreetly behind her. None of them could resist her soft, sculptured features or the glowing tresses of sun-kissed hair that flowed over her shoulders. She was not obsessed by her beauty or conceited about it. At seventeen, it had always been part of her life and by now she merely accepted it.

In all of St. Marin none could compete with her tawny, wide-eyed loveliness—except perhaps the seductive young woman who had been her rival since the day she left the cradle—the sable-haired, exquisite, green-eyed Carlotta DeCorba.

They were opposite in temperament as well as in appearance. Christina was a child of nature—fun loving, unpredictable and, as her stepmother often remarked, "not at all civilized." Carlotta, on the other hand, was the personification of smoothly calculated feminine charm. She never raised her voice above a provocative whisper, unless some unfortunate male aroused her rather ugly and lethal temper. The most important goals in Carlotta's life were finding a wealthy, respectable husband and appearing beautifully gowned at all times.

In contrast, Christina had no special set of priorities, never having outgrown the childhood habit of living from day to day. Together with Janie, her mulatto maid and close companion, she managed to get into mischief at frequent and alarmingly regular intervals. She had blocked Carlotta's well-laid matrimonial plans so many times that the dark-haired girl was sure that Chris had been sent by the powers of darkness to consign her to spinsterhood.

For the most part, Chris's interference was nothing more than unfortunate coincidence. The two girls had a knack for forming attachments to the same men. In the main, the lads chose Chris—chiefly because they felt more at ease in her company. Their preference was a source of unending consternation to Carlotta, who did not at all understand the cause. Yet, the reason was simple enough. As the pampered and cosseted daughter of an old and noble Spanish family, Carlotta, for all her soft, seductive charm, had in her nature a hard underlying foundation of autocratic superiority that two hundred years of family wealth and dictatorial power had refined into a haughty manner. Everything about her upbringing served only to heighten that already prominent family trait. Arrogance was considered a birthright by the DeCorbas. They were, after all, the oldest family on the island.

Theirs was an attitude that prevailed among the Spanish of the New World. Having successfully extended their sphere of influence wherever their galleons and carracks found land, they were both envied for their wealth and disliked for the cruelty they showed toward the people they governed. In fact, the Spanish were so rich and so resented in the Caribbean that privateering against Spanish vessels bearing gold to the motherland was considered an almost noble profession and had become so widespread that it no longer raised eyebrows.

At any rate, Carlotta had many ways of making her suitors feel awkward and improverished. It was not done intentionally, but it came as naturally as breathing. In her eyes it was only proper that they pay homage to her position and social importance, if she graciously allowed them to pursue her favor.

Christina was of a different mold—by nature, egalitarian to a fault. She had little use for suitors but dearly loved having young men as friends. This was not a common preference for a young maid on St. Marin. Christina had developed an early affinity for masculine company. Her mother had died when she was a young child, and early in her life her father had accepted the responsibility of raising his daughter alone. Despite his remarriage several years after her mother's death, he had still assumed primary responsibility for her upbringing. By the time she was thirteen she could hunt, fence, ride, and shoot as well as any lad her age. At fifteen she was an experienced sailor. There were few topics a young man could raise on which Christina was not conversant. She had a habit of smiling demurely as a young man talked knowledgeably about his favorite activities and then cheerfully adding several eye-opening anecdotes of her own. The trick never failed to intrigue—and it gave Carlotta one more score to even with her.

Yet Chris was not interested in collecting hearts. At the ripe old age of seventeen her passions ran more toward sailing, riding, and taking part in the much-loved, much-forbidden summer ritual of dance and song peculiar to the island on which they lived. She was so preoccupied with these pastimes that most young men abandoned their hopes for a romantic interlude in despair and again pursued Carlotta or turned elsewhere.

Often the competitive atmosphere between the girls had blossomed into open conflict, especially when they were children. Once, long ago, Christina had held a tea party for her two best friends—Marie Robillard and Veronique Lanier—and their dolls. Being in a charitable mood, she decided to invite seven-year-old Carlotta as well. They had been playing only a few minutes before little Carlotta noticed that Christina's doll was prettier than her own and fumed in silent offense.

At length, Chris and Marie left the little table to gather fresh flowers for the tea party. They returned to find Veronique and Carlotta in a heated argument. Marie and Christina looked at each other in confusion, and then Chris's mouth fell open as she saw her doll on the floor, its porcelain head shattered in several places.

"Carlotta broke Chris's doll!" Veronique piped in her high, chirpy little-girl voice.

"I did not!" Carlotta screamed indignantly. "It fell off the chair, you ignorant goose!"

"No it didn't! You picked it up and threw it on the floor—I saw you!"

"Ugly little donkey—you lie!" Carlotta yelled hotly. She stood up with admirable little-girl dignity and said, "I am going home. I do not have to stay here and be bored by your silly games. I have more important things to do." With that she turned and walked from the room with the regal hauteur of an offended princess.

When Veronique and Marie had gone, Chris put her head on the table and cried. Lisette was her favorite doll, a gift from her mother, Blaise St. Claire, who had died in childbirth.

A long time later, when all her tears were gone, she walked up the grand curved staircase to the upper floor of the Evrion mansion where her father's second wife, Hilda, questioned her as she passed in the hall. "What are you sniveling about, Christina?"

"Carlotta broke my doll."

"How do you know that? Did you see her do it?" Hilda questioned sharply.

"No, but Veronique said she did and Veronique wouldn't lie!"

Hilda was unconvinced. "We must not believe everything we are told, Christina, especially unsupported accusations against other people. Carlotta is a very well-behaved little girl—I only wish you were more like her. Now stop crying—go to your room and wash your face at once."

Chris left her stepmother, thinking, "She did break my doll . . . I know she did. I'll find a way to make her admit it—and apologize, too!"

The next day Chris asked Marie and Veronique for all their old dolls, the ones they no longer played with. She took several of them with her and disappeared into her room.

In a few days Carlotta DeCorba found a broken doll's head in her toy chest, among her other things. She looked at it, puzzled because it obviously hadn't come from one of her own toys. Unable to come up with an explanation, she absently put it aside.

Later that afternoon Carlotta and her mother prepared to go shopping. This was Carlotta's favorite activity and she climbed eagerly into the carriage ahead of her mother. After a moment she wriggled uncomfortably on the seat. A hard lump poked at her from beneath the velvet cushion. Tentatively she reached under her satin skirts and pulled a hard, round object from the carriage seat beneath her. Carlotta screamed long and hard when she recognized the object in her hand.

"What is it, Carlotta?" Doña DeCorba asked in alarm. She took the thing from her daughter, who had grown quite pale.

"Oh, my dear," Doña DeCorba smiled, "it is only a doll's head, though I cannot imagine how it could have gotten here. But there's nothing to be afraid of, my child." Carlotta looked at her mother and did not reply. That evening when they returned from their day of shopping, she was unusually quiet. Carlotta lay awake a long time after Doña DeCorba tucked her into bed.

In the morning, when she drowsily opened her eyes and focused on the room, Carlotta sucked in a great gasp of air and froze, immobile with fear. Suspended above her head on a small stick attached to the bed-

post was another doll's head—this one quite ugly—
with a note pinned to it that read:

Apologize and repent of your evil—or I shall
haunt you forever.

Lisette

Carlotta swallowed hard and left the bed to be sick.

That afternoon, before a solemn Chris, Carlotta
contritely apologized and offered to purchase a new
doll. Chris accepted the apology, declined the doll,
and left Carlotta in the study, a mysterious smile playing at the corners of her mouth.

Chris went to her room to fetch a lacquered rosewood box which now held the much-abused Lisette.
She walked through the rolling green lawns of Mimosa
Keyes, as the Evrion mansion was called, and stopped
at a flower-covered knoll near a small neat grace bordered by large green shade trees and lovely low
shrubs. Blaise Evrion's resting place was a small green
island of tranquility surrounded by marble benches
and graceful pastel flowers. Reverently, Chris dug a
little hole with her toy shovel and buried the box beside her mother's grave.

Tears fell silently as she remembered the bright,
laughing young woman who had given her the doll for
her fourth birthday. Several minutes passed before
Chris sensed that she was not alone. She turned
around to see the melancholy, handsome face of her
father, MacGraw Evrion, gazing down from his immense six-foot height, the red sunset turning his blond
hair to burnished copper.

"She killed my doll."

"Who little one?" her father asked, his voice deep and gentle.

"Carlotta. She threw Lisette on the floor and broke her. Maman gave her to me—" Chris's small voice broke and she started to cry in earnest.

MacGraw Evrion picked up his daughter and held her in his arms, murmuring soothing words until the sobbing stopped. Chris was silent for a time and then she said, "Hilda says Carlotta is a very well-behaved little girl and that I should be more like her. But I think she is mean and hateful. Look what she did to Lisette. Why should I try to be like that?"

Mac sighed. The gap between his second wife and his only child was deep and yawning. There seemed little common ground on which they could meet.

"She does not want you to be mean, skipper; she only wants you to learn the lessons she has been trying to teach you."

"But I have! I can play the spinet and do needlepoint now. But Hilda says I should not sail or practice shooting with you anymore, and that it is unfitting for a girl not to ride sidesaddle."

"Well, your stepmother is sometimes a little too strict, Chrissy, but she means well. Could you not compromise a little—for my sake? We will find a way to hide the sailing and shooting."

"All right," she conceded reluctantly with a sad little smile. "But it will be for you that I try, not her."

Mac Evrion took his daughter by the hand and began to walk back to Mimosa Keyes, musing over the circumstances that had seen him to this faraway island in the Caribbean. He knew well the conflict that stormed within the child. In her veins flowed his own rebellious blood.

* * *

The third of four sons born to a prominent Scottish family in the northern territory of Orkney, MacGraw Evrion was a descendant of the Norse invaders who came to Scotland in the twelfth century. In time they came to rule the highland territories of Orkney, Caithness, and Sutherland, founding earldoms and fiefs as they fortified their holdings. Gradually they incorporated themselves into the Scottish way of life, relinquishing the Norse customs and becoming more Scot than Viking. When the old Norse king, Haakon IV, failed in his attempt to reassert sovereignty over the Norse earldoms of northern Scotland by Viking invasion in 1263, the destiny of Mac's ancestors linked permanently with the Scots. The Treaty of Perth in 1266 severed the last formal ties with the Norse king and ended the age of Viking expansion along the northern coast of Scotland.

Life in the highlands was prosperous and the family fortune flourished, with an economy based on farming, salmon fishing, and linen weaving. The people were great sailors, plying the coast of Scotland with their ships and superintending thriving businesses in the burghs they governed. By 1700, Mac's family was an established force in the government and economy of Orkney.

Politically, the time was a turbulent one. England joined forces with the powerful Duke of Argyll to negotiate a union of the Scottish and English crowns so that one king, William III of Orange, would rule Scotland as well as England. But the decision was unpopular in the highlands. Many felt that James Stewart VI was the rightful king of Scotland because of an old and ancient claim to the throne. Frequent fighting broke out between Argyll's men and the followers of James VI. The Jacobites, as those who opposed the Duke were called, felt that when the English and Scottish parliaments were combined, Scotland lost much in the way of economic sovereignty, not to mention the ability to legislate policies favoring the national interest. The situation was aggravated by frequent religious conflict between Presbyterians, by and large supporters of Argyll, and the Episcopalians, whose sympathies lay with the Jacobites.

Through it all, MacGraw's father wisely preserved the family's neutrality, allowing the political conflict of the country to run its course. By the time the old earl's third son, MacGraw, was ready to attend the university, the Jacobites had all but given up the cause, and the Hanoverian succession of English kings was accepted for both countries.

The earl had two sons at Edinburgh University. MacGraw, his wild and handsome third son, was given to unrestrained behavior and loose morals. The earl thought that he needed strict discipline to curb his unorthodox nature and for that reason decided to send him to Oxford in England, hoping the institution would mold the lad's character.

MacGraw's departure from Scotland caused many a maid to sigh in wistful regret, for despite his father's opinion of his spirited antics, few of the young ladies of his acquaintance found cause for complaint. Mac-Graw was unquestionably the handsomest young man in the north of the land. His glowing blond hair was the color of the sun on a clear autumn day and his eyes were as blue as a September morning. He had a muscular physique, the grace of which belied its strength, and a way of smiling at a lass that was anything but soothing. Young Mac had a winning way with women and a charm he used to his advantage, often and well.

From the first day at Oxford he disliked the Spartan regimen and unyielding routine of his studies. MacGraw was an indifferent student—although he did excel in Greek and Latin because he favored the seafaring adventures of the ancient heroes. The restrictions the university placed on his personal movement chafed him sorely.

It did not take long for the beautiful young wife of an aging peer to capture his attention. Lady Elizabeth Wordley was a whimsical creature, quite bold in her way and more than a little bored with the sedate life she led. Their romance sailed along at full speed until a careless rendezvous, arranged by Lady Wordley, allowed her husband to discover the affair. Sir David Wordley challenged the young Scot to a duel and died later as a result of the wound MacGraw gave him. The ensuing scandal made it imperative that Mac leave England immediately. The old earl in Scotland sent instructions for his son to leave London for Paris at once and to stay with the earl's cousin, Girard Mauriere, the Marquis de Lasqueront. It was uncertain when, if ever, the lad would be able to return to Orkney, since Scotland was under the jurisdiction of English law.

Mac left for his elder cousin's Paris residence with little regret, for Lady Wordley made it clear that she wanted to enjoy her newly widowed status in the glamorous environs of London.

In Paris, Mac gave serious thought to his future and the alternatives open to him. With two healthy older brothers the likelihood of inheriting his father's title was remote, and he had always dreamed of acquiring a fortune of his own. The Marquis de Lasqueront had a son, Charles, near Mac's age. From the moment the cousins met, they got on well together. When Mac confided his ambition to Charles, his cousin suggested that he try his luck in the New World. There were substantial fortunes to be made in the profitable shipping trade that had developed there. The marquis had a close friend, Armand St. Claire, who ran a very profitable shipping business from an island in the Caribbean.

Years before, St. Claire, the son of a wealthy Louisiana plantation owner, had married Michelle Dumas, the most beautiful octoroon in New Orleans—much to the consternation of his family. As the eldest son, he would have inherited the St. Claire plantation, but he fell hopelessly in love with the wildly beautiful, sensuous Michelle, whose dark smouldering looks captured his imagination as well as his heart.

Armand waited until he obtained control of the trust his grandparents set up for him and then eloped with Michelle to St. Marin, the island Charles suggested to Mac. There, Armand set up the profitable rum and shipping business that was now the cornerstone of the St. Claire family's wealth. As Charles heard it, he had a young daughter, a magical creature with blond curls and green eyes, but no sons to aid him in his waning years. He had mentioned to the marquis, Charles's father, that he wanted a partner to help him supervise the vessels he owned.

MacGraw liked the sound of what he heard. He knew nothing else as well as he knew sailing; he came from a land where men used overturned ships as shelters for livestock.

The St. Marin upon which MacGraw Evrion first set foot so many years ago was much less densely settled then the island his daughter knew, although the promise of prosperity had filled the air even then.

It was a cosmopolitan island resplendent with palm-covered mountains and bays framed in miles of white sand. The ambiance was a blend of the French, Spanish, and Dutch groups who had crossed the sea in the early eighteenth century, bringing with them their culture and cuisine.

For decades they had come: noblemen in search of adventure and men of ambition who sought to build their fortunes in the New World. They settled the land and created a blossoming economy of agriculture and industry based on the sugar and rum trade. Fine old homes in pastel yellow and pink and blue graced the green hills and white beaches of the St. Marin coastline. The St. Claires were one of the island's first families, along with the Robillards and Laniers, the De-Corbas and Laveras, the Van Beurens and the Hornhausers.

On Mac's first day in St. Marin, the St. Claires welcomed him in the *grand salon* of Armand's stately island mansion, Mimosa Keyes. MacGraw was already enchanted by the velvet green beauty of the gently rolling hills and valleys, but once inside the impressive, vaulted drawing room of the Keyes, he was completely awed by the richness of the interior. Louis XV chairs dotted a salon whose walls were covered with large island murals. Pale-blue Sèvres bowls mounted in ormolu rested on a low-lying table of Russian malachite. A full-length portrait of St. Claire and his wife hung above a mantel decorated with several lovely oval shapes that at closer inspection proved to be Fabergé eggs.

Yet the real treasure of the salon was not an inanimate object, but the young woman sitting demurely before him on the brocade love seat near the French bay windows. MacGraw Evrion took one look at Blaise St. Claire's enigmatic, hauntingly lovely young face and experienced a rush of pleasure that struck him like a blow. She looked more like a whimsical fairy than a flesh and blood maid, with the sunlight dancing through the strands of her hair, spilling streams of light over the pale green folds of her silk morning dress.

Armand St. Claire surveyed the tall young man before him and decided that his choice had been a wise one. The handsome young Scot could have been mistaken for his own son—the prevailing difference in their appearance being only that Armand's eyes were a vivid green and the hair of the elder Creole several shades more fair than Mac's own wheat-colored locks. St. Claire stepped forward to grasp young Evrion's hand. He walked with a slight limp, the souvenir of a duel fought long ago in his impetuous youth.

With an effort MacGraw uttered an appropriate response to Armand's cordial greeting and turned his attention to the elegant, dark-haired woman who stood at his host's side. As Michelle St. Claire expressed her happiness that his voyage had been a safe one, he mentally catalogued the high-planed cheeks, arrestingly beautiful face and peach-hued complexion that identified her unmistakably as the mother of the maid seated at the window. He stole a glance at the girl. She was watching them silently with an unreadable expression on her face.

The older woman's amber eyes were speckled with honey flecks. They gave him the uncanny feeling that he was viewing a being whose previous life had surely been lived as a cat. Madame St. Claire was clad in a gown of soft tangerine satin with a white fichu modestly covering the bodice, held in place by a finely wrought cameo. She greeted him in the dulcet tones of Louisiana, softly accented with Creole French.

"Monsieur Evrion, welcome to St. Marin and our home. We are honored." At Michelle's side, Armand—lean, tall, and aristocratic—extended a thin, well-manicured hand.

"It is good to meet you, MacGraw. I have heard that your voyage went well."

"No problem, sir," MacGraw said, "save a small storm at sea, and that was little more than a spoon's stir in a teacup."

"Good. These crossings can be dangerous when the weather does not hold. Allow me to introduce the last member of my family. Blaise, my daughter."

Mac turned his head toward the sunny bay windows on his left. The vision was sitting with an air of casual disinterest, watching the distant sea beyond the rolling green. Mac was afforded a few heavenly seconds of her profile. The gently rounded curve of her bodice drew his gaze like a magnet as her breasts rose and fell softly with her breath. The heavy mane of hair that spilled over her back was a deeper gold than her father's, shot with strands of tawny wheat that wound artlessly through the thick flowing waves of honey.

She turned almost reluctantly to acknowledge his presence. Mac's breath caught in his chest as his eyes rose to take in her soft, enchanting mouth. Her skin was translucent—though not as fair or fragile as Armand's—and brought to mind thoughts of a budding tea rose.

Yet what caused Mac's blood to race crazily through his veins were the girl's eyes. The emerald irises had scores of small gold and amber flecks near their dark, liquid centers. They were so strange! They seemed to burn with a forbidden luminescence that was arousing . . . deep and knowing . . . and very mysterious. He sensed that something of the maid herself shone forth in those eyes, like reflections in a hidden pool. Mac felt as out of control as a small boat caught in a stiff quarter wind. She seemed magical . . . able to draw a man against his will. He felt a pull that was as unswerving as the moon with the tides—an invisible force molding his vague dreams into reality.

He was filled with a floating buoyance as he continued to watch her, a warm flow that rose inside until he felt himself smiling, beaming for no reason at all—save the pure headiness of having fallen in love.

Blaise watched him silently. She was motionless as she observed the parade of expressions on his face. Not given to idle chatter, she was waiting only for the proper moment to excuse herself so that she could pursue more diverting pastimes. As for MacGraw's fascination, it was not the first time she had witnessed such a reaction. Long ago Blaise had accepted the unusual effect she produced in men. By now she barely noticed.

Mac knew that he was uncommonly handsome—there were enough broken hearts in Scotland and England to verify that. This young woman, however, had shown no sign of interest. Blaise appeared not in the least affected by his masculine charm. He, on the other hand, was experiencing a rising excitement that had progressed rapidly from a pleasant tingling sensation in his groin to a discomfiting wave of heat that engulfed his whole body. It was terrible. No it was wonderful. And still she watched him with those golden-green eyes, her mouth a little sullen and a bit defiant—because now he was openly staring at her and she knew it. God, how very much he wanted to kiss that soft inviting mouth! Could she truly be as unaffected as she seemed?

He was vaguely aware of the need to acknowledge the introduction, which by now seemed a lifetime ago. "*Enchanté*, mademoiselle," he said in a deep voice that contained a note more vibrant than polite social convention required.

"I am delighted to meet you, monsieur," she said calmly.

Her voice was much lower than he had expected. It seemed to curl around the base of his spine like a warm hand. At that moment he would have given a galleon of Spanish gold to be able to carry her to a place of privacy and solitude.

"You are new to St. Marin, Monsieur Evrion?" she asked.

"Yes," he replied, watching the soft movement of her lips as she spoke.

"You have much to look forward to . . . the island is very beautiful."

"Very," he replied, although he was not referring to St. Marin. Blaise felt that she had adequately discharged her social duty and rose gracefully. "Papa, maman—may I be excused? I would like to go shopping in Lawrence this morning."

Armand nodded. "Of course, but you must return by this afternoon, *n'est-ce pas?*"

"How will you get there?" her mother asked.

"Gideon will drive me. He is waiting with a carriage."

Mac watched her go, feeling thoroughly confounded. Never had he encountered a more devastating creature—or one who had remained as unmoved in his presence as this one.

Here was a challenge he was determined to meet. Mac was suddenly elated as he realized how very much this elegant green Caribbean island suited him.

He tried to listen attentively as the St. Claires spoke to him over the afternoon tea. Presently, Madame St. Claire withdrew and left the two men alone to discuss the ship line. MacGraw found the information Armand was giving him very exciting, but his thoughts were elsewhere.

As she supervised preparations for the evening meal, Michelle St. Claire thoughtfully contemplated her daughter. Although physically Blaise had inherited more of Armand's appearance than her own striking looks, Blaise's volatile temperament was unquestionably her legacy to their daughter. Inside that young body burned a rebellious restlessness and desire for adventure that was as strong in the child as it was in the mother.

There were nights during the summer months when Blaise disappeared altogether. Michelle knew that she went to dance in the harvest ceremonies of the people who lived in the hills—the Rawani. Their music could be heard throughout the island during July and August. Michelle hid these occurrences from Armand, knowing they would upset him, but she understood completely her daughter's need for that diversion. Before Blaise's birth, during Armand's brief voyages to neighboring islands, Michelle herself had gone into the hills to dance, finding the ceremonies exhilarating. They were held before flickering campfires in palm-bordered glades and the beat of the drums was irresistible.

For some time the subject of her daughter's marriage had weighed heavily on her mind. Blaise had not indicated a preference for any of the young men of respectable St. Marin families who approached Armand for permission to address her. This new young man, Evrion, seemed an interesting possibility. The light in his eyes when he looked at Blaise had not escaped her. It was an intriguing thought, one that she would carefully consider. Michelle sighed as she completed the last of the menus. She hoped Blaise would consider it also.

CHAPTER TWO

Blaise St. Claire turned in the carriage to contemplate Gideon Baudien's hawklike profile. Gideon was a Rawani. Although he was not exactly handsome, there was something about his serene gray eyes, burnished walnut skin and tall, lean frame that attracted her. He was very mysterious. It was his habit to ponder the stars at night and hypothesize the laws of the universe—questions Blaise would never have considered on her own. He was a philosopher of sorts, and at times she doubted he was born of this world, for his thoughts were frequently too ethereal for her to follow. Yet she enjoyed listening to him, and he had always been her friend.

Gideon's grandfather had been a French mercenary who sailed for Spain. His mother, Madame Helene Baudien, was known throughout St. Marin as a midwife and fortuneteller. Blaise liked her, even though many people on the island considered her odd. She was a mystic, and the superstitious sought her out for her potions, cures, blessings, and sometimes curses. The Baudiens lived high in the St. Marin mountains in a secluded settlement, because they valued their privacy and did not like curious strangers. Since the death of Gideon's father, Madame Baudien's practice had made the family quite wealthy, but they refused to live differently. Gideon still worked as a coachman for Blaise's father when he was not away on one of his voyages to France. She had a strong suspicion that he continued to drive the St. Claire carriages as an excuse to be near her.

The stories she liked best were the ones he told her of Paris. Already Gideon had visited that city twice to study medicine at the Sorbonne. He was leaving again soon. From his descriptions Paris seemed the most desirable place in the world to live. Blaise had friends there, girls she had known as a child, whose families had left St. Marin to return to France. For two years she pleaded with her father to take them to Paris to live for a short while, but he refused. Armand was very settled in St. Marin after all these years and was reluctant to leave the shipyard for even a few months. He steadfastly denied her permission to go alone, dismissing her curtly by stating that she was far too young to undertake the voyage, even with a chaperone.

For a time Blaise had given up hope, but one night, at a Rawani celebration, a young dancer swallowed a potion made by Madame Baudien, which made him highly susceptible to suggestion. She watched in wonder as he did unbelievable things after drinking the liquid. Under the influence of Madame's potion, the young man approached a campfire and placed his foot momentarily on a glowing log without pain. Even more amazing was the fact that his skin was unharmed.

She was convinced that with a vial of this fluid she might persuade her father to be more reasonable.

As Gideon pulled in the reins and the carriage rolled to a stop in front of the fashionable dressmaker's shop in Lawrence, Blaise asked him to get a vial of the potion from Madame Baudien while she went shopping. He looked surprised and asked her pointedly why she needed it. She was vague, but he pressed her and finally she made up a story she was sure he did not believe. After a moment he shrugged and nodded.

She could barely contain her impatience as she suffered through a fitting, with Clothilde Tremont, her dressmaker, chattering away. Blaise listened absently as she babbled about trimmings and fabrics—how to prepare a proper *poisson en papillote*; whether *file* powder or okra was the superior thickener for gumbo; was it really true that the very rich Maria Isabella De-Corba, daughter of the island's most prominent Spanish family, had been kidnapped by a French pirate or could it be that he was her lover and she went with him willingly?

When Gideon arrived at his home in the hills he found his mother gone, but her assistant, Leah, was preparing a poultice in their large workshop. He told her of Blaise's request and sauntered into the parlor to wait while she prepared a vial. Leah pulled a large clay jar from one of the numerous shelves in the room. She opened it and stifled a cry of dismay as she found it empty. Madame Baudien would not be back for several days as she was attending a family ill with fever. Leah knew nothing about the herbs used for this potion and could not make more, but she did not wish to turn away Blaise's gold. She made a small commission on each sale. Swearing with exasperation, she filled a bowl with some weak herbs—spices she used for pickling fruits and vegetables. To that she added camomile flowers, honey and water—and then poured the whole of it into a small purple bottle wrapped carefully in plain brown paper.

Smiling, she brought the package to Gideon and

told him that if Blaise was not satisfied, she would replace the vial with another. "With any luck," Leah thought to herself, "she will not discover the substitution until Madame returns and it will be easy to replace it with the real brew."

Blaise was delighted when Gideon returned. With this bottle in her possession anything was possible. Yet for once she decided to be prudent. Her father's mind was sharp, and although the potion guaranteed receptivity to suggestion, she would need to be skillful to insure his ultimate compliance. She remembered that the liquid caused drowsiness, docility and a very happy feeling. If she could only practice with someone first . . . then she would know how to go about it. Ideally it should be someone who did not know her, who would suspect nothing at all. She looked at Gideon beside her, making quiet conversation. With his keen mind and quick wits it could not be him. But she must find someone.

During the coming weeks Mac was a frequent visitor at Mimosa Keyes. He had taken time to rent a few rooms at the Green Isle Inn, but that was only until he found a suitable house to buy in town, near the St. Claire shipping offices and the Lawrence counting house. In the meantime he came as often as his work permitted to take advantage of the excellent cuisine at Mimosa Keyes. Blaise was not much in evidence during his visits, and when he did see her, she seldom spoke. On the one or two occasions when they had talked to one another, their conversation had not gone beyond a discussion of the weather. It was frustrating to feel the longing and need grow daily within him and yet to feel so shy with her. That had never happened to him before and it made him swear beneath his breath.

One morning Mac found himself waiting for St. Claire in the vaulted mahogany-paneled library of the Keyes. Armand was extremely late, an unusual occurrence. The handsome young Scot was bored as he walked about the room, idly persuing the heavy leather-bound volumes and absently spinning a floor-mounted globe. The gnawing sensation in his stomach told him it was time for lunch. He was about to go into the dining hall when the library doors opened, and Blaise St. Claire walked into the room.

She did not notice him, so he moved deliberately from the corner in which he stood, taking small comfort as she jumped in surprise. He was damned if he would allow her to ignore him today.

"Oh, Mr. Evrion . . . I did not know you were here."

"Fortune has smiled on me at last this morning. May I say you look enchanting?"

She was wearing a lace-trimmed gown of peach taffeta with charmingly ruffled sleeves and a tiny peplum. Her hair hung loose and flowing, as usual. He noticed that neither Blaise nor her mother wore the lace-edged lingerie caps that were part of the habitual morning wear of many women.

Blaise looked at him with curiosity. "Are you waiting for my father?" He nodded and she smiled. "He was detained in Lawrence this morning," she explained. "Perhaps you should meet him there?"

Mac was nettled that Armand had forgotten to tell him about the change in his plans, but he hid it well. "Thank you. It is not like your father to be late, and I did wonder what had happened."

Blaise was regarding him with a peculiar speculative gleam in her eyes. Mac was pleased that she was finally beginning to see him, but her expression was so strange that he wondered what the devil she could be thinking. He waited for her to speak. When she did not, he smiled gently and said, "Does this show of interest mean that you like what you see—or has my nose sprouted a wart?"

She did not respond to that and looked quickly away. After a moment she said, "Have you been able to explore much of the island yet, Mr. Evrion?"

"No, I haven't, and please call me Mac. There is no need to be so formal. You will see me often enough."

"Today I planned to have a *déjeuner sur l'herbe*. If you have not yet eaten lunch, perhaps you would care to join me?"

Mac could barely believe he had heard her correctly. "I would consider that an extraordinary piece of luck indeed, mademoiselle."

"*Bien*. Please meet me at the stables in an hour, *n'est-ce pas*?"

He bent and kissed her hand. "It would take a typhoon to keep me away."

When Blaise left, Mac could barely contain the joy he felt that she wanted to be alone with him. Perhaps she was not as unaffected as she seemed—and how delightful that she was not shy!

Upstairs in her room, as her maid laid out her riding habit, Blaise was having second thoughts about her sudden plan to try out Gideon's potion on Mac Evrion. The leaping light she had seen in his eyes made her feel anything but secure. She shook herself mentally and reasoned that everything would be all right after she gave him the potion. He would be as docile as a kitten, and she would make sure he drank a glass of wine laced with the brew as soon as they sat down. Quickly, she donned a green silk riding habit, the jacket of which was trimmed with satin revers and cuffs. The gauze jabot at her throat was scalloped, edged with lace embroidery, and the full skirt was trimmed with green velvet.

MacGraw had been sitting on his horse a quarter of an hour before Blaise appeared on a spirited roan mare, her wild hair waving behind her like a flag in the wind.

"You are early, monsieur," she laughed.

"Mac," he reminded her. He could only stare back at her and smile—she looked incredibly beautiful. She laughed again, the sound like rippling bells.

"Come, follow me," she called, prodding her horse into a canter.

They rode for three miles before Blaise turned onto a narrow trail that seemed to lead nowhere. The foliage became so dense that they had to dismount and continue on foot. After a short time Mac saw a clearing through the trees and heard the sound of rushing water. As the herbage thinned and they stepped into a glade, the clearing revealed a lovely waterfall that poured into a deep pool surrounded by calla lilies and water irises.

"Oh, make a wish!" Blaise suddenly cried out.

"What?"

"Look!" she said, pointing to the waterfall. "It's a rainbow. Oh, quickly—before it disappears—make a wish!"

"I thought that one only did that with shooting stars," he smiled.

She looked serious for a moment as she considered

what he said. "But I have never seen a falling star, have you?"

"No . . ."

"Then it is better to use rainbows, is it not?" She bent down and removed her shoes. "I always walk barefoot here. The moss is very soft."

Mac looked down at the lush green carpet beneath his feet and decided to try it. He removed his boots and stockings and found that she was right. The stuff was cool and very springy. It tickled and made him laugh.

"You approve?"

"Very much," he grinned.

"*Bien.* We shall stop for refreshment here."

Blaise laid the special collation the cook had prepared on a linen cloth. There was cold lobster, roast Cornish hen, pâté molded into floral shapes, green crisp arugola and escarole, truffles in cream, fresh cherries lightly dusted with sugar, huge red apples, and a round of cheese. Smiling, she offered him a glass of wine well laced with Madame Baudien's potion. The entire bottle was filled with it, and Blaise knew that it would be necessary to distract him or risk arousing some suspicion regarding her lack of thirst.

Mac would not have noticed if an elephant sat down beside them. He was wholly preoccupied with the aura of sensuality that radiated from the curves of her lithe young body. With heavenly leisure he studied the firm, delicately carved planes of her face, the soft inviting roundness of her mouth, the slender column of her neck. Her cheeks were flushed a dusty rose—the predictable result of his caressing stare.

Blaise felt apprehensive about the unabashed ardor in Mac's eyes. She noticed with alarm that the wineglass remained ignored in his grasp. Quickly she said, "The day is warm, Mac, and we have had a long journey. Drink your wine . . . it will refresh you."

Contemplating her . . . refreshed, Mac grew warmer still in his regard. Obediently, he raised the glass to his mouth. As he drew the first sip, he reflected absently that the brew was inordinately dry, highly spiced, and not at all to his taste, but to please her he drained the glass. Blaise quickly refilled it. Mac smiled at her. The attentive concern she was giving him warmed his heart.

As he downed the second glass, she relaxed and felt more at ease. It would be best to give the potion time to take effect, and the whole exercise would probably work far better if he trusted her, so she began a conversation to put him at ease.

"My father said that you were from Scotland."

"Yes, that is right. My family lives in the highlands of the far north near Orkney."

"What is it like, your home?"

"Oh . . . very green with lots of rocky fields . . . rugged . . . misty in the morning . . . and very beautiful."

"Not so different from here."

Mac laughed. "It is very different from here. This island is much warmer than Scotland."

"Ah, I see. Do you miss it terribly?"

"Not at all. I am beginning to appreciate St. Marin more with each passing day," he said meaningfully.

"That is well. Father will be pleased to hear that."

Mac gently captured Blaise's hand with his own. "And what of his daughter? Are you pleased to hear that?"

Blaise thought for a moment. Saying yes would lead

to an overt flirtation and that was risky, but on closer consideration it was also probably the simplest way to lull him into the receptivity she wanted. She allowed the dark brown fringe of her lashes to hide her strange eyes for a moment before looking up at him. He sat watching her expectantly.

"Yes, Mac, I too am very pleased to hear that." She placed her hand innocently over his and smiled.

Mac kissed her hand and brushed the fingertips with his lips one by one. Blaise shivered. Her own reaction took her by surprise, and she discreetly withdrew her hand.

"Would you like a bit more wine?" she asked uncertainly.

He shook his head. Two glasses of that awful stuff was enough, and he broke off a joint of cold bird instead.

Blaise watched him patiently while she waited for the drowsiness to begin. This was the first opportunity she had had to study him at close range. He was exceptionally handsome, extraordinarily so. Mac's gray waistcoat lay beside his riding crop, removed in deference to the afternoon warmth. She could discern muscular arms beneath his silk vest and lawn shirt. He was very tall and his long, steel-hewn legs seemed to stretch out endlessly in their buckskin breeches and white stockings. Mac's skin now bore a healthy tan and the tropical sun had streaked his blond hair with light strands. The man had a certain careless charm that was very appealing. When he smiled—as he did frequently—even, white teeth flashed in a display so disarming that it was impossible not to smile in return.

Finishing his lunch, Mac stretched out on the grass,

resting his head on his arm. He thought happily that for the first time in his turbulent young life he felt at peace with the world, and he closed his eyes to savor the sensation.

"Ah, at last," she thought, pleased with herself. The drowsiness signaled that the brew was working. She reached over and touched his hand. Immediately, his lids rose, and she peered into a pair of warm and delighted blue eyes.

"You are relaxed and at ease now, Mac?"

He moved up on one elbow to look at her. His eyes never left hers as he nodded.

"And well rested?"

Mac's gaze flamed with a sudden wave of desire. It was better to show her than tell her! Slowly, he raised his arm and placed his hand gently at the nape of Blaise's neck, drawing her closer for a long, velvety kiss.

Minutes passed before he drew back and asked softly, "Was that what you had in mind, little one?"

Her reply came a little breathlessly. "That was very nice, Mac, but not what I was thinking."

"Oh?" he said, sitting up. He was slightly puzzled. Was she so impatient for him that she wished to forego even a pleasant kiss or two?

Blaise searched for a subject that would take them out of this disturbing territory and sharpen her skills of suggestion. "I was thinking. . ." She groped as she tried to think of something unusual. "Or wondering rather . . ." Blaise brightened as her mind chanced on the perfect test. It was so simple and easily performed!—"if you have ever had an urge to bark . . . like a dog?"

Mac stared for a second or two and blinked, wondering if perhaps he had fallen asleep and missed part of the conversation. He suddenly had no idea of what she was talking about. For a moment he was silent, and then he replied slowly, "Sometimes . . . as a little boy . . ."

"I thought so," Blaise smiled. "And you have an urge to do so now, do you not?" she said cheerfully.

Mac stared at her blankly for a long time before he replied, "Well . . . not . . . exactly . . ."

Blaise regarded him intently. "Oh, but think for a second. You really do want to bark, don't you?"

It must be an island game, he thought to himself.

He tried hard to get into the spirit of her play, but found it such a nonsequitur that he could only manage a weak and doubtful "Arf?"

Blaise smiled and nodded. The potion did indeed work, but so far he had not shown much enthusiasm. Perhaps he needed a more definitive command. She thought again. Ah, yes, of course.

"And what of ducks, Mac? I think they are most appealing."

He raised his eyebrows. "You do?"

"Oh, yes. They are exceedingly handsome creatures, don't you think?"

Mac drew in a lungful of air and let it out slowly.

"I have never really thought much about them. I suppose they can be rather nice." Ducks?!

Blaise nodded vigorously. "Yes, they are exceptional animals. Don't you wish you could sound like them?"

There was a long pause.

"Surely, you don't mean . . . quack . . ."

"Yes," she nodded enthusiastically, "that is what you want to do, is it not?"

He was totally at a loss for words. Mac had known

women who became aroused by unusual things, but he had never encountered this. He could do nothing but stare at her in wonder.

Blaise watched him with interest. The effect of the potion must be growing stronger—that would explain the confused expression on his face. He obviously needed more encouragement. She took one of his brown hands in her own and stroked it soothingly. In a quiet voice, as if speaking with a child, she urged him softly, reinforcing her words with a cajoling smile.

"Isn't that what you would like to do?"

Mac responded, not to her words but to the touch of her hand and the tone of her voice. The gold and amber flecks twinkling at him from the depths of her strange green eyes worked on his senses like a drug. Suddenly what they were saying was of little importance. He drew an uneven breath, and his deep voice vibrated above the sound of the waterfall as he said, "I will show you, Blaise, what I would like most."

Her eyes widened in surprise as he drew her into his arms and bent his head. His mouth closed on hers, and she felt him part her lips. His kiss was tender and prodding . . . deep and disturbing. She felt him softly probe the inner pads of her mouth, intruding with gentle insistence until she tingled with the unfamiliar sensations he awakened.

When he straightened and rational thought was possible, Blaise turned her head to hide a frown. Something was definitely wrong. It could be that Mac's body had not yet accepted the potion, that he was not yet completely relaxed. She was rushing him perhaps. Although his eyelids drooped sensuously, his gaze was very hot. She decided to double her efforts.

"Let me massage your neck, MacGraw. You must be tired after that ride and your busy morning."

Mac sighed. Now this was more expected. He surrendered willingly to her soft hands and thought truly that this was paradise. When she finished, he stretched his solid, firmly muscled frame languidly and smiled at her. "Now you must allow me to return the favor." he said.

"Oh, no! I mean . . . I am not tired."

"Ah, but I insist, Blaise."

She felt his gentle fingers on her neck. It did feel good, and she closed her eyes, but soon a pair of warm lips replaced his hands.

Her eyes flew open to find his handsome face inches from her own.

"Have I hurt you?" he asked softly.

"No, but . . ."

"Then relax . . ."

"I am, but Monsieur Evrion you must not do that!"

Mac was beyond denials at this point and all further comment from her was silenced by his warm mouth. With an effort, Blaise managed at last to draw away. "Monsieur Evrion . . . Mac . . . I think we should go home now. Do you not agree?"

Mac smiled, drawing her gently but firmly back into his embrace. "Most assuredly, Blaise, I do not."

Blaise heard him sigh as he covered her mouth with his own again and molded her so tightly to him that she wondered if the imprint of his body would remain when they parted.

His kiss was a dark velvet eternity of firm lips and warm arms. She felt as if he had taken a lighted taper and touched a candlewick deep within her.

When he raised his head at last to gaze at her, Mac

saw the beginning of passion alight in her eyes. He sighed and drew a finger softly across her kiss-bruised mouth.

"Blaise, darling," he whispered, "I love you."

Blaise's eyes widened in surprise. Before she could reply, Mac lowered his head once more. This time when he kissed her, her lips opened magically beneath his.

Blaise felt her meager defenses begin to crumble, chipped away by the longing that had grown inside her. She became aware of a warmth spreading over her breasts. With surprise she discovered his hand beneath her open camisole, the myriad fastenings presenting no barrier to him.

She knew that this was forbidden, but what he was doing was so pleasant, so gentle, that she did not want him to stop.

Time slipped by and presently they lay entwined as God made them, clothes scattered absently about and forgotten. The desire Mac felt for the exquisite form beside him was a deep pain gnawing his vitals. He groaned. "Blaise, Blaise . . . let me darling . . . I want you . . . so much . . . let me . . . please . . ." he murmured softly, brokenly in her ear. When she did not protest, Mac rose above her in triumph, impatient to join their bodies.

At first there was pain, but then a warmth slowly filled her. It seemed to start from a tiny point deep inside and blossom gradually throughout her entire body.

She began to experience a strange peace, as if something long missing had been found . . . a new wholeness. She looked up at the handsome man above her, and their eyes met. As he whispered endearments there was a need and urgency in his voice that vibrated throughout her being. She touched his cheek and slowly, almost languidly, traced his features with her fingertips. Evrion grasped her small hand with his own and pressed his lips to her palm.

He felt a boiling inside, as if his being had concentrated in one central place and knew an overwhelming urge to embrace her as tightly as possible—to thrust his seed deep within her. His arms tightened reflexively as he pressed her closer.

Blaise watched with something akin to wonder as Mac's handsome face became taunt and fixed. His eyes seemed to focus on some point in the future . . . she felt his body grow rigid . . . expand powerfully. Blaise was conscious of his arms growing tighter around her, and a small fear that he might crush her stirred in her mind, but as she lay in the warm confinement of his arms—feeling the solid thickness of him thrusting deep inside—a flame engulfed her and all thought disintegrated in a soft mist. They strained together and found in each other a happiness far beyond mere mating. A dam of emotion burst inside them, and they returned to the present through a tunnel of pleasure.

Mac sighed. He realized that he had not known what love was until he coaxed this soft, whimsical girl into his arms. Blaise lay quietly, absently watching the clouds in the sky. She was not expected home until late afternoon, so there was yet time to rest—and a good thing because she was completely exhausted.

Noting her understandable languor and feeling a pleasant lassitude himself, Mac drew Blaise against him, and he was gratified when she promptly curled up in his arms and went to sleep. For some odd reason the simple sight of her beside him was delightful. Mac stroked the downy hair at the nape of her neck for long moments before he yawned and joined her in slumber.

CHAPTER THREE

They met often after that day for passionate, leisurely couplings. Blaise forgot her desire to see France, and Mac felt for the first time in his life a much-needed sense of balance and harmony. He was at peace with himself at last, and, above all things, he wanted to make certain this new-found sense of well-being continued. One sunny, love-filled afternoon he asked Blaise to share his life. Her green eyes glowed with an uncanny twinkle as she smiled mysteriously and nodded yes.

Their announcement was greeted with joy by Armand and Michelle. For Armand it was added assurance that he would be able to count on the astute young man who had quickly become a vital asset to him. It also solved the problem of his fey, precocious daughter. All in all, he was delighted.

Word of the impending nuptials reached the hills of St. Marin quickly. Gideon Baudien could not believe his ears when he heard that young Blaise St. Claire was to marry. She was only a girl, yet a child! It was her lack of maturity that had kept him for so long at bay, in spite of the fact that he loved her. For years he'd planned to claim her one day as his own. And now she was to wed! He could not allow that to happen without telling her what was inside him. Perhaps he still had a chance.

Gideon rode quickly down from the high, green island hills, urging his horse over the road that led through the acres of manicured greenery surrounding

Mimosa Keyes. He found Blaise in the *salle de jardinière* with her mother.

"Madame," he began in a voice strained with emotion, "may I have a word with Blaise, alone?"

Noting the look of quiet desperation on his face, Michelle hesitated, but the two of them had played together as children and her intuition told her that this unexpected appearance had been prompted by the now imminent wedding plans. She responded with tact. "Of course, Gideon."

As she left the room she whispered *sotto voce* to Blaise, "I shall be nearby, on the terrace."

Blaise regarded Gideon with some apprehension. She sensed the reason for his visit and dreaded hearing his words. She did not want to lose him as a friend and desperately hoped he would accept her love for MacGraw, but his discomposure was not a good sign.

"What is it, Gideon?"

"Is it true what I have heard—that you are to marry?"

"Yes," said Blaise, and nodded.

Gideon closed his eyes in pain. When Blaise saw the sadness in his face, she added quickly, "I always want you to be a part of my life. Please believe that. I value everything you have taught me, and you have been my dearest friend."

Desperately he looked at her. "Blaise, you cannot do this. You are only a child."

"I was, yes. But you are wrong—I have not been a child for several years."

"I don't want you to do this."

She walked to the other side of the room. "Gideon, I love MacGraw Evrion, as he loves me. I'm not a child, no matter what you think. Please try to understand that and do not worry. Believe me, this is what I want." Softly, she added, "It will bring me great happiness, Gideon."

Baudien took a deep breath. His solemn gray eyes glowed with the intensity of his emotion. "Blaise, do not marry this man. I love you. It has been my intention to wait until you were of age to tell you—but obviously that is impossible. Please listen to me. I believe I can make you happier than this Evrion. What do you know of him really? I have loved you since we played together as children."

Blaise closed her eyes, unable to bear the look of longing on his face. "Gideon," she said, and the pain in her voice made his heart sink, "it is too late."

In desperation he crossed the room and grasped her by the shoulders. "It is not! You are not yet his wife. Do not make this mistake!"

"No, you do not understand," she said as tears filled her eyes. The expression on his face was terrible to behold, but she continued doggedly. "I love you as dearly as I would a brother—I always will. But the love I feel for MacGraw Evrion is different. It fills my entire heart. And . . . there is more between us. I also bear his child."

Blaise felt his hands fall from her shoulders. He stared at her as one would view a friend who has died. Gideon looked like a man suffering the torture of the condemned. Without a word he turned and walked away, leaving Blaise with a painful constriction in her throat. The desolate droop of his shoulders, the slow and heavy tread of his footsteps, were more than she could bear.

"Gideon, wait!"

He was too far away to hear. Blaise started after

him, but she felt a gentle hand on her arm. It was her mother.

"Let him go, my child. There is nothing more you can say."

Blaise looked into her mother's gentle, understanding face and gave in to the sudden urge to cry.

Mac and Blaise were married, and in short order little Christina was born. Those first few years were filled with happiness. They were a family. Armand fairly doted on his granddaughter, so much so that Michelle stated flatly it would be his fault if the child was spoiled. He retorted that he would be happy to lessen the attention he gave the little girl as soon as his daughter presented him with a grandson. At these times Mac would grin broadly and wink at Blaise, who discreetly avoided her parents' knowing glance. It was all so perfect that Mac wrote his father to reconcile their differences, explaining to the old earl that he was at peace with the world and had found his destiny at last.

Blaise thought at times of Gideon, who had disappeared shortly before the wedding. She heard from Madame Baudien that he had gone again to France—to study medicine and philosophy at the university in Paris. Wherever he was, she wished him well.

For three wonderful years everything prospered with them, but happiness so perfect could not continue forever. One day, at the Lawrence counting house, while Mac supervised the loading of the *East Wind*, a ship bound for England with the quarter moon, he received word from the St. Claire-Evrion shipping offices that one of their frigates, the *Bon Ami*, had missed her landfall during the night and crashed against a reef near St. Lucia. There were no survivors.

MacGraw froze in his chair as he heard the news. Both Michelle and Armand had been aboard that ship on holiday.

He dreaded telling Blaise, but she took it well under the circumstances, half hoping that her parents would be found alive. As the days turned into weeks, however, and it became apparent that they were lost, a depression overcame Blaise that pained Mac to witness. The only thing that brought light into her eyes was their child, and the nights when they made love.

Mac became extremely attentive. He was convinced that another life, a new baby, would bring her out of the dark well of sadness that gripped her.

Before long, Blaise had grown large with their second child, and Mac proved right. The pregnancy did take her thoughts away from the pain of her loss, and Blaise brightened again into the mischievous creature he had married. For months she blossomed under the pregnancy's influence, and their home became a happy place. But during the fifth month it became apparent that something was wrong.

Despite the finest medical help in the Caribbean, her condition deteriorated so rapidly that doctors suggested ending the pregnancy. Blaise would not hear of it, and she steadfastly insisted she would have the baby and carry it full term.

In the end, though, the child came early. Mac could still remember her face just before the birth. She was very weak, but she smiled and teased him by saying that if he had done a proper job, they would have a son in the morning. Mac returned her smile, but he was too worried to banter.

Sometime during the night she developed a severe hemorrhage. The pain gradually drained her depleted strength, already low from a bout with fever. Before dawn Blaise's heart failed. They worked furiously to save the child, a little boy, but he was too small to survive the shock of birth.

For many months after that night Mac could not accept the reality of her death. He walked through the house and heard her laughter, went into their bedroom and saw images of her face on the walls. He tossed in his sleep, dreaming of her warm presence beside him. At times he awoke with wet tracks of tears on his face.

The sight of his impish four-year-old daughter almost broke his heart. She was so like Blaise! Yet, it was a comfort to know that something of his wife lived on in their child. Little Chris was a magical imp with blond curls and twinkling, cerulean-blue eyes. All St. Marin knew and loved the little girl.

She was an unusually bold child and had to be constantly watched. Chris often wandered into potentially dangerous situations, as if she lacked the natural caution born of fear. Gradually, Mac transferred all his love to Chris. Her funny antics did much to ease his pain. He taught her to ride, hunt, and fence, so that before her thirteenth birthday she could throw a knife with deadly aim and kill a fly with a dueling pistol at thirty paces.

He saw to it that she learned French, Spanish, and mathmatics—and tried to teach her philosophy but found that Chris resisted abstractions she couldn't use. She studied only to please him. By nature she was an outdoor person, and her favorite pastime in all the world was sailing with her father on business trips along St. Marin's coastline.

Mac sought feminine companionship when he needed it in the discreet establishments on Rue Avillier in Lawrence. There were several young matrons and many scheming mothers who did all they could to attract the handsome widower's eye, but he seemed to move through polite social gatherings like a specter, coming late and leaving early.

Mac hated going to the homes of friends he had frequented during the happier days when his wife was alive. The memories of those gatherings were almost unbearable. It was at one such painful time a few years after Blaise's death that fate delivered him his second wife.

He was at a large, opulent ball on the Van Beuren estate. There was laughter and gaiety, but in the midst of it all he felt only a gnawing, unrelenting emptiness. The night was warm and soft. A breeze from the trade winds blew across the island, permeating the hall with the scent of tropical plants, flowers, and the sea. He left the ball to get away from the noise and the laughter, laughter which assaulted his ears and tore at his bowels because it was just not in him to participate.

He went walking along the beach, soberly watching the moon as its reflected light swirled in the dark waves washing over the sand. A noise behind him made him turn about. A woman, tall, with Junoesque proportions, standing a short distance away, was watching him silently. She wore a pale yellow ball gown of watered silk with voluminous panniers and a lace jabot that accented her generous bosom. He recognized her now from the ball. She had been watching him for sometime inside, and now she'd followed him onto the beach.

He was later to regret it, but sadness, liquor, and desire made him walk the short distance between them and take her in his arms. She made no protest, and Mac, too inebriated even to see her face clearly, drew her unresisting form onto the sand.

It was over in a few moments. Groggy with the heat of passion and holding his aching head, Mac realized with chagrin that she had been a virgin, yet as he looked down at the face beneath his own, he could tell that this was no young maid but a mature woman who appeared even older than himself.

"Who are you?" he asked as he rolled from her reclining form.

"Hilda . . . my name is Hilda Lesky."

In the morning, as he lay in his own bed staring at the ceiling, he remembered little of the night before. Yet, he did remember the woman and that she had been a virgin. He also remembered proposing, as honor required. And she had accepted. Blast! But it was too late to call it all back now. Mac dressed and went to Lawrence with the intention of visiting the Van Beurens to find out more about her.

Hilda proved to be their cousin. Her uncle, Maarten Lesky, was a wealthy Dutch merchant whose family fortune was based on herring fishing in the North Sea.

Mac thought somberly on the future that stretched before him. His heart seemed permanently numbed— he would probably never know again the kind of love he held for Blaise. At least this Hilda offered a willing body with an attractive form. Perhaps it was just as well that he take a second wife. His daughter would have a mother.

* * *

Two years after their small, unpretentious wedding, Mac stood holding young Chris in his arms, fighting the stab of pain that gnawed at him as he remembered the past. He looked at the sleepy little girl in his arms and smiled. She was very like her mother. It was a great source of comfort to watch her antics and know that although Blaise was beyond his reach, a part of her would always be with him in Chris. It made life more bearable somehow, knowing that.

Slowly, he walked through the swaying trees and tropical plants of the courtyard back to Mimosa Keyes. Chris was fast asleep, oblivious to the quiet sadness in the human being she loved most in the world.

Mac merely existed now, rather than lived, for despite his second marriage, Blaise St. Claire was the only woman he had ever loved.

CHAPTER FOUR

A young man, naked to the waist, wheeled a barrow of fish along the winding, cobbled street that bordered the quay of St. Marin Bay in Lawrence. It was crammed solid with oysters, small dolphin, spiny lobster, and red snapper. He was clad in clean breeches and little else; his dark skin glistened in the noonday sun. The street was lined with stores in soft pastel hues—eggshell yellow, light blue, salmon pink—sitting side by side like matrons sharing afternoon tea. Small wooden booths of food and wares dotted the quay as busy marketers stopped here and there to buy bread, meat, and fish.

Beneath the watchful eye of her mother a young woman sat in a booth with a tricolor canopy, selling candles, raw wax, wicks, and lamp oil to the passersby. A group of Dutch housewives whose husbands sailed in the many ships that set forth from the island strolled along the quay, laden with parcels of bread, vegetables, and island fruit. They paused to buy several ounces of wax and twenty wicks, enough for a week's supply of candles. The young woman carefully counted their change while her mother sat watching the quay with quiet interest.

At an adjacent booth beneath a canopy of yellow and green, an elderly Rawani woman sold anise, basil, camomile, and ginger—herbs to be mixed in a poultice for swellings and pain. She competed with other men and women—some young, some not so young—who balanced baskets of cinnamon, sage, thyme, bay leaves, rosemary, marjoram, and mint on their arms as they milled through the crowd.

The women who shopped at the market wore long cotton dresses of floral prints with the requisite three petticoats visible beneath their skirts—one of lace, one of silk, and one of fine, starched cotton. Gauze fichus adorned their shoulders, held by small gold pins or fine cameos.

The wives of the merchants and sea captains rode in well-sprung carriages while their maids and servants stopped at the stalls to make the day's purchases. They favored morning gowns of tulle or silk, trimmed in velvet ribbons and satin ruching, tucking their hair beneath bonnets of straw, gauze, or taffeta adorned with ribboned bands, rosettes, and ostrich feathers.

The smell of fresh baked bread blended with the savory scent of smoked meat pies and the sea as the milling crowd moved along the quay. Several vendors wound through the throng, crying their wares in a singsong voice—potions, blessed or hexed, as one preferred, and charms to aid life's passing.

A small crowd gathered to listen and throw coins to a young French lad who played the flute while a small fluffy poodle danced on its hind legs. For a sixpence his brother sketched a portrait in charcoal while the music played.

The quay was teeming with men in well-cut waistcoats and breeches in sober hues of charcoal, blue, and tan. As they threaded their way toward the dock, the silver and gold heads of their polished canes gleamed in the afternoon sun. The men formed eager knots before ramps leading to newly docked ships from Spain, Portugal, France, and the neighboring islands—waiting impatiently to contract for the cargoes of hides, woven cloth, oil, and lumber.

A brawl had broken out among the men jostling for position before two sleek carracks from the nearby island of Bajora. MacGraw Evrion sat in his carriage, watching the rather unusual sight of dignified St. Marin merchants flailing each other with fists and canes. He was comfortably dressed in a white linen suit and cream silk vest, suitable garb for a warm July day. Despite his advancing years, MacGraw remained an uncommonly handsome man. His blond hair had turned a distinguished silver, giving him an air of sagacity and wisdom. Quietly he told his driver, Alphonse, to find out what the excitement was all about.

The driver, a man of mixed Spanish and Indian descent with the build of a young bull, soon worked his way through the crush of merchants to a harried ship's steward and made inquiries.

"Well?" asked Mac, when the young man returned after a brief time.

"The ships are Bajoran, sir, under the command of two captains—Jacques LaCroix and Logan Armor—who apparently sail the carracks for the owner, one Kade Renault, a powerful man of affairs in Bajora. The goods they bring—gold, silver, and jewels—are like nothing I have seen before. The merchants and shopkeepers are killing each other to get in to see the captains and contract for their wares."

Mac chewed the stem of his pipe thoughtfully for several seconds before he said resolutely, "Tell Captains LaCroix and Logan that they are invited to dine at Mimosa Keyes this evening and are welcome to remain as my guests while in this port."

He was curious about these Bajoran captains whose

goods so far exceeded the norm, but he was even more curious about the man who employed them— Kade Renault.

A few hours later the household was a flurry of activity in response to the messenger Mac dispatched to the Keyes to announce that guests would arrive for dinner.

Christina could see that there were special visitors coming to the Keyes. She had been helping Juan, one of the Evrion grooms, care for her horse, whose foreleg suffered a strained tendon in an ill-taken jump that morning. Chris still wore a white shirt of fine lawn and a lad's tan riding breeches. They fit snugly over the well-formed curves of her legs and more than one pair of servant's eyes watched in discreet appreciation as she walked by, oblivious to the admiring glances cast her way.

There was so much activity around the main dining room that she remarked to herself that the guests must indeed be important. Christina walked carefully around the busy clusters of maids, through the *salle de jardinière* and into the *petit salon*. She was about to bound up the grand curved staircase of the Evrion mansion when Hilda emerged from the main dining room in an austere gown of striped blue and gray cotton trimmed with well-starched white-lace collars and cuffs.

"Good morning," Christina said pleasantly.

"Good *afternoon*, Christina," Hilda corrected, noting the girl's breeches with distaste. She made a mental note to speak to MacGraw about Christina's attire when he returned. Those breeches were indecent and totally unfit for a young maid. The child was growing less manageable with every passing year and if something was not done, she would never develop the docile, biddable temper befitting a proper wife.

Undaunted, Chris said, "We are preparing an especially elaborate dinner tonight, I see. Are there guests returning from Lawrence with my father?"

"Obviously, Christina."

"Who are they?"

"That does not concern you," the older woman replied. "They are men from Bajora with whom your father has business and that is all you need know. You will not be present tonight, of course. You and Janie will dine in the *petite salle à manger* so that your father can conduct his business without interruption."

As always, Christina was rankled by the peremptory tone of Hilda's voice but conceded that her presence was not needed, after all, and would perhaps prove distracting. She was generally excluded from these large dinners unless the male guests were over fifty years old. Any younger than that and the frequent glances toward her end of the table proved a formidable obstruction to serious discussion.

With a sigh and a nod she bounced up the stairs to her room to change, having noted the faint look of disapproval that crossed Hilda's face as she entered the room.

An hour later Mac arrived with his guests. The sound of robust male laughter filled the hallway as Mac burst through the door, with LaCroix and Armor close behind. They exchanged pleasantries with Hilda, and Mac asked politely how her day had fared. She responded formally that all had gone well and indicated that dinner awaited their pleasure in the dining room. She withdrew discreetly and left them to their affairs.

After a formidable meal of rare roast beef and strong ale, with a groaning sideboard of meat pie, kidneys, Yorkshire pudding, and fresh island vegetables, the table settings were whisked away and replaced with a large crystal decanter of fine port.

Mac laughed heartily at a ribald tale that Jacques LaCroix recounted. LaCroix was tall and auburn-hired, with a ready wit. Weeks at sea had tanned his skin a nut brown, and a full beard covered much of his face. He was a jocular Creole from New Orleans, and Mac liked him immensely. Logan Armor was a taciturn, brooding man who said little while he sat, quietly sipping his port. Armor's hazel eyes surveyed Mac, weighing and assessing all he did. Mac knew Logan was taking his measure, just as he in turn measured LaCroix.

Mac was curious about the man who commissioned these men—the one they referred to as Renault. After a short interval he raised the subject. "How long have you sailed the *Anna Dayle*, Mr. LaCroix?"

"For two years, *mon ami*, and she is a magnificent vessel. I received a command from Captain Renault in appreciation for a certain service rendered during a perilous time in our lives."

"This Captain Renault you sail for . . . you say he is from Scotland?"

"*Oui*, but he has not lived there for years. He left that isle when he was but a young *garçon*. *Très jeune*."

"I hail from that part of the world myself. Where is his home there?"

Jacques LaCroix and Logan Armor exchanged glances, and Armor answered cautiously, "The Great Glen, near Lochaber."

Noting their reticence, Mac decided not to pursue that topic, and the three men drank in silence for a time. At length LaCroix ventured, "And you, Monsieur Evrion, are a builder of ships, are you not?"

"Aye, that I am. We import a great deal of lumber as well as some of the other materials we need, but on an island as dependent on the sea as this one, 'tis a trade that's sorely needed."

"What sort of timber do you favor?" asked Armor.

"The various kinds of oak for the most part: post oak, smooth white and gray bark, butter oak and a bit of hickory, pine and birch—all of which we bring here from the mainland. We do the planking and masts ourselves, of course, and our woodcutters use pitch pine for tar and rosin for the beams, wale pieces and knees. We import copper fastenings from England. My fastest frigates, though, are made from live oak."

Armor nodded. "Aye, we have heard of your ships."

Mac smiled and lit his pipe, drawing in a leisurely puff. "I think it is time we came to the point, gentlemen. I own a number of the stores along the quay, and many of the merchants in Lawrence prefer to obtain wares for their shops from me, rather than contract with incoming ships at the dock. I manage cargo operations for my own stores everyday—so it costs me little effort to unload goods for them as well. An economy of time, if you will. Having watched the pandemonium your arrival caused on the dock today, I would like to suggest a business arrangement that will prove profitable for us both. Allow me to act as—distributor, let us say—for your goods in St. Marin. You will be able to come and go more swiftly, having only to deal with the Evrion line, and I can assure a good and fair price for your goods—which are superior."

He paused, allowing them time to digest his proposal. Jacques LaCroix's reaction was swift and enthusiastic, his dark eyes gleaming. He'd spent the day untangling endless details and would give anything to avoid a repetition of that madness.

"A most excellent idea, Monsieur Evrion," he beamed. "It will surely save us a host of problems. You can well imagine, *mon ami*, what we went through today. *Mon Dieu!*"

"We can agree to nothing without Captain Renault's approval," Logan Armor stated bluntly in his clipped, laconic voice.

Mac cast a penetrating glance at the taciturn man. "Of course. There is plenty of time for you to obtain permission from your employer and all of the local Bajoran officials, if need be."

"It will not be necessary to consult 'local officials'. Renault is the authority on the island. Nothing is done there without his approval."

Mac nodded. He was consumed with curiosity regarding how this Renault had managed to acquire the riches he saw at the quay.

"Yes," Mac said amiably, "but surely you will want to clear things with the Bajoran government. There is the matter of tariffs to settle, taxes for docking and the like."

Logan Armor smiled for the first time. "Mr. Evrion, Captain Renault is the government of Bajora."

Mac stared at the two men, who were now openly exchanging smiles. "I see . . . er, well . . . in that case . . ."

Jacques LaCroix broke in. "We very much appreciate your offer, Mr. Evrion. I am sure Renault will himself be interested once we explain all that has taken place here. It will not be long before you hear from us."

The men continued the meal in genial conversation until the hour grew late. Then Jacques and Logan rose to bid MacGraw farewell, explaining that they wished to sail with the morning tide, and there were accounts to settle and balance, that would take the rest of the evening.

"Have a care, gentlemen, on your way back. With the load of gold you'll be carrying in exchange for those goods, you're a prize worth taking. At times the pirates in these waters can be as dangerous as the ones in Tortuga."

Jacques LaCroix grinned and Logan Armor appeared bored. "We are not worried, monsieur. We are not strangers to the pirates you speak of or, for that matter, the ones in Tortuga. It is they, not us, who have cause to fear."

Mac's eyebrows rose reflexively. Logan, stifling a yawn, confirmed the query in Evrion's eyes. "Yes, we trade with the Tortugans. Disgusting band of brigands, but worth the trouble and more."

Mac's mind raced. If this Captain Renault was fool enough to frequent those waters, it would indeed explain the difference in the quality of the goods he traded. The most bloodthirsty rogues on the sea were found around the Isle of Tortuga. Their bounty was beyond imagining—but they were such a murderous lot that none were willing to assume the risk of bargaining with them. So that was why the man offered such fantastic treasures! He must be crazy to deal with those cutthroats. Mac was impressed. Their captain was indeed a rare breed.

Earlier in the day, Christina had ridden along the beach in the warmth of the St. Marin afternoon with Marie Robillard and Veronique Lanier. The salt spray was cool and tingling on their skin and the beauty of the day, coupled with the intoxicating nearness of the ocean, sent their spirits soaring. Their mounts were affected also, prancing about, straining at the bit, fairly begging for a free rein. At last the girls relented and, spying a large palm grove at the end of the beach, Christina suggested they race for it.

"What does the winner get?" giggled Veronique.

"Her choice of baubles from the market at Lawrence," Chris answered.

"And the loser?"

After a few seconds of consideration, Marie replied, "She must go into the rain forest tonight on foot and bring back a lock of Gideon's hair." They all laughed and, with the stakes set, at the count of three they galloped away.

The palm grove was a mile away. Christina's horse Xerxes was a born racer, and she led easily after a quarter mile. Chris was beginning to choose a trinket when suddenly, amid the shouts and squeals of her friends, something went wrong with Xerxes. He stumbled, slowed, and began to limp.

"Now what?" she thought. Dismounting, she watched with some disappointment as the two girls caught up and galloped by. Looking at her mount, she chided, "You would choose this moment, my friend, to get a pebble beneath your shoe."

When she arrived at the grove, Marie and Veronique were resting on a grassy patch of sand beneath the shade. "What took you so long?" Marie beamed.

Chris mumbled a disgruntled reply and flopped down on the grass beside them.

"I hope you have more luck with Gideon than you had with this race," Marie quipped, "or you may wind up with your bones stewing for one of his cures."

Veronique laughed. "Oh, Marie, you know Christina will not really go into the rain forest and steal a lock of that old wizard's hair. Why, he is supposed to be quite mad and . . . well . . . dangerous."

But Christina shook her head and said, "A bet is a debt of honor."

Marie smiled. "Don't be silly. I was only teasing. The contest was but a jest. We won't hold you to the penalty."

"No, the race was ridden in good faith and I lost. I must honor the wager."

Chris was smiling and there was a mischievous gleam in her eyes. Marie and Veronique laughed uncertainly and changed the subject, half-suspecting Chris was leading them on—but then again, they were not quite sure.

Later that evening, after dinner, Christina dressed for her task in her maid's room to avoid attracting Hilda's sharp-eyed attention. Janie, the lovely young mulatto who had been in the Evrion's employ since her family died of fever, was a frequent accomplice to Chris's chicanery and a close friend as well. She stared in abject consternation as Christina donned a short green shift, trying in vain to grasp the necessity of this mission as she watched her young mistress tie a small leather pouch to her waist.

"Mis' Chris, you must be ill. Why don't you lie down?"

"I'm fine, Janie. Please understand, I have to do this to honor a wager. And to be honest, I have always been curious about Gideon. It will be an adventure. But don't worry, I'll be all right. I know a short cut to Gideon's retreat on Andier Mountain."

"But why must you go there? That man is dangerous. They say he makes things happen . . . you know . . . with his mind. And he makes all kinds of strange potions. People who live on Andier Mountain say he is big magic. They are afraid of him and only go there when they are sick and there is no hope."

Chris shivered a little. When it thundered in St. Marin it was said that Gideon snored in his sleep. The man was considered a mysterious force of sorts. Adults whispered his name and children were frightened of him. Chris had heard rumors that long ago Gideon had walked the streets of Lawrence like any other man. Someone once said that he had even worked for her grandfather long before she was born . . . but that was so many years ago that people seemed to have forgotten he had ever been one of them. Gideon never came down from the mountains. His activities were so strange and hidden that no one thought of him in normal terms. It was rumored that people who went to Gideon's retreat on Andier Mountain sometimes did not return. But Christina thought that was no more than an old wives' tale.

She solemnly extracted a promise of silence from Janie, then conceded that if she was not back by morning, it was all right to tell.

As Chris opened the door to leave, Janie's little brother Robby bounded into the room, hopping onto his sister's bed as he eyed Chris's strange costume with curiosity. He was an adorable child with melting brown eyes, curly black hair, and an impish smile.

"Are we playing a game tonight?" he asked in his little boy voice.

"No, Robby—and don't you dare tell about this," Janie said quickly. "Just pretend you never saw Chris here."

Robby nodded with an elfin grin. He was used to pretending that he hadn't seen what he saw with his sister and her mistress.

Chris wound her hair beneath a green scarf and crept silently through the long hall, pausing once or twice to duck into an open doorway as she heard voices in the parlor or footsteps on the curved staircase. In a few moments she reached the gardens of the Keyes without being spotted. She broke into a light run, setting off toward Andier Mountain, soon disappearing into the dense wood. She followed the winding road that cut along the beach and veered into the forest.

Jacques LaCroix and Logan Armor were impatient to continue the long journey back to Lawrence. The coach that MacGraw graciously lent them had halted along the roadside to allow the horses a rest. But LaCroix and Armor found the pause wearying. The moon was already high in the sky, and they had plenty to do aboard ship before they could turn in for the night.

Restlessly they walked from the road and wandered into the woods. The moon was so full that it was easy to see the still beauty of a small glade beyond the trees. There was a silvery pond a few feet before them, and they sat down idly on a grassy knoll near its edge, talking of nothing in particular as they waited for the coachman's call.

Suddenly LaCroix's sharp ears picked up the sound of light footsteps running in the brush, steps that drew rapidly nearer as he listened. LaCroix motioned Logan Armor to silence and pointed toward a group of trees, where they quickly concealed themselves.

As they peered into the clearing from their hiding place, a lovely young girl in a short green shift appeared in the glade. She removed a bit of cloth from her head and shook free a long mane of wavy hair as she bent toward the pond for a drink.

Christina had been running for half an hour. Her throat was terribly dry, and she bent to swallow a few sips of cool water from her cupped hands.

A sudden noise from the bushes made her freeze instantly. She watched in surprise as her eyes discerned the shape of two men emerging from the trees. In the blink of an eye she turned and was gone.

"Hold, maid! We mean you no harm," shouted LaCroix, but he found himself addressing only the still night air and felt quite silly. Armor stared at the woods as though he had seen a ghost. The two men looked at each other in bewilderment and laughed.

Had they not been so tired, or the night's work ahead of them so arduously long, they would have pursued and caught the young nymph, but time and circumstance intruded. LaCroix sighed. What a vision the sprite had been! Who the devil was she, and where had she come from? He was glad that Armor was with him—it confirmed at least that he was not merely a tired seaman whose imagination was playing tricks.

The coachman's voice rang forth from the road, reminding them of the work that lay ahead. With reluctance and a weary tread the two men left the clearing and returned to the waiting coach at the roadside.

Christina had been startled when the two men emerged from the bushes but quick reflexes and agility saved her. After bolting from the clearing she streaked through the woods at top speed, thankful that the incandescent summer moon illumniated her way. It was exhilarating to speed through the night, far away from everyone and everything that might say her nay. She had traveled this path many times, but she had never been bold enough to explore the actual cottage where Gideon lived.

Yet everyone in St. Marin knew of this place. One could find him by following the huge flowering plants that bloomed along the path that led to his retreat. Nowhere else on the island did the calla lilies and tiger irises grow to such enormous size. Gideon did something to the plants that charmed them, but no one had been able to find out what.

He lived among the Rawani and Arawaks, meditating alone when he was not attending the sick. His activities were wholly secret, but whispers of his doings were a favorite topic of gossip on the island. The Rawani and Arawaks believed that everything he did was magical.

Stealthily, with little noise, she climbed the path that wound up Andier Mountain to Gideon's cottage. The remains of small fires over which food had recently been cooked could be seen along the way. The small village was settling in for a night's sleep. Chris spotted a thatch-covered cottage much larger than the rest, situated at some distance from the others. The descriptions she had of Gideon's retreat fit that hut.

She waited until the last of the fires had been extinguished and the villagers had gone in for the night. Crouching low, she slipped past the other huts and peeped cautiously into one of the windowless openings of Gideon's cottage.

Inside, she saw a man with shock-white hair and startling gray eyes adjusting the flame in a copper lantern that swung from a rope in the roof of the cottage. He was very tall and thin. Gideon's face was illuminated by the lantern's light for a brief moment before he extinguished the flame. He had the features of a hawk, lean and predatory. There were no furnishings in the room—just a chair, table, and bed. But on a long shelf that covered one wall, Chris saw rows and rows of bottles filled with multicolored liquids, and books with French titles that appeared very old.

As he put out the light Chris could have sworn that he looked straight at her and she ducked quickly beneath the opening. Her heart pounded in her throat for long moments as she crouched absolutely still, not daring to draw a breath.

When she again found the courage to peer into the opening, she saw Gideon lying out on the bed, breathing deeply in sleep.

Very quietly, she slipped through the opening and withdrew a pair of shears from her pouch. She had never been so afraid in her life. If he should awaken and the whisperings of him were true . . . her mind refused to complete the thought. With painful slowness she advanced to the bed and bent over his sleeping form. Quickly, she snipped a lock of white hair and with trembling fingers placed it in the pouch strapped to her waist.

Gideon turned restlessly in his sleep. It took an extreme exercise of will not to scream in fright. She skipped to the opening and jumped out, running as fast as her nimble young legs would go.

Gideon awoke and sat up, listening intently to the sound of running footsteps in the night. He stood and walked to the door of the cottage, opening it to peer into the tropical night. He saw no one, only the still huts in the moonlight.

Thoughtfully, with an expression of bewilderment on his lined, wizened face, he walked back to his bed and went to sleep.

CHAPTER FIVE

The *Anna Dayle* and the *Trade Wind*, captained by Jacques LaCroix and Logan Armor, reached Renault's private dock on a secluded bay in Bajora in good time, less than two days later. Knowing that Renault would still be busy with civil matters on the morning they arrived—a portion of his time was devoted to settling legal disputes in Bajora when he was in residence on the island—Jacques and Logan availed themselves of the opportunity to attend to creature comforts in Vistabuena, the small village on the bay.

When their duties aboard ship were done, they shared a waiting coach to the Red Boar Inn, a convenience thoughtfully provided by their employer.

Located on the outskirts of Vistabuena, the Red Boar Inn was a frequent meeting place for Kade Renault's men. It was favored for its excellent ales, mead, rum, and the comeliness of its serving wenches, though not always in that order. The tavern that housed the inn was a large, white stucco structure with wide beams of dark wood visible in the walls and ceiling. The upper floor held rooms for overnight guests; the lower was cluttered with oak tables, ornate high-backed chairs and cushioned mahogany stalls, the latter used for private conversations away from the noisy, crowded taproom.

The windows were constructed rhomboids of glass with small lozenges held in place with lattices of lead. The multicolored panes were fashioned into shapes of animals, unicorns, and mythical figures. Four graceful archways were completely doorless to allow the cooling trade winds to circulate the inn's air, always heavy with the aroma of spirits, food, and strong Bajoran tobacco.

Patrick Joseph, the Red Boar's innkeeper, bustled noisily about with his portly girth as he supervised the dispensation of large silver tankards brimming with the Boar's potent brew. Like Logan and LaCroix, he was in fact Renault's man. In exchange for his services as proprietor he retained a percentage of the profits and part ownership of the premises.

Inez and Mary, two of the Red Boar's attractive serving girls, hurried to attend the two tall captains as they settled at one of the inn's comfortable corner tables. Patrick smiled as he saw them come in. The Corsairs, as the men who sailed for Renault were called, were the Red Boar's most favored patrons. Bajora had a sizable population of shopkeepers, tradesmen, and professionals. Many of them had a mercantile connection with Renault or were actively engaged in his service. But the Corsairs, the men who captained and manned his ships, were his maritime companions and, by virtue of that, closer to him than the rest of Bajora's male population.

The tavern was also crowded with men from Bajora's remote, wild hills. Few of them had money, but none would deign to farm the land or work for hire. They came from all countries—Spain, Portugal, England, France. Many were former prisoners, voluntarily indentured in exchange for freedom, escaping long sentences for robbery, theft, or murder. Once their respective ships put into island ports, they were free men, allowed to come and go at will. Many of the Caribbean islands had such men, but Vistabuena had more than its share. They favored Bajora's raw, sparsely populated hills.

Piracy was a popular occupation among them, and when a ship with the skull and crossbones put into port, it found no problem in raising a crew. Between such voyages the men eschewed the expensive pleasures in Vistabuena and took to the hills, where wild boar and tropical fruit were readily available. They were fond of roasting boar on a spit in the French manner known as *le boucan*. Women who could be coaxed to do so lived with them in the hills, and the boucannings were rowdy affairs with games and goings on that had little to do with cooking. So prevalent was this form of revelry that they and others like them in the Caribbean earned the nickname *boucaneers*. Though the Red Boar tolerated their patronage, Patrick Joseph always watched them with a wary eye, for they were a volatile lot. Joseph was certain they would have robbed the inn long ago had they not known that it belonged to Kade Renault, whom they feared.

The rowdy laughter and bawdy behavior of the boucaneers contrasted sharply with the well-modulated conversation of the merchants and tradesmen, adding to the general air of confusion and high spirits in the tavern. Tankards of ale and rum passed quickly from tray to table. The squeals of the serving maids punctuated the low-pitched din as wandering hands fondled sensitive portions of their anatomy.

Amid the amiable mayhem, Jacques LaCroix and Logan Armor sat drinking buttered rum and munching juicy slices of sticky, sweet papaya. They watched in good spirits as Patrick Joseph ambled to their table with a cold collation of pudding and souse, a tasty Bajoran forcemeat.

"Good morrow, gentlemen," Joseph greeted them. "How fared the voyage?"

"A very profitable venture, all in all. I deem that Renault will be pleased enough," Armor answered.

" 'Tis good to hear that. I dinna care much for his temper when some bit o' business strikes him ill."

"Aye, it's a dark day on the island when the man's displeased," Logan agreed.

"Tell me, what transpired here while we were away?" asked Jacques.

"Ah, 'twas busy, truth to tell. Several run-ins with the boucaneers. Not those that's here now," Joseph quickly added, seeing Armor's appraising glance sweep the room, "but the real bad ones, ye know, who never come down from the hills. A good home burned and all the goods taken. Daughter of the house kidnapped as well. The men what did it were found and brought to himself. They were put from the island— their belongings went to the families of the dead. 'Twas a big to-do. Took nearly a week to track them down. Sorry you missed the fun, lads."

"We often do, *mon ami*," LaCroix sighed. He stretched and tried unsuccessfully to stifle a yawn. Logan watched him and turned to Joseph.

"All very interesting, Pat, but where can we find Renault now? We have a long report to make and as you can see, my friend is having difficulty focusing his eyes."

Joseph chuckled. "You'll find him at Falcon Hall."

Jacques LaCroix stopped in mid-yawn, and his face brightened considerably. Renault's home—named for his leadship, the *Falcon*—was famous for its excellent cuisine. The captain had gone to some trouble to acquire an experienced chef from France, coaxed with a princely sum and a bit of physical coercion. For LaCroix the evening had taken a decided turn for the better. At Falcon Hall they could expect to dine royally as they gave the captain their account.

"Aye, 'tis there I'm sure you'll find him, but not alone, I think. The young Spanish marquesa's carriage stopped here to water its horses less than an hour ago. Bound for Falcon Hall she was. On this part of the island there's only one place she would be agoing."

LaCroix smiled. Marquesa Francesca De Subias was one of many beautiful women on the island who willingly surrendered her favors to their esteemed employer, but Renault would tell the marquesa to be patient when they arrived, Jacques was sure. He was strict in attending to matters of business and government first, those of pleasure and comfort second. The marquesa would be piqued, but she would wait.

LaCroix, being perceptive in matters of the heart, could understand why. Renault was the sort of man that even beautiful women found irresistible. Exceptionally tall and broad of shoulder, with dark blue eyes and black hair, the captain was so favored by the fair sex that LaCroix suspected there were times when Renault found women a serious nuisance.

The two men said their good-byes, anxious to reach their destination before nightfall. They decided to travel on horseback rather than coach to shorten the journey.

In an hour they trotted up the long, palm-lined thoroughfare that led to Falcon Hall. Far from the flurried activity of Vistabuena, with its shops and trading streets, on a beautifully green roadway on the outskirts of the bay stood Falcon Hall, the center of Renault's domain and the place from which most of the Corsairs' activity was directed. The winding passage that led to the Hall was dotted with flowering vines, hibiscus, and moss-covered trees. It was fashionable among Bajora's leading merchants to build their own homes along this thoroughfare, when they were able. If not, they built along smaller roads that branched from the Falconway; consequently, lovely dwellings with curved archways and wrought-iron balconies decorated the lower bay, extending over the valley to the foot of the rugged Bajoran mountains.

Jacques and Logan spurred their horses as their destination came into view, a graceful, white stucco structure with a slanting red-tiled roof, built in the Spanish manner. The upper windows were bordered by latticed iron balconies with delicate wrought-iron railings, festooned with trails of moss and ivy. Massive carved doors of polished mahogany marked the entrance way, their bright copper handles shining in the sun.

LaCroix and Armor galloped rapidly by the jauntily sprung black carriages of the merchants and their families. It was nearly sunset and their bellies told them that the dinner hour was approaching as well.

A uniformed steward answered the door as Jacques and Logan arrived. "Good evening, gentlemen. Captain Renault is in the library. Let me announce your arrival. Do be seated."

This was the usual procedure at Falcon Hall, and they were shown into a tastefully furnished salon near the entrance. The steward rang for tea. Jacques and Logan were by now used to Renault's fondness for this new British custom, although they preferred less formality with their repasts, and tea was not on the whole very high on their list of favored beverages. The sandwiches and cakes that appeared on a heavy silver serving tray were, however, most welcome. There was a rich profusion from which to choose— tasty morsels filled with shrimp paste, thinly sliced to- mato with bits of grated cheese, and a sideboard of heartier fare—sausage rolls, pork pie, thick slabs of beef and ham, and a savory meat pie still steaming. Scottish oat cakes, baked steaming and dripping with fresh butter, covered one platter, and black bun—a rich fruitcake encased in pastry—adorned another. Gingerbread fingers and scones filled the last silver platter the steward produced, which he set down and discreetly withdrew.

Armor and LaCroix hungrily downed the food, find- ing that their appetites had been increased by their ride. They felt refreshed after eating, even fit enough to tackle an evening of detailed business with the cap- tain. Armor reflected wryly that Renault was wise to give them sustenance before subjecting them to one of the grueling interrogations it was his habit to inflict. A full stomach made for a sweeter temper.

Shortly after they finished, the steward announced the captain's arrival, and Renault appeared at the en- trance of the sitting room. Both Jacques and Logan were tall men, but Renault rose above them by a head.

He stood there before them, a formidable figure casually clad in a white lawn shirt, cream-colored breeches and shining black boots that LaCroix knew to be polished daily with champagne. Renault's great size often proved an asset with his men. His presence triggered a respectful silence that was pure reflex.

Seldom was it necessary for him to shout an order, but when he did, the bellow that issued from his muscular chest shook the rafters.

But from long experience Jacques and Logan knew that the captain preferred cunning to force. Over the years they had developed a healthy respect and admiration for the man's shrewd skill as a trader. The wisdom he showed in their business endeavors was uncanny.

Just beneath the gentleman on the surface—beyond the courtly manner and disarming smile—was the smooth, calculating intelligence of a true profiteer.

He was a hard man to work for and he made a dangerous enemy, but it was not all toil in his service. If the voyage was successful, they could expect a royal celebration once back in port. Then the steely-eyed tradesman threw discipline to the winds and allowed his freewheeling nature free rein.

The revelries often lasted for days, with lovely wenches so abundant that a man could die of pleasure. Renault was overtly gentle and courtly to women, but rather ruthless in his actual use of them. Surprisingly, they didn't seem to mind. Logan Armor had often wondered whether it was the captain's good looks or winning ways that made them blind.

He recalled that what struck him most when he first met his employer was the man's youth. To have amassed so much in so brief a span of years had greatly impressed him. Armor surmised correctly that the captain had been on his own in the world since he was a lad.

"Greetings, gentlemen," he said. Renault's conversational voice was a warm rumble somewhere between low baritone and deep bass. "You have good news to report, I trust?"

Logan and Jacques took careful note of the inflection in his voice as he posed the question. His tone implied that their news had better be good.

Logan Armor drew a deep breath and cleared his throat. "Yes, we were able to sell the entire cargo for a profit of two-and-a-half times the cost of the goods to us."

Renault's mood improved visibly. The sternness in the handsome face melted away, leaving in its stead an engaging grin. "Well done, lads. How did you manage that?"

"Not without considerable difficulty, *mon capitaine*," Jacques replied. "We were besieged when we arrived at the dock. Evidently, word of our coming had been widely circulated there—the result, I suspect, of your initial voyage to survey the island. At any rate, we were mobbed by St. Marin merchants at the quay. *Nom de Dieu*, I have never seen such madness!"

Renault nodded, smiling as he imagined the mayhem. "The St. Marin shop owners have not previously traded with ships bearing Tortugan bounty."

Logan Armor concurred. "They bought all we bore with us and shouted for more—but something must be done about that mob on the quay."

Renault walked over to one of the large morocco-leather wing chairs and sat down, comfortably propping his muscular legs on a nearby footstool. He was certain that Logan had some answer in mind. His men were well trained in that regard. No one posed a problem in his presence unless he'd first considered all the possible solutions and decided which was most likely to succeed. Renault poured a glass of brandy and took a healthy swallow. He aimed a penetrating look at Logan and said quietly, "Well?"

"We suggest that before we again attempt to trade there, we arrange a meeting with MacGraw Evrion, a gentleman of some substance and the owner of the largest shipyard in St. Marin. He has offered to vend our goods on the island in his own shops and to distribute our goods to other St. Marin merchants as well. It would eliminate the necessity of conducting our own auctions on the wharf and assure a fair profit in the bargain."

"What did you think of him?"

"He seemed an honorable man."

Jacques LaCroix shifted uncomfortably while Renault remained silent, noting that the captain's smile had faded. He rose and crossed the room, stopping before an ornately carved armoir from which he withdrew two beautifully worked silver goblets.

Renault gave one to each of the two men, allowing them to pour their own brandy as he stood before a window and mused aloud. "An interesting proposition—but not without its drawbacks."

Jacques and Logan took a nervous swallow of the exceptionally fine brandy and waited.

"Before we proceed further on the matter, we will sail to St. Marin and speak at length with Evrion." There was a brief pause before he added, "In truth, I have been planning to return there at the first opportunity, and the thought of making the trip does not displease me in the least."

Jacques and Logan exchanged glances, puzzling over his reasoning, as well as the distant look in his

dark blue eyes. Renault seemed lost in thought as he
stood there with the curling black locks of his hair re-
flecting the candlelight.

After a long moment he looked at them as if just
remembering they were still in the room. His smile
returned. "You will be staying for dinner, of course?"

Logan Armor and Jacques LaCroix relaxed at last.
He was pleased with the voyage.

Dinner was a sumptuous blend of French cuisine
and island fare. Renault eased into the relaxed camaraderie that typified his association with the Corsairs
once business was done. As their meal concluded,
their now amiable host said, "I take it you have im-
parted everything of note?"

Logan Armor nodded solemnly, but Jacques
grinned. "Everything save one detail, Captain." Renault reclined in an ornate high-backed chair at one
end of the long dining table, negligently sipping a
glass of port. As Jacques spoke he cocked one eyebrow with casual interest.

"On the night before we sailed, as we returned to
Lawrence from Evrion's home, we stopped along the
road for a change of horses. While waiting, we wandered into a small clearing in the forest to stretch our
legs a bit. Barely two minutes passed before a most
extraordinary thing happened. A young nymph clad in
a wisp of green cloth no bigger than this," Jacques
made an indication with his hands, "slipped forth
from the woods. It was too dark to see clearly, with
only the moon for light, but she was a *jeune fille* . . .
a vision. I have never seen such in my life. We came
forward for a better look—but when she saw us she
took flight and vanished. Indeed, if Logan had not

seen her also, I would swear I imagined the whole of it. These moonlight fantasies when one has been away at sea can be very real, eh, Logan?" Jacques laughed.

Armor did not respond. He was watching Renault intently with a perplexed look on his face. The captain, who had been casually drinking his port with an air of detached interest, had moved to the edge of his chair by the time Jacques finished the tale. "Where did you see this . . . vision?" Renault asked sharply.

Jacques was taken aback by the note of command in his voice. "We cannot be sure," he replied cautiously. "It was dark and hard to tell." As Renault's eyes narrowed he added quickly, "Somewhere along the road that leads to Lawrence from the Evrion estate. I think it is known as Mimosa Keyes. We might have imagined the whole thing," he finished lamely, more than a little uneasy under the captain's scrutiny.

The steward broke the tension in the room as he entered the dining hall.

"Begging your pardon, sir, but the Marquesa De Subias is here." Renault stared at the steward as if he were trying to remember who the marquesa was.

"Tell her we will be a while yet."

He was casual once more as he asked in a tone that bordered on indifference, "And what did she look like, your nymph?"

Logan Armor answered carefully. "Long of limb, beautifully shaped and wrought. Silver hair around her shoulders . . . but that was perhaps a trick of the moon."

The two men became more amazed by the minute as Renault plied them with questions for half an hour. Then he said nothing for a time, leaving them to wonder in silence, for they were hard put to find further conversation.

He rose at last and stretched his tall frame, yawning and congratulating them on their successful voyage. Renault invited them to stay as his guests, knowing they were too tired to go to their own homes.

Although both Jacques and Logan were anxious to return to their own establishments, each luxurious in its own right, they recognized the truth in the captain's words and thanked him for his hospitality.

As Logan and LaCroix left the dining hall, they noticed a small salon and saw the marquesa pacing the room impatiently as she waited for Renault. Stealing a look over their shoulders into the dining hall behind them, they saw the captain gazing through a latticed window, lost in thought.

A most extraordinary occurrence, thought Logan Armor, and not explainable by half.

CHAPTER SIX

There had been trouble in the waters around St. Marin of late. A few ships bound for Spain from other islands were taken by pirates after leaving Lawrence Harbor. For that reason, and the fact that a display of strength never hurt when arranging a business association, Kade Renault took the *Falcon*—a full galleon—to St. Marin for the meeting with Evrion. Guy Savant, Renault's first lieutenant, sailed on the voyage as well. Commanding the *Falcon* was a complicated affair—at full crew she carried well over seven hundred experienced seamen.

They weighed anchor at the quay in Lawrence on a fine day in June, and Renault was struck at once by the beauty of the island, the graceful old hills that rose and fell in the distance dotted with large homes in pink, green, and blue. The St. Mariners built their houses in colors, which reflected less sunlight and therefore were as kind to the eyes as they were beautiful. Renault had made arrangements to stay at Mimosa Keyes as the guest of MacGraw Evrion, while Guy and the men remained aboard ship to auction the coffee, spice, and linen cargo the *Falcon* bore.

The smell of honeysuckle drifted through the open window of Chris's bedroom. It was late evening in St. Marin, and the sun sank in a golden arc across the blue and pink of the island sky. Chris sighed and finished her toilette.

"What, still sitting? Mis' Chris, you been there for a

half hour! If you don't get yourself into them lace petticoats so I can lace your dress, your father will skin us both!" Janie Tresgros scolded with exasperation.

Seventeen-year-old Chris looked fondly at the girl who had been with her family since her tenth birthday. They were inseparable friends—and had gotten into more trouble together than she could remember.

"I don't want to go, Janie. Mac wants me to marry well and, because I love him I have put up with this nonsense, but I don't believe this is going to work. That wife of his . . ."

"She is your stepmother, Mis' Chris, and she is trying," Janie offered.

". . . cannot abide me any more than I can her, and she is making my life miserable with these endless parties." Chris lowered her voice to a conspiratorial whisper. "I would rather go with you to Night Festival and dance, as I have not been able to for months. You know, Janie, I do not think I am at all suited for marriage."

Janie was shocked. "Mis' Chris, you must marry— you have no brothers or sisters. Who will run your father's business when he is gone if you do not marry and have children?"

Chris sighed. "I know. Why do you think I put up with this and my stepmother's marriage candidates? I swear, she chose each one with an eye for the worst possible match and then convinced my father of the opposite."

Janie sighed. Hilda Lesky was an austere, withdrawn woman with brown hair and leaden gray eyes. Although her figure was full and statuesque, Janie had seen none of the passion suggested by those ample curves. On the contrary, Hilda seemed to have an aversion to physical expressions of affection. She was aloof, detached, and unyielding. It was inevitable that she would clash with MacGraw's whimsical, impetuous daughter. Aloud Janie said, "Mis' Chris, I'll be back to lace you in fifteen minutes. Hurry now."

Chris moved to her bath, now tepid. If only my real mother were alive, she thought. She remembered very little about Blaise Evrion—just a beautiful woman who smiled and held her—the soft, bubbling sound of feminine laughter punctuating her father's voice.

Janie came in with her gown, a white dress with billowing silk panniers and satin ruching, very *jeune* and befitting a girl making her debut. Quickly, Janie laced her into the gown; the guests had already begun to arrive.

"Mis' Chris, you look beautiful in that dress. Your father will be very proud of you tonight," Janie beamed.

She did look stunning. Her dark gold mane flowed in heavy silken waves to the middle of her back . . . soft, sun-lightened curls which framed her temples and cheeks. A fringe of dark lashes outlined her turquoise eyes and smooth, flawless skin covered the high planes of her cheeks, flushed a soft, glowing pink by the swelling anticipation she felt in spite of herself.

The gown was cut lower in the bodice than most of her other dresses, an adjustment she had persuaded Janie to make in deference to the increasing warmth of the St. Marin nights. The young curves of her high, round breasts swelled gracefully against the soft white silk. She had the smallest waist on the island. The full, cloudlike skirts hid her long, graceful legs, but trim ankles and small slippered feet were just visible beneath the hem of her gown.

Chris heard the distant patter of small footsteps. In a moment Robin skipped into her room, bounced onto the bed, and grinned mischievously at them.

"You look very guilty, Robin," Chris smiled. "Where have you been?"

Robin's grin widened. "In the garden."

"Not pulling flowers again . . ." Janie said sternly.

"Chasing butterflies. I caught two," he said proudly.

"Whatever are we going to do with you, imp?" Chris sighed, but she was not really annoyed. On the contrary, it was good to see him well and active again. Like Janie's parents, Robin had been a victim of the high fever. Most of their family had succumbed to it—she and Robin alone survived.

His sister seemed immune to the dreaded illness, but for two years Robin had been plagued by bouts of alternating chills and fever, until desperation had made Janie seek Gideon's help. The old man had given her a bottle of evil-smelling yellow liquid for the boy—and amazingly, the attacks had lessened, then disappeared completely. Now, he was never ill unless he forgot to take the tonic.

Robin picked up a bonnet from Christina's bed and promptly placed it on his head, scampering to the mirror to laugh at the effect. Janie took it from him and admonished, "You are far more trouble than you are worth, young one."

He cast his sister a look of reproach and reached into his pocket. Skipping over to Christina, he produced several slightly crumpled flowers and pressed them into her hand. Chris smiled and kissed his forehead.

"You have solved my problem, Robby. I will wait until you grow up and marry you."

Robin laughed and ran away, off again for the garden.

There was a knock at the door and tall, charming MacGraw Evrion entered his daughter's room. Despite his advancing years he was ever the distinguished gentleman—handsome, dignified, and endearingly perceptive. Chris rose on tiptoe to plant a kiss on her father's cheek.

"You look enchanting, dear," he said.

"Thank you, Mac," she smiled.

"I have a gift for you. It would please me to have you wear it tonight," Mac said, looking at her with the special pride he showed whenever she was near. "It belonged to your mother."

Chris took the black velvet case from him and opened it. A slender golden chain with a single bluewhite diamond sparkled in the case.

"Oh, Mac. It's beautiful." She looked up at him as her eyes clouded with tears. Mac sighed.

"Now, now. There will be no red eyes at this soirée." He smiled, and said, "You'll be happy to know I've made some additions to Hilda's guest list, as you two seem to have remarkably different tastes. I think you'll find the young men more to your liking tonight, daughter."

Chris's sea-blue eyes widened with appreciation. "Thank you, father." As always, his insight into her thoughts surprised her.

Turning to leave, he said, "Your friends Marie and Veronique are waiting for you in the garden room."

Chris fastened the necklace into place and smiled conspiratorily at Janie. Mimosa Keyes was built on a grand scale and her room was in a wing on the opposite side of the mansion. She ran quickly down the stairs and hurried past the fine paintings, tapestries, and statuary her father had collected in his travels. Through a wide hall to the left of the *petit salon* was the room her mother had christened, *la salle de jardinière,* or the garden room. It was a large salon bordered on three sides by graceful archways that let in the sun. Deep green plants and baskets of hanging ivy filled the room. Several small couches covered with bright floral cotton prints lined the walls, and small tables were situated in the middle of the room for light meals or card games.

It had been Blaise's favorite room for entertaining, and Chris liked to receive her friends here in its cheerful warmth. Outside the garden room lay the long rolling greens of Mimosa Keyes. One simply walked onto a small veranda and down a graceful wrought-iron staircase to get to the main gardens of the Keyes.

Inside the room Chris found Marie Robillard talking with Veronique Lanier. Her two best friends had grown up to be very different in appearance. Marie was tall, dark, and softly mysterious, with a quiet voice and slate-gray eyes. Veronique was short, redheaded, and a trifle plump. She talked a lot and Chris liked her bubbly, enthusiastic ways.

"I still can't believe you really went to Gideon's cottage! It was just a jest—our race—but you took it seriously. Why did you want to go?"

Chris looked at Veronique and smiled. "Because I knew it would be . . . exciting . . . and fun."

"Fun! I would have been frightened to death!"

"So was I."

"Then how can you call it fun?"

There was no adequate answer for that question, and Chris shrugged.

"Well, it wasn't nice of you to keep us waiting here, Christina. What took you so long?"

"I was talking to Mac," Chris said.

"Ah, that good-looking father of yours. Is it true he invited half the young male population of St. Marin here tonight?" asked Marie Robillard.

"That's what he told me," Chris replied. "The more interesting half, of course."

"I heard that he invited Lord Haverston's son Charles," Veronique interrupted in an excited voice.

"Oh, Chris, did he?" Marie chimed in. "Charles Haverston came here from England just two weeks ago to visit his father, and already all the girls are saying he's the handsomest young man on the island!"

Chris started to answer, but a voice from behind said, "Forget about Charles Haverston. He's mine."

Carlotta DeCorba walked into the orange and gold room like a rainstorm on a summer day. She strolled over to their table and sat down, her smile deceptively sweet.

Chris grinned. "Carlotta, I'm glad you could come. Without you these affairs are so unbearably pleasant."

"I knew you'd be overjoyed, Christina. But do listen to me seriously and save yourself the trouble of trying to attract Charles Haverston. He came to my debut fête last week and was very taken with me. I assure you that since he has seen me, your efforts would be wasted."

Veronique sucked in her breath. "Carlotta you have always been the most conceited—"

"No, I am merely truthful." Carlotta ran slender fingers lightly through her straight, sable-colored hair and seductively blinked her dark green eyes. She was indeed beautiful, and Chris didn't doubt that Charles found her attractive. "And because this affair is costing Mac so much money, I don't want to see Chris waste the opportunity." She looked from Veronique to Marie and said, "She isn't getting any younger, you know."

Angrily, Veronique started, "Carlotta, you are a real b—"

Chris interrupted. "Veronique, Carlotta's intentions are always . . . admirable. Besides, this will prove very entertaining for all of us. If Charles is as taken with you as you say, Carlotta, then he won't notice me tonight. On the other hand, it is my intention that he shall notice me, and when he does, we'll all enjoy seeing him ignore you the whole evening."

Carlotta's green eyes narrowed. "I intend to have him, Christina. I've made up my mind to be Lady Haverston some day."

Chris smiled coolly. "It would take more than a title to make you a lady."

Carlotta's eyes flashed cold green sparks. She said evenly, "Insolent slut."

Chris grinned and replied, "You have me confused with your mother."

Carlotta's hand rose as if to strike her, but Chris's icy blue eyes made her stop in midair.

"Unless you'd like to miss this soirée entirely, I wouldn't do that," she said quietly.

Carlotta stood up and swept out of the room.

Marie let out the breath she had been holding. "She has an evil temper. You shouldn't make her so angry."

"But I enjoy getting her angry." Chris laughed.

"Are you really going to try to take Charles Haverston away from her?" Marie asked.

"With every ounce of femininity in me," Chris replied.

"You might find that he does not interest you, Chris," said Marie.

"It doesn't matter. Most men don't interest me. At least this one will be a challenge." Chris sat back in her chair and looked out the open doors that led to the veranda toward the rolling lawns and stately trees of Mimosa Keyes. The estate was bathed in the soft glowing light of the St. Marin sunset. "The majority of men in the world are sweet fools," she continued. "Any intelligent woman can wind the best of them around her little finger. English lord or not, I think this Charles Haverston will not prove to be any different from the rest."

Marie and Veronique looked at each other. Must be the Dumas blood, Marie thought. Veronique laughed. "You know, Chris," she said, "the problem with you is that you're really just an awful flirt."

Smiling, Chris looked at her friend. "Yes," she said, "I know."

Chris watched as the two young women stood up and left to join the growing crowd in the ballroom. "If you don't hurry up, you're going to miss your own debut!" Marie called from the foyer.

"I will come in a minute. I just need a breath of air," she said. She turned and walked through the double glass doors of the garden room onto the balcony. Outside to the right, she could see the verdant mountains and white beaches of St. Marin awash with the glow of the orange and pink sunset. Far below the high vista of Mimosa Keyes, the ocean surged and ebbed against the St. Claire beach, blue and mysterious in the dusk.

She was never to remember how she knew someone was standing behind her, but a prickly feeling along her arms and goose bumps on the back of her neck made her turn around. She looked down the stairs and saw the dark outline of a tall man. In the evening light he was little more than a broad-shouldered silhouette. A tiny ripple of apprehension danced up and down her spine. "Where did he come from?" she wondered. Standing there, framed in the sunset, he looked like some dark god risen from the sea.

She walked down a few of the steps to get a closer look and stopped. His dark blue eyes appeared black in the dusky St. Marin twilight. She watched as he walked to the foot of the stairs and leaned casually against the wrought-iron railing. He moved with the natural grace of a dangerous animal . . . with dark, glowing eyes that were vigilant and alert even while he seemed at ease.

She'd never seen such a superb specimen of mature manhood. His skin was swarthy—like a man who spent most of his time in the sun. His features were clean-cut and well carved—as if some ancient master had chosen the perfect stone and created the work of his lifetime. He had wide-set, deep blue eyes and a strong, square jaw. There was an intriguing cleft in his chin, and Chris noticed that his lips were firm and sensually shaped.

That forceful mouth had the undeniable look of a rogue. The well-shaped lips promised pleasure to be enjoyed today and regretted tomorrow. She couldn't tell how old he was, but he looked mature and masculine, different from the lads who flirted with her every day.

Chris felt uneasy. It was disturbing to realize that he was the source of her agitation. A raw magnetism radiated from him and it was distracting.

He seemed annoyingly at ease, leaning against the railing, a suave, mocking look on his face. Unhurriedly, his eyes traveled from her face to her breasts, pausing to take in the soft swelling curves before moving downward to boldly speculate what lay beneath her billowing skirts. He raised his gaze again to her breasts and then, with a smile, looked directly into her snapping turquoise eyes.

How dare he, she thought.

She was embarrassed, but she didn't want him to know it. Ignoring the blush that crept into her cheeks, she stared back at him. At last she couldn't stand it any longer and said, "It's rude to stare."

"Very rude," he agreed amiably in a deep voice.

Chris waited for him to say something else, but he remained silent. She felt an uneasy qualm in the pit of her stomach, the beginning of a suspicion that she faced with great reluctance. Had this dark stranger heard what they had said?

"Who are you, monsieur?" she asked.

He smiled and swept her a cavalier bow. "Kade Renault, mademoiselle, at your service."

She thought the look in his eyes belied his words. "How long have you been standing here?" she asked quietly.

"Long enough to hear an interesting conversation between four young ladies." He grinned sardonically.

Reprobate, she thought to herself.

"Tell me how you came by enough experience at your tender age to conclude that all men are fools?" he said.

She wanted the ground to swallow her or, even better, to swallow him.

"Come. You spoke with such authority. I, too, wish to learn."

"What I said is true," she mumbled.

"Perhaps Charles Haverston will not want you. Your vanity will no doubt tell you he is too big a fool to know what he is missing," he said gravely. There was so much amusement in his eyes that she grew annoyed. Who was this man to make fun of her? She thought he needed a lesson.

"Not want me? But, monsieur, how can you know, having nothing to judge by?" she said. On a whim she moved closer to the stranger. Putting her arms around his neck and rising on tiptoe, she pressed her lips to his.

It was a soft kiss—young, fresh, and innocent. She had from time to time been kissed by young men who were inexperienced in the art of love, and her own knowledge of such matters was limited.

His response was so swift that it startled her. She began to move away, to end the kiss, but found his arms about her, as strong and hard as iron. She grew alarmed and put her hands against his chest to push him away, but it was like trying to move a wall. She felt his mouth move against hers, parting her lips as his tongue entered to caress her own. For a time he seemed to drink in her essence, pressing her closer as she squirmed and attempted to evade intimate contact with his hard, unfamiliar body.

"Jake's ribs!" she thought. "This man will never let me go!" Finally he did. Her eyes snapped indignant blue fire, mad as hell that he'd taken far more than she'd wanted to give. She looked at him and tried to guess what he was thinking, but his blue eyes were unreadable. "I'm not going to give him the satisfaction of seeing how mad I am," she thought. She forced herself to compose her face, unaware that her narrowed eyes crackled with blue sparks. She looked irresistible with her mouth pink and soft from his kiss and her cheeks flushed with soft color.

"Well, do you still think Lord Haverston's son will be indifferent?" she asked. As the first flash of anger passed, she had to admit that he'd done a fine job of turning the tables on her. She looked at him with a mischievous glint in her eyes. This was a man to be reckoned with.

Kade Renault was quiet as the sea-blue gaze enveloped him. It was a moment before he replied. At last he raised an eyebrow and said with amusement, "Actually, I feel a great deal of sympathy for that young man."

She was not sure what he meant, but it didn't seem complimentary. She wrinkled her nose at him and, turning, walked regally up the stairs toward the veranda. She paused to look down at him and said coolly, "Don't be so certain that your concern is not misplaced."

He looked up at her sardonically. "It isn't. Rest assured, I have no sympathy for you whatsoever." He grinned as his eyes slowly caressed the young curves of her body.

Disconcerted, she turned quickly and walked

through the garden room into the foyer. I have to find out who he is, she thought. She had the inescapable feeling that she would see him again. And she wasn't sure she liked the idea.

CHAPTER SEVEN

Chris stood at the entrance of the ballroom. Mac was resplendent in a waistcoat of beige satin that complemented his fair hair, now mingled with strands of silver. He came forward to lead his daughter into the room. True to his word, the handsomest young men in St. Marin filled the grand ballroom of the Evrion mansion. Chris was beset with invitations to dance. The night passed in a whirl of pastel skirts and high-spirited young laughter.

Before long she was out of breath and dying of thirst. She sent her attentive young escort to the punch bowl, her eyes searching the room for Marie Robillard. She spotted her in a corner, laughing and gossiping behind her fan with two other girls.

"Marie, a word with you alone?" she asked. Marie excused herself and walked toward her.

"Are you tired of dancing so soon?" Marie teased.

"Yes, I wish I could leave now," Chris sighed. "But that is not what I want to talk about. Marie, have you ever heard of Kade Renault?" If anyone knew of him, it would be Marie. For all her young years, few things on the island escaped her notice.

Now her eyes widened in surprise. "That man! Yes, I know him. Why do you ask?"

"I met him in the garden," Chris replied.

Marie said, "He is a privateer who sails against Spain. Their ships carry more gold than most. He has business with my father and was a guest at our home this past week. If you saw him here, then Mac must trade with him also. Chris, he has the most awful reputation with women. I was not allowed to dine in his presence or see him at all. It is too bad too, because it is said that he comes from a good family in the British Isles. But for some reason they no longer have anything to do with him. It is even said that he is proud of being a scoundrel. Chris, I think you should stay away from him."

Chris said nothing. She was watching Carlotta. "Who is the young man with DeCorba?"

Marie looked toward the couple and smiled. "That's him. Charles Haverston."

He was a handsome young man with light brown hair, hazel eyes, and an open, honest face. His eyes crinkled at the corners when he laughed. "Excuse me, Marie," Chris said.

Marie watched her go. Slowly, she shook her head. She felt almost sorry for Carlotta.

Charles Haverston listened as Carlotta described several dresses she'd bought recently. He had to concentrate to keep his mind from wandering. She was lovely to look at, but after listening to her pretentious drawl for an hour, he wanted to escape.

"I hope you're enjoying the ball, Carlotta."

Charles turned to find the source of that low, soft voice. Carlotta's green eyes turned cold as she saw Chris regarding her calmly. "We were," she said, emphasizing the last word, "weren't we, Charles?" When there was no response, Carlotta turned to look at the young man beside her. He was looking at Chris . . . as though he'd found something he'd lost.

"I'm glad," Chris said unperturbed. "I'd like all my guests to have a good time. I don't think I've met your friend."

When Carlotta did not reply the young man said, "Charles Haverston, Miss Evrion," bending to kiss her hand.

"I have not seen you before, Mr. Haverston. You are new to the island?"

"Yes," he replied, smiling brightly. "I arrived last week. My father is teaching me the ship-building business."

She nodded. "An interesting and very difficult art. Perhaps next week, if you have time, I can arrange for you to visit my father's shipyard. He has several vessels that are known in St. Marin for their speed and unusual design."

Charles was surprised. It was unusual to find a debutante who was interested in ships. "You know something of sailing, Miss Evrion?"

She nodded. "My father feels that everyone who lives on an island should be able to sail."

He laughed. "Your father is a wise and practical man. I have heard of him. Someday I would like to meet him."

"That is not hard to arrange." She smiled.

Carlotta stood silently smouldering. "Charles, I feel a little dizzy," she said, smiling her most seductive smile. "You will accompany me to the garden for a breath of fresh air?"

Charles looked at her levelly and said, "I'm sorry, Carlotta, that you're not feeling well. I say, wouldn't it be better to lie down for a bit?"

She frowned and then quickly caught herself. "Oh, no, I am sure that it is only air I need."

"My dear," he said, "you really do look a little fatigued. And in the tropics, well, you can't be too careful. I insist. You must sit down and be quiet for a while." Putting his arm through hers, he piloted her to a nearby couch. Two matronly chaperones began to fan her sympathetically. Turning to Chris, he smiled and said, "It would be rude of me, Miss Evrion, not to dance with the guest of honor. Shall we?"

An hour later they were still dancing. Young Charles Haverston was quite taken with MacGraw Evrion's daughter. Laughing, they went to the punch bowl, and Charles handed a crystal glass to Chris. As she raised the glass to her lips, the back of her neck began to tingle. It must be a night breeze, she thought. She was getting tired and she wanted very much to leave and go up to her room. Absently, she turned toward the entrance of the ballroom. Her eyes widened in recognition, and she started.

Kade Renault stood in the doorway, leaning nonchalantly against a marble column—a knowing light dancing in his dark eyes. He looked from her to Charles and back. Chris felt her cheeks burn. He grinned disagreeably, white teeth gleaming against his tanned skin. Chris bristled under the amused scrutiny of his gaze. Casually, Renault inclined his head in a wordless salute. Then, with a soft laugh, he turned and walked silently off into the night, whistling carelessly to himself.

CHAPTER EIGHT

Christina was annoyed by Kade Renault's desultory look. That man was destroying an otherwise pleasant evening. She found herself nodding to some question Charles asked. Chris almost jumped with surprise as he took her toward the open French doors. She realized that he had asked if she would like some air. Normally she would have declined. Now it was too late.

As it happened, there was little cause for worry. Charles remained a gentleman, and while it might be said that he aimed a few too many glances at her demure décolletage, his conversation was impeccable. At length, tiring of their inane banter, she asked him to retrieve her fan from a banquette in the ballroom.

He left and she was alone for a moment in the peaceful quiet of the garden. She stared at the tips of her kid slippers, brooding over nothing of consequence, troubled by a vague sense of discontent she was hard put to name.

When she looked up at last, a pair of shining black boots came into view. With a sinking sensation in the pit of her stomach, Christina's gaze traveled up a pair of steel-hewn legs encased in light tan breeches, to a trim, hard waist, powerful chest, and shoulders—until she looked directly into two wickedly amused blue eyes.

"We meet again, Miss Evrion," Kade Renault said. "I believe you are called Christina, are you not?"

"Only by my friends, Monsieur Renault."

"Well . . . Christina," he said with an emphasis

that caressed the name, "you surprise me. After what I overheard earlier today, I did not think you would send your young friend away so soon."

"Do you make a habit of eavesdropping, monsieur?"

"Yes. It makes life very amusing indeed."

"It is insufferable."

"But highly entertaining."

"You are a boor, Captain—and I find you intolerable."

"Such abuse from one who appears so gentle and soft. You surprise me, Christina—you look so obedient and well behaved."

"My mother died when I was a small child, Captain. I learned most of what I know from my father, and he greatly values honesty and independence."

Renault regarded her with a mischievous twinkle in his eye. "This . . . independence . . . that you value interests me. Please do enlighten me further."

Why she should bother with this odious person was beyond her, but with an uncharacteristic show of patience she explained how important it seemed to live life without constraint, to feel free, and do that which came naturally, without fear or hesitation.

Renault smiled as she finished. Something about the look in his eyes made her wary, and she stiffened as he stepped nearer, so close that his tall, muscular frame brushed her own. The expression on his handsome face was too warm by half.

Resolutely she put her hands on his chest to push him away, but far from improving matters, she lost ground as Renault put his own warm hands over hers and gently entwined their fingers.

"Monsieur . . ."

His voice was deep and teasing as he smiled at her

and said, "This independence—of which your father approves—does it include swimming alone in the nude?"

Christina froze. Her mouth formed a round "oh" of surprise, and she stared at the captain in mute shock.

Renault found the softly parted lips too inviting to resist. Christina's dismay doubled as he drew her into his arms and kissed her lingeringly. It was altogether the most unsettling moment of her young life.

It took minutes of struggling before the bold captain set her gently down. She couldn't remember ever being so angry—or embarrassed. She raised her hand to strike him, but Renault caught it quickly in his own and grinned.

"Oh no, kitten, I always return the favor when someone deals me a blow—and I'm sure you don't want that."

The devilish look in his eye increased. "Besides, I feel certain that no matter how leniently your father has raised you, you've not told him of your passion for swimming in the altogether. 'Twould take but a few seconds to mention it once our business is done."

Chris looked at the man in silent horror—and cursed the fates that had put him in her path.

"Nay, on second thought perhaps your stepmother would be a better choice . . ."

"_Mon Dieu_, Captain Renault you must not tell her!"

He smiled charmingly.

"No, I won't. But then again, perhaps I shall. I suppose we will just have to wait and see . . . will we not?"

Chris was beset with alternating waves of anger and frustration, coupled with the nauseating realization that she had given him a considerable weapon.

How in God's name had he found that well-hidden spot? It was a half-day's ride on horseback—then a full hour on foot. She cursed aloud.

Renault raised his brows in mock dismay. "Mademoiselle, you abuse my tender ears."

"Christina, is everything quite all right?"

It was Charles Haverston, back from the ballroom with her fan.

"Yes, Charles. Please take me in. I . . . that is . . . I've had quite enough air."

"Miss Evrion," Kade Renault said as he bent over her hand in a courtly bow, "I do hope that I'll be seeing more of you in the future." With a deep chuckle, he bid them good-bye and strode away. Chris knew a decided urge to kill.

She went back to the ball with Haverston, feeling troubled and depressed. Lord, but she regretted the impulsive kiss she had given him on the terrace. It had been hasty—and she realized now, quite foolish. He was different from the lads she knew, and beyond her ability to control, a dangerous person indeed. Kade Renault would have wide berth from her as long as he was in St. Marin.

A very wide berth, she thought, as she remembered the impossibly strong arms that had rendered her immobile in his embrace.

CHAPTER NINE

The next week passed quietly, and by its end Christina was thoroughly bored. She asked Marie Robillard to come to Mimosa Keyes to relieve the ennui of the still afternoon.

As they sat in the *salle de jardinière* drinking tea, Marie asked Christina what she planned to wear to Carlotta's ball.

"Carlotta is planning a ball?" Christina asked.

"You mean you didn't know?" Chris regarded her friend quizzically as she continued, "Carlotta persuaded Doña DeCorba to give a special fete for Charles's father, Lord Haverston. Of course, Charles will be there as well, and Carlotta plans to finish the game she started before you interrupted last week."

Chris was silent as she considered the probable outcome of Carlotta's plan. Unless she did something to intervene, DeCorba would yet manage to ensnare that nice young man. She could, of course, simply sit back and let fate shape events as it would, but what would be the fun of that? Besides, it was impolite of Carlotta to have excluded her from the ball. She needed a lesson in manners.

Thus, on the day of the ball Chris and Janie rose before dawn and dressed in pants, with loose-fitting linen shirts. Tucking their hair beneath blue kerchiefs and broad-brimmed hats, they made their way stealthily downhill to St. Claire Bay, dressed as lads. They were totally unrecognizable, and Christina had no problem in renting a small boat from an old fisherman on the wharf. She was an expert sailor, and it took only a few hours to reach the small port on the other side of the island where she could purchase the wineskins she needed.

They returned to the Keyes, each carrying three goatskin bags filled with dark red wine. Chris and Janie spent the better part of the afternoon attaching leaves and twigs to the bags with tar until it was impossible to tell what they really were. They hid them in the courtyard of the Keyes, where they could return after nightfall and retrieve them easily.

The only problem that remained was sneaking into the house without being spotted. It was late afternoon and the parlors and salons of the household were bustling with activity. Chris smuggled Janie into her quarters on the lower level, just in time to avoid a group of St. Marin businessmen leaving her father's study. She ducked behind a hanging drape as they passed her in the hallway. Stealthily, she tiptoed along the inner wall, hoping to make a quick run up the curved stairway to her room on the second floor.

Chris had almost succeeded in reaching the foot of the stairway when she heard quick footsteps above her and the sound of Hilda's voice as her stepmother began to walk down the stairs. Chris was trapped. She couldn't go forward without being seen or backward without running into the men who had just left the study, so she darted quickly through the door to the library on her right and closed it with one swift motion of her foot. Chris listened for a moment with her ear pressed to the keyhole as Hilda's footsteps tapped rhythmically past the door of the library. Only then did she turn around to glance at the room behind her.

When she did, her heart leapt into her throat at what she saw.

Sitting silently in two large leather wing chairs across the room, watching her with peculiar expressions on their faces, were Mac and Captain Renault. Her father's eyes narrowed slightly as he said in a voice that was a trifle strained, "Christina . . ."

Chris closed her eyes, hoping that the simple act of blinking would clear their presence from the room. But it didn't work.

"Oh, hell," she swore silently, her mind working quickly to fabricate a plausible explanation for her attire. She turned to face them with unhurried grace, as if she had not just come running into the study like a fleeing house thief. Kade Renault was grinning at her in a very disagreeable way. With one hand she removed the hat and kerchief from her head and walked forward with ladylike dignity to greet her father.

"Good morning, Papa," she said formally.

Mac arched an eyebrow at her. Renault was trying to suppress his mirth without much success.

MacGraw Evrion regarded his daughter with consternation. "What in heaven's name are you about, and why are you dressed in that outrageous outfit?"

Fortunately, Christina had by now come up with a reasonable excuse. "Xerses was limping badly this morning, Mac, and I stayed in the stables while Juan tended her leg. I was worried that it was going to be serious."

"Was it?"

"No, just a bad splinter. It must have been painful though."

"Still, that is no reason to go flying through the house as if it were burning over your head."

"Yes, Father, I'm very sorry—I didn't know you had a guest," she said, glancing at Renault.

Kade watched Chris with an inner smile. He could tell by the glimmer in her eyes that she was up to mischief. She had worn the same look the day she beguiled young Haverston into abandoning that beautiful dark-haired maid. There was something about the way she stood there before her father—an air of tension, like a deer poised for flight—that reminded him of the day he had watched her on the cliff. Though he hadn't known her long, Renault was perceptive enough to realize that beneath the dimples and aqua eyes lay a true hellion. He was quite sure Chris was lying. Yet the smile she wore now was like a sunrise, all bright morning light. Worldly though he was, Renault felt himself succumb to the pull of its charm.

MacGraw continued. "From now on, Christina, you are to let Juan attend your horse when it is hurt. He is very capable and can work far better when you are not in the way. Understand?"

"Yes, Father," she replied sweetly. "Uhhh, may I go now? It's time to change for dinner."

Mac smiled. "Off with you then, but remember what I said."

Chris kissed him quickly and hurried out of the library. She knew he was far more startled than annoyed, and in a few minutes he would forget the whole incident. After dinner she and Janie would take the wineskins from the garden and get everything ready for the little surprise she planned for Carlotta DeCorba's ball.

MacGraw Evrion turned back to Kade Renault. "You will have to excuse my daughter. She can be very unpredictable at times." Renault made a polite reply, thinking that he would like to find out himself just how unpredictable. The business relationship that had developed between them had thus far proved very profitable for both. Renault had never considered bringing it to an end, and after seeing Christina at close range he had an even more important reason to make sure it continued.

Mac Evrion thought highly of Captain Renault, which was not surprising, for they were much alike. The pursuit of adventure and the promise of excitement propelled them both, and each had found in the Caribbean a world more to his liking than the one he'd left. Like Mac, Renault was a middle son of a thriving Scottish family with lands that lay south of Orkney, in Lochaber, near the Great Glen. Although Renault had never precisely said so, Mac had the feeling that he had left the highlands very early to seek his own way in the world, for the man was too independent to defer his will to that of his elder male relatives.

Though Renault was a privateer and therefore somewhat disreputable, Mac thought him a fair tradesman and an excellent captain. As long as their business dealings went well, Renault's politics were his own affair.

Besides, MacGraw liked Kade on a personal level. He found the young man's style easy and controlled, something he always appreciated in a business associate. He was contained, yet responsive, and one had the feeling that he could cope with the worst life could give and steer his ship and his men to safe harbor. The young man was resourceful; he knew how to build. There was a confidence about him that suggested reliability and commitment—a quiet power that augured well for the future and the air of a man who controlled his own destiny.

Christina bounced up the stairs, good-naturedly plotting Carlotta's demise. She was so engrossed in pleasant anticipation that she nearly collided with her stepmother walking down the hall.

There was something about Christina that irritated Hilda, no matter when she saw her. Perhaps it was the way the child walked, or the sound of her voice. Whatever it was reminded her of her cousin Johanna— bright, laughing Johanna whom Hilda had bitterly resented throughout her girlhood in Holland.

Johanna's father, Maarten Lesky, was the most successful herring merchant in their village. Hilda's own father, Piet, was Maarten's partner in the business and possessed the same business acumen that had enriched his brother, but lacked the former's concern for decency and human kindness. Piet felt limited and restrained in the herring trade. After years of coaxing he persuaded his brother to let him extract his share of their profits to make a sizable investment in the growing Dutch linen industry.

Before long, Piet Lesky ran a highly lucrative linen workshop—one that was infamous in the town of Ottenzie for its intolerable conditions and harsh hours. The crowded one-room space was freezing in winter and oven-hot in summer. Piet preferred to use children as workers—they were less apt to complain about working eighteen hours a day and could be more tightly packed in the weaving room. He fed them a meager fare of the cheapest French cheese and bread, for which a sum was deducted each month from their wages.

Piet was a true miser and hoarded his money in various banks, spending little on his wife, two sons, and daughter. His prosperity and reputation as a merchant grew, but his family benefited little.

As a girl and therefore a liability, Hilda fared worst of all. She received virtually no schooling beyond a rudimentary knowledge of domestic skills. Seldom was she permitted the company of other children her age, and with the exception of her brothers, who were several years older, Johanna was her sole companion.

Johanna possessed everything Hilda deemed worthy of having in the world. She wore new dresses, was allowed to play with other children, and was never punished by being locked in her room for hours on end.

It was hard for Johanna to believe that Hilda's life was as bad as she said, and she often teased her cousin about her dour demeanor and surly personality.

Hilda resented Johanna's insensitivity and lack of understanding. The girl's utter lack of comprehension and belief angered her beyond endurance. Without realizing it, Hilda began to blame Johanna for the inequity of their lives.

One day when the two girls were alone in Johanna's small boat on the River Weiss, the wind blew her young cousin's hat into the water. As Johanna stood and bent to retrieve it, she lost her footing and fell over the stern. The voluminous skirts of her dress quickly took on water and weighed her down. Johanna flailed in agony against the sodden material and frigid water, trying frantically to grasp the side of the boat as she called to Hilda for aid.

Hilda could easily have extended an oar to the girl as the boat drifted downstream, but she did not. Instead, she watched and waited, idly noting that it took Johanna almost twenty minutes to drown.

Unfortunately for Hilda, Johanna's brother Nels was out for a stroll along the river that day. He was too far away to reach them in time but close enough to see that Hilda made no attempt to help his sister. Nels watched the scene in horror from shore.

After Johanna's funeral Nels revealed what had occurred. Hilda was sent to St. Marin to live with their relatives, the Van Beurens, who were given spurious but adequate reasons for the visit.

Now, watching Christina as she struggled to regain her balance, memories of Johanna flitted like ghosts through Hilda's mind.

She resented the closeness between Mac and his daughter. During her first days at Mimosa Keyes she had tried everything she could think of to stir Mac-Graw Evrion's heart, but nothing had changed the detached politeness he showed her, and over the long years of empty nights, she had become bitter and hard. It was a source of inner shame to her that she could be totally in love with a man who was so obviously indifferent to her as a person. She was a very proud woman, and Mac's affairs, however discreet, wounded her sorely. Despite it all, she would have walked a hundred miles to his bed gladly—had he but asked. The bitter truth was that, as Hilda well knew, the only thing that mattered to Mac at Mimosa Keyes was his daughter.

Damn them both! She vowed that someday she would repay them for the unspeakable pain they had caused her.

Chris watched several expressions play across Hilda's face. Nothing she saw in her stepmother's eyes surprised her—she had never known them to hold affection or kindness when they peered in her direction.

"Just where have you been all day?" Hilda asked.

"I was with Xerses in the stables. She hurt her leg this morning."

"I should think that Juan would be able to take care of that."

"I wanted to be certain that it was not serious."

"Were you thrown this morning?" Hilda asked.

Chris thought a moment and then embellished the tale. "Yes, but Xerses was hurt worse than I. She will be fine in a few days, though. Juan says we were both lucky." Chris shifted her weight uneasily under Hilda's scrutiny. "Well, if you'll excuse me, I must change for dinner."

Hilda watched as Christina walked away. Quietly she thought to herself, what a pity she didn't break her neck.

Later, in the soft twilight cover of the St. Marin sunset, Chris moved about the DeCorba garden like a quiet shadow. She had enlisted Robin's aid and now was having great fun with the fat wineskins as they silently set the trap. Chris was well acquainted with the way Carlotta stalked her prey. There were six marble benches in the courtyard and each was beneath a large shade tree. When Carlotta had chosen her favorite for the evening, she would find a way to lead the young man to one of these secluded alcoves, where she could employ the full force of her charms. When Chris and Robin finished their work, a fat wineskin was secured among the branches above each one of the lovely white marble benches.

Robin smiled conspiratorily and returned to Mimosa Keys, while Chris concealed herself in the tall, manicured shrubbery near the entrance to the courtyard. Once or twice she thought she heard footsteps nearby, but when she cautiously raised her head to look, no one was there, so she settled down in the shrubs, holding the pistol she had brought with her cradled in her lap, humming a little as she waited for Carlotta to arrive with Charles.

Chris did not have to wait long before Carlotta appeared with him in tow. The young man looked a bit reluctant and more than a little uncomfortable, but Carlotta was unquestionably at her loveliest, magnificently dressed in a rich green silk gown with voluminous panniers. A high neck of frothy lace augmented her dark curls, and she smiled coquettishly behind a beautifully made fan inlaid with mother-of-pearl.

"Ah, Charles," Carlotta said in her most seductive whisper, "why don't we sit here for a minute. The breeze is so soft, and we can see the bay from here."

They walked to a bench that overlooked the long stretch of pale beach, far below the DeCorba estate. The little alcove was well lit by golden candles in copper lanterns and bathed in a hazy yellow light. "Isn't this lovely," Carlotta purred, sitting down on a marble bench while fastidiously arranging her skirts around her. "Have you ever seen a more beautiful night?"

Charles Haverston stood looking at the bay, somewhat bemused by the unexpected splendor of the view. When he turned to answer her, Carlotta favored him with a voluptuous gaze from her liquid green eyes. Haverston began to walk toward her, a glimmer of desire alight in his eyes.

Chris took careful aim, raising her pistol deliberately. She pulled the trigger with confidence and like a bolt of summer lightning, a loud crack of gunfire cut through the tranquil silence of the garden. Carlotta shrieked with fury as the wineskin burst above her head, showering her hair and gown with the sticky, wet brew.

Haverston froze, not quite understanding what had changed the lovely girl before him into the messy creature he now beheld. Somehow Carlotta had suddenly become a mass of soggy wine-stained green silk.

"Don't just stand there you fool, do something! Stop gaping and help me!"

Charles turned in confusion to stare at the myriad shrubs and trees, then raised his eyes to the branches above Carlotta's head. "I don't understand how . . ." he began.

"It does not matter how! Call for help—take me away at once . . . someone help me! I'm with an imbecile," she whined. "Charles Haverston, if you dare to laugh . . ."

But Charles began to smile in spite of himself as Carlotta danced about, raging incoherently. The smile became a laugh, and Carlotta's fury knew no bounds. She was still shrieking at him when they disappeared through the courtyard gate.

Chris laughed out loud after their departure and left the shrubs for a closer look at her handiwork. As she reached up to retrieve the wineskin, she heard a deep chuckle rumble from the tall shrubs on her left. Her eyes were as wide as saucers as she watched, in paralyzed shock, as Kade Renault walked forward with a wide grin on his handsome face. Chris's mind spun wildly. The noises in the bush hadn't been her imagination—they were sounds he'd made! She cursed her loathsome luck. How in heaven's name had he managed to follow her?

Christina swallowed hard as Renault said, "Good aim," and doubled up with laughter. She had an impulse to cover his mouth with her hand. She was awfully afraid that Charles or Carlotta might come back. Finally his laughter subsided and he looked at her, blue eyes dancing with wicked amusement. "Do you always scheme so thoroughly to make the world come out your way?" he asked.

"I try," she replied, disgruntled. Chris was annoyed; she realized that his discovery of her plot was going to cost her something.

Kade's eyes twinkled with dark mischief. She watched him with increasing apprehension. Renault regarded her with what she could only describe as evil amusement. Softly she murmured, "Are you going to tell Hilda?"

"That depends. I'm sure that you, being such a resourceful maid, can think of a way to persuade me to hold my tongue." Chris watched in silence as Kade closed the distance between them. She looked up at him as he loomed over her, wishing fervently that he had never been born. "Any ideas, sweet?" he asked, smiling.

Chris thought quickly but found no reasonable bribe to put before him that he might accept, save of course the obvious one.

Renault watched her closely, one eyebrow cocked in wry amusement. Chris shuddered to think of how unpleasant her life would be if Hilda learned of this escapade while Mac was away. She regarded Kade dubiously, doubting that he could ever really be trusted. There was no assurance that he would not tell Hilda when it suited him, no matter what she did. Yet, it was well worth the effort to pacify him—because anything was preferable to the awful seclusion Hilda could impose on her while her father was away on business.

With a small sigh of resignation she put her arms around Kade's neck and pulled his head down for a deep and thorough kiss. Renault's arms slipped around her waist, and as he straightened, Chris felt her feet leave the ground. He held her, enfolded in his arms for a long moment, and then set her back to earth, releasing her with a reluctance that was not reassuring.

"That was a most persuasive and satisfactory bribe. Your imagination does you credit."

"Well . . . that was what you had in mind, wasn't it?" Chris snapped. The man was a curse, in the extreme.

"Maybe. What pleases me is that it was obviously what you had in mind. Not that I blame you. There are not many maids who can resist my charm. There is no reason to be ashamed if you cannot control yourself while we are together . . ."

Christina didn't hear the end of Renault's sentence; she was already walking away.

Kade was laughing again. "Leaving so rudely? Aren't you afraid I will change my mind?"

"Go ahead and tell," she flung back over her shoulder, "and go to Hades as well."

Renault's answering laughter rang in her ears and ground on her nerves. Lord, but that man is beyond endurance, she thought irritably. He does everything but disappear. She looked back at the tall shrubs where he stood—and saw that he was no longer there.

Perhaps he can do that too, she thought glumly. She crossed herself as she had seen Janie do, and fervently hoped she would never see him again. Renault's discovery had taken all the fun out of her play and her ill humor lasted the rest of the day.

CHAPTER TEN

MacGraw Evrion sat in one of the petite dining rooms of Mimosa Keyes. It was his habit to breakfast alone in one of these smaller rooms in the morning before driving to Lawrence to the Evrion shipping offices. Long ago he had begun to rise at dawn and leave just as the sun crept over Andier Mountain. On the surface he did it because it was good for business, yet he knew that the real reason for his early waking habit was to avoid his wife.

Beyond the first night they lay together, try as he would, Mac had been unable to rekindle the arousal he had felt. At best, he could not blame Hilda. She was as she had always been. In the beginning she came to his bed willingly enough, and he was not adversely disposed to their union. But during those first tentative couplings—though he tried in vain to stop himself—he repeatedly uttered the name of his first wife.

How often he had whispered Blaise's name while his first love lay beneath him, softly telling him of the joy and pleasure he gave her. It was as natural to him as the act itself.

But when he had continued to murmur her name when making love with his second wife, Hilda, understandably, had withdrawn and then withheld herself from him completely. Mac had not pressed her further. In time they had reached a reasonably satisfactory living arrangement. Hilda ran Mimosa Keyes in an efficient, well-organized manner, and the domestic details of the Keyes were entirely her domain. Mac left daily for his work in Lawrence and was frequently away on business, managing to conduct his *affaires du coeur* with discretion and tact. Hilda seemed content with their way of life and was outwardly as satisfied as MacGraw himself. Her seething resentment was wholly unknown to him.

Mac quickly downed several slices of cold roast beef and eggs, washing the whole of it away with strong island coffee as he finished the last bite of a well-buttered muffin. He was about to rise from the table when footsteps in the corridor caught his attention, and he watched his wife approach.

Hilda did not disturb his morning repast unless a pressing household matter needed his attention. Her light brown hair was neatly, though somewhat severely, drawn from her face and secured with a deep green ribbon that matched her plain, linen morning dress.

Noting briefly that MacGraw had finished his repast, Hilda began to address him regarding the matter on her mind, characteristically without preamble. "I would have a word with you regarding your daughter."

Mac nodded. He knew that Hilda bore no particular affection for Christina. But the task of raising a little girl to womanhood had fallen heavily on his shoulders with Blaise's death. He knew nothing of the manner in which young girls were raised, coming as he did from a family of four strapping lads. As it was, he mused, he probably had done the girl a woeful injustice, being selfish enough to enjoy her company and thereby instructing her in his favorite pastimes— sailing, riding, hunting, and the like. The advice that

Hilda had tendered on Chris's upbringing he had received gratefully and implemented forthwith.

Hilda knew of her husband's vulnerability in this regard and used it to ease her frustration when she felt so inclined. On many an occasion it had given her great pleasure to cause that peppery young woman grief with a well-timed comment regarding her "lack of restraint" or "wanton ways."

But today Hilda had outdone herself. She had overheard a conversation among Chris and her friends in the *salon jaune*. Marie Robillard had commented that a young man by the name of Timothy Wyncliffe had been paying an inordinate amount of attention to Chris. Christina had smiled and said that her fortune, not her person, was the reason for Wyncliffe's interest. The young man was more favorably disposed toward lads than girls, but his family sought to extend its influence by linking their holdings with the Evrion wealth. That had given Hilda a truly delightful idea.

She looked at Mac's waiting, expectant face and continued.

"Christina is seventeen years old, MacGraw. It is time for you to think much more seriously than you have about her future and a husband that will be both suitable and dependable for her. There is a young man on the island who has made known his desire to address Christina formally. His name is Timothy Wyncliffe and his father owns a sugar refinery, as you know. I would urge you to encourage his suit."

"This young man Wyncliffe is personally known to you?"

"No, although I have seen him many times, as have you. His mother, Orelia Wyncliffe, has been a member of my sewing circle for some time. She is a very decent woman of admirable character."

MacGraw regarded Hilda thoughtfully. "And how does Christina feel toward this young man? Have you discussed the possibility with her?"

"Christina has seen young Wyncliffe on many occasions. I have no reason to believe that she would not look favorably upon him," she lied.

MacGraw nodded thoughtfully. After a moment he said, "I have to go to Dionville Island for a few days regarding a cargo problem with one of our ships. We will speak of this again when I return. As always, Hilda, I appreciate your concern."

"I would like to give young Wyncliffe some sign of encouragement, MacGraw. It would not do at all to put the lad off by seeming opposed to the match. In your absence I suggest we invite the young man for a luncheon here. Christina will be given the opportunity to become acquainted with him while I act as chaperone."

"Very well. Once again, thank you. We will discuss the matter at length upon my return." He favored her with a smile of gratitude and, picking up a slender cane of oak and whalebone, left the dining hall.

Hilda watched his retreating form with a smile of quiet satisfaction on her face.

Morning came bright and early the next day, too early for Chris. She opened one eye as Janie came in and threw back the curtains to let in the sun. Chris winced at the light. "Janie, what did I ever do to you to deserve such cruelty," she grumbled.

"Time to get up, Mis' Chris," Janie laughed. "Your

daddy got up at dawn and left on a business trip. And here you are still in bed."

"I can't stand people who are cheerful in the morning," Chris said, pulling the pillow over her head. Suddenly she sat up. "Did you say Mac left on a business trip?"

"That he did," said Janie as she straightened the room.

He had just returned from one trip—in jocular spirits because of its success—and now he was off on another without a word. Drat, Chris thought. She could still remember the fun they had had when Mac taught her to navigate as a little girl. In those days he never left on a trip without her. That had changed with his second marriage. Hilda told Mac that it was improper for Chris to go sailing or be knowledgeable about such things as business and navigating. She had convinced Mac that most of the things Chris liked to do were improper.

I'm in such a foul mood now that I may as well get up, she thought. She put on the short pink satin maillot Janie had laid out for her. It was delicate and feminine, trimmed with white Belgian lace. It clung to the swelling curves of her high young breasts and graced the line of her trim hips, stopping just above midthigh, leaving her legs bare.

With Mac away on business, no male servants would be upstairs, so Chris didn't bother with a dressing gown. In the summer, St. Marin mornings were humid and warm.

"Christina!" Hilda Lesky's voice cut through the peaceful morning like the sharp blade of an axe. Reluctantly, Chris walked to Hilda's bedroom. A summons from Hilda in the morning was unusual. She and her stepmother made a point of maintaining a polite silence. When they did speak there was usually trouble.

"Good morning," Chris said, determined to be friendly.

"Well, you finally woke up, I see," Hilda said irritably. "I have good news for you."

I doubt it, Chris thought.

"Today I arranged something special," Hilda continued. "Timothy Wyncliffe approached your father last night for permission to call on you. His family is quite wealthy, as you know. Your father and I discussed it, and I have convinced him that Timothy should be allowed to address you."

I'm sure you did, Chris thought drily. Timothy Wyncliffe was effeminate, spoiled, and arrogant. Chris found him wholly repulsive. She said, "Hilda, did it ever occur to you to discuss it with me?"

Hilda ignored her. "He will be here for lunch. We'll receive him in the green salon. And Christina, it is time for you to wear your hair up like a young lady rather than streaming down your back in that wanton fashion you favor."

"Hilda," Chris began, "I appreciate your efforts on my behalf, but I really don't think that Timothy and I will deal very well together."

"Christina, I don't have time to argue with you. It's almost noon. Get dressed," Hilda snapped.

Chris stood in the doorway trying to decide whether or not the issue was worth the fight she felt brewing. After a moment's hesitation she decided it wasn't and walked back to her room. Sitting down on her bed, she sighed to herself, "Lord, there's no solution to this tangle. There's not a man on this island I want to marry."

She thought of Charles Haverston. He was nice. She liked him, and he was very attentive. She knew that if she gave him any encouragement, he would soon ask Mac for permission to pay his addresses. She laughed to herself. I have his eternal gratitude for saving him from Carlotta, she thought. The problem was that she liked him too well to see him married to a woman who didn't love him, even if it was her. All she wanted to do was to keep him out of Carlotta's grasp.

Her thoughts turned to Timothy Wyncliffe. He was haughty, selfish, unmanly. She felt no scruples about him.

Janie had begun to put up Chris's long hair. The pins hurt her scalp.

Mac may be able to stomach him for a son-in-law, but how could I abide him as a husband? she asked herself. What if our sons grew up like him? Surely Mac wouldn't want that. And Hilda has probably all but assured him of my acceptance. How am I going to get rid of him?

She was still thinking when Hilda marched into her bedroom.

"What? You're not ready?" she said loudly.

Chris sighed. "Hilda," she began, "I'm afraid it's not going to work with Timothy and me. To be honest," she tried to put it delicately, "I really don't think he likes girls."

Hilda looked at Chris for a long moment. "I wouldn't be so quick to judge, miss. A girl of your questionable background would be lucky to get him."

Christina regarded Hilda with eyes of bright blue flame. She was seized with a burning urge to slap the

woman's face. Hilda was fortunate to be out of striking distance. Chris was proud of her lineage, of the
black blood she had inherited from her octoroon
grandmother. She felt it made her special and unique.
But Hilda had a narrow view of the world, and her
sensibilities were pricked by everything her stepdaughter represented. Christina was part of a world
she neither understood nor wished to know.

"I'm not going to marry that prancing popinjay,
Hilda, and the two of you can go to Hades for all I
care!" Chris said hotly.

In a cool, measured tone and with great satisfaction,
Hilda replied, "You are no better than your grandmother, little slut."

Convulsively, Christina snatched a vase and threw
it squarely at Hilda's head. The woman barely ducked
in time. Chest heaving with uncontrollable anger,
Chris thought wildly that if she remained in the same
room with Hilda, she might commit murder. Whirling
on one foot, she ran from the room, nearly colliding
with Janie, who was carrying her dress.

Janie watched open-mouthed as Chris ran toward
the staircase clad in only her silk maillot. "Mis' Chris,
wait! We have company downstairs. Captain Renault
is . . ."

But Chris didn't hear her. She pulled the pins out of
her hair, letting it spill in waves of honey brown and
gold over her shoulders and down her back. Running
through the house made her feel wild and free again,
like a little girl. She reached the top of the stairs. The
railing was made of mahogany. She'd used its smooth,
wide length for a slide as a child, too impatient to
walk slowly down the stairs. On impulse she hopped
onto the rail. With her long bare legs extended in front

of her, she slid down laughingly, picking up speed as she neared the bottom.

When Captain Renault's tall, broad-shouldered figure emerged from the parlor, it was too late to stop. He was directly in her path.

"Look out!" she cried a second before the collision. He turned just in time to catch her, but the impact knocked the wind out of her. She felt as if she'd run full speed into a rock. It was all she could do just to stand there, with her arms around his neck—trying hard to get her breath.

Jake's ribs! I wish I'd known he was here, she thought, dazed. She had practically nothing on. His arms were around her, warm and hard. She could feel his hand on the bare skin of her back while the other rested at the small of her waist. Her legs pressed intimately against his steel-muscled thighs. She looked up into his face and saw two laughing dark blue eyes. He smelled of brandy, tobacco, and leather. Like a snake charming a bird, he gazed back at her as he slowly closed the distance between them. She felt his mouth close over hers. Idly she thought that it was odd for lips that looked so hard and firm to feel so soft. When he released her some of the teasing glint had left his eyes, replaced by the glowing light of something deeper.

She moved away from Kade. Out of the corner of her eye she saw Timothy Wyncliffe emerge belatedly from the parlor on the right, curious about the commotion at the staircase. His eyes went huge as he stared at the sight of Chris in her scanty attire.

A glimmer of pure malicious mischief sparkled suddenly in Chris's sea-blue eyes. I know how to get rid of Timothy once and for all, she thought to herself.

Pretending that she hadn't seen Wyncliffe, she put her arms around Renault's neck. Gazing tenderly into his eyes, she said, "Darling I couldn't wait any longer. Every minute without you is agony." Then, using all her imagination, she gave him a passionate kiss.

She heard Timothy Wyncliffe's angry gasp behind Kade's back, and opening one eye, she watched him stalk back into the parlor and slam the door. Good riddance, she thought, amused. Her attention went back to Kade. She was still locked in his arms. "Let me go," she said against his lips.

If he heard her, he didn't show it. His embrace had been strong before, but now it was like iron. She tried to move away, but he tightened his hold. Caressing and warm, Kade's lips moved over hers. There was hardly a part of her body that was not closely pressed to his. Her breasts seemed melted to his chest, and she could feel the hard warmth of his manhood against her thighs. His kiss was bold, demanding, and hungry. She felt as if he were drawing the breath from her body.

Suddenly she heard a gasp from the top of the stairs. "Mis' Chris! What are you doing?" It was Janie. She felt Kade's arms relax.

"Now will you let me go?" Chris said.

"If you insist," he replied, his voice low and deep.

She bolted up the stairs, looking back over her shoulder just long enough to see his mocking blue gaze alight with a glow she didn't stop to analyze.

CHAPTER ELEVEN

"Oh, Mis' Chris," Janie said, shocked and dismayed. "You must stay away from that man. Trouble walks with him. He's very bad. Even pirates are scared of him. I have a cousin who knows the cabin boy on Kade Renault's ship. He said the man does not know what fear is. He goes after Spanish ships, takes their gold to Bajora with him, and laughs. The Spanish—they would do anything to catch him."

"He's from Bajora?" Chris asked, remembering Marie's words about his origins in the British Isles.

"Not born there," she said, "he just live there. He come here to trade for rum. His real business is in Bajora. Women there chase him all day, but he loves no one. Stay away from him. He will be bad for you," Janie finished, shaking her head.

Women did find Kade Renault irresistible. It was more than just his looks. With his black hair, swarthy skin, and disarming smile, he was ridiculously handsome, but his real appeal lay in a kind of elusive charm—the deep blue eyes that danced with electric sparks when he laughed, or turned dark as midnight when he was angry. His attitude toward women made them respond almost against their will. In passion he was bold, direct, and honest. When he desired a woman she knew it. This man played no games. Women found his reactions both flattering and disturbing.

Renault was ever-available, elusive, and unattainable. It seemed that no manner of woman was immune to his magnetism. Ladies and tavern girls found him equally irresistible, and when summoned, all were more than willing to give. Men marveled at his amatory exploits, and his conquests were both legendary and legion. The female population regarded his women with grudging respect and admiration, as though an honor had been conferred on those who won his favor. The challenge of catching his eye was one to which few failed to rise.

For women, Kade was the prize of prizes—a force to be tamed. His very name was synonymous with sexual vitality and compelling sensuality.

The pirates made it a point to stay away from his ship—wary of his reputation with a sword and a gun—yet it was known that he ran legitimate businesses, too. They were, in fact, the mainstay of his fortune, but for his own reasons he sometimes waylaid Spanish vessels, freeing them of their heavy cargoes of gold and jewels. Rumor had it that he spread most of this booty among the poor, but when confronted with the tale he laughed and said that charity was not in his nature. Still, the rumors persisted.

Janie's warning to stay away from Renault went unheard. Chris had other problems on her mind. She was of marriageable age, her father wanted her to make a good match, and there was no one on St. Marin she felt she could love. The only man who came close to stirring passion in her young heart was Captain Renault—a uniquely unsuitable husband and a reprobate, to boot. Her head hurt. She felt confined, and if she saw Hilda again today, she would undoubtedly strike out at her. Her wild young soul cried for release.

"Janie, I have to get away. I can't stay here tonight. Come with me to Night Festival. Let's go and dance."

Janie looked nonplussed. 'Twas not easy to follow Chris's mercurial moods. She said uncertainly, "Are you sure you want to do that?"

"It's the only thing that can help me now. I've got to relax. I'm so tense and upset. If I don't dance tonight, and let all of this out, I'll explode. I don't want to upset Mac, if I can help it."

Janie sighed. Just like her mother, she thought.

Night Festival in St. Marin was a ritual of dance, music, and laughter. The revelry was derived from African ceremonies of long ago, transplanted to the New World by members of those ancient tribes. Blaise Evrion had gone periodically to the festival to dance, like her mother before her. It was as if the Dumas blood in their veins drew them to the low beat of the drums and the dark warm night.

"Janie, please," Chris pleaded.

"Yes, all right," Janie smiled. Her own blood cried out for the music as much if not more than Chris's. Neither girl ever went alone. They felt safer together.

A wide expanse of virgin rain forest ran adjacent to Mimosa Keyes. The lush green mountains behind the estate had long been the gathering place for the Rawani celebration or the Night Festival, as Chris and Janie called it. It was a traditional ceremony of dance and song done ostensibly to celebrate the summer months and insure a good harvest, but its religious importance had diminished over the years, and now it was held primarily for the pure enjoyment of the Rawani. When Chris felt civilization pressing down on her, she went to Night Festival to dance and let go.

Anyone could go to the Rawani celebration. It was

open to all on the island, but it had developed chiefly from ceremonies carried forth by members of the tribe who had come to the island a hundred years ago as slaves and bondsmen. Most of the participants were either Rawani descendents, pure Africans, or mulattoes. Nearly all of the descendents of the original Rawanis had bought their freedom by the time Chris was born, but they still proudly maintained many of the old customs of the mother tribe. Chris thought Night Festival was the best custom of all.

At ten o'clock, when the rest of the household was asleep, Chris and Janie slipped out into the warm tropical darkness. The moon was high in the summer night, and it was easy to follow the path through the rain forest toward the bright fires glowing in the distance. They could just make out the sound of the music and the drums.

"*Lowani . . . lowani . . . adume . . . adume . . .* all of my children . . . come . . . to . . . me . . ." The sound of the doman's voice drifted to them through the trees. There were other people beside them on the path now. Young men and women their own age, mature adults in mid-life, and women who were obviously grandmothers—everyone mingled together. The salt smell of the sea mixed with the sweet scent of tropical flowers as they threaded their way through the green foliage.

They reached a clearing in the trees. A small fire burned in each corner of a large square clearing, while at the center of the square another large fire burned as well. To the left of it, food and drink were spread on palm leaves for the revelers—kingfish and yellowtail with melted butter, the spiny island lobster called langouste, and grouper fillets beside huge bowls of okra, avocados, plaintains, bananas, and limes. Two big barrels of St. Marin's most popular brew framed the spread at either end. The drink was known simply as "spice" and was made by boiling cloves, cinnamon, aniseed, fennel, and rum into a smooth liqueur.

For long hours people danced and drank, ate and laughed. The old were young again. The young knew no sadness, had no cares. The women wore clean, loosely cut white cotton blouses and full skirts with white ruffles along the hem and yards of petticoats. When they whirled and turned with the men, who were clad in white pants and shirts, their long brown legs gleamed in the firelight—bare arms, bare fingers, and bare feet making quiet, rhythmic sounds in the tropical night.

They were soft spirits in white—dancing, singing, moving, chanting, transported by the beat of the drum. The drum moved all things, made all things move. The drum and life were one—like the heartbeat of the universal mother above her unborn child, sustaining, maintaining always. Safe, secure. Happy and carefree.

They came to the part of the ceremony where good and evil meet and do battle. Good wins and evil disappears. Thus the harvest grows well. The spirits didn't actually come, but everyone had fun pretending.

Tonight, Christina was the dancer who would invite the spirits into the camp. For no particular reason, evil was always summoned first. The drums began a steady, low beat. She moved toward the center fire. Her long, tawny mane swirled softly about her shoulders in the night breeze. She wore the white blouse and full skirts of the Rawani. Her blouse was not new and she had nearly outgrown it. The short sleeves were still puffed and full, but the bodice had become tight across her developing bosom, and the swelling curves of her young breasts rose invitingly above the soft material. All Rawani skirts stopped at the knee—it made dancing easier. Although rarely seen, Chris's well-formed calves and small feet were clearly visible tonight.

It was time to do the Dance of Evil. The drums grew louder. Chris felt the beat in every part of her body. Her hips moved slowly in time . . . from left to right and then around . . . around . . . left . . . and around again. The others began to clap in time, softly with the music. A chant to call the evil one began. The drums beat faster. Chris responded to the quickened tempo. The clapping grew louder. The end of the dance was near—Chris would signal to the others that evil was present by falling to the ground at the end of her dance.

Her hips moved faster, sensually increasing the spiritual erotic involvement of the onlookers as she herself grew more emotionally involved with the drums—the beat, the night, and the fires. Anger, frustration, and pain all slipped away. The emotions spent themselves in the wild, free rhythm of the ancient dance. Her soul began to feel free; she was flying. Her body moved with the chanting, moved with the drums, and then it was over. She had released the tension and the private demons that haunted her. She fell to the ground. Evil was now present in the camp—the dark demons of her young soul released by the cleansing rhythm of the drums.

On a normal night, silence was expected at this point as the dancer quietly renewed her strength on the palm-strewn ground to prepare for the Dance of Goodness. But not tonight. Chris knew something was wrong when she heard a hushed gasp from the crowd, followed quickly by the sound of running bare feet. Scared but curious, she raised her head and opened her eyes. Chris crouched by the campfire, white ruffles and skirt aglow with reflected firelight, too fascinated to run.

A tall figure, well over six feet, stood before her. It had appeared from nowhere and was entirely clad in black, with a long black cape and . . . oh, no . . . it had no head! Chris screamed and scrambled to her feet to run, but the menacing black spirit grabbed her arms. She struggled, screaming. Just as she was about to faint she heard an amused deep voice ask calmly, "Do you do this often?"

It was Renault. She sighed. For a moment she was too relieved to be angry. The cape fell down around his shoulders, revealing a wicked, mischievous grin on his handsome face. "Kade. I'm so glad it's you. Has anyone told you how very much you look like the devil?" she asked.

He threw back his head and laughed. His white teeth gleamed as he smiled at her, blue eyes flashing with amused sparks. "Serves you right—invoking the spirits. And with such a dance," he said as his eyes traveled slowly over her lithe young body, lingering on her shapely bare legs. "What would you do with the devil if you met him?" he asked with that teasing glint she was beginning to recognize aglow in his eyes.

"I'd introduce him to you," she said saucily. "He'd be frightened to death." He laughed. "How did you find this place?" she asked. "No one knows of it except us."

But instead of answering her, he said softly, "You didn't answer my question."

"What question?"

"Do you do this often?" he said again.

"Often enough," she said cautiously.

"You amaze me. I didn't think girls of your upbringing had a yen for this kind of adventure."

Chris sighed. She didn't know why, but she felt she could be open with him, tell him the truth. "It isn't that," she said. "There are just times when something deep inside me cries to let go, when something in me has to get out. There are days when I can't stand polite conversation, restrained music, or forced laughter. Something bursts in me. I have to get away, and come here to the drums and the music and the dancing. I have to know the freedom of letting my body move as it wants to." She looked at him, feeling certain he would not understand, but he was looking at her with something like admiration on his face.

Renault said nothing for a long time, looking intently into her eyes as though he were reading a book. Finally he smiled and said, "Yes, you would need to do this, wouldn't you, tiger?"

Chris didn't reply, wishing for once she could read his thoughts. His eyes did not seem to condemn or judge. He just looked friendly. She wondered if it was because he felt the same way.

She walked over to get a drink. It was hot, and she was suddenly thirsty and tired. This had not been so relaxing after all. She was tense again. She suspected strongly that Renault's presence had a lot to do with it.

"How did you come by this habit?" he asked.

"My mother, Blaise. She had the same need. She'd come here when my father and I left on business trips. She got the habit from my grandmother, Michelle Dumas. She was a Creole—an octoroon from New Orleans. My mother told me Michelle could outdance every woman at the Rawani celebration. I have always longed to be like her."

"Well, I never saw your grandmother, but I did see you, and offhand I'd guess you're damn close to matching your grandmother's record."

She looked up at him to see if he was teasing. His smile was warm but not mocking. She dipped a cup into the barrel and pulled it out, filled to the brim with the cool, sweet liqueur called "spice." Chris drank it quickly. It should be sipped, but she was very thirsty. She dipped the cup in again.

Kade raised an eyebrow. "Isn't that barrel filled with spice, young one?" he asked.

"I am aware of the contents of the barrel, monsieur," she quipped. "It is hot tonight, and I am thirsty."

Kade watched her drain the second cup. The corner of his mouth went up as his face assumed its usual suave, mocking expression. "Your capacity is admirable. Spice is a potent brew. Many men three times your size find that two cups are one too many."

Her head did feel light. Chris was beginning to float on a soft pink cloud. She giggled softly and said, "Men. What care I for their capacities?" The last word came out a little slurred. "Not even that much do I care," she said as she snapped her fingers lightly.

"Ah, yes," he said with mock gravity, "I remember

now. How did you put it? We are all fools. That is what you said, isn't it, Miss Evrion?"

"Yes, that is precisely what I said," she said precisely. She thought.

She turned to get away from Kade. He was such an annoying person, always showing up at the wrong time in the wrong place. Didn't he have anything better to do? She began to dance again, differently from before. This time she waltzed. One . . . two . . . three. Turn . . . turn.

Kade watched the small figure in white float around the campfire, a strange smile on his handsome face. He laughed softly and said to himself, "I always forget, kitten, how young you really are."

Chris ignored him. She waltzed until she finally got dizzy and stopped. She heard a small whisper from the bushes.

"Mis' Chris, over here. Quick, run!" It was Janie.

"No, Janie. It's okay. It is only Captain Renault." Janie looked unconvinced. "Come on out. Everything's all right," Chris encouraged. Janie stepped shyly out of the bushes, not looking at the black-clad figure of Renault. He seemed very amused at her behavior.

"Captain Renault, Janie Tresgros, my maid and personal companion."

Renault bowed politely. Too politely, thought Chris. He's making fun of me again.

"At your service, Miss Tresgros," he said in his deep voice.

"Captain," Janie said, bobbing a brief curtesy. Chris caught the apprehension in her voice even if Kade didn't. She meant to say something reassuring, but she felt so sleepy. "I guess I overdid it tonight," she thought. "Well, we better be getting home," she said aloud. "Janie . . . let's . . ." She never finished the sentence. The last thing she remembered was her whole body sort of melting. . . .

Kade Renault caught the soft, slender figure in his arms as she slipped into unconsciousness.

"Oooh," Janie said, surprised. "She never did this before."

Kade was staring at the face of the sleeping young woman in his arms. "Don't worry, Miss Tresgros," he said, lifting his gaze to Janie. "Which way is Mimosa Keyes from here?"

Janie led him to the Keyes. They tiptoed in through the kitchen and up the back stairs to avoid waking the sleeping household. "Where is her bedroom, Janie?" Kade said. Janie pointed to a door. Kade slipped in with Chris in his arms, but when Janie tried to follow, he gently closed the door with his foot until it locked. Janie's mouth formed a round "oh" of surprise, and she ran to get the key.

Kade walked toward the canopied bed and laid Chris on it gently. With one finger he softly traced the line of her cheek. She stirred slightly, fighting for consciousness against the alcohol and fatigue.

Through a fog Chris heard the sound of low, resonant laughter. She felt a pair of warm lips cover hers and a tongue caress the soft recesses of her mouth just before she slipped into a deep, dreamless sleep. Far off in the distance a voice said, "Goodnight, tiger."

A moment later Janie came back with a key. With trembling hands she opened the door to Chris's bedroom. When she entered, no one was there except Chris. Janie looked around the room apprehensively.

Satisfied that there was truly no one else present, she walked across the room and, humming to herself, quietly closed the window.

CHAPTER TWELVE

MacGraw Evrion was impatient to leave the tiny island of Dionville for St. Marin. His stay had proved less than fruitful as his business representative, René Ardielle, was not sufficiently prepared for his visit, and the papers which were to have been ready for his approval were far from complete. Another trip would be necessary, and Mac was not happy about it. To make matters worse, the sleek frigate in which he had made the trip from St. Marin to Dionville had taken the worst of a voyage in rough weather and would have to remain in Dionville for repair. He would return for her later, but in the meantime René was supplying a carrack—a rather old one at that, which still featured immensely high castles fore and aft—for his journey home. Cumbersome thing, but nothing else would be seaworthy within the week.

The *Mariadonna* set sail with the morning tide. The day was cool for the season and the winds were high, but the *Mariadonna*'s captain seemed confident that they could reach St. Marin in two days' time with favorable winds. Mac was not so certain. He'd noticed that the *Mariadonna* had a disturbing tendency to handle ill with a stiff wind bowling her along, and the captain had difficulty steering her. Not surprising, for she lacked the proper head and jib sails that would have truly eased her handling.

They had been on the high sea only a few hours when the first dark clouds appeared on the horizon. The rain began an hour later. The morning sun was completely gone, and the winds whirled about them like the scream of a demented god. The sea became a nightmare—an angry, boiling blue mountain range with disaster in the treacherous valleys between the giant waves that crashed above them.

Mac had been in his cabin, but he came on deck at the first sign of trouble. It was the worst storm he had ever seen. They fought it for hours, but at nightfall, when the intensity of the winds showed not the least sign of abating, Mac conceded with a heavy heart that the *Mariadonna*, old and tired as she was, could not hope to see this one through. In the seething darkness that surrounded the weakening ship, a mountain of a wave crashed mercilessly against her deck, snapping two masts like dry twigs.

Mac watched, desolate but resigned. It was now only a matter of time before the *Mariadonna* sank to her grave. With a sigh, he decided it was fitting that the end should come here for him—at sea.

Another giant wave caused the ship to capsize as men screamed and scrambled for worm-eaten lifeboats. MacGraw Evrion alone seemed at peace. His last thoughts were of Blaise.

Three young women sat before a table of tea and sweet breads on the terrace of the garden room in the Evrion mansion. The morning sun bathed them in its clear, bright light, enhancing the special beauty of each. Marie Robillard's dark locks gleamed under its glowing rays, and Veronique Lanier's coppery tresses looked fiery enough to burn the fingers.

Chris smiled at the two young women, who were engrossed in an animated discussion of the DeCorba ball.

"Carlotta was raging at Charles when they returned, and he was chuckling so hard that he had to retire to regain his composure," Veronique bubbled. "You should have seen her gown! It was covered with red wine. And she had boasted that it came all the way from Paris."

"I wonder where the wine came from?" Marie mused. "She babbled something about it falling from the sky." She regarded Chris with a speculative look. "Do you know anything about it?"

"The sky in St. Marin does not rain wine, only water," Chris said with a smile. "Tell me again how Carlotta looked as she came back to the ballroom."

They described again the remarkable scene that had taken place, wondering if Christina didn't know much more than she would admit.

Marie said casually, "You know, you might do well to avoid her for a while. I overheard Timothy Wyncliffe tell Carlotta that Charles lost interest in her charms. She spoke of you with real malice and said she would get even if it took forever."

Chris looked thoughtful and shook her head. "No. I can't go around hiding every day. This isn't the first time we've clashed. It probably won't be the last."

Chris looked out over the green lawns and rolling hills of Mimosa Keyes. It was good to see the sun again. The last week had brought a terrible storm to the island. Hurricanes were not uncommon in the Caribbean, but this one had been specially fierce. And there had been no word from Mac. He should have returned from his business trip three days ago. Chris was worried.

"You know, Chris," Veronique was saying, "Charles has been telling everyone that he loves you, but to look at you, you don't seem to care. Don't you want him to offer for you?"

Chris sighed. "I like Charles very much, but I don't love him. He deserves to be married to someone who can honestly return his love and I . . ." Just then Chris heard a man's voice politely clearing his throat.

Standing in the doorway was Andrew Hardy, the Evrion's lawyer. Chris had known him for many years and regarded him as a sort of surrogate uncle.

"Andy," she smiled, "will you join us for tea?"

Something was wrong. She had never seen Hardy look so drawn and gaunt. The little man was usually pleasant and genial. "Is something bothering you, Andy?" Chris asked, concerned.

"Miss Evrion, may I see you privately in the library as soon as possible?" he asked.

"Of course," she said. Her stomach began to knot. Aloud she said, "Excuse me, Marie, Veronique. Please stay and finish your tea."

Chris followed him to the green parlor. Inside she saw Hilda seated in the large Louis XV chair, eyes staring at the window, unseeing. She turned to Andy.

"Miss Evrion," he said gravely, "it is my unpleasant duty to inform you that your father's ship was lost in the storm."

Christina froze, regarding Andy in stunned silence.

"The vessel was approximately thirty miles from Lanier Harbor when it hit a reef. There were no survivors. I can't tell you how sorry I am. Your father was one of the finest men I've ever known. He . . ."

But Chris didn't hear him. Mac! Her beloved Mac. Gone forever? It wasn't possible. She heard her own voice say woodenly, "You're sure, Andy? There's no possibility that . . ."

Andrew Hardy shook his head. He'd dreaded this moment and the look he now saw in her eyes. He wanted to say something comforting, consoling. "Miss Evrion, you and your stepmother will be provided for. Under the provisions of your father's will, you are to inherit two-thirds of his commercial and private assets. Control of your inheritance will pass to you upon your marriage. Until then, your stepmother is your legal guardian."

She'd never again see his smiling, weathered face, or hear that calm, reassuring voice. Never. She was alone. She looked at Andy.

"I understand. Excuse me . . . I . . . have to . . . retire for a while."

Christina climbed the carved stairway in a daze. There was a biting ache in the region of her bosom and a numbness over the rest of her body, as if she moved in a dream. Many times she had watched her father sail away and waved happily to him from shore. She knew her mother worried at these times, but not she. She knew that no matter what the sea had to offer, her father could meet it and come out the victor. Yet in the end the sea had won.

The realization that he was truly gone tore through Christina like a rending blade. With a cry of pure agony she collapsed on the floor, crying as if she could drain the grief from her heart with the sheer volume of her tears.

Just when she thought she would die with the pain, and her whole being seemed racked by sobs that threatened to engulf her, she heard a soft rap at the door, and Janie Tresgros, drawn and silent, entered the room and walked wordlessly to Christina's prostrate form. Listening to Janie's soft words of sympathy, Chris wept throughout the night—drifting at last into a troubled, dreamless slumber.

In the bleak days that followed, Christina and Hardy tried to keep the memorial vespers simple, knowing MacGraw would have wanted it that way, but all of St. Marin wanted to pay its respects to a man who had been so important to its history and development. For three days people filed through the chapel at Mimosa Keyes, expressing their grief and offering quiet support.

Almost immediately thereafter, life for Christina changed for the worse. Hilda was determined to run, or ruin, Chris's way of thinking, her life. She found fault with everything Christina did. Sailing was immediately forbidden. Visits with Marie and Veronique were limited so that Christina would have more time to "contemplate the evil nature of her ways and renounce unchaste thoughts and wicked excess."

With somewhat malicious pleasure, Hilda bestowed her full blessing on Wyncliffe, and the young man became an almost daily visitor. He cherished the notion of gaining control of the Evrion interests from his bride shortly after the wedding and made a pact with Hilda that the Keyes itself would remain in her hands.

Christina could barely face each new day with the thought of once again seeing Hilda's aloof, unyielding countenance. There were repeated quarrels, fights, and ultimatums. Chris knew she couldn't continue to live at the Keyes with Hilda as her guardian.

Kade Renault peered with unseeing eyes through the heavily leaded stained-glass windows of his huge bedroom in Falcon Hall. The news of MacGraw Evrion's death was a heavy blow. He had liked and respected the man. Indeed, had he a choice in the matter, his own father would have been gifted with the sensitivity and sight of that fine gentleman. Now that he was gone, Kade wondered about the fate of the maid whose beauty had haunted his dreams these several months past.

Though he had been in Bajora less than a week, Kade felt a compelling urge to return to St. Marin. He wondered what Chris would do now that the stability of her life had been altered. Renault was sitting before an ornately carved French *écritoire* in his private suite. With a movement of careless grace, he pulled the bell rope near a fourteenth-century Florentine bed. Quickly, his steward appeared.

"Yes, sir?"

"Gordon, ask messieurs Guy Savant and Jacques LaCroix to come in immediately."

Renault smiled pleasantly at his two officers when they entered.

"Good morning, gentleman," he remarked pleasantly in his deep voice. "I've asked you here for two reasons. First, it would please me greatly to have your company at my table this evening, and second, I want you to begin preparing one of the ships—a small frigate like the *Joliette* would suit well—for a short voyage."

"Certainly, Captain," Guy Savant replied. "Might I ask where we sail?"

"St. Marin," Renault replied cryptically. "Now off with you. We will leave as soon as possible."

Once outside, Guy turned to Jacques for an explanation. "Why is he sailing for St. Marin again so soon when we have already secured our trade there?"

"Ah, only God can say, *mon ami,* but I think our

captain has found something much to his liking on that green island."

Guy Savant's eyes lit with comprehension at the knowing look on Jacques's face. "You mean—someone."

Jacques laughed. "But yes, *exactement*." With that amusing thought they went to the stables to find their mounts.

The trip to St. Marin in the sleek, fast frigate *Joliette* took less than two days. Once in Lawrence, Renault lost no time in arranging a meeting with Andrew Hardy at the Evrion shipping offices.

He entered the low, chalk-white Spanish building on an elegant side street branching from Lawrence's busy quayside market and rapped discreetly at the richly carved oak door. A moment passed before Andrew Hardy, somberly clad in a suit of simple black broadcloth, answered. The little man had grown thinner.

"Oh, Captain Renault. Do come in."

Hardy led Renault to his office. The drawn curtains shut out the bright St. Marin sunlight, and Renault's eyes strained to focus in the dim light.

"You have heard, I presume, of the tragedy?"

"Yes, Andy, your dispatch reached me."

"You are curious, of course, about our trade agreements. I can put your mind at rest on that point at least. Everything will remain as it has been, and we will continue to act as your agent here. Of course, we are a bit backlogged now; the services have disrupted our normal routine . . ." Hardy's voice wavered a bit, "but we expect to resume business shortly, certainly in time for your next voyage."

"I'm relieved, Andy. I knew your partner for only a

brief time, but I had great respect for his abilities, and I liked him very much."

Hardy cleared his throat and, taking a handkerchief from his pocket, pulled his glasses from his nose and took a long time in cleaning them.

"Yes, Captain," he replied at length. "Everyone liked MacGraw."

Renault tactfully changed the subject.

"Glad and relieved though I am about our continuing business association, it is not at the moment my most urgent concern. What I would like to know, Andy, is how is she faring in this?"

From the look in Renault's eyes there was little doubt in Andy's mind of whom the captain was speaking.

Hardy began slowly. "Well, Captain, Christina has fared, I would say . . . not badly . . . under the circumstances . . ."

As Andy faltered for words, Renault prompted none too patiently, "Yes, go on."

"You may be aware that Christina and MacGraw's second wife have never been . . . well, close . . . and now that he has passed on, the tensions between them are much worse than before. To be blunt, Captain, in my opinion Christina is miserable."

Renault sat down in a nearby chair and stretched his long, powerful frame comfortably.

Hardy continued. "The terms of her father's will state that Christina will inherit two-thirds of the commercial and private assets, but control of the estate remains in Mrs. Evrion's hands until such time as Christina chooses to marry."

Andrew Hardy thought that Kade Renault actually

smiled. He cleared his throat. "That presents a problem for her. Christina has been absolutely opposed to that idea for a very long time, but now it is obviously necessary that she marry. It is something of a quandary for the child. In order to become independent of her stepmother, she must relinquish control of her life to a stranger. The problem has left her very distracted, to put it mildly."

Renault nodded. "I see," he said, getting up from the chair.

Andrew Hardy raised an eyebrow as Kade Renault walked to the door. "Captain, would you not like to go over the necessary changes in our trade agreements?"

"We can review that later, Andy. I want to express my condolences at the Keyes."

Renault's sleek Arabian mount took less than an hour to reach the rolling hills and green lawns of Mimosa Keyes. As his horse was led to the stables by one of the grooms, he saw a petite young girl with golden skin and a myriad of silver bangles on her wrist, dressed in a green sprigged cotton dress and white fichu. She looked upset as she carried a basket of ripe avocados toward the lovely pastel mansion, and she toyed nervously with the heavy braid of black hair that hung over her shoulder. Kade suddenly recognized Janie Tresgros. He called out and Janie started, as if surprised from a daydream.

She squealed and instinctively started to run, but Renault was faster and gently caught her arm.

"Miss Tresgros, I am hardly here to harm you. I only want to pay my respects to the family. I hear that Mr. Evrion was lost at sea. Tell me, how is your mistress?"

Janie stared at Kade Renault for a moment, and then her face fell and she looked more upset than ever.

"Oh, Captain Renault, it is awful here. Mis' Chris and Hilda fight all the time. And when they are not fighting, she just stares out of the window in her room or cries in there with the door closed. She miss her father very, very much."

Renault asked quietly, "And what of marriage, Janie? Has she considered anyone?"

Janie shook her head. "Many came to inquire, but Chris turned most away, and Hilda say no to many others. Charles Haverston, he come often, but Timothy Wyncliffe is here every day.

"Haverston," Renault said thoughtfully. "Tell me, Janie, why is she declining all offers?"

"She wants to be married, but she does not want a husband. She says she needs a husband who won't be around to be one."

Renault chuckled deeply.

"I would like to see her, Janie. Will you ask her to come out?"

Janie hesitated for a moment and then nodded. Perhaps a visit might cheer her. She asked Renault to wait in the *petit salon* and ran upstairs to Chris's room.

After what seemed to Renault like a very long time, Christina appeared. She looked gaunt and pale in a severely cut black gown with long sleeves and a dark apron buttoned stiffly to the neck. She did not smile when she greeted him, and Kade thought that he had never seen her look more despondent. Yet it was good to fill his eyes with the sight of her, and he waited a moment before he spoke.

"I am sorry, little one, about your father," he said.

Christina had taken a seat near the entrance without lifting her eyes. "Thank you." She looked up and seemed to gaze at him without seeing him. When at last she focused on his face, she said, "Is there something you require? I . . . I'm not yet myself, but I could ask Andy to help you with whatever it is. Why are you here?"

"To bid you farewell."

Chris's brow wrinkled. "I don't understand. Are you going away?"

Renault smiled. "As apt an expression for facing one's demise as any other. In a short time my men and I face an old enemy, one who has been itching for the sight of my blood for many a year. This time he will bring a quarter of the Spanish Armada with him. I'm not at all sure we will prevail."

Christina looked at him. "You don't really mean to say that you think he will beat you?"

Renault shrugged and raised an eyebrow in an expression that was infinitely stoical.

This was totally unlike the confident, swaggering captain of the galleon *Falcon*. Chris looked at him with open curiosity.

"Let's just say that it is fortunate that I am an unmarried man. 'Twould be a shame to leave some pretty maid a widow in her prime."

Christina blinked at him. "Yes, a shame . . ." she repeated.

He grinned. "I believe, Miss Evrion, that for the first time in our acquaintance we have agreed."

Standing up, he smoothed an imperceptible wrinkle from his tan riding breeches and tapped a muscular thigh with his riding crop. "Well, I do not want to tire you unnecessarily, my dear, so I'll be off. If there is anything you need, I am at your service—you have only to let me know."

She thanked him and bid him good-bye as he started down the long hall toward the entrance way.

Kade Renault walked toward the stables with a smile playing at the corners of his mouth, whistling a merry tune.

CHAPTER THIRTEEN

Renault's visit had given Chris new hope. She needed a marriage of convenience, but she had no intention of being a quiet, dutiful wife. Charles was out of the question; she felt it would be unfair to marry him when he loved her and she felt nothing. And it certainly could not be Timothy Wyncliffe. She couldn't do that even to be rid of Hilda.

What she needed was a sophisticated, worldly man who might be persuaded to enter an attractive business arrangement. She knew only one such person. Chris asked Andy to arrange for passage to Bajora immediately.

It took hours of pleading, but she finally obtained Hilda's consent to visit that island on the pretext of visiting the daughter of one of Hardy's close friends. Chris knew that Hilda was merely being difficult— and would be happy to be rid of her stepdaughter a few days.

The trip to Bajora took two days. Chris thought the island looked a lot like St. Marin, except that the people looked rougher, hungrier somehow. The men's eyes were more naked, and the women seemed freer. There were few homes like the Evrion and Robillard mansions. People seemed to come and go in a rush.

Andrew Hardy had arranged for Chris to stay at the home of a relative near the center of Vistabuena. She was glad that Hardy was with her—something about the men here disturbed her. She suspected that half of them were pirates.

After they had been on the island for a week, she made discreet inquiries regarding Captain Renault's whereabouts. She was shocked to learn that he was being held prisoner by the Spanish. Apparently he had not lied, and this time the Spanish were serious in their intent to put an end to his plunder. She learned that a ship of soldiers had landed on the island, surrounded his home, and taken him by force. It was thought that they planned to execute him for his longtime raiding of Spanish ships.

Chris arranged for a carriage to take her to Renault's residence. Her gown was soft rose, a shade that accented her creamy skin and tawny mane. The carriage stopped in front of an elegant white stucco home with two floors, a red-tile roof and a wrought-iron balcony on the upper floor that faced the street below. It was a striking building, strongly beautiful and somehow like Kade.

As she looked closer she saw two Spanish guards on either side of the massive carved wooden doors. Alighting from her carriage, she instructed the driver to wait for her and walked toward the house.

The guards barred her way. She showed them a pass she'd wheedled Andrew Hardy into getting for her. She was shown immediately to a magistrate, who asked her purpose for being there. Chris poured out her well-rehearsed story. She was the captain's fiancée, and she had to see him. Couldn't the magistrate understand what it was to be in love and have compassion? The man frowned and declined, but Chris was persistent. Finally, she resorted to bribery, giving the little man ten gold pieces. He agreed to let her have two hours alone with the prisoner.

She followed the red-uniformed guard to the second

floor. The house was beautiful inside, the furniture heavy and solid, done in the elegantly ornate Mediterranean style. The chairs were massive, obviously built to hold men of considerable bulk. On the walls, antique swords and arms of war were mounted among tapestries and oriental rugs of considerable age. Chris was fascinated by a shield she saw mounted on the wall just below the staircase. It had an ancient coat of arms, and she wished there had been time to inspect it at close range.

On the second floor the guard stopped before a large doorway and nodded. Chris waited until he had walked several feet away down the corridor and assumed the sentry position. She knocked on the door. From inside a deep voice said, "Come in." She took a deep breath, turned the knob, and walked in.

The bedroom was large, spacious, and elegantly furnished. On one wall stood the most beautiful carved wood armoire she had ever seen. It was huge, over eight feet high and six feet wide. There was an intricately woven Persian rug on the floor and several very valuable antique Spanish chairs in the corners of the room. A massive writing desk faced the armoire on the opposite side of the room. No one can say the man doesn't live well, Chris thought wryly.

The drawn curtains blocked out much of the bright afternoon sunshine. What light there was cast a hazy golden aura over the room as it came through the material. The soft light gave the room an other-worldly quality, outlining the chairs and furniture in misty dimness.

Chris focused more closely as her eyes adjusted to the light. Kade was sitting lengthwise on a massive bed centered in the middle of the most distant wall.

His black hair was tousled and his face held an odd mixture of sardonic amusement and pleasure. She was shocked to see iron manacles on his wrists. His hands were chained on either side to the brass tubing of the bed's headboard.

She looked at him with wide eyes and said, "They certainly don't trust you, do they?"

"An understatement, Miss Evrion." His smile was self-mocking.

She walked toward the bed and took a seat near the desk. He was wearing a white linen shirt unbuttoned to the waist. His rugged chest was covered with soft curling black hair. His waist seemed ridiculously small for his broad shoulders. Plain black pants covered his heavily muscled thighs, and calf-length black leather boots were on his feet. He looked as tan and healthy as ever. He couldn't have been confined for very long.

"Surely they don't keep you locked up like this every day," she ventured.

"No. I was particularly indiscreet last night. I tried to escape. Unsuccessfully."

"Oh, I'm sorry. Were they—did they hurt you when you were caught?" she asked.

He shook his head. "No. Actually they were relieved. You see, they expect me to try and get nervous when I don't." His eyes traveled the length of her rose-clad figure, taking in the lovely planes of her face, the sea-blue eyes, and dark golden hair. "Perhaps not as charming as your last outfit, but beautiful nonetheless," he murmured. "Forgive my bluntness, but what the deuce are you doing here?"

There was a lump in her throat and her voice caught, but she took a deep breath and began. "The terms of my father's will state that my stepmother will inherit one-third of the Evrion holdings, and the remainder will go to me upon my marriage. But until that time, my stepmother is my legal guardian.

"My stepmother and I have never gotten along. She is from a different world. I can't live the way she thinks I should. We can't be in the same room ten minutes without fighting. I can't stay with her. When I marry I'll have enough control to run my own life. Mac taught me all he knew about the rum business. I want to become actively involved in our holdings." She paused for breath and looked at Renault. He was sitting back, relaxed and listening. She continued. "But first I have to marry."

Now the hard part, she thought to herself. I may as well dive in.

"Kade, you're a businessman. How would you like to open your own shop in St. Marin—even go into the rum business if you like—set up your own operation instead of paying high prices to buy from other people? I could help you get started. My father had many friends. It would be easy. All you have to do is help me."

"I don't mean to be obtuse," he smiled, "but how?"

"I can't do anything without Hilda's permission until I'm married. If you'd consent to that—marrying me, I mean—I could almost guarantee you an easy start." There. She breathed a sigh of relief. She'd said it.

He looked at her. His expression was calm and unreadable. Only a faint sparkle in his eyes betrayed that they were talking about anything more significant than the weather.

"Your proposition is . . . most intriguing, but have you considered my present position?"

She lowered her eyes.

"Ah, I see that you have. Do you also know that I am to be executed within the week?"

She wondered how his voice could remain so even. He must have ice water in his veins, she thought. Aloud she said, "Well, there is a rumor going around that gives you an even chance."

"But you know that my having a rum business in St. Marin would do me very little good if I'm rotting in my grave," he said, faintly amused, watching her.

She sighed and drew a deep breath. "If they're going to execute you, Kade, then you really don't need your name anyway, do you?" She looked at him.

He raised his eyebrows. "What a cold, calculating woman you are, sweetheart," he said.

"Kade, I'm desperate. Even if you die, I'll honor our deal. I'll send the money to anyone you want. Just tell me where. And if you do live, you won't have anything to worry about from me. You can go anywhere, do anything you want. We'll go our separate ways and not make demands on each other. We'll get a divorce." She looked at him hopefully. This was her last chance and it was a very slim one.

Kade Renault remained silent for a long time. His deep blue eyes seemed to look into her very soul. She wanted to lower her eyes, but she returned his gaze, willing them not to waiver. Later she could go to her room and shiver with nerves, but now she had to remain cool and at ease. He shifted his gaze from her face to the window. A smile played around the corners of his mouth. She looked at his broad, deeply muscled chest and his strong brown hands. She noticed idly that the back of his hands were lightly covered with curling black hair.

He turned toward her again. "As you said, little one, I have nothing to lose." His voice was quiet. She felt elated. It was more than she'd dared hope for. She had never really thought he would agree. But he had. She flashed him her most dazzling smile. Small, pearl-white teeth beamed at him. Her turquoise eyes turned as radiant as the sea in St. Claire Bay. Happiness flushed her cheeks rose-petal pink, and her breath came and went quickly. "Kade, you won't be sorry, I promise."

Reacting to the transformation occurring in front of him, Kade smiled back at her. Then he said deliberately, "I'm sure I won't be." His eyes took on a wicked glow. "You see, they will probably execute me before the end of the week, but even so, I won't have missed much in the way of entertainment by being deprived of our marriage bed. You are far too young and ignorant to have been much of a diversion on that score."

Chris could hardly believe her ears. Her mouth dropped open, and she just stared at him.

"Don't look so shocked. I have never met a young woman whose vanity exceeded yours, but as your fiancé, I feel it my duty to help you get to know yourself better. And as we will have so little time for instruction, I'm being painfully frank out of necessity."

She sat back in her chair and looked at him squarely. Why did he have to be so perverse? She listened glumly as he continued. "To begin with, you truly think you are the most beautiful, desirable woman in the world. Well, *petite*, I have been around the world twice, and let me assure you that you are not. You also think that any man who looks at you wants you on sight and lies awake at night pining for your warmth. Wrong again. Actually your charms are nice but unremarkable. If you're going to be my wife, for however short a time, I want you to see yourself as you really are," Kade finished. He seemed to be waiting for something. If Chris hadn't been so angry, she would have seen the glimmer of anticipation dancing in his eyes.

She didn't see it. She was seething. That cool, mocking voice insulting her so calmly—it was too much. Hadn't she swallowed all her pride to come here to this reprobate's house with her offer? It was, after all, an attractive and perfectly reasonable business arrangement. Why, saints above! Men married for less every day. She was an heiress, a very wealthy one! And rather than appreciate what she had placed in his lap, this fool in chains was attacking her womanhood. Her aquamarine eyes crackled with angry sparks. She'd show him.

Getting up from the chair, she walked over to the bed and looked down at him. Her long, honeyed locks fell in soft waves to the middle of her back and her pink mouth looked delightfully kissable in its soft, sulking pout. She sat near him and looked directly into his midnight blue eyes. "Monsieur, this is not the first time you have hinted that I am not very attractive to men, to you." She put a soft hand on his broad chest. "You speak with such conviction, such certainty. Again I must ask, how can you know? How can you be sure that you do not like what you have never known?"

She bent forward slowly as she asked him the question and very lightly pressed her lips to his until she felt him just begin to respond. Then she pulled away. She let her hand move caressingly over the muscles of his chest. He felt hard and solid, like granite. She was so close that the scent of him floated around her. He smelled of sandalwood, clean cloth, and masculinity.

Actually, he was right about her youth and ignorance. She knew little of men and was really quite innocent. But so bold a slight to her womanhood could not go without reprisal, and she determined that she would satisfy her curiosity about the male body today, with him, while he was so conveniently confined in chains.

Chris put her other hand on Kade's chest. It was solid and warm. She could feel his heart beating. Again she placed her lips on his, this time parting them slightly. His mouth opened magically beneath hers. She decided she liked the taste of him—brandy, tobacco, and mint. She put her arms around his neck and pressed closer, so that her soft young breasts melted against his bare chest.

Chris felt his muscles tense a little and heard a low sigh come from somewhere deep within him. She drew back to look at his face. His eyes glittered like dark blue sapphires. She wondered what made them shine so. Desire, maybe? Passion? What would make a man's face look so intense? His chiseled features were perfect in the hazy golden sunlight, and she began to enjoy the game.

She looked at his chest again, so different from her own. It fascinated her. Tan, solid, and muscled—it seemed to invite her touch, and she ran her fingers slowly through the curling black hair, over and over. Softly, she kissed the center of his throat, pressing the warm flesh between her lips and then lightly between her teeth. Chris could feel his muscles strain with tension beneath that calm exterior. There was a feeling of carefully leashed power emanating from him that made her shiver and want to draw back. She had to remind herself that he was chained before she dared continue.

She raised her gaze to his eyes and smiled mischievously. Chris felt an anticipation and excitement that was like nothing she had ever known. Suddenly she was very brave, like a kitten playing near the jaws of a lion that was bound and harmless.

Her gaze fell once more to his chest. Beneath the hard muscle and corded tendon that invited her touch, she could discern the solid presence of his ribs. With an agonizingly slow and unhurried movement she began to trace each rib with her fingertip, watching his eyes as her hand lightly explored. Kade's gaze was steady and intense—the blue eyes dark and unfathomable, alight with a glow she did not comprehend. On impulse she lowered her head, adding the warm brush of her lips to that of her fingers. She felt Renault's muscles grow rigid and flex involuntarily as she leisurely traced the outline of each rib. Chris paused to steal a glance at him. Kade's eyes were completely closed now, his handsome face rigidly devoid of expression.

A little nettled by his lack of response, Chris decided that closer contact was in order. Again she put her arms around his neck, molded her upper body to his and kissed him deeply on the mouth. Again she sensed the tightly controlled power of his muscles straining against her and the chains.

She drew back and sought his eyes. They were open and burning with what she was sure was desire. At least he could no longer claim indifference. She grinned at him. But he didn't smile. He continued to regard her with that intense, blazing gaze. Passion smouldered there and something more. She looked at him for a long time, but she couldn't identify what it was she saw in those smokey, dark blue depths. She waited a few seconds for that heated regard to cool, fascinated by the way the blaze in his eyes seemed to peak and then subside.

Pleased with herself, Chris leaned carelessly across his legs—elbow bent, propping her head on her hand. She looked up at him and smiled.

"I think that is sufficient, don't you, Captain? I am, of course, ignorant of such matters, but I don't think you can stand much more."

Renault refrained from comment, not trusting his voice at that moment. Instead, he cocked one black-winged eyebrow with a sardonic air. Despite his outward calm, he was both literally and figuratively tied in knots, yet he would rather be damned for eternity than reveal the full extent of his need. After a long pause he said, "An interesting performance—within its limitations, of course."

Chris sat up abruptly, and her eyes sparked. What limitations! She started to tell him that she knew he had not remained as unmoved as he seemed—but gradually thought better of it. Why bother? She had what she came for. Instead, she slowly but deliberately trailed one fingernail lightly across his chest with a lazy, repetitive motion. At length, she replied coolly, "Please, Captain, compliments like that will turn my head."

With a light spring she stood up from the bed. Smoothing the rose gown, Christina said as she turned to leave, "I'll make arrangements for the ceremony to take place tomorrow."

When she paused to open the door, Kade called out

to her. His eyes held a speculative gleam. "For an innocent, you have an unsurpassed lack of modesty. Are you as brave when your subject is not chained?"

She looked back at him and smiled sweetly. "You will probably never know, *cher* Captain."

"Maybe not, but then again, we shall see, Tiger."

Christina lowered her eyes to a spot in the center of Renault's powerfully muscled chest, staring pointedly. She began to smile with real amusement and was still smiling when she closed the door.

Kade looked down at the spot on his chest that had drawn Chris's gaze. There, clearly traced through the rugged mat of hair was a large, and very noticeable, "C."

Kade frowned. He moved his hand to brush away the letter and cursed when he found the chain was not long enough. When the Spanish soldiers came back, their jests would be intolerable. Kade leaned back against the brass headrail of the bed, making himself as comfortable as he could. He had a large score to settle with that impossible minx, and settle he would.

The sooner, the better, he thought to himself with wry amusement, wondering how he would find the patience to wait.

CHAPTER FOURTEEN

In two weeks time, Andrew Hardy arranged passage for a priest from St. Marin to perform the ceremony. An enormous amount of gold was paid to the Spanish to insure their cooperation. They insisted that the ceremony take place in the town house where Renault could be closely watched.

Christina sat in the carriage beside Andrew Hardy, feeling twinges of apprehension and guilt as the jauntily sprung phaeton moved through the winding streets of Vistabuena toward the wide thoroughfare on which Renault's home was located.

Deep inside she felt that it was abominable of her to use him this way. Yet time and circumstance provided an opportunity to end the conflict with Hilda over the inheritance once and for all, and Kade Renault was the focus of that solution. There was not a ghost of a chance that the Spanish would release him. Renault had plundered far too many of their gold-laden ships to permit that. They had waited for years for his capture. Now that he was in their hands at last, they discussed his execution in the same jovial tones that other Bajorans used to talk of holidays and festivals. It sent a chill through Christina when she listened.

Although it was the perfect solution to her problem, she really did not want to see him executed. He was infuriating and outrageous and given to appearing in exactly the wrong place at precisely the wrong time, but his wit and intelligence were a constant source of stimulation. She would miss his rapierlike wit more than she cared to admit.

The carriage stopped before the massive, imposingly carved double doors that marked the entrance to Falcon Hall. The wood had been painstaking polished to a mirror gloss that made the dark wood gleam in the afternoon light. Andrew Hardy rapped fastidiously at one door with its heavy gilded knocker.

Renault himself opened the door, tall and smiling. He wore a deep blue waistcoat of the finest velvet, the simple lines of which called attention to the wide breadth of his shoulders and the powerful muscles of his arms. His legs were encased in snow-white breeches and shining black boots polished with champagne. A sapphire nestled in the folds of an impeccably tied cravat. Chris had never seen him look more handsome.

Yet it was not Kade's attire that made Christina's breath catch in her throat. Beyond his social smile, Chris saw the same burning flame in his eyes she had viewed that day in his bedroom, a look that intensified as his gaze swept slowly over her, from head to toe.

Chris stepped backward reflexively. Something radiated from the man that seemed wild, barely controlled, and very frightening. Kade looked like a dueling pistol—primed and ready to explode. She regarded him with frank wonder. He hadn't spoken a word.

To the others present he seemed nothing more than a handsome young groom very pleased with his bride-to-be. But Chris recognized the barely restrained power that hovered beneath the surface calm. She felt a prickling along her skin—just as if she was standing too close to a fire. She started to walk away, thinking it prudent to put a few yards between them, but found the way blocked by one of Kade's strong, warm arms. He drew her closer without once allowing his eyes to leave hers.

His skin seemed to burn her fingers, and no woman could misread the look on his handsome face. Too late she realized that the game she played with him had gone too far. Christina chided herself for feeling afraid. After all, as soon as the ceremony ended she would be off for St. Marin and the safety of home. Yet, that knowledge could not keep her from trembling in his arms. She wanted at that moment to be anywhere else, to run as far from Renault as possible.

Kade smiled as he felt the small form shiver in his embrace. He knew she read his thoughts, and her nervous reaction did not at all displease him. He raised her chin and lowered his head to take a kiss, but she pulled away.

"Kade, please . . . not until we are wed," she pleaded.

"But the wedding shall take place in a matter of minutes, so there can be no cause for alarm," Kade said easily, drawing her again into his arms.

His mouth was warm—very warm—on hers, and his kiss was gentle, a light and lingering pressure that was more of a caress than a kiss—all the more upsetting to Chris, who knew the restraint he used and wondered nervously how long it would last. She shifted her weight anxiously when he withdrew and, to her annoyance, could not suppress a nervous tremor.

Kade's smile was affectionate and teasing as he said lightly, "I hardly imagined that you would play the part of the nervous bride, Christina."

She blushed in spite of herself.

"But don't stop," he laughed, "I rather like it. As you can well see, I am a very eager groom."

Chris looked askance at him. Marshaling her resolve, she rallied and made an attempt to smile, but found she could not quite manage it. Still, she did regain some of her composure. She had come too far to let her nerve fail her now.

Andrew Hardy, who had stood watching patiently at a distance up until now, cleared his throat when it seemed the tall young man had no intention of releasing Christina or moving from the spot where they stood.

Renault turned and smiled at Hardy. "You're quite right, Andy. By all means, let's begin the ceremony—immediately."

With an inward sigh of relief, Chris allowed Kade to lead her toward the room where they would be wed. She marveled at Renault's calm. He laughed and joked with the guests and seemed perfectly at ease.

"It's as if everything were perfectly normal, and he was not about to be hung," she thought. Chris was so preoccupied with her musings of Renault's sang-froid that she failed to notice that she was herself the object of much attention.

The eyes of every man in the room followed her, particularly those of the Spanish soldiers. She was stunning in a long white gown of Belgian lace, the veil of which framed her long hair as it hung in heavy, sun-lightened locks. Soft ringlets framed her temples and her aquamarine eyes sparkled mysteriously, drawing the glance of every man in the room like a magnet.

The Spanish officers envied Renault the beauty he was to marry, but pitied him as well because he would have little time to enjoy his treasure. They had orders to execute him the following day. Yet, in an uncharacteristic show of generosity, they had not announced the impending execution.

Christina's eyes began to dance with suppressed merriment. It was exciting to be getting married, even if the man of her choosing was not long for this world. The ceremony was brief and lovely. She would remember it fondly, in spite of the untimely end awaiting the man beside her.

"You may now kiss the bride," she heard a voice say. It seemed distant. She felt Kade's hands on her shoulders, turning her to him. His eyes burned with the intensity of some emotion he was feeling, something Chris couldn't put a name to, but knew she had seen on his face before. Fascinated, she watched as he closed the distance between them and then his lips met her own. It was a soft kiss—so soft that she couldn't help thinking to herself that this tall, gentle stranger bore little resemblance to the Kade Renault she had come to know and mistrust.

The rest of the afternoon passed in a blur. She greeted their guests—laughing, talking, joking, and teasing, as if the man she had just married was not about to be hanged. She wondered idly why Kade had chosen this very public way of consummating their business arrangement. If she had been in his shoes, she'd have done it quietly, with no fanfare at all. But Kade was often beyond her understanding.

Across the room, she stared at the tall dark-haired man she had wed. Feeling her gaze, he turned and their eyes met. He smiled at her and raised his glass in a silent salute.

Chris crossed the room and stood beside him, wondering what one should say to a husband who faced not a wedding night but the gallows. Secretly, she admitted to a vague feeling of relief at that. Brave though she was, her courage failed her at the thought of spending a night in this man's arms. Still, as she looked up at him now, standing so quietly above her, she felt a stab of regret that he would die in so ignoble a manner.

"Kade," she said softly.

"Yes?"

"I would save you this ordeal if it lay in my power."

"Coming from you, that is very gratifying, *petite*," he smiled, raising her hand to his lips. "But you surprise me. I could have sworn that you have spent the better part of the afternoon avoiding my touch. Don't blush. You've jumped ten feet each time my hand brushed that soft skin."

She looked away, biting her lip.

"What I want to say is that I appreciate your help, and it distresses me to think of your . . . being . . ."

"Executed?"

"Yes. Is there no hope for you at all?"

"None."

Kade took her hand and drew her across the room to a corner partially hidden by a large, exquisitely painted oriental screen. For a brief moment their eyes met, and Christina was puzzled by the expression on Kade's face. It held an odd mixture of mischief, excitement, triumph, and the deeper glow of . . . what? Affection, she thought. She felt close enough to this man to call him a friend. Infuriating as he was, he more than any other knew and understood her.

Under his direct gaze the old uneasiness began again, and she was about to suggest that they leave the secluded spot, when Kade drew her into his arms. His mouth descended on hers in a kiss that was warm, possessive, and stirring. After a few heady seconds, her knees gave way and refused to support her, and she clung to Kade's well-muscled shoulders for support. Renault's arms tightened reassuringly about her as he slowly raised his head and smiled with satisfaction. Chris was annoyed by the small spark of triumph she saw in his dark blue eyes and angry with herself for being unable to stand alone.

Kade seemed perfectly content to hold her while she struggled to regain her composure, although he prolonged the process by lowering his head and nibbling her ear lobe.

When her composure returned it was a smiling Renault that led her back to their guests and the reception line that was forming.

There was no time for a real good-bye. She bid him farewell with Andrew Hardy standing nearby and wished him good luck. Privately she doubted she would ever see him again, which left her feeling a mixture of relief and disappointment. She never knew what to expect with Renault around. Indeed, she couldn't even predict what her own behavior would be in his presence. He took complete control of things with no effort at all.

The next day Christina and Hardy boarded the *Nelly Ann* and left for St. Marin with the morning tide. She watched as Bajora receded into the sunset, an emerald jewel against the Caribbean sea. With a sigh, she turned and walked below deck to her cabin.

How odd, she thought to herself, to become a bride and a widow in almost the same day.

CHAPTER FIFTEEN

Jacques LaCroix and Logan Armor sat in the taproom of the Red Boar Inn toasting their captain with ale. For ten years they had sailed with Kade Renault aboard the *Falcon* and had become very rich in the process. Yet all the adventures they had shared with the captain paled beside the sheer audacity and potential reward of tonight's escapade. It had taken months to plot this undertaking, and everything was proceeding according to plan. Only one thing disturbed them. They didn't know what to make of the incredible rumor that the captain had been married yesterday at Renault House, complete with the governor of Bajora and the whole damned Spanish guard!

It wasn't true, of course. Whoever spread the rumor didn't know Kade Renault. The captain would never marry anyone. As Joshua Boman, an escaped slave from Virginia and third mate of the *Falcon* had once said, "The captain is the kind who loves well fo' a spell and then tells 'em to go to hell." Jacques LaCroix and Logan Armor thought it was as apt a description of him as they had ever heard. LaCroix remembered the lovely young widowed duchess who had offered Renault a fortune last year to leave Bajora and return with her to England.

The captain had smilingly declined, telling her that he recognized no man as king and that long ceremonies of state bored him. And this year, Señorita Maria Del Vega, a wildly exciting Spanish dancer, had thrown herself at his feet when he told her he had to go to St. Marin on extended business. She threatened to commit suicide if he left her behind. On the night before his departure she did indeed cut her wrists. Luckily, she was found in time. Renault came to her, gave her a severe lecture on the value of life, and told her to come to her senses or he'd beat her until she did. When he left she was crying, but rational. He sailed with the morning tide. No, thought Jacques LaCroix and Logan Armor. The captain would no more marry than scuttle his own ship.

They laughed and joked about the *Falcon* and the good times with the Corsairs, as Kade's men were called, impatiently wiling away the afternoon hours in the Red Boar's taproom. Guy Savant, another of Kade's men, walked into the Red Boar and joined them.

"Well, men, I knew I could count on finding you here toasting the captain's new bride," he said jovially.

Jacques LaCroix's mouth flew open almost as quickly as Logan Armor's did. Guy Savant looked nonplussed. "Surely you heard that our brave leader has fallen prey to a fair charmer's web?"

"We heard the tale," Logan finally managed, "but we didn't believe it. Are you sure, Savant?"

"Positive," he answered. "I was there. You would have been too had there not been more urgent work for you to do here. The maid is a vision, and judging from her bearing, the captain has found himself quite a handful."

LaCroix looked dazed and shook his head, saying, "I can't believe it. Renault married?"

Savant nodded. "With my own eyes, I saw it."

Just then Mary and Inez, the Red Boar's two pretty serving girls, entered with large earthenware platters of meat and vegetables in their arms.

"Well, well . . . the sea dogs are back. It's been weeks since we've seen the likes of you in this place," said Mary.

"*Si.* We thought the ocean, she swallow you," agreed Inez.

They made a charming picture as they floated around the table, pouring ale and filling the Corsairs' plates.

"I don't see that good-looking captain of yours," said Mary as she strained her neck, searching the room.

"We saved some choice roast beef for him, the kind he likes," Inez said hopefully.

Jacques and Logan looked at each other. The captain was their favorite. How were they supposed to break the news to them that he was married? They took the coward's way out. "He'll be in later, *mes petites.* Now run along. We have important things to discuss," said LaCroix, tossing three gold coins to each. They bobbed a curtsy and left smiling. The Corsairs were always generous.

LaCroix turned to Savant. "Well, Guy, is all waiting and ready at the house?"

Savant nodded. "It is all as planned. The governor will arrive at seven o'clock tonight."

It had taken months of careful planning to bring about the events that were about to take place. They had allowed the Spanish to find out the exact location of Renault's stronghold and made sure his comings and goings were known. The Corsairs went wildly about the town, spending their gold and drinking heavily. Soon it was said that the men of the *Falcon* had grown soft with women and drink. There were even rumors that they were divided among their ranks and no longer supported their captain. Some people said it would be easy to take his house—that the men would not come to his aid. Fantastic stores of gold were said to be hidden in the cellars of the captain's home. The trap had been carefully set to convince the Spanish that now was the time to put an end to the menace that was Kade Renault.

The Corsairs spread a rumor one day that most of the men who guarded the town house had been ordered away for the night—the captain wanted to entertain a guest alone. The Spanish jumped at the chance to seize the house. Kade Renault was imprisoned inside.

The captain and the Corsairs had counted on the fact that a helpless Renault would be too much for the governor of the Spanish interests in the New World to resist, and it was him they wanted to kidnap. Governor Orlando DeVilla didn't know it yet, but not only would he be forced to pay handsomely for his freedom but he'd also graciously provide full pardons from the Spanish government for all the Corsairs before he was returned to his palazzo in Mexico.

Kade Renault paced the floor of the master bedroom. In precisely one hour Jacques LaCroix and Logan Armor would arrive with ten other Corsairs and join him via a secret passageway that led to the bedroom. By that time the remainder of his one hundred men would travel through the hidden system of underground tunnels he had laid five years ago to surround the town house, unseen by the Spanish. Thirty men had already stationed themselves in a room adjoining the cellar, where a company of Spanish guards were playing cards.

Acting the part of the docile prisoner had been an irksome task. Happily, that was all behind him. He sat down and poured himself a drink.

At six o'clock the doors of the massive armoire in Captain Renault's bedroom opened. Kade looked into the grinning faces of Jacques LaCroix and Logan Armor. "Punctual as always, my friends," Kade grinned back.

"Nothing would keep us from missing this," Logan said, smiling.

The men disappeared into several prearranged hiding places around the room. Renault resumed his relaxed position and poured another brandy.

At seven o'clock an ornately appointed carriage replete with liveried servants pulled up in front of the wrought-iron gates of Renault House. The Spanish governor, a portly, middle-aged courtier, stepped heavily down from the carriage. He had looked forward to this for years. To think that at last he had the accursed captain of the *Falcon* right where he wanted him. The little man could hardly contain his excitement as he thought of how he'd torture Renault into revealing the location of the stolen treasure. A week of diligent searching in the town house had turned up nothing at all. But no matter. When Orlando DeVilla was through, *el capitán* would beg to reveal its hiding place.

DeVilla was so impatient to get at Renault that he declined the refreshments his lieutenant offered. Instead he climbed the stairs toward the upper floor with his heavy tread, eyes gleaming with anticipation.

The commotion below alerted Renault and his men

to the governor's arrival. When DeVilla and three guards opened the door, Renault was calmly sipping his second brandy.

"Ah, Don DeVilla, come in," Renault drawled politely.

"So we are face-to-face at last, you spawn of a jackal," DeVilla said menacingly. "You have cost me much, Renault. Tonight I shall enjoy watching you pay with your blood." Renault regarded him coolly and smiled.

DeVilla continued. "For years I have watched you raid my ships, stealing the gold and taking it to this lawless island. But that is all over, Renault. Tonight your screams will ring like fine music in my ears. I shall enjoy watching you die slowly, begging for mercy." The governor walked closer to Kade. "You are totally in my power. Where are your fine Corsairs now, Renault? Have they all deserted you?" he taunted. "Scum of the sea, on your knees before your master!" he growled.

Renault slowly put his glass on the table. He said calmly, "I think not, DeVilla. You see, it is really you who are in my power."

Like silent ghosts, the Corsairs appeared. They formed a menacing ring around the governor and the two cowering guards. Their guns were aimed at De-Villa's head. They moved swiftly to disarm and bind the three stunned Spaniards.

Leaning one foot on a chair, Renault grinned at the governor. "You will notice, DeVilla, that five guns are aimed at your miserable throat. I advise you not to try to call for help, or you will find that you have two mouths."

"What do you want?" DeVilla croaked.

"While I would rather enjoy killing you . . ." Kade began and smiled as the paunchy governor blanched, "you are more useful alive than dead. My terms are as follows—one hundred thousand gold ducats and full pardons for myself and my men from the Spanish government. You will be returned to Mexico when the gold and the pardons are delivered here."

Renault thoughtfully raised his sword in the direction of DeVilla's arm. The little man's face broke out into a sweat. With his sword Renault slowly cut the cloth covering the governor's shoulder. Perspiration began to pour down DeVilla's face, and he squirmed uncomfortably in his chair.

"It would be no trouble at all to separate you and your arm, DeVilla," Renault said amiably. Don De-Villa opened his mouth to speak, but Kade signaled him to be silent. "Perhaps there is another piece of information you would consider helpful in making a decision. If you refuse my terms, we will let the Spanish government know just how much gold you've shipped out of Mexico to add to your personal stores in St. Marin. You see, several of your loyal sailors have talked. We know the gold we took from you and brought to Bajora was gold you were stealing from the coffers of the Spanish government in Mexico—tax money you . . . diverted, shall we say . . . for personal use."

DeVilla paled and swallowed. "And if I do as you ask?" he said weakly.

"We return you to Mexico in one piece," Renault replied, smiling sardonically. "And if you're thinking of trying to escape, forget it. My men outnumber yours three to one."

A trap, DeVilla thought dully. A well-planned, inescapable trap. Aloud, he said in a tired voice, "You win, Renault. I will concede to your terms."

"A wise man," Renault said drily.

Three weeks later, his excellency, Don Orlando De-Villa, was on his way back to Mexico, having signed a full confession for the Corsairs' safekeeping. Renault and his men celebrated their victory at the Red Boar. The men were in high spirits and the scene in the tavern was raucous, full of rowdy gaiety.

Mary O'Hare laughingly poured ale down the throat of Logan Armor while perched on his lap. Across the table, Jacques LaCroix roared as his friend sputtered, missed a swallow, and wound up with the sticky stuff all over his face. Inez Ramada walked by with two tankards in her hands. Guy Savant pulled her unceremoniously onto his lap and kissed her soundly.

Renault sat across the room with his tankard in front of him, strangely subdued in the midst of this revelry. He fingered his mug idly as his thoughts carried him far away.

Logan looked up as Mary wiped his face and saw the captain's eyes focused on nothing in particular. Thoughtfully he said to Jacques, "Do you suppose the captain will give half his share to the Bajorans in the interior again?"

"Probably," answered Jacques. "But don't ask him about it. He never likes to acknowledge that bit of charity." Jacques frowned and added, "And he's very touchy these days."

"Aye," Logan agreed. "'Tis a strange mood he's in."

Jacques called across the room, "Ahoy, Captain.

Come over and share a tankard with three wayward men."

Renault looked up. Smiling slowly, he got up and sat at their table. A shapely brunette with olive skin walked into the room. Logan recognized her as the Red Boar's new serving wench. "Mignon, come over here and brighten our table," he called with a grin.

Mignon turned to regard Logan with cool brown eyes. Then her face brightened with interest. Sitting next to that buffoon was the handsomest man she had ever seen. He looked very tall, over six feet four, she guessed. Mignon watched him for a second as he sat—silent, dark, and brooding—but magnificent in a white linen shirt open to the waist and a black leather vest. A sword was laced to his side and black leather boots encased his muscular legs. She recognized him from the whispered daydreams of Mary and Inez. He had to be the legendary Captain of the Corsairs—Kade Renault.

Mignon wasted no time in quickly walking over to the captain and depositing herself in his lap. She snuggled against him and pressed her shapely bosom to his chest as she cooed suggestively, "Would you like to order now, Captain, or after?"

Renault gently lifted the well-endowed lady from his lap as if she were a feather. "Sorry, sweet. I . . . ah . . . ordered . . . before you came."

"Oh," said Mignon, disappointment all over her face as she walked away.

Renault stood and stretched like a great black panther. He yawned as he said, "Better turn in early tonight, lads. We sail with the morning tide."

LaCroix and Logan exchanged glances. "Where?" asked LaCroix.

"St. Marin," Renault replied. Suddenly he grinned, and his white teeth gleamed rakishly against his skin. "I have unfinished business there with a certain young lady."

CHAPTER SIXTEEN

Chris was happy for the first time since Mac's death. When her carriage rolled into the long driveway at Mimosa Keyes, she alighted so quickly that the startled groom barely had time to help her. Once inside, she forced herself to walk calmly into Hilda's room, where she found her seated comfortably at an *écritoire*, upbraiding a maid for dropping a dish.

"I have not given you leave to enter my apartments, Christina—and I do not have time for your ramblings this morning."

"Oh, I think you do. You will be very interested in what I have come to tell you."

Hilda frowned. "I doubt that very much. Whatever it is will have to wait—I don't have time for you at all today," she said with an impatient gesture of dismissal.

"Hilda, you will listen," Chris said softly. "Now, at this moment."

Hilda's eyebrows drew together ominously. She was about to deliver a long tirade, but something in Chris's eyes caused a small, cold knot of fear to form in the pit of her stomach, and she said a trifle shrilly, "What have you to say?"

"Simply," Chris smiled, "that I have wed."

Hilda sat down hard on a nearby chair. "What?!"

"I am married, Hilda," she repeated. "You-are-no-longer-my-guardian," Chris said, pronouncing each word clearly.

Hilda was silent for so long that Chris wondered if

she had lost her voice. Then her face contorted angrily, and for a moment it seemed as if they would come to blows. But Hilda fought to regain her control and at length she said icily, "I see."

There was so much malice in her voice that Chris shivered, but she decided that it was, after all, a bad shock—and Hilda had no choice but to reconcile herself.

"I knew you would," she said. "Please excuse me while I unpack. The voyage was long and, as you have seen, very eventful."

Chris left the room with a smile. Hilda sat on the bed, a frightful frown spreading across her stern features.

In the week that followed, Hilda left Mimosa Keyes to live with the Van Beurens, her cousins. Chris reveled in the headiness of her new freedom, wanting to share her happiness with the world.

Soon after her return, she told her two closest friends, Marie and Veronique, what had happened in Bajora. When she told them whom she'd married, they thought she was crazy.

"Oh, Christina, you didn't!" wailed Veronique.

"Is it too late to have it annulled?" asked Marie.

"No, but why would I want to do that?" she laughed.

"Oh, Chris, of all the men you could have chosen, why him?" asked Veronique, still wailing.

"Well, he's not too unbearable and . . . well . . . we're alike. We have agreed to leave each other alone. It will be the perfect marriage. He wants his freedom as much as I want mine," she said.

Maria and Veronique looked at each other and then

at Christina. "Then why in heaven's name did he marry you?" asked Maria.

That question had bothered Christina for some time. On the voyage back to St. Marin she had pushed it out of her thoughts. But now that she was home and had more time to wonder, she felt a little uneasy on that score. She wanted to believe that her business offer had been too good to turn down, but Renault was already a very wealthy man. The thought that it might not have been business alone that prompted his unexpected compliance made her more nervous than she would admit.

She lost no time in getting a grip on the Evrion business interests. With Andrew Hardy at her side, she made it plain to her father's partners that she would take an active role in managing her holdings. At first they balked. It was unheard of. A woman running that kind of enterprise, and one as young and beautiful as Christina? Never.

But she showed them she meant what she said. It soon became apparent that she knew more than they did about the operations. They grudgingly conceded that Mac Evrion must have passed on everything he knew to his daughter, and that she had gone beyond that foundation with her own imagination and vision. They grew accustomed to the sight of her small figure on the wharf, watching over cargo as it was loaded on ships bound for America. It became a matter of course to find her with Andrew Hardy, carefully reviewing the inventories and accounts. When Chris presented a plan for several new additions to the existing Evrion facilities that could be done for two-thirds of the normal cost, she won over the most hardened skeptic of the lot.

All in all, life was going beautifully. The business was prospering. She would be able to increase wages next year if the profits continued as they were. Christina decided to celebrate the good fortune with a ball. The guest of honor, she decided, would be Andrew Hardy. She would present the bespectacled little man with a gold replica of the first Evrion ship. The thought of his surprised and blushing face made her smile.

Chris engaged a housekeeper, Madame Ouvre, to look after the domestic side of the Evrion mansion. She was a genial, efficient woman nearing fifty. Small of stature and a trifle plump, she bustled about the house making preparations for the ball. Time flew by, and just as it seemed as if nothing would be ready in time, the night of the ball arrived. Madame Ouvre followed Chris around the house all day with questions such as, "Madame, shall we serve the langouste with or without a salmon bisque?" and "Would you prefer shrimp rémoulade or *salade de conch* before the *rôti de veau?*"

Christina buoyantly settled the minor decisions. Characteristically, she lost track of time. Most of St. Marin would be in the Evrion ballroom tonight, and she was not yet dressed.

"Janie, quick!" Chris called, lifting her skirts to run up the stairs. "We've got one hour before the ball!" Janie grinned. She was used to this by now. Christina Evrion dressed for parties like a mad whirlwind, waiting until the last minute to begin. Janie suspected that it gave Chris an excuse not to put up her heavy dark gold hair. Chris hated the pins and perferred to let her hair remain loose in its own natural waves.

Janie laced her into a lovely gown of gold silk

trimmed with voile. She looked enchanting in the dress. The peplumed bodice framed the graceful curves of her bosom, and the soft sheen of the material accented the creamy roundness of her young breasts. The filmy voile lay like a cloud over the wide expanse of her golden skirt. She wore the star diamond Mac had given her around her neck. The effect was enchanting, and Christina had never looked more lovely.

Janie fastened a petite cluster of tiny white flowers to the center of her bodice. "Lord, Mis' Chris, it is too bad you are married. Otherwise, the way you look, you sure would have fun tonight." Janie grinned, not believing for a minute that Chris would let her married state spoil the party. Chris smiled back conspiratorily. Pinching her cheeks to give them color, she went to the grand staircase and walked regally down the stairs.

The ballroom of Mimosa Keyes was aglow with the light of a hundred starlike candles. Tropical flowers from all over the island decorated the marble columns and myriad corners of the room. Mac had imported graceful mirrors from France to line the walls. The flowing gowns of the ladies and formal attire of the gentlemen were reflected in a dazzling array of colors and shapes in the gilt pier glass that decorated the ballroom.

When Christina entered the room, there was an audible gasp of pleasure, followed by seconds of silence. Although she was hardly shy, she felt herself blush as little butterflies fluttered in her stomach. Then she straightened and, smiling, walked forward to greet her guests.

She saw Andrew Hardy, with a group of St. Marin

businessmen, looking ill at ease in formal attire. She walked over and joined him, putting a graceful hand on the little man's arm.

"Andy, I'm so happy to see you. Come with me. There is something I want to show you," she said, smiling.

A little surprised, Hardy followed her to the middle of the floor. She signaled the musicians to stop playing. Then she began. "All of you know that we are here tonight to celebrate the new prosperity we have had in the last few months. Tonight I want to thank Andrew Hardy for working so hard to make that possible." Madame Ouvre brought out the gold replica of the *Fleetwood*, the first ship Mac Evrion had ever built. "Forty years ago Andy helped my father set up a company whose purpose was to design the fastest ships on the sea. If he were here today, Andy, he'd want you to have this." She kissed the little man on the cheek and gave him the beautifully crafted model ship. "A small token of our love and appreciation for all you've done. You will stay with us for another forty years, *oui?*"

Andrew Hardy's eyes were moist as he nodded. The shy little man uttered a barely audible thank you and would have melted into a corner, but a rousing round of applause came from the guests, and he was surrounded by a crowd of friendly St. Mariners.

Chris eased from the group and found herself beside a man she had not seen before. He was good-looking with regular features, blond hair, and friendly gray eyes.

"Do I have the honor of addressing Madame Christina Renault?"

The new name sounded odd to her ears, but she smiled and said, "Correct, monsieur."

"Then you must dance with me, madame. I have been waiting all evening to meet you."

He led her onto the floor as the music began again. They waltzed for several minutes around the room. She decided she liked the way he danced. "You have the advantage, monsieur. You know me, but I do not know you."

He chuckled. "I'm James Marston, madame. And there is something about which I'm very curious." She looked at him, waiting. "Where is Monsieur Renault tonight?"

She smiled enigmatically. "My husband is frequently away for very extended periods of time on business."

"And now?" Marston asked, his voice hopeful.

Christina lowered her long lashes demurely. "Fortunately, he is away in Bajora attending to a very urgent matter, which I expect will take him a very long time to complete."

Marston smiled and was about to speak when a wrenchingly familiar voice behind her said in deep, resonant tones, "Too bad one's expectations do not always come true."

She turned to stare at the sardonic countenance of Kade Renault. Her mouth fell open in surprise, and she breathed in a barely audible whisper, "Kade?!"

"The same, Madame Renault." He gave an exaggerated bow. "Your loving husband has returned," he said in a suave, mocking voice. Turning from her to James Marston, he said quietly, "Excuse us, please. I have an unaccountable desire to dance with my wife." Marston reluctantly released her.

She could not conceive of how he had escaped. When she left him he was practically on his way to the gallows. But here he was, standing before her with that calm sardonic smile, very much alive. Though she was surprised by the fact that he had survived his capture, she resolved not to show it.

Chris felt Kade's strong arms enfold her and sweep her onto the dance floor. The familiar feeling of uneasiness crept up her spine and she snapped, "Why didn't you let me know you were coming?"

"Because I didn't want to waste any time in getting here, sweet." He smiled down at her.

She looked at him dubiously. "What, in heaven's name, was so urgent?"

His white teeth flashed in a heart-stopping grin that would have melted most women at his feet. "I knew that you were alone and helpless, so I came to give you my protection," he said sardonically.

She was silent for a long time. Her stomach felt upset. "Does that mean you intend to stay?" she asked.

"Of course, kitten. Why would I leave you?" His deep blue eyes twinkled with outrageous mischief.

"How long?" she asked.

"Hmmm?" he looked innocent.

"How-long-will-you-be-here?" She pronounced each word slowly and clearly.

"Oh, I don't know. One or two years—three maybe. By the way, have you ever been to Paris?" he asked.

Chris felt sick. This was definitely not the evening she had in mind. She looked around the room, which was beginning to spin. She saw Carlotta DeCorba smiling at her with feline malice. "Excuse me . . ."

she said. "I . . . I'm very dizzy. I think I'd better retire early."

"All right, sweet," he said affably.

He walked her to the grand staircase. She turned and said, "Thank you. I can make it from here."

"You're sure?" he asked in a gentle, concerned voice.

"Yes," she said. She turned slowly and climbed the stairs. On the way she left specific instructions with Madame Ouvre and the two male servants that absolutely no one but the household staff be allowed upstairs. When she got to her room, Janie was there with tea and smelling salts.

"I don't believe it, Janie," she said dully. "Kadel Here! He's supposed to be dead by now."

Janie shook her head sympathetically as she helped Chris out of her dress into a guazelike white night shift. Her young mistress just hadn't known what she was getting into. Captain Renault was a living legend. Unfortunately, Christina had not heeded anyone's warnings. Now it was too late.

"Don't worry," Janie sighed. "Things will work out in time. You better get some rest. You look like you seen a ghost," she said, barely able to contain a giggle at her own jest.

Chris looked at her, but Janie's face was innocent. "I do not find that amusing," she muttered and sat down in a chair near a small table laden with tea and sweet breads.

"Good night, Mis' Chris. Remember, it'll work out," she said, closing the door.

Chris sat for half an hour, gazing thoughtfully out of her window at the moonlit night. "Well," she sighed, "there's nothing I can do about it tonight." She was about to get up to put out the candle when the door of her room opened. She gaped open-mouthed as Kade Renault, still resplendent in his evening clothes, strolled into her bedroom and closed the door. His smile was as calm as if he'd done the same thing every night of his life.

By contrast, Chris was livid. She sat bolt upright, glaring at him. "How did you get in here?"

"I can be very persuasive, kitten," he smiled. She looked so incredulous that he added, "I told them I was your husband."

She swallowed. "Kade, we have to talk about this . . ."

"Of course, sweet," he said, starting to undress. "We can talk about anything you like when we're alone."

"What do you think you're doing?"

"Getting ready for bed, little one," he replied.

"Surely you don't think you're going to sleep in here? With me?!"

"My dear little girl," he smiled indulgently, "men usually sleep with their wives—unless the wives are old and ugly. You are neither."

"You can't sleep here!" she cried, her control breaking.

"I can and I'm going to," Kade replied calmly.

When she remembered how she'd teased him that day in Bajora, her courage failed. Chris bolted for the door, but Kade anticipated her action and was there seconds ahead of her. It took all her strength to keep from careening into him. He reached out and pulled her against him, turning quickly so that she was pinned between his hard body and the wall.

"Wouldn't you like to finish what you started that day in Bajora?" he asked in a low, amused voice. Then his eyes lost their teasing light and seemed to glow. Christina trembled as his mouth closed over hers.

She felt his lips part hers in a burning kiss. His tongue ravaged the soft recesses of her mouth, drinking in the honey there. As he breathed in, she felt his rock-hard chest expand, and she started with surprise as her tongue was drawn into his mouth. He sucked it gently, stealing her breath as well. A warm, tingling sensation rose deep inside her. With great effort she turned her head and escaped his absorbing kiss, only to feel his lips caress the line of her cheekbone. He nuzzled her neck, and his hot breath seared her ear. She relaxed in his arms and made her body go pliant against him. Unconsciously, his steel embrace softened, and he eased his weight from her somewhat. She brought her knee up sharply. But he'd felt her tensing muscles and deflected the blow before it could do much damage. She ran across the room.

"Well, tiger, I see you haven't changed." Kade's voice was deep with amusement and passion.

"Listen to me, you demented pirate! What I proposed was a business arrangement. This marriage was supposed to be in name only. I offered you a start in the rum business. Nothing else!"

Kade smiled indulgently. "Don't let that bother you, sweet. You didn't know it when you came to me, but I was planning to steal you anyway as soon as I got rid of the unwanted guests in my house. I've wanted you, badly, since that day in the garden. Our brief contacts were so pleasant that I knew I had to have you—the sooner the better. It was obliging of you to come to Bajora and save me the trouble of plotting your abduction."

For a moment Christina was speechless. Then she

found her voice. "You knew they would release you! You never had any intention of sticking to our deal!"

"True," he nodded. "It was reprehensible of me," he admitted generously.

"You should be in Spain awaiting trial before the Inquisition."

"But instead I'm here—your husband—alive, willing, and very eager." He grinned wickedly.

She turned and ran for the balcony, but he caught her easily. Christina couldn't believe what was happening. After everything else that had gone wrong, now this. Mac dead and this madman alive—how unfair! And now he was here claiming all the rights of a husband! She started to scream, but she felt his mouth silence her and at the same time her feet left the ground. He was carrying her to the bed.

"Kade!" she said desperately, "This is not a real marriage!"

He kissed her again, easily subduing her squirming form, and said, "You're right, darling, but it soon will be."

She started to fight him in earnest then, striking wherever her small fists could reach.

"Ouch! Easy, tiger, you'll hurt your hand trying to break my ribs." She bit him. "Now, that's enough," he said firmly. Carrying her kicking, struggling form across the room, he grabbed a long shawl from her closet and wound it around her arms. Then he picked her up and sat in a chair, positioning her in his lap. She struggled furiously, but did him little damage. Finally she stopped, her chest heaving and her body miserably tired from her effort. It had been ludicrous to fight this tall, iron-hard man. She had only succeeded in exhausting herself.

"Look at me," he said softly.

She was leaning against his shoulder, too overcome with fatigue to sit upright. She kept her eyes lowered.

"Christina." The sound of his deep voice caressing her name made her raise her gaze.

"I know that I frighten you, little one . . ." he began. She started to protest, but he put a finger to her lips. "Hush. You *are* frightened. Of what you don't know . . . of what will happen tonight." She lowered her gaze again. Kade lifted her chin gently with his hand. She was very lovely. Her sea-blue eyes were bright and shining, and her breath came and went quickly, causing her full, young bosom to rise and fall hypnotically. The transparent white shift had been torn from her shoulder in their struggle. It exposed the swelling roundness of one firm breast. What little there was left of the thin garment revealed more than it covered. The diminutive waist, graceful hips, and long tapering legs were clearly visible to his discerning eyes.

He looked at the soft pink lips that drooped a little at the corners and drew her closer against him. Christina squirmed weakly in his lap. During the battle, most of the buttons of Kade's trousers had come away. She was uncomfortably aware of the warm, pulsing hardness beneath her bottom. She felt his lips caress her temple as he said, "For all your natural flirting and coquetry, kitten, I know you are an innocent. You have little experience in the ways of love."

His lips softly followed the line of her cheek to her mouth, and he carressed her lips with his own, lightly tracing their delicate line. It was a heady sensation that made her giddy. "A kiss is for tasting, Christina—

like so. I love the way you taste—like honey with a drop of cream."

She frowned at him. She couldn't believe what she was hearing. But his deep blue eyes were serious. His handsome face was devoid of its mocking expression; it was open and earnest. He kissed her then, and again her tongue found its way through his parted lips. She had not put it there; he'd breathed it in. He kissed her for a long time, tasting her as he would a glass of champagne. He drew back and she relaxed. Unknowingly, she'd held her breath.

Kade's hand carressed her cheek and moved downward over her shoulder. He kissed the hollow of her throat, and his hand moved to gently cup her exposed breast. He brushed the nipple beneath the filmy material with his fingertips, teasing it into tautness. "Some day when you are with child, your breast will fill with mother's milk in preparation for the young one. But for now, Christina, they are only for pleasure," he said as his hands stroked the swelling curves. "Did you know that men and infants are much alike in that respect, sweet? Let me show you." He moved the shift aside and bent his head. Softly, he kissed her breasts all over, and, to her wide-eyed surprise, he pressed his lips first to her right and then to her left nipple and suckled her gently. A warm rush of sensation surged inside her, and she felt lightheaded.

Kade lifted Christina from his lap and left for a moment. She sat tensely in the chair and watched him warily. He took off his shirt and pants. She blushed as she looked on the first man she had ever seen completely nude. He was solid and hard, all muscle. There was nothing soft on him anywhere. The curling black

hair on his chest trailed down his hard stomach to . . .
oh . . . she had never seen anything so huge, not
even that day in Bajora had he looked this big! Why,
he would kill her if he tried to . . . Chris averted her
eyes and shivered. Kade returned and carried her to
the bed. Her aquamarine eyes sparkled with rebellion
and fear. She moved to the far side of the bed and
half-knelt there, with her weight on her heels, legs
tucked under her.

Amused, he noticed her protective posture and annoyed her enormously by lying next to her on his side,
enclosing her in the C-shaped curve of his reclining
body. His head rested on one hand as he pleasurably
filled his eyes. Her dark gold hair tumbled around her
shoulders and her shift was completely askew. It lay
as open as he had left it when he carressed her
breasts. She had very little resistance left, but in a last
gesture of protest she shifted her position slightly so
that her back was partially turned to him, providing a
brief respite from the smouldering examination of his
magnetic blue eyes. Not a very good move, she soon
found out as he casually reached out an arm and drew
her against him. She jumped as his warm manhood
touched her back. Soothingly, he stroked her bare arm
and kissed the nape of her neck. Each time he
touched her now, warm surges of feeling assaulted her
senses in nerve endings she hadn't known she possessed.

"I love your scent," he said. "It's soft and delicate
and very feminine."

She shivered. "God, will I live through the night?"
she thought frantically.

Very gently, his arm tightened around her so that
she was pulled from her kneeling position and her legs

parted slightly. Almost casually, his hand caressed her stomach and thighs. Her skin burned beneath his fingers. Then lifting the hem of her shift, his hand softly touched the downy, dark gold fur of her womanhood. She groaned and strained away from him, but his arm held her fast.

"The greatest pleasure in love, tiger, begins here," he said, touching the center of her being, "for both of us. You're hot and wet and tight here," he said, subtly shifting the position of his fingers.

"And for a man, that's very exciting." His voice was deep and husky. She trembled and shuddered as his hand continued to touch her, caress her. She wanted to jump out of the bed and run away. She wished fervently she had never heard the name Kade Renault. Her thoughts were mirrored in her eyes, and he whispered against her ear, "Relax, kitten." He pressed his lips softly to her shoulder, touching it with his warm tongue. She started. "No, don't move away from me," he said. He grasped the hem of her shift and removed it. Kade seemed to drink in the sight of her for a long moment—the heavy, dark honey waves, the shining sea-blue eyes, her full young breasts, the firm flat belly, the long graceful line of hip and thigh. He seemed to hold his breath. Then she heard him exhale in a long, deep sigh as he said, "You're very beautiful, tiger."

She looked up at him. His eyes were filled with the smouldering embers she had seen many times before, but now they were so intense that she caught her breath. Renault groaned and drew her to his chest. His lips devoured hers in a passionate kiss. His control had broken, and she knew there was no hope. Kade's arms crushed her against him as if he sought to mold their bodies into one form. She tried weakly to evade the hot, searing contact of his manhood against her belly, but his hand moved to the small of her back and pressed there until the lower halves of their bodies were as intimately entwined as their lips.

Against her will she was drawn into a vortex of feeling. Warm, piercing tides of sensation flooded her body. She would float into space if she did not hold tightly to this man who was the source of the storm. If only he would stop, so she could catch her breath and come back from the deep well into which she was sinking. But he didn't stop. He took her into its depths . . . and then surged toward the stars. She had to cling to him tightly or she would come crashing back to earth and die.

Dimly through a haze of sensation, she watched him rise above her, and felt him part her legs. His eyes were as dark and shining as two blue sapphires. She was too drugged with feeling to be frightened, but she knew that he would hurt her. It was inevitable. She felt a pinching tightness as he located the entrance. The first deep thrust drove him home to his nest, and her cry of pain was lost in his kiss. He moved inside her and the walls of her womanhood tensed and flexed without her willing it. She was totally unable to control anything that was happening.

As if she were outside of her body and across the room, Christina watched as Kade's mouth locked demandingly to hers and his arms enfolded her ever closer to his muscular form. She drifted back into her body and felt him surging powerfully inside her, her own muscles gripping him as if it were his will and not hers that controlled them. She felt him tense, and suddenly all his weight bore down on her there, centered in that dark secret place where no one else had dared intrude. She began to cry, not so much in pain but with some other powerful sensation she did not understand. Then, mercifully, she sank into darkness.

When she awoke, Kade was holding her in his arms, quietly murmuring soft endearments. He drew her to him and kissed her deeply, whispering quietly, "That was wonderful, kitten—for me. It will be better for you soon—the first time is more difficult than the others." He stroked her hair. "Go to sleep now, sweet."

She was tired, her body ached all over and she wanted to go to sleep, but by herself. She wanted to tell him that, but she was too tired to form the words.

Christina was so new to the game of love that she did not realize the time and care he'd given her. Nor did she appreciate the patience he'd shown. She only knew she was sore and uncomfortable, and she wished she could sleep alone.

When she thought he was asleep, she eased from his side. But even as he dreamed, he put his arm around her and drew her back to him. She looked at his handsome face, now boyishly innocent in slumber, and she sighed with resignation. She quietly promised herself she'd get out of this somehow. Chris spent the night with her back nestled closely against Kade's chest, disturbingly aware of his warm breath as it fell softly against her cheek.

CHAPTER SEVENTEEN

The sun shone bright and golden through the curtains of Christina's bedroom. She dreamed that she was swimming in the bay. Suddenly the ocean turned warm and solid. She couldn't move her arms. Christina struggled to consciousness and drowsily opened her eyes to find herself wrapped in the embrace of Kade Renault. His smile was disarming.

"Good morning, sweet," he said. He lowered his head, and she felt his lips play gently over hers. "How do you feel?" he asked softly, raising his head to gaze into her eyes.

"Sore," she said matter of factly as she looked up at him. His handsome face broke into a grin. "That will pass quickly, tiger." He kissed her nose lightly. "We've only begun your education. And I've never had a more beautiful pupil."

"Thank you," she said drily.

Kade yawned and stretched. She watched the muscles play over his tan chest and stomach. He rose from the bed and said, "Regrettably, I have some business to attend to that will take most of the day. Try to keep yourself amused without getting into mischief." He shot a playful glance her way.

She quickly swallowed a sharp retort. The sooner he left, the better—she wasn't about to start a fight that might prolong his presence in her room.

Humming to himself, he dressed without further comment. He looked as impeccable as ever in a cream waistcoat and brown trousers. "See you at dinner, *pe-*

tite," he said as he kissed her good-bye and left the room.

Chris sat up in bed and tried to collect her thoughts. This wasn't a nightmare she would wake up from. It was real. He seemed to have every intention of staying. But Renault was by reputation a man who did not let grass grow under his feet. Perhaps he would get bored in a few days and leave. He had to have many mistresses on Bajora. At the moment she was a novelty, a challenge. But that would change with time. Chris hugged her knees and smiled. If she had waited this long for her independence, she could certainly wait a little longer.

In the meantime she had work to do. She got up, dressed quickly, and ate a light breakfast of croissants and black coffee. A carriage was waiting downstairs to drive her to the Evrion offices in Lawrence, St. Marin's capital. It was a beautiful, clear blue day. The drive to Lawrence was so pleasant that she almost forgot about her problems. As they neared the center of town, she was brought abruptly back to earth by the sight of a broad muscular back in a cream waistcoat. It was Kade. She told the driver to stop.

Chris watched as he walked down the street. People turned as he passed. The women seemed especially reluctant to let him out of their sight. He greeted some and stopped to talk with others, but most he passed with a smile. When he walked into the bank, Chris signaled her driver to move on.

Andrew Hardy was already hard at work when Chris walked in. "Hello, Andy," she smiled. "Any luck with the new mast?" For several weeks, they had been working on the design of a new clipper that, if successful, could double the speed of the Evrion line.

"No," Andy said ruefully. "It still snaps like a twig under sail." So far the best ship designers in St. Marin were unable to come up with a mast strong enough to support the enormous weight of the sails, yet light enough to preserve the clipper's speed.

"We'll work on it today," she said cheerfully. Being here with Andy gave her a sense of well-being, almost as if things were normal. Chris spent most of the day with him trying to work out the design problem, but the solution eluded them, as usual. They decided to stop for the day. Chris said good-bye and headed for the dressmaker's. She was in good spirits as she told the driver, "Wait outside the shop, I'll only be a few minutes."

Madame Defaux was very efficient with customers who hated long fittings, and in less than a quarter of an hour Chris emerged from the shop singing a little tune. When she looked at the carriage her voice caught in her throat. Sitting nonchalantly at the reins was Kade Renault.

The driver was nowhere to be seen.

She walked slowly to the carriage. Kade's face was innocent as he watched her approach, but his eyes were faintly amused. "Where is Alphonse?" she asked accusingly.

"I told him to go back with my horse," he replied.

"How did you know . . ." she began.

"I recognized the carriage," he said, climbing down to help her up.

There was nothing to do but get in. They drove a few miles in silence before he said, "What did you do today?"

"I spent the day with Andy. There's a problem with the new clipper," she replied.

"What kind of problem?" he asked, interested.

"Well, we've got a new design that will outsail anything in the water once it's done, but we won't build it until we can devise a mast capable of supporting the large amount of sail the design requires."

"And that's a problem?"

She nodded. "Oh, we can always use the usual material. But that's heavy, and we would lose the speed of the design."

They talked of ships and sailing for the rest of the drive. Chris was almost surprised when they reached Mimosa Keyes. Renault knew much of the ship-building craft, and their discussion had been diverting. Kade stepped down from the carriage and walked to her side to help her down. His hands were firm and strong on her small waist as he lifted her from the seat. He took her from the carriage, and she found herself enfolded in his arms. She felt him brush her lips softly with his own. Then his mouth opened, and he kissed her hungrily. When at length he lowered her to her feet, her knees were not quite steady.

She went upstairs to change for dinner, thankful that he'd stopped in the library to go over some figures. She put on a simple gown of sprigged green muslin that modestly framed the swelling curves of her breasts. The sun-lightened curls at her temples were charmingly windblown, and her cheeks glowed with color from the agitation she felt.

When she entered the small family dining room, Kade was already seated, calmly studying a sheet full of numbers. He stood up and smiled as she walked in, his eyes taking in her appearance with appreciation. They talked quietly about dozens of insignificant things as they were served. Chris was uncomfortable and wondered if he sensed it. He was being uncharacteristically soothing, not like the irritating rake she'd become accustomed to. She might have relaxed, had it not been for the way his dark blue gaze caressed her bodice from time to time. At length they finished their meal, and she left him to his port.

Chris undressed and donned a diaphanous pale pink shift. She suddenly wished she owned some more substantial bedclothes. She would have to remember to have Madame Defaux make some long cotton nightgowns. Apprehensively, she climbed into bed. She considered locking the door, then thought better of it. In a few minutes the door opened, and Kade walked in. He was wearing a dark blue brocade robe, open to the waist, revealing his brown muscular chest. She could barely see the handsome, sculptured planes of his face in the dim candlelight. He walked toward the bed and sat down near her. Looking deeply into her eyes, he took her face in his hands and slowly kissed her, his lips moved over hers lingeringly, bringing back the warm tingling sensation she was powerless to stop. His hands moved beneath her shift and as his lips left hers, he drew the shift over her head and carelessly tossed it aside.

His eyes roamed unhindered over the young, shapely curves of her body as he removed his own robe. He joined her beneath the light satin bedcover and took her in his arms. His mouth claimed hers in a kiss that made her tremble with its intensity. His chest crushed her breasts. She felt her body melting into his tall, hard form. It was as if she was losing her identity—somehow becoming part of him and disappearing from the room, the world. She was afraid and began to struggle. A faint tremor shook his body, and he groaned softly. Her panic increased until at last he raised his head and gazed down at her. "Christina," he whispered, "you do not possess the strength to keep me from taking what I want." His blue eyes glowed strangely in the dark. "In time, you will learn to experience love's full joy, but for now, just lie quietly as I hold you. It will not hurt this time, sweet, if you do not struggle," he said as his lips caressed her throat, moving downward to gently and softly bite her breasts. "Trust me, kitten," he said.

He kissed her demandingly then, and she felt a hot flood of warmth as he joined their bodies. He moved inside her rhythmically, like the ebb and flow of the St. Marin sea. She caught her breath against his powerful surges and gripped him tightly for reasons beyond her knowing. Kade's muscular loins pressed warmly against hers as he continued the forceful thrusts for what seemed an eternity. His hand kneaded the soft curve of her breast as he held her close.

Suddenly his body seemed to expand with raw power. She felt his weight bear down on her, filling her completely with his manhood. A rush of heat swelled from her loins and rose to her breast. Every nerve in her body seemed to burst. She gasped with a shudder as she felt Kade explode inside her. Then, exhausted beyond words, she slept.

CHAPTER EIGHTEEN

When Chris awoke the next day the sun was high in the St. Marin sky. Janie pushed the curtains apart and opened the window to let in the sea breeze. "S'pose you'll be sleeping mornings now that Captain Renault keeps you up half the night," Janie giggled.

Chris shot a dark look in her direction and said, "What time is it?"

"Almost noon," Janie replied. "Seems like just yesterday you used to be the first one up in this house," she grinned.

Chris muttered something unintelligible.

"Yes, sir, that captain sure is a powerfully built man," she teased. "Guess any woman'd have the right to sleep late after a stallion like that had—" She was cut short by a flying pillow. Laughing, she left the room for a minute and returned with croissants and coffee. Janie poured two cups and sat in a chair near Chris's bed. "Like I said, things have a way of working themselves out."

Chris bit a criossant. Then, for the first time, she realized Kade was gone. "Is Renault still in the house?"

Janie nibbled a roll and said, "No, he left for Lawrence early this morning and said to let you sleep because you had a hard night." She hid a grin behind her croissant.

"Considerate of him," Chris said drily. "Did he say what he was going to do in town?"

"Well, he mentioned something about talking to Andrew Hardy, but nothing more than that."

Chris sat bolt upright in the bed. The thought of Kade Renault unattended with Andy at the Evrion offices was a disturbing notion. She gulped down her coffee and dressed quickly.

When she arrived she found Andy and Kade discussing the new mast.

"You know, Captain Renault, I think you're right," Andy was saying. "This piece of wood from Bajora is stronger than anything the draftsmen have tested so far and light enough not to slow down the frigate. It just might work!"

"What might work?" said Chris as she walked through the door.

"Miss Evri . . . eh . . . pardon me, I mean Madame Renault . . . ," a smile covered the slip, "your husband has just come up with a remarkable specimen of wood from Bajora that looks like just what we've been searching for."

Chris looked at Kade. He favored her with one of his heart-stopping smiles. His face wore a pleased expression, and his obvious good humor was contagious. She walked over to them and looked at the sample Andy was holding. It did look promising, strong enough to withstand weight, but with a lightness they hadn't seen before. "Has Van Auchs seen this?"

"Not yet," Andy replied. "He should, I think. You agree?"

"Yes," she said firmly. "As soon as possible. If he agrees with us, we'll start on the model ship immediately."

Andy Hardy looked euphoric. The mast problem had caused him many sleepless nights in the past months. "Christina," he said, lapsing into their usual informal way of addressing each other, "I wonder if you'll do me the honor of allowing me to hold a reception in honor of you and Captain Renault. As your wedding took place on Bajora, your friends in St. Marin have not had the pleasure of greeting you and your husband properly."

Chris was silent for a few seconds. She wanted to get out of this marriage, not celebrate it, but Andy was right. There should be a reception of some kind for St. Marin. "That would be lovely, Andy. Don't you think so, Kade?" she asked.

Renault was watching her with a twinkle in his eyes. "Very lovely," he replied. The amusement in his voice was considerable. She'd been neatly trapped, and he knew it. He walked over to Christina and brushed her cheek with his lips as he said, "I have to go, *petite*. I'll see you at dinner."

Christina frowned inwardly as he left. She wished she could get inside that black-haired head and find out what he was thinking. How much longer did he intend to stay? How long would it be before the novelty of marriage faded and his attention turned elsewhere? She hoped it would be soon. She couldn't stand much more.

Chris spent the rest of the day with Andrew Hardy, making plans to begin building the model clipper. Later that evening she returned to Mimosa Keyes. As she passed the library she heard laughter and the sound of male voices she didn't recognize. Curious to know who was in the house, she walked into the room.

Inside, she saw Kade seated in the brown leather wing chair. Three men sat across from him. She recognized one of them from her wedding day in Bajora—a tall, powerfully muscled, fair-haired man named Guy Savant. The other two she'd never seen before. They stopped talking when she walked into the room. Renault was the first to speak.

"Hello, *petite*," he said. "Let me introduce you to three gentlemen you will see a lot of. You've met Guy. This is Jacques LaCroix and Logan Armor."

"*Enchantée, messieurs*," she said.

The one called Logan Armor bowed and kissed her hand lightly. He was almost as tall as Renault, with sandy brown hair that matched his hazel eyes. "The pleasure is mine, madame," he said.

Jacques LaCroix had dark auburn hair and his skin was nearly as tanned as Kade's. He bowed also and said, "The captain is a very lucky man, madame. There are few women whose beauty rivals that of the sun, but yours makes it seem dim by comparison. I have never seen . . ."

Renault laughed and put up a hand. "That's enough, Jacques. I find it difficult enough to live with her vanity without your increasing it." He grinned broadly.

Chris shot him a withering look and turned back to Jacques LaCroix. She sighed tolerantly and said, "Some men are so much more perceptive than others. It is pleasant to be in the company of a man of such good taste, Monsieur LaCroix."

Guy Savant and Logan Armor laughed at her retort. She noticed that these men had a kind of wild charm. There was an aura of danger in the way they moved and a suggestion of violence in their bearing that was both attractive and a little frightening. It was as if the civility was a mask to hide natures more savage than they cared to reveal. She often thought the same thing about Renault. Obviously he chose his men in his own image.

"Will you gentlemen be staying for dinner?" she asked.

"Unfortunately not, madame," Logan Armor replied. "We just arrived in St. Marin, and as we plan to stay for quite a while, there are several matters we have to attend to."

"I understand. You must come to the reception then. You will be able to meet many of the people who live here. The captain will tell you about it. Please excuse me, gentlemen, and finish your discussion. It was a pleasure meeting you." She nodded and left the room.

Renault's eyes followed her retreating form. When she was gone he turned to Guy Savant. "So DeVilla has vowed revenge," he said thoughtfully.

Savant nodded. "He says he will kill you within the year."

"It was to be expected," Renault said, unperturbed. "Any other information—have you heard what he plans?"

Guy Savant shook his head. "Not yet. But our friends in Mexico will keep us informed."

Renault nodded and smiled. "This promises to be a very interesting year." He appeared to be looking forward to it. Savant smiled to himself. There were few things Renault enjoyed more than a good fight.

Andrew Hardy wasted no time in arranging the reception. It was held at Hardy's home in Lawrence, a gracious house filled with the fine antiques the little man favored. Christina chose a striking gown of vivid green silk trimmed with exquisitely delicate lace in a matching shade. She considered pinning up her hair and almost as quickly dismissed the thought. It was allowed to fall as usual in long waves over her back and shoulders, and the soft golden tendrils rested in their natural position at her temples. She was about to call Janie to lace her into the gown when a deep voice said, "May I be of assistance?"

Kade Renault leaned casually against the doorway. He looked elegantly imposing in a severely cut blue waistcoat and trousers. His black hair gleamed in the candlelight, and, before she could decline his offer, he walked toward her with the easy grace of a jungle animal.

Warm hands grazed her skin as he unhurriedly closed the myriad fastenings on her gown. When he was done she moved away from the unsettling nearness of his presence. He seemed not to notice, or if he did, he gave no indication.

"Thank you," she said uneasily.

Kade smiled enigmatically. "You're a vision in that dress, as you well know," he said, "but something is definitely missing. I think, perhaps, it is this." She stared at the case in his hand for a moment and at last took it slowly. Inside was the most beautiful emerald necklace she had ever seen. She was silent for so long that he sighed and, taking the necklace, clasped it around her throat. It was framed perfectly by the rich green lace bodice of the dress. She raised her fingers to her throat and softly touched the stones. Then she lifted her eyes and looked at him. They stood gazing at each other for a long moment. Neither spoke. At last, Christina, unable to bear the tension that was building inside her, broke the silence. "Kade, I . . ." she began, but a knock at the door interrupted her.

"Mis' Chris, shall I lace you up?" asked Janie from outside the door.

"No, Janie. Captain Renault saved you the trouble," Chris said.

A giggle was the only reply as Janie walked away.

"Thank you, Kade. It's magnificent," Chris said. She brushed his lips lightly. It was more of a touch than a kiss. "We'd better go or we'll be late . . ." she said. She sounded like a small child wheedling a favor. His lips curved in a slight smile as he took her arm and escorted her to their waiting carriage.

Andrew Hardy greeted them at the door. "You both look splendid," he said jovially. "Come in, come in. Everyone is waiting." Beaming broadly, he led them inside. For the next few hours Christina smiled, talked, and generally played the role of the happy, blushing bride. She felt Renault's gaze from time to time, but looking at him, she found it impossible to read his thoughts. As her eyes wandered around the room, she saw him talking with one of the men she'd met in the library, Logan Armor.

When the clamor around had died down a bit, she made her way to the punch bowl. She found Jacques LaCroix at her side.

"Our captain has more luck than a mere mortal deserves, madame. You must certainly be an angel, for no normal woman could look so radiant."

She smiled and was about to reply when Veronique Lanier walked up to her and beamed, "Christina, my dear friend. I would wish you every happiness, but with such a handsome husband, you cannot possibly be otherwise."

Chris grinned when she noticed that her pert friend

was regarding LaCroix with something beyond polite attention.

"Thank you, Veronique. Allow me to introduce you to a friend of my husband, Monsieur Jacques LaCroix."

"*Enchantée*, Monsieur LaCroix," Veronique said demurely as Jacques bent over her hand.

Jacques's eyes held Veronique's somewhat longer than was required and he said, "I see that Captain Renault did not capture the only angel in St. Marin after all, mademoiselle."

Veronique blushed and favored him with a smile. Aptly judging the probable direction of their conversation, Christina excused herself and discreetly left to join Marie Robillard, who seemed to have already met Guy Savant. She was laughing at some funny remark Savant had made. Marie hugged her. "Oh, Chris," she said, "we are *very* glad you and Captain Renault are wed. And it's so wonderful that he is moving his business interests to St. Marin to be with you. We will all be like a big family." She was talking to Chris, but her eyes were more often than not on Guy Savant as she spoke.

Savant was very amused by this and enjoyed it thoroughly. He made a great flourish over Marie's hand as he kissed it and smilingly excused himself to join Renault and Logan Armor.

Marie exclaimed as soon as he was gone, "Christina, you are so lucky. I met Captain Renault a little while ago for the first time. I had no idea that he was so . . . so . . . oh, I don't know. But you are very fortunate, Chris, to have such a man."

Chris looked at her. Was this the same young woman who had warned her away a few short weeks ago?

Veronique Lanier joined them. "Oh, Chris," she cried, "Captain Renault is sooo good-looking. He has such charming friends."

Marie grinned. "But Chris, you had better lock him in a closet or the ladies of St. Marin will kill him with attention. Look over there."

Chris followed the direction of Marie's glance. She saw a crowd of attractive young women surrounding Renault, Guy Savant, and Jacques LaCroix. Carlotta DeCorba was gazing at Kade with obvious longing. Her eyes seemed to undress him while he regarded her with an amused expression on his handsome face.

"I've never seen Carlotta look so hungry before," said Veronique. "Like a starving woman gazing at a banquet," Marie remarked drily.

Carlotta did look like a cat watching a bowl of cream. Christina fought down the impulse to kill. She reasoned that if Kade were attracted to Carlotta, he would undoubtedly lose interest in her. And that would be wonderful. She abhorred Carlotta, but she wished her good hunting. It wasn't that she disliked her husband. On the contrary, she often found him wildly exciting. That was the whole problem—she didn't want to lose her heart. It took most of her will now to resist his sensual assault on her body, and the effort was beginning to sap her strength. But she was determined to travel and enjoy her youth. She had spent her entire life on the island. She itched to expand her small world—to learn new things and visit new places.

The reception was drawing to a close. She was near the refreshments when an unpleasantly familiar voice said, "Well, Christina, I see you wound up with a pirate."

She turned to stare at the unwelcome face of Hilda Lesky.

"Left to your own devices, you refused all your decent suitors and chose a thief and a murderer. I told Mac what would happen if you had your own way, and I was right."

Christina's eyes turned to slivers of blue ice. "Whatever Captain Renault . . . my *husband* . . . is or is not has nothing to do with you, Hilda. It concerns me and no one else. If you think that your pure mind will be soiled by being near us, then leave."

Hilda's voice dripped with venom as she regarded Chris malignantly. "You and your precious father. Always so close, so loving. I was his wife, but he barely knew I existed. I tried everything to make him notice me, to care . . . if only a little. Nothing worked. Because of you! And your damned dead mother! And what were you, nothing but a worthless—"

"Hilda!" Chris said through bared teeth. "This is not my house, and you may be a guest here, but if you say anything more, you will regret it, I promise you!"

Hilda's face grew ugly with rage. Before she could speak, Andrew Hardy walked up to them. He had been watching the two of them from a distance, and he sensed trouble brewing.

"Christina," he said, "shame on you leaving Captain Renault alone to deal with that herd of admiring women. Go and be a good wife and rescue him. I'll keep Hilda company." Chris hesitated a minute, noting the hatred in Hilda's eyes. Then she sighed and walked toward Renault.

Andrew Hardy looked uncertainly at Hilda. "Would you care to dance, madame?" he asked.

Hilda did not reply. She was still glaring at Christina's retreating back. "She does not deserve to be happy," she said softly. Then she seemed to notice Andy's presence for the first time. "She does not deserve it!" she sneered at him. Turning on her heel, she stalked away.

When Chris walked over to join Renault, Carlotta DeCorba was talking to him, and her eyes still had that hungry, seductive look that only DeCorba could deliver with such deliberate intensity.

"I see that you have met Kade, Carlotta," Chris said simply.

"Yes, I have had that pleasure," she said, putting soft emphasis on the last word. "You are very fortunate, Christina. I wish you much happiness," DeCorba said sweetly.

Chris doubted that she meant it, but tonight she and Carlotta were on the same side. Slipping an arm through Renault's, she said pleasantly, "You know, Carlotta, now that I'm married and we're not fighting over the young men of St. Marin, I think we should be friends. I hope you'll come and call on us—very soon."

DeCorba's eyes widened slightly at the unexpected opportunity, and, thinking Christina a fool, she smiled and said predatorily, "I would love to, Christina."

"Good." Chris smiled. "Don't wait too long." Turning to Renault she said, "Could we go home now, darling?"

Kade's expression had been impassive and unreadable as he listened to the exchange. They said their good-byes and left. The ride home was spent in silence. Chris was tired and despondent by the time they reached Mimosa Keyes. The contact with Hilda had depressed her, as seeing the bitter woman always did. The melancholy emptiness caused by her father's death was still with her. She missed him deeply. She'd lost her mother early in life. Most of the love in her small world had come from Mac. Now Janie was the only link she had with the past. She sighed sadly. Then she felt an arm around her shoulders, drawing her close. She looked up, and Renault smiled down at her—a simple smile, devoid of passion or guile. She leaned back against him and he held her for the rest of the journey. She felt strangely grateful for the reassuring warmth of his arms.

As the carriage neared the Keyes, Chris heard the sound of the Rawani drums. Night Festival was beginning. She knew an instant aching deep inside. The drums always made her want to run to them, to feel the sea breeze in her hair and dance in the firelight. She said nothing to Renault. She only listened, wishing quietly that it was a few short weeks ago, and that she could run with Janie toward the flickering light in the forest, as others were doing at this very minute.

Upstairs in her bedroom, she put on a long peach-colored gown. It was transparent, but not as revealing as her short shifts. Still, it left little to the imagination since the sides of the gown were slit to allow the wearer to move about more easily.

She could still hear the drums clearly. The Rawani celebration was very close to the Keyes tonight. She could even hear the sound of the doman's voice as it drifted through the night.

"All of my children . . . come to me . . . *Lowani* . . . *Lowani* . . . *Adume* . . . *adume*.

Chris began to move. The music started. Her senses were filled with the soft song of the reedlike flute, the throbbing melody of the guitarlike instrument called the *bunya,* and the deep stirring beat of the drums. It all drifted through her window with the breeze. She closed her eyes. The music was soft. She was floating on a cloud. The sound became more intense, demanding. Her body began to undulate in the ancient movements of the Rawani ritual. She felt relaxed, at ease. The movements made her feel free and whole again. The music grew wilder. It soared. So did she. Spiritually, she was above the trees—looking down at the world from somewhere among the stars. Then as quickly as it had begun, the music stopped. Chris dropped on the bed, breasts heaving and out of breath. The first part of the ritual was over, and the dancers were resting.

A movement in the doorway caught her eye. Kade walked into the room and stood looking down at her. She knew from the smouldering fire in his eyes that he had been standing in the doorway while she danced. She was too drained to fight him. His blue gaze held hers. Then he said in a voice deepened with desire, "I want you." She looked at him. "It's impossible to be near you without wanting to hold you—and touch your softness." He seemed to be waiting for her to speak. But she didn't respond . . . she couldn't . . . she was too weak. For the moment, Chris was emotionally and spiritually exhausted.

When Chris remained silent, his handsome face grew stern. "Nothing to say? I'm sorry, *petite*. I will not stand here and burn to ashes with my need of you." He smiled sardonically. "We are going to put out the fire you started in me, Christina—together."

She watched as he moved over her. Then she felt his hard body cover her own. His mouth came down on hers, crushing her lips with his. He had never kissed her this way before, with such consuming urgency. His robe was open to the waist and she felt the crisp curling hair on his chest brush her breasts through the soft material of her gown. His hands moved under her to knead her buttocks as his mouth ground into hers. He had not lied—his body was on fire. She could feel waves of heat from him wash over her.

She felt an answering warmth welling up inside herself. Dimly she struggled against the swelling tides of sensation that threatened to engulf her.

His mouth left her bruised lips to place burning kisses along her throat. Impatiently he ripped her gown to the waist and his lips locked on her breast in passionate hunger. She felt a gripping sensation deep within her as if he were turning her inside out.

Vaguely she heard the sound of tearing cloth as he pulled the rest of the gown from her. She watched as he flung his own robe across the room. Then she felt his iron body again cover her own, and she flinched as the hardness of his passion flamed against her belly. His hands moved to the small of her back and pressed, molding her close to him. Then gradually his hand slipped between their bodies.

Christina felt white hot surges of fire race along her spine. It was too much. Determined to preserve her sanity, she put her hands on his shoulders to push him away, but just as she felt the firmness of his well-muscled arms, the Rawani drums resumed. The ritual to summon the spirits of good harvests had begun. Christina became still as she listened. It had been so long since she had experienced the entire ritual. The music started, and she felt the pounding of the drums creep into her soul. She lay with her eyes closed as the rhythm and the chanting captured her spirit.

When she opened her eyes she looked straight into Kade's sapphire-blue gaze as she felt him part her thighs and join their bodies. Something inside her melted. In her mind's eye the man and the music and the drums fused into one. As if she were dancing, her hips began the undulating movement of the Rawani ritual. Her body moved in the ancient motions of the ceremony that had brought peace and release to its dancers for centuries.

Through a soft haze she heard Kade groan deeply as she began to move and felt his embrace tighten. Joined with him as she was, his body countered her movements with his own forceful, rhythmic thrusts. She shuddered as he covered her lips with his, molding her to him. She squirmed a bit. When he held her too tightly, she couldn't move. And she had to move, with the drums and the music. They compelled her to. Without realizing what she did, her hands caressed his neck and her fingers spread themselves in his thick, curling black hair.

"Christina," she heard his deep whisper. "Ah . . . kitten . . . yes . . . that's it."

The drums became faster. The ritual was nearing its close. Christina's rippling motion grew faster. The tempo of the dance was always controlled by the drums. "Oh . . . god . . . yes," she heard Kade whisper as he kissed her again. She felt a searing flame spread through her loins. She couldn't stop what was happening to her. Always there was a soaring feeling at this time, but never before had it threatened to steal her will and send her shooting into the darkness without return. The drums and the music grew faster as did the rhythm of her undulation.

"Sweetheart," he groaned deeply. "My wild . . .

warm . . . soft . . . little girl," he sighed against her ear. The feeling inside her was stronger than she was. It was taking over, and she couldn't stop it.

"No!" she cried, frightened of what was happening, shivering as the strange new sensation possessed her.

"Yes," she heard his deep whisper, "God, yes . . . come with me, kitten . . ." he sighed. She did . . . she couldn't help it.

CHAPTER NINETEEN

Chris awoke the next morning to find Kade asleep beside her, one arm thrown carelessly across her waist and his leg entwined with hers. His face looked boyishly innocent in slumber. She noted the clean, classical lines of his face and the thick, black lashes that lay on his cheeks. His mouth curved upward in a slight smile that was almost angelic. How harmless he looks, she mused. For a moment she felt an unfamiliar softness towards him, but she shrugged it off. Appearances are deceiving, she thought wryly.

Mentally she reviewed the past few weeks. All in all, things were not progressing as well as she had expected. By now she had hoped that the novelty of their relationship would be gone and that Kade would be restless enough to leave the island for other pleasures. Instead, there were rumors that he was moving his base of operations to St. Marin, and when that happened she might be stuck with him for good. She had to prevent that. She had married to gain her freedom, not lose it.

Christina knew there was one ace in the hand fate had dealt her. Kade Renault was irresistible to women. There were enough attractive females in St. Marin to keep him busy for a quite a while, if he could only be tempted. Christina intended to see that he was. She would start with a temptation called Carlotta De-Corba.

As if her thoughts disturbed him, Kade yawned and opened his eyes. His azure gaze roamed over the creamy roundness of her breasts, then leisurely rose to take in the veil of waving tresses that flowed wildly over her shoulders, moving at last to the fine planes of her lovely face. "Good morning," he whispered as he drew her into his arms and kissed her deeply.

Knowing the trend of his thoughts, she quickly started a conversation to distract him. "You know, Kade, I think it would be fun to ask Marie and Veronique to dine with us tonight. Would you mind?"

He smiled one of his melting smiles. "Of course not. Your two friends are charming," he said as he nuzzled her neck.

"That tickles," she said.

"I know," he grinned. He rolled over and his weight pressed her into the soft bedcovers.

"I would also like to ask Carlotta. It is time we put aside the bad blood between us."

"A good idea," he said. He was planting soft kisses in the hollow of her shoulder. "If you intend to make this a banquet, I should invite Guy and Jacques to round out the party."

"But if you invite them, we will have to find chaperones."

"*We* will be the chaperones, sweet. We are married, remember?" Christina attempted to rise. "And just what, madame, do you think you are doing?" he asked, amused.

"I'm getting up to make dinner preparations. We've slept half the day away and there is much to do," she said pleadingly.

The glow in his eyes was unmistakable, and she felt a sinking feeling in the pit of her stomach. "I'm afraid the preparations must wait a little longer, Christina," he said in his deep voice.

* * *

Much later Christina sent the invitations by messenger. Carlotta DeCorba had a previous engagement with James Marston, so Chris suggested that they both come. Carlotta agreed. She wasn't going to miss the opportunity of seeing Renault again.

Madame Ouvre carried out the preparations for the sumptuous dinner menu Chris planned. A succulent *filet du boeuf* would be the main course, preceded by several savory island seafood dishes.

The gown she chose was pale blue silk, devoid of lace and simply cut. It was her plainest gown. She wanted all of Kade's attention to be on Carlotta, not her. Her tawny mane went unpinned as usual, a rippling waterfall of dark honey and gold. She went downstairs to make sure everything was ready. They would dine in a small walnut-paneled room used for small parties of less than twelve.

A cloth of French lace covered the long mahogany table in the little dining room. Silver candelabra decorated a table set with fine bone china. A large, covered tureen of lobster bisque lay waiting on a small cart in one corner of the room. Chris smiled with satisfaction and sighed softly. An elegant trap—now, if only the bait worked! She silently wished Carlotta luck.

She heard footsteps in the hall and turned to watch Kade enter the dining room. He was roguishly handsome in a white ruffled silk shirt, sea-green waistcoat, and buff-colored trousers. She had to admit that he was devastatingly attractive. Carlotta would definitely be drawn to him. He walked over and lightly brushed her lips with his. He looked into her turquoise eyes penetratingly for a moment. Then he asked her levelly, "What mischief have you planned, Christina?"

Taken aback, she opened her mouth to deny the question when she heard Madame Ouvre's graveled voice in the distance saying, "Step into the parlor, Miss Lanier, Miss Robillard. Madame Renault and the captain will be with you in a moment."

"None at all," she answered belatedly and watched as he raised one black eyebrow dubiously.

"I'm glad for your sake," he said cryptically, as he took her arm and led her into the green parlor to join their guests.

Guy Savant and Jacques LaCroix were engaged in animated conversation with Marie and Veronique. Chris noted that the normally reserved Marie was smiling brightly at the debonair Guy Savant. For a time they laughed and talked about the events of the last few weeks. Logan Armor was in Bajora handling the details of moving Renault's business interests to St. Marin.

Then she heard the butler announce, "Mademoiselle Carlotta DeCorba and Monsieur James Marston."

Carlotta swept into the room, and Chris silently complimented her taste. She was wearing an emerald-green gown that perfectly matched her almond-shaped eyes and enhanced the dark sable beauty of her hair. James Marston looked elegantly dapper in a gray satin waistcoat and light brown trousers. Chris thought the combination was particularly pleasing with his blond hair and gray eyes.

Carlotta, however, had eyes only for Kade. From the moment she walked in the door, that seductive green gaze had followed him subtly around the room. Christina was sure that he noticed her. Any man would have. And Carlotta was looking especially beautiful tonight.

As the hosts, Chris and Kade were seated at opposite ends of the dining table. Chris had made certain that Carlotta was seated at Kade's right. James was positioned next to the talkative Veronique, which left Carlotta free to concentrate on Renault. Chris noted with satisfaction that Carlotta was using one of her favorite tricks. She spoke softly so that Renault had to bend his head to hear her, bringing him closer to her arresting cleavage and probably, Chris mused, surrounding him with her seductive perfume as well. It would not be easy for Kade to resist her invitation.

Pleased with the way things were going, Chris turned her attention to James Marston. He was a very attractive man. She had wanted to get to know him the night he asked her to dance. Unfortunately Renault had interrupted their conversation, but now the opportunity presented itself again.

"What brings you to St. Marin, monsieur?" she asked.

"I'm an architect, madame," he replied. "Lawrence is a growing town. The government has commissioned me to construct several buildings. In a few years the center of town will be very different from the way it is now."

"Oh," she smiled. "I'm sure you will make it so beautiful that we will not recognize it," she said.

"Not half so beautiful as our hostess, madame." He smiled, gazing directly into her aquamarine eyes.

The dinner was superb. The *filet du boeuf* was so tender that it fairly melted in one's mouth, and the vegetables with their sauces were delicate, tender, and fresh. When the meal was finished they moved from the dining room to the garden, where the St.

Marin sea glistened in the twilight. Graceful palm trees framed the courtyard, and in the center a large goldfish pond dotted with lily pads lay like the eye of a living green jewel. Wine and after-dinner cordials were served on carts.

Chris noticed that Carlotta had chosen a chair near Kade's and was subtly managing to monopolize his attention. James Marston was standing a short distance away, quietly neglected. She walked over to him, smiling to herself. "After all, I do have to be a good hostess," she reasoned.

"Do you find St. Marin to your liking, Monsieur Marston?" she asked.

"How could I not, with inhabitants like yourself, madame?" He looked at her significantly.

"Where do you call home, monsieur?" she said.

"Home is where I hang my hat, madame. But I was born in Philadelphia," he replied.

"Philadelphia. That is in Pennsylvania, is it not?"

He nodded.

"Tell me, are the women here very much like the women of Pennsylvania?"

"There is one woman here who makes the women of Pennsylvania seem drab in comparison."

"Ah, yes," Chris smiled, glancing in DeCorba's direction, "Carlotta is very lovely."

"I was speaking of you, Christina," James Marston replied, gazing deeply into her eyes.

She looked at him quizzically. Then she said, "The women of Philadelphia must have been very sorry to see you go." Marston regarded her warmly. Very warmly, Chris thought to herself. She was about to ask him another question when she felt something cold and wet splash down the back of her gown. She squealed and turned in surprise to find Renault behind her with an empty wineglass in his hand.

"Oh, how clumsy of me," he was saying. "Sorry, darling—I've ruined your dress," he drawled as he dabbed her with a handkerchief. She could tell by the amused glint in his eyes that the scoundrel had done it on purpose.

Kade looked at her dress with feigned regret. "Oh, well, no harm done," he said. "Just go upstairs and change." She noted the disappointment on James Marston's face, and she glared at Kade. He was all kindness and innocence as he said, "Don't worry. I'll keep our guests amused while you're gone." More than anything, she longed to wipe that smug, self-satisfied expression off his face, but at the moment there was nothing she could do. She vowed she'd get him later. Chris turned on her heel and walked toward the house. Guy and Jacques took advantage of their hostess's departure to ask Veronique and Marie to accompany them on a stroll around the garden. The two young women agreed eagerly. Kade signaled Jacques with a glance to take Carlotta with them. Reluctantly, LaCroix complied.

Renault and Marston were left alone in the courtyard. "You know, Marston," Kade began as he casually lit a cigar, "flirting with a strange woman is a risky business. It can be very bad for your health."

Renault drew on the cigar and exhaled a long puff of smoke in Marston's face. "If the woman is Christina," he said quietly, "it is downright dangerous. Your life will be a good deal less . . . complicated . . . if you stay away from her."

If Marston had known Renault better, the steely

glint in the azure eyes would have warned him to mind carefully where he trod and speak only after much thought. But he did not know him, and as a result he did precisely the wrong thing. Marston looked defiantly at Kade and replied haughtily, "That, my good man, is entirely up to the lady."

Before he could blink twice, he felt himself being thrown through the air. He knew only a second of fear before a loud splash and the sensation of cold water around him caused his mind to go blank. Sputtering and choking, he dragged himself from the fish pond, his feet and hands leaving soggy little puddles in his wake. The color of his beautiful gray waistcoat was running all over his sagging brown trousers.

He glared at Renault, who was calmly regarding his dripping figure. Defeated for the present, Marston walked through the garden to his waiting carriage. When he was out of sight, Kade sat down and chuckled to himself while he downed a brandy. Then rustling steps on the grass behind him made him turn his head. It was Carlotta. She was alone. Renault glanced around and asked, "What have you done with your companions, Carlotta?"

She smiled provocatively. "I could ask you the same thing about James," she said.

"He was catching a cold so he went home," Kade replied.

Carlotta stared at him. In her entire life she had never met a man as handsome or as magnetic as Kade Renault. A raw sensuality seemed to flow from him and surround anyone who stood near. She knew this was not the time or the place, but she had to speak, for who knew when there would be another opportunity?

"Kade," she said, moving toward him, "I have known a great emptiness since the first day I saw you. I should not tell you, but I can't help it. I long for you—only you can restore the peace that has deserted me." She was very close to him, and he sat looking up at her, his blue gaze curious and impassive.

"I yearn for you," she sighed as she lowered herself to his lap. Boldly, she put her arms around his neck. "There is much I could give you," she said, pressing her body close to his. "You are too much man for that childish girl," she cooed. "Next to me, she is nothing. A baby. She does not have a brain in her head, or fire in her body—not compared to what I can give you. You need a woman, a real one." She pressed her lips to his and kissed him hungrily, then drew back to look at his face.

He regarded her with silent amusement, and she felt him gently ease her arms from his neck. "I thought you and Chris had decided to be friends," he said.

Carlotta made a small sound of impatience, putting her arms around him again. "We have been rivals for years. We are used to it. But that has nothing to do with you and me. I would love you and want you even if you did not belong to her. Do you not feel how I burn for you? Can't you sense the need in me?"

Renault's cool gaze met Carlotta's fiery green eyes. "And what do you suggest we do about it?" he asked.

She released the breath she had held. "We can arrange to come to each other. There must be times when you can get away. Surely you are not always together. You will not be sorry. Beside me, she is a ghost, a phantom. I am twice the woman she is or will ever be. When?" she said, kissing him again. "Tell me so I may know and anticipate our love."

"I'm afraid never, Carlotta," he said.

Carlotta looked at him as if she hadn't heard clearly.

"What did you say?" she asked.

"We probably won't be, ah . . . seeing . . . each other," he said.

She looked at him incredulously. "Do you know what you're saying?" she asked. "You can't possibly prefer that underfed, willful, spoiled child to me. You don't know what you're throwing away."

"I think I do," he replied calmly.

She rose from his lap and looked down at him. "Do not answer me now. Think about it first. You may find that you'll change your mind, very soon."

He was about to reply that it was likely he wouldn't when the laughing foursome returned. Carlotta moved guiltily away from him to sit in a chair a short distance away.

Christina came down wearing a light silk gown of buttercup yellow. Lace inserts revealed her softly rounded bosom and lay in soft ruffles on her sleeves. The entire effect was a provocative innocence that was entrancing. She looked around for James. "What happened to Monsieur Marston?" she asked Kade suspiciously.

"His spirits were somewhat dampened after you left, and he went home," Kade's amused voice replied. Christina seethed inwardly.

It was late and the guests made their good-byes after extolling the wine, the food, and the company.

Upstairs in their room, Chris brushed her hair angrily. A soft sea breeze rustled the curtains of the open window. It was cool and a little chilling, but Christina was so incensed that she felt nothing, though she wore only a short beige shift. There was a knock and Renault walked in, as coolly sardonic as ever. He was wearing a long robe of sable velvet.

"I want to talk to you, Kade," she began.

He looked at her calmly. "I mentioned before that we can talk about whatever you wish when we're alone," he said.

"You spilled that wine on my dress deliberately," she accused.

He looked at her for a moment and then smiled. "That's right," he said amiably.

"You're not even going to bother denying it?" she said, surprised.

He shook his head. "Not if we both know I did it on purpose." He grinned.

"Damn you, Renault. Why?!" she yelled.

His smile faded, and his blue eyes gleamed coldly. "If you know it was no accident, then you know why."

"Oh, I can guess," she said, gritting her teeth. "But I want to be sure."

He went over to a small table near the bed with a crystal decanter and glasses lying on it. He poured himself a stiff brandy. When he spoke she noticed a slight edge in his voice. "It was obvious to me, Chris, if to no one else, that you were in the midst of charming the pants off poor Marston when I intervened. Excuse the phrasing, it's crude but accurate." She made a movement of protest. "No, don't bother denying it. I have been the object of your efforts myself, and, my sweet, I remember them well. As a result, I can recognize the signs." Christina got up to pace back and forth restlessly.

Somewhat distracted by this treat, Renault looked appreciatively at the long, well-shaped legs and slim hips beneath the transparent material of her shift. The flimsy garment covered everything, but hid nothing from his gaze. Undaunted, he sat on the bed and put his feet up. "I remember being chained in a rather compromising position," he said lightly, "that you lost no time in using to your advantage." The teasing mockery in his voice annoyed her. "And I, being the trusting, gullible sort that I am, allowed you to come to my room because I thought you were a lady. I naively expected you'd act like one. You didn't, of course, because you aren't."

She wished a very unladylike curse upon his mocking black head.

He continued, "You had no idea, innocent that you were, what torture you put me through. When your education is a little more advanced, you will learn that a man can stand far less of that sort of play than a woman without experiencing considerable pain. *Mon Dieu*, tiger. I had been imprisoned for more than six weeks," he laughed. "I only wish you could feel the kind of torment I went through." He grinned again.

"You certainly aren't suffering those pains any longer," she snapped in retort.

"Not at all," he agreed caressingly. "The joys of your bed are most rewarding in that aspect." Chris glared at him. Kade thought idly that if she knew how provocative she looked, pacing the room like a tawny young animal with her indignant eyes shooting turquoise sparks, she'd sit quietly in a chair and stop tempting fate.

"Are you trying to tell me you did it because you felt sorry for Marston, you pompous ass?" she yelled.

"My, such language from a gently reared maid," he said. "Yes, that is more or less what I'm saying. You see, Christina, we fools of the male gender have to stick together for protection. The female of the species is always more deadly than the male. Fortunately, our instinct for survival is pretty well developed," he said as his eyes roamed over the swelling curves of her bosom.

Christina stopped pacing and stood dead still as she yelled at the top of her lungs, "Damn it! I've stood all I intend to take from you. I'll assist you in moving your business interests to the island, as I promised, but then it's over! I do not intend to go on living with you. That wasn't part of our deal! I will not be a slave to your lust!"

He frowned slightly. "What an inelegant and inaccurate turn of phrase. Have you forgotten that you asked for this arrangement?"

"I did not ask for this!" she flung at him. "You deceived me! If you had any kind of decency, you'd let me get a divorce."

He shook his head. "I never agreed to that. Divorce was all your idea. And frankly, it doesn't fit my plans at the moment," he said calmly. Her eyes shot icy blue daggers in his direction. "Cheer up," he said. "You've learned a valuable lesson. The danger in thinking someone a fool is being made a fool of oneself."

She stood near the bed and looked down at him. She wondered if they would really hang a woman for murder.

Kade sighed with feigned disappointment. "Actually, I'm a little unhappy with your progress thus far. Granted, I'm no longer in danger of execution, and we have more time for your education, but I had hoped that you would have learned much more by now." She regarded him quizzically. "You should try to be more like your friend Carlotta."

Carlotta! she thought wildly. If ever a man waved a cape in front of an angry bull . . .

"Now, there is a woman who knows how to please," he said. If Chris had not been furious, she would have seen the teasing light in his dark blue eyes. "She's beautiful, seductive, and a good deal more charming than you are. She knows how to make a man feel . . . wanted. You would do well to observe how she does it. Your edges are still rough and, while I'm happy to point out some of the areas you ought to improve, by watching Carlotta you'll learn how to . . ."

Christina forgot to be pleased that he'd noticed Carlotta. In her emotional state she only heard him praising the virtues of her lifelong rival. The deep drawl of his voice was making her head spin. Something inside her exploded, and before she knew what she was doing, she slapped him.

Kade's calm voice stopped immediately, and Christina watched in horror as his handsome face hardened, and the dark blue eyes grew cold. She wanted to apologize but the words froze in her throat. He reached out and tore her shift in half. She screamed and turned to run, but he caught a handful of her tawny hair and pulled it cruelly, forcing her down on the bed. Kade's mouth descended on hers with violent intensity, crushing her lips in a bruising kiss. She struggled as he ground his mouth on hers, attempting without success to break his iron embrace. Their movements parted his robe, and Christina felt the solid hardness of his desire press against her trembling thighs. He tore his mouth from hers and rained hard kisses on her breasts, nipping them with his teeth in the heat of his passion. Christina lay writhing in his arms, trying to escape the insistent mouth that ravaged her. The air seemed to vibrate with the feral vitality that radiated from him as his hands traveled demandingly over her hips and thighs.

She cringed as his fingers entwined in the tender hairs of her womanhood. They moved inside her, probing, insistent, making her ready for him even as she willed it otherwise. She tried to evade his demanding caress, but Kade lowered his weight on her, pressing her into the soft covers, not allowing her to get away from him. His other hand rose to grasp her breast, squeezing and kneading it to his pleasure.

Christina felt Kade's knee part her thighs. She was penned by his solid manhood as he thrust forcefully within her. His eyes smouldered as he watched her, struggling beneath him. Gradually her struggles ceased, and she lay mesmerized by his dark gaze as his body surged into hers, again and again, filling her with the burning warmth of his desire. She closed her eyes as her hips began to rise and fall compulsively to meet his thrusts. She felt him place her arms around his neck and she no longer had the will to remove them. Kade held her tightly, molding her to his hard, lean form. When she looked at him again, his eyes were knowing and triumphant. She felt him strain inside her, releasing his seed deep within her. Her own body reacted instinctively to the consummation of their passion as she sank into a semiconscious state, barely aware of her own fulfillment.

Kade kissed her eyes, lips, and throat with a touch that was curiously gentle and caressing. His face held what seemed to Chris a bewildering mixture of gratification and satisfaction. He shifted his weight and drew her against him. In a little while she knew from his even breathing that he was asleep.

The next day Christina sat in the garden, absently watching the tide as it glistened in the morning sun. Janie Tresgros joined her with a silver pot filled with tea. Christina looked at her and said, "Janie, does the captain seem like the kind of man who can be persuaded to change his mind?"

Janie shook her head. "Oh, no, Mis' Chris, he's about the last man in the world who'd let go of an idea once it took root in his head. Why, it'd probably take an earthquake or a hurricane to get it out of him. That's what men who sailed with him say."

Chris sighed to herself. It had been silly of her to strike him. She promised herself never to make that mistake again. In the meantime there was the more immediate problem of getting rid of him. She still had high hopes for Carlotta, despite the frustrated anger she'd felt last night. Still, it would be wise to formulate an alternate strategy in case Carlotta failed.

Christina knew she had relatives in France. "When you are a young lady, Christina," her father had often told her, "we will visit my cousins in Paris. You will enjoy meeting Charles Mauriere and his family. There are several young cousins for you to play with." She had never forgotten that promise. It was one of the things she had always intended to do. Somehow she would find a way to leave the island without Kade knowing. Andrew Hardy would run the Evrion business affairs in her absence. She vowed she would get the best of that black-haired rogue yet.

Renault had gone to Lawrence early that morning.

The Corsairs were a familiar sight in town now. Kade purchased an attractive two-story building near the Evrion offices and went there daily to run his affairs. Chris fervently hoped that some pressing item of business would make it necessary for him to leave on a long sea voyage, but so far there had been no such plans. Still, the possibility was promising. It would be much easier for her to leave the island if he were away for a few days.

She turned to Janie, who was curiously watching the play of expression across her face, and smiled. "Janie, let's go into town today. It's been a long time since we went shopping together."

Janie grinned. Shopping with Chris was always fun. She bought things for everyone and didn't mind being asked for specific items if they were needed. Janie hopped up. "That's a fine idea. I'll go upstairs and get things ready right now," she said. Humming a little tune, she scampered off.

Chris stared moodily at the ocean. Suddenly she heard the sound of deep male laughter and heard footsteps in the courtyard behind her. She turned to see Renault and the Corsairs come into the courtyard. She could tell they had been riding. Kade wore a pair of light brown breeches that closely followed the muscled tendons of his thighs. His feet were encased in brown riding boots, and he wore a white linen shirt, which accented his clean good looks and sun-bronzed skin. When he saw her his face softened, and he smiled intimately.

"Good morning," he said as he bent to kiss her. Chris wondered at the emotions he stirred within her at that brief contact.

"Good morning," she said. "You are back from Lawrence so soon?"

"Yes," he replied. "We've an important matter to discuss that should not be heard by unfriendly ears," he said calmly.

She looked at him and rose from her seat. "You'll want privacy then. I'll finish my tea upstairs."

He smiled. "No, stay. You brighten the courtyard and what we have to say concerns you too, though indirectly."

He annoyed her by sitting in a nearby chair and pulling her onto his lap. He waited a fraction of a second for signs of open rebellion and, when she wisely decided to acquiesce, he grinned. "A lesson well learned, kitten," he whispered, nuzzling her ear. Chris chafed under the amused, approving eyes of the Corsairs, but kept silent.

He turned to Logan Armor and said, "Tell me more about this man Anjuez."

"Last night Anjuez was found aboard the *Falcon* in the hole where the guns are stored. He was carrying papers written in the code used by Don DeVilla. We suspect he is a spy sent by DeVilla. We know DeVilla wants to attack us badly, but he cannot take us on in St. Marin without losing most of his men in the battle. We believe he is searching for a vulnerable point of entry, a way of getting around our main defenses," Armor said.

Renault looked pensive. "Have we gotten anything more from Esprada, the spy we captured a month ago?"

Jacques LaCroix shook his head. "DeVilla covered himself well. Esprada knows nothing of the governor's plans."

Kade was silent for a while. The look in his eyes chilled Christina's blood. "Under no circumstances will I allow him to attack us here," he said. "We are going to pay DeVilla a little visit of our own."

CHAPTER TWENTY

Their departure was just what she'd been hoping for. It would be the perfect time to put Kade Renault and their unwanted marriage far behind her. Kade and the Corsairs would be gone in two days, and Chris wanted to leave for France on the same day they did. That left her little time. Janie enthusiastically agreed to come along. The young girl had always wanted to see Paris. Like Chris, her sheltered life had revolved almost entirely around the island. Janie thanked the stars for the day she'd come to work for the Evrions. From the first, Christina, who was four years her senior, had been more like an older sister than a mistress. Janie had a great deal of affection for her.

The two young women conspired together to pack their baggage without attracting suspicion in the household. They decided not to take very much in the way of luggage since Chris thought it would be easier to buy new wardrobes when they arrived.

"Where will we stay?" Janie asked as they folded their belongings into valises.

"With my cousins, the Maurieres," Chris answered. "Andrew Hardy is sending word of our coming to them."

"Won't they be surprised? They will not have much notice," said Janie.

Chris shook her head. "No, Mac planned to take us to France long ago. They've been expecting a visit. Only it will be just you and me, instead of three of us."

Janie raised her eyebrows. "The captain's not coming?"

Chris's lips tightened into a thin line. "No, Janie. Captain Renault will be in Mexico by the time we leave."

Janie looked at her with sudden understanding. "You don't love him, do you Mis' Chris?"

Chris looked at Janie and knew she had guessed the truth of their relationship. "I can never hide anything from you, can I?"

Janie shook her head and smiled.

Chris sighed and sat down on the bed. "I don't want to love any man, Janie. I think if Mac hadn't died, I wouldn't have gotten married at all. There is so much to do in the world, so much to see. My father taught me many things. I want to use them. I'm not like Marie and Veronique. I can't just get married and stay at home and make babies. Life can be so much more than that," she said passionately.

The next day Christina went into town to see Andy Hardy. When she got to the office, he was busy reviewing the specifications for the new mast.

"Morning, Andy," she said.

"Good morning, Christina," he answered with a smile. She looked like spring itself in a dress of lilac muslin trimmed with white lace and green ribbon. Hardy was disturbed by her request for passage to France. He liked Renault and believed that the captain cared a great deal for the fiery, headstrong young beauty who stood before him. In spite of what he'd heard about Kade, he found the man to be decent and intelligent. And of all the men he knew, Captain Renault was the only one he thought remotely capable of handling this tawny-haired tigress.

"My dear," he said, "are you still determined to go through with this escapade?"

Christina glanced at him sharply. "Andy, we've already discussed this, and my mind is made up. Anyway, it's not so terrible. I'm only going to visit my cousins."

"Then why don't you tell Captain Renault you're going?" he asked.

She sighed impatiently. "He has other things on his mind, and his business in Mexico may take some time. I don't want to wait until he returns to leave. Now, were you able to book passage on the *Northern Cross?*"

It was Hardy's turn to sigh. "Yes, Christina. Everything is arranged. You sail tomorrow."

Chris smiled. The thought of leaving was sweet indeed. When she returned to the Keyes she wrote a long letter to Kade. She thanked him for his assistance in gaining her inheritance and stated again that she did not want to interfere in his private life or curtail his freedom in any way. She hinted that she would be gone for a very long time. She was confident that he would turn to others. He was not known as a man with a celibate nature. Andrew Hardy, she wrote, would assist him in entering the rum business. Chris made several suggestions regarding enterprises whose owners were known to be searching for partners. She wished him luck and mentioned that he could contact her through Andrew Hardy, but only if it was absolutely necessary. Then she said good-bye and, satisfied with the overall effect, sealed the letter.

At dinner she took pains to be unusually charming to Renault. She smiled as he talked casually of his upcoming voyage and nodded sympathetically in the right places. Her mind secretly dwelled on her own departure in the morning, and her eyes twinkled with suppressed excitement. More than once she felt Renault gaze at her with quiet speculation. When dinner ended she walked over to him. Putting her arms around his neck, she drew his dark, handsome head to hers and kissed him ardently. He raised a dark eyebrow and regarded her quizzically. He was about to speak when suddenly there was a knock at the door of the dining room.

"Come in," she said, moving away from him.

It was Madame Ouvre. "Oh, madame," said the woman with a distressed look on her face, "Janie is ill. She is asking for you. She refuses to let anyone else come to her."

"Excuse me, Kade," said Christina. "I must go and see what is wrong."

She felt his blue gaze penetrate the depths of her being as he nodded silently. She hurried to Janie's room and found her moaning in bed, holding her stomach as she thrashed from side to side. Madame Ouvre stood behind her, worriedly wringing her hands. Chris bent over Janie briefly and turned to Madame Ouvre saying, "It is all right, madame. I recognize these symptoms. She ate green plantains even though she is allergic to them. I will stay and watch her. Please inform Captain Renault that I'll be sleeping here tonight."

The worried look left Madame Ouvre's face, and she went to convey Chris's message to Renault. When the door closed, Janie sat up in bed and grinned at Chris. Chris smiled conspiratorially. Everything was proceeding according to plan.

Early that morning Christina rose to have breakfast

with Kade and bid him farewell. He seemed unusually quiet. Chris decided he was angry that she had stayed away on the night before his departure. She made light conversation to cover his silence and ate an enormous quantity of croissants with jelly.

Later she walked with him to his horse and kissed him good-bye. "Have a safe voyage, Kade, and be careful," she said.

He reached out a hand and traced her lips with his finger. "Your life would be simpler if I did not return, wouldn't it, kitten?" She regarded him warily. He smiled cryptically and said, "But I will return, Chris." Without saying good-bye, he mounted his blooded stallion and rode away.

Christina sighed with contentment as she watched his retreating figure. She raced back to the house and ran to Janie's room. There, baggage hidden in various nooks and crannies was quickly assembled and hastily loaded into a large carriage. Madame Ouvre was surprised to learn of Christina's departure, but bore the news with admirable calm.

Chris and Janie rode to the harbor in high spirits, laughing and giggling like two truant children. They boarded the *Northern Cross* and settled in their cabin with much girlish silliness.

The sun was high in the sky before Christina sensed that something was wrong. Ordinarily, the *Nothern Cross* sailed before noon. By Chris's reckoning it was nearly that time already, but she couldn't detect any preparations being made for the departure. Janie grew apprehensive as well. They sat for a few tense moments, hoping they were both wrong. At last, Chris could stand it no longer. She was about to go above when a knock sounded on the cabin door.

Chris opened it, and her heart skipped a beat as she looked straight into the solemn faces of Logan Armor and Guy Savant.

"Begging your pardon for the intrusion, ma'am," Logan said pleasantly, "but the captain sent us to escort you to the *Falcon.*"

It took an extreme exercise of will not to scream. Behind her, Chris heard Janie catch her breath. Resolutely, she fought the nausea in her stomach and forced herself to remain calm.

"If you'll take our bags, Monseiur Armor, we will be ready in a few minutes," she said. Her mind frantically went over the details of the past week. *Que le diable!* How had he known?! There wasn't a clue. It was beyond all bearing. By the time they boarded the *Falcon,* Christina was seething.

They escorted her to the captain's cabin, where she found Renault seated at a desk poring over his navigation charts. He looked up when Chris walked in, and his expression was not kind. For long moments they stared at each other. Neither of them spoke. At last, unable to bear the tense silence, Christina said in a voice that was hardly more than a whisper, "How did you . . . how could you have found out?"

He looked at her without replying. His face held an expression of mild contempt. "As I told you, Christina, all men are not fools."

She turned from him and walked to the porthole, wondering what to say. What could you say to a husband you had just tried to leave? She turned to look at him. Renault's face was impassive, but there was something in his eyes that checked the angry words of frustration that threatened to spill forth. Where had she seen that look before? Images of a wounded animal floated quickly through her mind. Was it pain she saw in the dark depths of his eyes? Chris stared at Kade, feeling uncomfortable now and more than a little guilty.

Under her scrutiny he sighed impatiently. "Did it ever occur to you to find out who owned the *Northern Cross* before you so impulsively booked passage on her?"

Christina's eyes widened in shock. "You mean you . . . you're . . ."

"The owner. I bought her two months ago," he said.

She shivered at the coldness of his voice. Frowning, he folded away the charts. Renault's steely gaze bore into her. "You are far more trouble than you're worth. We have lost a great deal of time because of you. Since I can't trust you to remain in St. Marin while I'm gone, and I can't spare any men as guards, you and Janie are coming with us."

Christina gasped.

His mouth went down at one corner as he said sarcastically, "I take it you're not thrilled by the idea of an ocean voyage with me?" The note of self-mockery in his voice escaped her.

"You can't be serious," she exclaimed. "I can understand your being angry with me, but how can you drag Janie into the middle of a battle?" she asked incredulously.

"Janie has impressed me as a girl with a very strong nature. I'm betting she'll be able to take care of herself."

"What right do you have to bet her life? Oh, Kade, put us ashore, please."

"No. We are almost underway now."

"But this situation is impossible!"

"Well," he said wryly, "at least we agree on that count. You should have stayed home."

Christina slumped dejectedly on the bed. Tears began to fall from her eyes, despite her efforts to control them. "You're a fiend, Kade Renault. I hate you. I hate you for finding me and dragging us into this."

He looked at her coldly. "Unfortunate that you didn't consider the possibility of discovery before you decided to run away, isn't it? I'm afraid you'll just have to suffer the consequences."

She started to cry in earnest then, overcome by anger, frustration, and disappointment. Kade's face softened a little as he watched her.

"Paris is a beautiful city, Christina. I would have taken you there, if you'd asked," he said quietly.

She raised her head listlessly to stare up at him with angry, tear-reddened eyes. "I didn't ask you," she said slowly, "because I wanted to go alone—without you."

A hooded expression crept into his eyes. Silently, Renault stood up and left the room. When he was gone, Christina was more wretchedly miserable than ever. Overcome with fatigue and exhausted by her emotions, she fell into a restless, troubled sleep.

In the morning Christina awoke to find herself dressed in a man's linen shirt. She didn't remember changing. It dawned on her that Kade had come back to the cabin during the night and slipped her into it. Blushing a little, she looked around. There was no one else in the cabin.

A knock at the door disturbed her thoughts. Janie walked in, looking a little haggard. "Morning," she said weakly.

"Oh, Janie," Chris said quickly, "are you all right?"

"Yes, but I'm seasick. Don't think I ever been on a boat before. Not that I remember. " The ship lunged forward on a particularly strong wave, and Janie groaned, closing her eyes and holding her troubled stomach.

Chris stifled a smile. She knew she shouldn't laugh, but Janie looked like a little girl who'd eaten too much candy.

"Don't know why I ever let you talk me into this . . ." Janie moaned softly.

"Because you wanted to see Paris," Chris grinned. Then she added seriously, "And someday we will too . . ."

There was another knock at the door. "Ladies," said a deep, unfamiliar voice, "I brought breakfast."

"Who's there?" Chris called.

"Joshua Boman, ma'am" he answered, "third mate of the *Falcon*."

Janie opened her eyes long enough to look at Chris. "It's all right. I met him yesterday. Josh is a real nice man." She made a gallant attempt to smile. "He may be the best part of this trip for me." The ship lurched again, and she moaned.

Joshua brought in a tray filled with coffee, rolls, butter, and fruit. "Good morning," he said cheerfully. His eyes lingered for a brief second on Janie. He was a tall, powerfully built black man. It was a hot day, and he wore tan breeches with no shirt. His only adornment was a gold earring worn casually in one ear. Chris observed wryly that Janie's eyes roved appreciatively over his rippling mahogany chest.

Joshua set the food on a table nearby. Janie's face wrinkled when she smelled the food, and her brown eyes shut tight. Joshua grinned at her. "Yo' look a little seasick, but eat and yo'll feel better d'rectly. Captain says yo' ladies is makin' the voyage wit' us. Anythin' I can do, just let me know." He looked at Janie. "Old Josh'll never be far away," he said, smiling.

Christina called to him as he was leaving. "Joshua, where is the captain now?"

"He be on deck, ma'am," Josh replied. "Lot of work to be done on a ship, 'specially one as big and fast as the *Falcon*," he said. Then he left.

Janie bravely nibbled at her food for a few minutes, but eventually admitted that she was too ill to be about and went back to her cabin. Christina put on a dress of white muslin, sprigged all over with tiny green flowers, and looked through the porthole. The sea was blue and shining under the bright morning sun. It was a gorgeous day. She decided to go above.

The deck was astir with frenzied activity. Men moved quickly from one point to the next, tightening ropes, securing cargo, assembling guns, and checking ammunition. A voice beside her said, "All settled in, Chris?" It was Guy Savant, looking lean and formidable in the Caribbean sun. All of the Corsairs had a sensual, predatory aura about them, Guy Savant no exception.

"Very nearly," she replied.

"I hope you don't mind if I address you by your Christian name. We will be seeing each other often in the next few weeks, and it seems more friendly to be informal."

"No, I don't mind. I'll call you Guy," she said.

"Good. I'd like to be your friend. You're a very unusual lady. I've never met anyone who got the better of Renault," he chuckled.

She frowned slightly. "What do you mean 'got the better of him'? He stopped me before we could get away."

Guy laughed. "You miss the point. The remarkable thing is that you wanted to *leave*. Women don't run *away* from Kade Renault. They only run toward him. Chase him, would be more like it." He smiled. "I'd have given a chest of ducats to see his face when he found out what you did."

Chris frowned and muttered softly, "What bothers me is why the devil it mattered to him."

Guy looked nonplussed. "You mean you don't know? Why, Chris, the captain is . . ." His voice trailed off as he looked into her eyes. "That is . . . he thinks of you a great deal." He'd been about to say something more, but he thought better of it, never being one to interfere in other people's lives.

Chris said nothing, but she didn't believe for a minute that what Guy said was true. She thought Kade was an outrageous rogue and had felt that way long before their marriage. Now she knew he had another fault, one that was more serious in her eyes. Not only was he a perverse scoundrel—he was possessive as well. She was about to voice her opinion of the celebrated captain to Guy when they were joined by Jacques LaCroix.

"As usual, Guy, I find you wiling away the time with a beautiful mademoiselle when you should be working. Be careful, *chérie*. It is not safe to be too long in Guy's company, " LaCroix said jovially.

"Belay that, you scurvy sea scum. It's not I, but you she should watch out for," Guy laughed.

"Under any other circumstances, *certainement*," Jacques agreed amiably. "But not under the watchful eyes of Renault—*non, mon ami,* the mademoiselle has nothing to fear from you or me. *C'est regrettable.*"

Near the bow, Logan Armor was plotting the *Falcon*'s attack while Kade Renault directed the men to position the cannons toward the stern of the ship. A bit bewildered, Christina watched the men move the guns.

"Do we intend to attack DeVilla from the rear?" she asked.

LaCroix smiled. "There is always a reason, little one, for what Renault does before a battle, though to us it often looks insane. Rest assured that when the time comes, you will understand." Guy Savant left them to join Renault and Logan Armor at the helm.

Chris was curious about these men. Where had they come from, and who were they really? She knew so little about them. For that matter, she knew very little about Kade. She looked at Jacques LaCroix and said, "Jacques, tell me how you met Renault. Have you always sailed with him?"

LaCroix shook his head. "*Non,* I was a silversmith in New Orleans before I joined him. I had a small shop on the Rue de Reviens. I had a fiancée, Adrienne; we were soon to marry. But . . ." Jacques sighed. "Forgive me, mademoiselle, it is difficult to speak of it, even now."

Christina interrupted gently, "If it's too painful, Jacques, I'll understand."

"*Non,* I don't mind telling you. You're one of us now. My fiancée was killed. Adrienne was brutally murdered by the son of one of the leading families in New Orleans. Gaspar was insane. He was very clever—he could appear normal when he wished. Yet he had murdered before and would have again if I had not killed him. Afterwards I could not remain in New Orleans. I stowed away on an outgoing ship. I didn't know it at the time, but the boat was bound for Bajora. When we arrived at the island, I looked for work without success, and I didn't have enough money to buy silver for my trade. For a long time I just existed from day to day—hungry and exhausted. One night I wandered into the Red Boar Inn and saw a tall, dark-haired man laughing over a game of cards. The other men at the table were in good spirits too, and I was drawn to them. They were playing the king's game. I wasn't good at cards, but when I joined their hand and learned the game, I started to win. I had the luck of the beginner, you see. We got to know each other during the game. I won a great sum of money from them. At the end of our play, Kade offered me a place on the *Falcon*." Jacques paused thoughtfully. "That was seven years ago," he finished.

Logan Armor called Jacques's name and motioned for him to join them at the helm. Jacques nodded to Chris and excused himself. Chris wandered toward the bow of the *Falcon*. For a long time she stood looking out over the blue-green waves of the Caribbean.

Standing there in the sunshine, her heart felt lighter, her troubles more bearable. She found that she was even more curious about Renault. Chris looked around the *Falcon* as her eyes sought him out.

He was at ease in the sunshine, talking near the helm with Logan and Jacques. The two Corsairs were not small men, but Renault was nearly a head taller than both of them. His black hair was tousled and windblown. One unruly lock lay in the center of his forehead. Like the Corsairs, he wore only breeches and a white linen shirt with his sleeves rolled short.

Chris could see the muscles of his arms, healthy and rippling under his tanned skin. He laughed at something Armor said, and his white teeth gleamed in the sun. That contagious smile lit up the strong, chiseled features of his face and made him look suddenly young and boyish. Chris reluctantly acknowledged a discernible tug at her heart as he walked from Jacques to the mast of the *Falcon*. His body moved with a fluid grace that was remarkable in so large a man. She grudgingly remembered the perfect proportions that allowed him to move in such smooth strides.

Testing a line, he took a knife and put it between his teeth as he began to climb the rigging. He didn't bother to use a nearby ladder, preferring to scale a single length of rope to the crow's nest. At the top he took out a telescope. Placing it against his eye, he looked north toward the Mexican coastline. He stood there for a long moment, the blue, cloud-filled sky all around him. Guy Savant's words floated back to her: "Women don't run away from Kade Renault . . . they run *to* him." Watching him there in the sun, it was not hard to understand why.

As if he sensed her looking at him, Kade glanced down, and his eyes met hers. She looked away quickly, a hot blush coloring her cheeks. Renault climbed down from the crow's nest and walked over to her. Chris looked like a small sea sprite in her green and white dress, skirts and hair blowing in the wind. "Are you feeling better?" he asked.

"Yes, no thanks to you."

"Ah, I see that you're as sweet-natured as usual."

"What do you expect? We are prisoners here."

"Hardly that," he said mildly. "You can move about as freely as you wish. I don't plan to keep you tied up in my cabin, although that might be the wisest course, since you seem so determined to disappear."

"And where would I go—out here in the middle of the sea?" she asked irritably.

"True," he agreed. "In any case, you had better get used to it and learn to keep a civil tongue in your head. I've got enough on my hands fighting DeVilla without adding you to the list. I'm already tempted to throw you overboard, Christina—don't give me any more reason."

She didn't believe he'd toss her over the side, but he could make life very unpleasant for her in any number of ways.

It took an extreme exercise of will, but she asked calmly, "How long will it take us to reach Mexico?"

"Not long. Two, maybe three days. We're almost there already."

"Why is DeVilla looking for you? I didn't understand that conversation in the courtyard. What does he have against you and your men?"

His face hardened, and Chris thought she saw contempt there. "DeVilla and I are old enemies. When I left my home in Scotland to come to the New World, I stayed with a young Spanish nobleman in Mexico. Juan Miralda and I had been friends since our school days. I was a guest at his hacienda for a year while I purchased a ship and set up a business on Bajora. In those days the governor of the Spanish territories was an honorable man, respected by the landowners. Not long after I left, DeVilla replaced him. The man was completely dishonest. He doubled the taxes of the farmers and kept the new revenue for his own use, building a great personal fortune. My friend Juan and several of the other honorable landowners opposed him. DeVilla ordered the Spanish garrisons to burn them out. Juan died in a military prison. His wife and children were brutally murdered by DeVilla's personal guard."

Chris was horrified. "What an awful man!"

Renault smiled cynically. "The world is unfortunately full of such men, Christina. Many of them find ways to exploit those who cannot defend themselves and kill to protect their little empires." He continued grimly, "DeVilla killed Juan's family to make sure that no one remained to seek revenge, but he didn't consider Juan's friends. The governor is a man who has no friends, so he overlooked that possibility. For years DeVilla's ships have come to St. Marin filled with gold to trade for the luxuries he craves. Many times Juan's friends in Mexico have been able to get word of their voyages to me in advance. The *Falcon* has often given his vessels a little surprise." He looked down at her. "That is why, Chris, my men and I are known as pirates."

She looked at him levelly. "But you keep the money, don't you?"

"No," he said simply. "Most of it is smuggled back to the farmers DeVilla stole it from. The problem is that when DeVilla sees that the farmers survive despite his robbery, he raises their taxes."

"How awful," she said softly.

Renault smiled. "Yes, he is. And that is why it is very important that this trip be a success."

The days passed in busy preparation. Never before had Chris seen so many swords, knives, guns, and assorted weaponry. She was glad her father had taught her the use of arms. From the looks of things, that knowledge would come in handy.

Chris was amused as she watched Janie with Joshua Boman. Her young compainon was completely fascinated by the tall, black Corsair. They made a handsome couple. Joshua's large, muscular frame complimented Janie's small softness. Janie sought him out during the day when he wasn't working and talked for long periods of time.

One afternoon in Renault's cabin, Janie said wistfully to Chris, "That Joshua, he the nicest man I ever met. You know what? He got a little store on Bajora. Sells dry goods and things. Joshua is real smart. He saved all his share of the *Falcon*'s haul. And now he say he has enough for another store." She blushed a little. "Yesterday he told me he might build the store on St. Marin." Janie walked to the porthole and looked out wistfully.

"Do you like him, Mis' Chris?" she asked.

"I think you like him," Chris replied. "And that's all that matters."

Janie grinned at her. "I do. I like him—very much." She smiled.

One day when Chris was strolling on deck, she saw Guy Savant sharpening a rapier. She walked over to him. "I would run away if I saw you come toward me with that in your hand," she said.

Savant laughed. "If I came toward you, I would not have this in my hand."

"Have you always been a pirate, Guy?"

Savant roared. "No, and to be honest, I don't consider myself one now." Guy went back to sharpening his blade. "Kade and I go back a long time, Christina. All the way back to Scotland. I've worked for his fam-

ily since I was twelve. We grew up together. When
Kade left to seek his fortune, I left with him."

"Did you know Juan Miralda?"

Savant nodded. "Juan was the finest man I've ever
met. He'd do anything to help a friend. When I think
of what DeVilla did to him, well, I hope I find him
first."

The look on Guy's face made her shiver. She
changed the subject. "What was Kade like when he
was a little boy?"

"A lot like he is now—clever, restless, proud. A demon when he's angry and ruthless when someone he
loves is hurt. He's the smartest man I've ever known.
If you're thinking of crossing him again, I wouldn't."

She saw very little of Renault except at a distance.
He rose before she did in the morning and returned to
the cabin long after she retired for the night. He
worked all day and all night with such single-minded
purpose that it seemed almost sinister and made Chris
uneasy. But she grew to love the way the ship
looked under full sail. It was a breathtaking sight.
Though battle scarred, there was a masculine elegance about the *Falcon* that was stirring and beautiful. The lines were massive and stately, the wood
highly polished and lovingly cared for.

In subsequent conversations with the Corsairs, she
found out that the *Falcon* would arrive off the coast
of Mexico at night and anchor far offshore. The men
would set out in small boats and rendezvous with a
small partisan force on the land.

Chris planned to escape after the Corsairs left the
ship. Janie didn't want to come, and Chris could
hardly blame her. She had fallen in love with Joshua
Bowman and had no wish to leave him. It would be

nearly impossible to set out in a small boat on her own, so Chris planned to disguise herself as a man and stow away in one of the Corsair's boats when they left the *Falcon*. Once she was in Mexico she felt sure she could find a ship sailing for Paris. That was all she needed.

On the night of the attack, Renault drew her aside. Putting his hands on her shoulders, he looked at her intently and said, "If we have not returned in four days, the *Falcon* will cast off for St. Marin. I am leaving enough men behind to see you safely home." She thought in that moment that this was perhaps the last time she would see this enigmatic man—the last time she would look into his azure gaze or feel his smile tug at her heart. Unaccountably, Chris felt a burning sensation behind her eyes. Why, I'm crying, she thought with amazement. Kade's handsome face was immobile with surprise. He brought his hand to a tear and wiped it away. He drew her into his arms and held her for a moment. She could feel his cheek resting against her hair. It all seemed so unreal—she couldn't get over the fact that she had actually cried when she realized he might be killed. Her feelings toward this sardonic stranger were so contradictory.

Kade moved away from her slightly and raised her chin with his hand. He kissed her lingeringly, as if he didn't want to leave. He looked down at her and smiled. "I'll be back, tiger," he said softly. She watched as he leapt into a boat filled with Corsairs. In a moment he was gone.

Chris struggled with the emotions warring inside her. Half of her wanted to stay and cried out that she was a fool not to love this man who seemed so desirable. But the other half shouted that a whole world was waiting to be discovered and if she stayed, she was likely never to see it at all. Even if she did, it could only be under the keen and watchful supervision of Renault.

With that last thought she resolutely turned and hurried toward the captain's cabin. Inside, she rushed to Kade's sea chest and pulled out the outfit she had secretly assembled from clothing Janie had helped her steal. She bound her breasts and donned a man's linen shirt and jerkin. She put on a pair of loose-fitting, rough brown trousers and tucked her hair under a red scarf with a black tricorn over it. With a bit of brown soot she smudged her upper lip in something resembling a mustache and rubbed her cheeks with the stuff to simulate a beard. In the dark night she suspected no one would spot it as false. Then Chris hastily tucked a rapier and gun into her belt and went above.

On deck the last of the small boats was boarding. With her best swagger she approached the nearest boat. The mate in charge eyed her briefly, then went back to checking over the weaponry in the boat. She sat between two burly Corsairs who seemed preoccupied with their own thoughts. It was as she hoped—the men were too absorbed in pre-battle nerves to notice her.

The boat moved slowly toward the coast, about five miles away. As they drew nearer she could see a small group of men standing on the beach. When they reached the shore, the Corsairs pulled the boat on the land and dragged it into the bushes. Chris scanned the group with her eyes. She sighed with relief to see that Kade was not among them.

There were horses waiting in a small clearing not

far from the beach. Chris mounted a spirited roan. She was thankful that she was a good rider. The horse was fresh and needed a skillful hand at the reins.

They moved through the night toward distant lights that appeared to be a town. She gradually allowed most of the Corsairs to pass her until she and her mount were near the rear of the group. When they reached the town, she allowed the remaining riders to pass her. Then Chris quickly reined in the roan and turned into a small, dark side road.

When the Corsairs were gone, she coaxed her mount out of the alley and turned toward a small saloon near the center of town. Dismounting, she drew in a deep breath, squared her shoulders and walked in.

The bar was filled with Spanish soldiers. They were everywhere—laughing, drinking, talking, and fondling the women. She willed her churning stomach to be still and walked up to one of them, saying in her deepest voice, "Sir, can you tell me where I might book passage on a ship bound for France?"

The soldier eyed her strangely and said in Spanish, "Who are you? I have not seen you in this town before. All travelers are required to register with his excellency, the governor, if they will be in town more than one day."

She answered him in his own language. "I assure you that my intentions are harmless. I will remain here only long enough to book passage to France."

"The next ship bound for France will not leave for several days," he said ominously. "I must insist that you come with me now, señor, to see the governor."

The soldier put a rough hand on Chris's shoulder to push her toward the door and then drew back as he yelled with pain. Quick as lightning, she had drawn her dagger and the man's hand was now dripping blood. "I do not wish to meet the governor, señor." Suddenly, Chris felt a sharp pain in her head—followed by absolute darkness.

The red-uniformed soldier cursed as he wound a handkerchief around his bloody hand. He looked at his friend, the lieutenant, whose gun butt had struck Christina from the rear, and nodded approvingly. "Good work, Miguel. We will take this one to Don De-Villa immediately. There is something about him that disturbs me. What it is, I don't know, but his excellency will certainly find out, eh?" The two men laughed as they dragged Christina's limp form to her horse and tossed her carelessly over the saddle.

CHAPTER TWENTY-ONE

Christina felt a dash of cold water in her face and struggled to consciousness. Her head ached, her ribs felt bruised, and her whole body was as unresponsive and cold as lead. Groggily, she opened her eyes and stared at a small, thick-set man with thinning brown hair and small, beady, black eyes.

She tried to sit up, but groaned as her tender ribs resisted the motion. Her hat had fallen off during the ride and her red scarf was askew, revealing several long tendrils of tawny hair.

"Remove that rag," she heard a man's voice say. Chris struggled, as her arms were pinned to her sides, and she felt the scarf snatched from her head. The long waves of hair tumbled over her back and shoulders. She felt a cloth rubbed roughly over her face. When she opened her eyes the repulsive little man was peering at her with obvious relish.

"Well, the señorita has a most novel way of dressing," the voice said. "We are curious to know why. Who are you and why are you here?"

Chris opened her mouth to speak and then thought better of it. It might be wiser to let this man draw his own conclusions.

"Come, come. You will answer me, sooner or later. Are you in trouble with the law?"

She shook her head.

"Running from your lover?"

That was very close to the truth, and she smiled in spite of herself. The thick-set man, DeVilla himself, found the beautiful face irresistible. His eyes narrowed with lust as he said, "You are fortunate that I found you, señorita. I am sure that we can make some agreeable arrangement regarding your protection. It is such a long way to France. Someone as beautiful as you need not travel so great a distance . . . to fulfill her needs."

Suddenly the sound of gunfire exploded outside. The Spanish soldiers looked startled, and half of them ran through the open door to investigate the noise. DeVilla barked an order in Spanish to a young lieutenant nearby, and the soldier firmly took Christina's arm and led her from the room.

She found herself in an adjoining bedroom with a small window. She didn't bother trying the door. She heard the lieutenant lock it as he left. The sound of guns and men fighting at close quarters was almost deafening now. She looked out the window. Although it was difficult to see in the darkness, the palace she was in seemed to be situated far inland, somewhere in Mexico's desertlike interior. The fighting was centered in a large courtyard. Evidently the soldier who had hit her in the saloon had brought her to DeVilla's stronghold.

Everywhere she looked she saw grappling bodies. Some of the men looked like farmers; others were in well-tailored clothing and could only be sons of the landed gentry Kade spoke of. She recognized the Corsairs immediately. They fought like savage animals, mercilessly cutting down the red-uniformed men who dared to fight them. In battle they moved with deadly grace, like cobras charming their prey before the kill. Chris shivered and turned away. She had to get a horse and leave this madness before Renault found her.

In a few hours it became apparent that the Corsairs and their compatriots were winning. The fighting had moved into the first floor of the hacienda, and she could hear the battle raging below. Chris quickly braided her hair and wound the thick plaits around her head. If she had to fight, she didn't want it to get in the way. She picked up a heavy water pitcher from a table near the door and waited.

She didn't have to wait long. A Spanish soldier, looking desperately for a place of refuge, shot through the lock of the bedroom door and burst through. Chris hit him with all her strength and heard a muffled crackling sound as the heavy pitcher crushed his skull. She quickly stopped to pick up his gun and sword, and ran from the room.

Outside the corridor was dimly lit by sputtering candles. It appeared empty. She heard the sound of men's voices behind one of the closed doors. Quietly, she tiptoed near the door and listened. It was DeVilla and his lieutenants.

"There is no way, we can hold them off, Your Excellency," one of them was saying. "We must escape while there is still time."

"Ruiz is right, Don DeVilla," a second man offered. "In a little while, that devil and his men will be up here. There will be no time to use the tunnel. If we leave now, we can gather our troops in the mountains and attack the palace later with a full force."

DeVilla cursed with feeling. "I will kill him! I will place his head on a post for the vultures to pick at! The demon will not get away with this!"

"Yes, Excellency," said one soldier with growing impatience. "We must hurry."

Chris peeked through the keyhole and saw DeVilla turn a small statue on a pedestal several times. Slowly the wall behind the statue drew back to reveal a passageway, which DeVilla and the lieutenants entered quickly. She waited ten minutes before she shot the lock off the door. She went directly to the statue and managed with difficulty to turn it in the same direction as DeVilla. The wall slowly receded. She grabbed one of the candles and stepped into the dark, narrow passageway.

She heard the wall close behind her. Only the faint light of the small candle kept her from being plunged into total darkness. She swallowed the instinctive fear that welled up in her throat. Carefully she moved forward.

At the palace, Kade Renault disposed of an unlucky colonel who dared to challenge him. He looked around and saw Guy Savant and Jacques LaCroix engaged with two grizzly-looking soldiers who were tiring rapidly. Renault watched as Savant and LaCroix dispatched the two men to eternal rest and then shouted a signal that the two Corsairs recognized instantly. Savant and LaCroix joined Renault, and the three pirates climbed the now unguarded stairs of the palace to the third floor, where DeVilla maintained his private apartments. They searched everywhere, but the floor was deserted. The Corsairs sat thoughtfully in a room that served as a library. Kade Renault sat in dejection for long moments. Then suddenly his eyes opened wide. He felt dry desert air blowing faintly on his skin. Quickly he looked at the window.

It was tightly shut. The air had to be coming from another source.

Following the sensation with his eyes, he looked at the wall behind a statue that was sitting in an odd position on its pedestal. He peered closely at the wall. Very slightly but distinctly, there was a dark line of separation between the wall and the ceiling above. Instinctively he put his hands on the statue. It couldn't be lifted. He turned it around. The wall began to recede.

Savant went downstairs to look over the prisoners. One of the men was a colonel in the governor's private guard. The man was brought upstairs and tied to a chair. It took only a few minutes to persuade him to reveal the tunnel's surfacing point. As Renault had suspected, the passageway twisted and turned beneath the ground for several miles, and the fastest way to reach its end was above ground on horseback. Renault and the Corsairs left the colonel in the chair and ran to their mounts in the courtyard.

They rode like three madmen through the night. The first light of day was beginning to dawn as they reached the tunnel's exit point. LaCroix quickly searched for tracks near the exit, which would mean their arrival was too late—but the ground remained clear and unbroken. Renault and his men settled down to wait.

In a short while, a large rock moved, and a red-uniformed lieutenant winced as the bright sunlight hit his eyes. A second followed, and then DeVilla himself stumbled out.

With their guns trained on the three men, Renault and the Corsairs stepped into the clearing. The two lieutenants gasped and drew their swords. Savant and

Renault, seeing that the Spaniards lacked guns, drew their own swords and laid their guns aside. With a blood-chilling yell the Spaniards rushed at Guy and Renault. Renault took a gash in his arm as he swiftly stepped away from the charging soldier. Kade lunged as the soldier careened past him, unable to check the momentum of his charge. Renault's sword buried itself deep in the man's side. The Spanish lieutenant screamed and crumpled into the dust at his feet.

The other lieutenant warily circled Guy Savant, looking for a point of weakness. Unwisely, he decided on a flank attack. Guy easily parried the man's lunge and, quick as lightning, redirected his rapier with a mighty sweep of his arm and sent it deep into the man's throat. The soldier's eyes bulged and his lips moved wordlessly as he fell to the ground.

Renault turned to DeVilla, who stood trembling in the passageway. "I'll give you gold, Renault, more gold than you have ever imagined, if you let me go. Leave Mexico and return to St. Marin, and I'll make you rich beyond all your dreams."

Renault looked at DeVilla with so much contempt that the man began to shudder convulsively. "I am already rich, DeVilla. I wouldn't soil my hands with your gold. Do you think I'd take money you got by murdering women and children? Your hands are stained with Juan Miralda's blood.

"There is nothing I would enjoy more than killing you, but I know that the Spanish government can devise a much more exquisite death for you than I. Therefore, you and the confession you signed are going back to Spain, to the court of your king. Rest assured, DeVilla, that the document will be your death warrant."

DeVilla screamed and tried to run, but Guy Savant slammed a fist into his portly gut, and DeVilla sank to his knees, crying in soft, disgusting sobs. Through a crack, Christina stood watching the grisly scene in the dark passageway, but her mind was on the three horses she saw tethered to the trees. The Corsairs had their own mounts, and two of the Spanish soldiers were dead. If only Renault and his men left the extra horses behind!

Renault turned away from the sobbing man in the dust. "Come," he said to LaCroix and Savant, "let's conclude this business. It has begun to turn my stomach." They tied DeVilla to his horse and mounted their own.

"Shall we bring these mounts with us?" asked Savant.

"No, they'll only slow us down. Leave them. I'll send someone later," Renault replied.

Christina gave silent thanks. She watched as they rode away. She left the black passageway, mounted a chestnut mare, and steered her horse to the right of the town. She would have to ride through desert, but this way there was less chance of meeting unwelcome strangers. Taking a deep breath, Chris clicked her heels against the mare's side. The powerful horse reared and galloped off into the distance.

Kade Renault was grimly pleased with the scene that greeted him back at the hacienda. DeVilla's forces were totally beaten. The prisoners were incarcerated in the cellar, and the grisly remnants of the fighting had been cleared away.

Upstairs in the study, DeVilla elaborated on the confession he'd previously signed, detailing when, where, and how much he had stolen over the years from the Spanish government. To Kade and his men, it was little enough retribution for the wrongs the man had done, but nothing could bring back the lives he had taken. The revenge, however hollow, was complete. The one satisfying fact to come out of the bloodbath was the knowledge that DeVilla would never again force the innocent to suffer for his greed.

DeVilla was taken to a small bedroom on the third floor and placed under guard. Renault and the Corsairs shared a drink in the study, each quietly thinking his own thoughts. There was an urgent knock at the door.

"Come in," Renault said.

"Captain, I have bad news," said Joshua Boman as he entered the library. "Robin Grenby just arrived from the *Falcon*. He say your lady is gone, and they can't find her anywhere."

Christina vanished—alone in this wild country! The little fool, Kade thought angrily. God, she'd be dead before he found her. Renault was on his feet before he finished the thought.

"Need some company, Kade?" Savant called after his retreating form.

"No! Stay here and make sure DeVilla gets dispatched on the next ship. This is something I must do alone."

He saddled Ravascar, his black, pure-bred Arabian stallion and mounted. Joshua Boman stopped him as he was about to ride away. "Captain, one mo' thing. Ned Wilton says he couldn't find all them horses you sent him fo'. They wasn't but two, not three like you thought." Renault stood still for a second. It was a chance, not more than a wild hunch, but it was the only lead he had. Renault turned the stallion toward the desert and rode like a bolt of lightning for the clearing at the end of the tunnel.

When he found the exit he searched for tracks. He quickly picked up the ones he and the Corsairs had made earlier that day, and the tracks of Ned Wilton, who'd returned for the remaining horses. Then he spotted another set. Small footprints led to the spot where the third horse had been tethered, and hoof prints trailed off into open desert country. Kade lost no time following them.

Christina had ridden a long time. It seemed safe to stop and pitch a campfire for it appeared that she had indeed escaped. Once she arrived in town, she'd book passage on a ship bound for France, and her troubles would be over. She shot a rabbit for dinner and cooked it over her small campfire. The mare grazed in the sparse grassland nearby. Several hours went by, and at sunset Chris felt almost peaceful. The dinner was good, and everything seemed to be going well.

Then she heard the mare whinny with fright in the distance. Chris picked up her gun and started to run toward the horse. "What's the matter, girl?" she said, running as hard as she could. The horse started to gallop into the desert. She cursed to herself. There had been nothing to tie her to in this open, treeless country. She ran after her, hoping she wouldn't wander far. Suddenly she heard an ominous rattling near her left foot.

Chris stopped, paralyzed with fear as she gazed down in horror at the large rattlesnake under her boot. It took only a split second for the snake to strike. She screamed loudly, hobbling a few steps before she turned and shot the rattler through the head. Her leg felt as if it weighed a ton. Molten rivers of pain flowed from the snakebite to her hip. Groaning, she sank into the sand and struggled to remove her boot. She did what Mac had taught her, praying that she would get out most of the poison. When she finished, Chris began to laugh hysterically to herself when she realized her efforts would make no difference. Poison or no poison, she would die alone in the desert—from lack of water because she couldn't walk. She closed her eyes in utter defeat, waiting for the black cloud of unconsciousness to put an end to her pain.

CHAPTER TWENTY-TWO

Chris drifted in and out of consciousness. She felt as hot as the desert one minute and as cold as the sea the next. Renault's face haunted her dreams. She kept fighting the vision, but again and again it came—a worried, drawn-looking face that didn't smile or grin. She wondered at that—Kade was always smiling—shouldn't he smile in her dreams? In her delirium she willed the face to grin. It would not.

Sometimes when her eyes were closed she thought she heard worried voices. They spoke in low, concerned tones. What are they concerned about? she wondered. And always she was so hot; she couldn't stand it. She felt something cool against her brow, brushing her face. Thank you . . . whoever, however. And then she was cold, shivering. A smile played at her lips. How convenient to imagine a warm blanket around her and two strong arms to enfold her shaking form. She kept expecting to wake up in a world of white clouds and singing voices or red flames and fumes of sulphur. But each time she opened her eyes, it was Kade's face that floated in the fog—grim, concerned, and serious.

Then one day or night, she couldn't tell which, when she opened her eyes, her vision was clear, and the room was in focus. She looked around, feeling dizzy and weak but fully awake. She was in a bedroom that she didn't recognize. There was a fireplace on one wall and a large open window on another. A chair was next to the fireplace and a tall, bearded man was dozing in it. Dark circles ringed his eyes, and his face looked gaunt, as though he'd had very little to eat in several days. As Chris looked closer, there was something familiar about the square chin, the straight nose, the chiseled planes of the jaw and forehead. Was it possible that . . . could that untidy-looking stranger be Renault? She squinted and focused harder. Yes, there was no mistaking the thick fringe of dark lashes or the black hair that was now so long that it curled softly at his ears and neck. But the beard? The rumpled shirt? Kade was never anything less than immaculate. Perhaps DeVilla had won after all. Only losing a battle could make her husband look like this.

"Kade?" It was a croaky whisper. Her throat was so parched that it hurt to speak. Chris closed her eyes and swallowed. She tried again: "Kade."

His head rested partially against his shoulder and partially against the back of the chair. He stirred. Not realizing what woke him, he looked desolately at the window. The expression on his face was so sad that she longed to say some words of consolation, but she lacked the strength. All she could do was murmur his name once more.

His head jerked around in the direction of the bed. When he realized she was awake, that she'd spoken, his face held a mixture of surprise and profound gratitude. He walked over and sat down carefully on the bed, bending over her as if he couldn't believe what his eyes saw.

"How do you feel?" he said at last.

"Terrible," she rasped, but she managed a smile. For a minute, his features were flooded with relief. Then his face transformed into solid stone. The change was so complete that it took her breath away.

"Good. You deserve to feel terrible," he said. Then he turned and barked a name she didn't recognize. A little man wearing spectacles walked into the room and looked surprised to see her awake. He checked her pulse and vital signs and then beamed at Kade.

"I don't know how she did it, Captain Renault, but she pulled through. She's a very lucky girl. Most people don't survive a rattlesnake bite as serious as that." Kade muttered something under his breath about "fools and children" and thanked the doctor for his help.

"Try to get her to eat something. It will be a while before she's strong enough to be moved," the doctor said as he left.

Kade walked over to the bed once more and stood looking down at her. Anger and concern warred on his face. Chris wondered whether he would strike her or hold her hand. It gradually occurred to her that he'd somehow found her out there in the desert and brought her here—wherever they were. He must have been near during her illness . . . that's why she had kept dreaming of his face. Only she hadn't been dreaming. He'd really been there. She owed him her life.

She was suddenly ashamed that she'd caused him worry. It was difficult to look him in the eyes. She lowered her gaze and whispered in a hushed voice, "I'm . . . sorry."

"You should be." His tone was ice itself.

"Did you find me and bring me here?"

"Yes," he said, "but I should have left you for the vultures."

"Kade, I feel . . . awful . . . about the trouble I've caused you."

"Don't lie. You can't feel, and you don't have a heart."

She sighed. Dejectedly she said, "We don't have to keep hurting each other. Let me get a divorce. I'll stay out of your life. We can both start again."

Bringing up the subject again was a mistake. The expression on his face made her start to shiver all over again. Fiery blue sparks exploded in his eyes as he said, "If you had not almost just died, I'd kill you myself." He turned on his heel and left the room.

Chris grew steadily stronger during the next few days. Often Jacques LaCroix or Guy Savant would visit and chat. One afternoon when Jacques was amusing her with his ribald tales, she sighed sadly. He paused, noting her lack of attention, and asked, "What's the matter, *chérie*?"

She looked up at him with melancholy eyes. "I'm feeling sorry for myself I guess, because I'm married to a man who hates me."

Jacques's face was incredulous. "Renault? *Mon Dieu*, whatever gave you such an idea?"

"He does. I don't blame him. I've tried to leave him twice."

LaCroix shook his head. Why was it that people could not see what stood right before their eyes? "Christina, *chérie*, Kade Renault does not hate you. *Au contraire*, he . . . well . . . if you could have seen how he looked when he found out you were missing, you would not run away again. He was like a man demented. We are still amazed that he found you, lost as you were in that vast desert. The look on his face when he brought you back and carried you upstairs in his arms . . . I myself have never seen a man so stricken with grief. No, little one, whatever it is the man feels for you, it is not hate."

"But he said if I hadn't almost died, he would kill me for the trouble I've caused him."

Jacques smiled. "We men often say rash things in our anger. But you were not there to see the anguish you caused him."

"When I awoke I often thought I saw his face."

Jacques nodded. "He would not leave you, even though we tried to get him to eat and rest. He didn't budge from this room until he knew you were out of danger."

"How strange," she said softly.

LaCroix looked at her oddly. "Did you know that during your fever you often called his name?"

Her eyes widened with surprise. "No . . . I didn't . . . I couldn't have," she said uncertainly.

"But you did. At those times during your illness, he held you in his arms like a little girl. It pleased him, I think, that you called for him while you were help-less—at those times he would almost smile. I think, *chérie*, you care for him more than you know."

During her recovery Renault was in a foul temper. On the rare occasions when he came to her room, he either coldly asked about her health or growled at her irritably and left. It was almost as if he came to the room against his will and stayed only long enough to note her condition. It was very disheartening.

In a few days Chris was well enough to travel. Still weak, she had to be carried to a brougham. Renault came to her room and unceremoniously lifted her in his arms. His handsome face was stern and set as he walked down the stairs.

She looked at the cold blue eyes and knew a sudden, irrepressible urge to tease him for ignoring her. Christina allowed her arms to steal around his neck and then nibbled softly at his ear. She felt him stiffen, and he pulled away from her sharply. Chris regarded him innocently and smiled. His glare was most unfriendly, but she was elated. Angry he might be, but that slight stiffening belied total indifference, and she wondered what it would take to destroy the barrier between them.

On the *Falcon* she found that she did not share his cabin as she had on the first leg of the voyage.

Once they arrived in St. Marin, Chris regained her health rapidly. Renault was seldom home. Christina suspected that he spent most of his time in Lawrence with the Corsairs, forgetting her existence with wine, women, and gambling. On those few occasions when he came to the Keyes and she tried to engage him in conversation, he remained annoyingly withdrawn, his deep blue eyes regarding her with cool detachment.

Kade came and went like a phantom. Christina hardly saw him. After endless days of such neglect, she was determined to break through the impasse between them. One morning she invited him to join her at lunch. He greeted the idea with indifference but agreed.

During the morning she took special pains with her toilette. Janie helped her don a gown of pale apricot silk with an entrancingly low bodice. The smooth, delicate planes of her face glowed, thanks to the sun and the air she'd received from long walks along St. Claire Beach. Her hair fell in thick waves down her back and framed her temples with sun-streaked curls. Inspecting the effect in the mirror, she decided that it would take an extreme effort of will on Kade's part to remain indifferent to her.

Lunch was served at noon, and he was late by a quarter of an hour. She sat serenely as he entered the dining room, elegantly clothed in a cream waistcoat with tan trousers and a white linen shirt. His dark blue eyes swept over her, and he quickly veiled the look of appreciation that briefly lit his face. He could not, however, prevent his gaze from dipping to her bodice as they ate in silence.

She began to talk of little things, trying to breach the ice between them. He responded in terse monosyllables that were barely polite. Chris fancied she could see the tension building inside him—caused by the undeniable attraction they held for each other. In a minute, he'll explode, she thought.

Still hoping to smooth the waters, she said, "I haven't thanked you for saving my life since we came to St. Marin. I do now, Kade. I can never repay you for what you did."

He looked at her with eyes of blue steel. "And I haven't told you what I think of what you did that day," he said. "I had to leave my men in the midst of an important battle because of you. That was unforgivable, Christina. How could you be foolish enough to ride into wild country you knew nothing about and expect to come out alive? It was such a childishly stupid and insane thing to do that it almost makes me laugh. What a fool you are, my sweet. You nearly got your precious freedom by killing yourself." His dark blue eyes smouldered, and he gazed at her with real anger.

Christina regarded her hands thoughtfully. Everything he said was true. She *had* been stupid and childish *and* overconfident. She was very lucky that he had found her in time. She looked up at him and smiled ruefully. "I am a fool. And an idiot. I know I didn't deserve to have you find me, but I'm glad you did. You may not believe me, but I regret the trouble I caused—if I could relive the day, I would not leave the *Falcon*. I'm sorry, Kade. I am grateful, and I do thank you for saving me." On impulse she stood up from the table, walked to him, bent her head, and kissed him lingeringly. She didn't expect him to respond and he did not, but neither did he pull away. Encouraged, she placed soft kisses on the hard, chiseled line of his jaw and gently over the bridge of his strong, straight nose. She stood up again and regarded him. His face was set and inscrutable. It was impossible to guess his thoughts. She could think of nothing more to say so she traced his lips gently with her fingertips and smiled at him. Then she turned and left the dining room.

In her bedroom upstairs she felt depressed. It was an unusually hot day. Even the sea breeze was still. Not far from St. Claire Beach there was a lagoon where she had swum every day as a child. It was an enchanting blue and green jewel nestled among tall palm trees and brightly colored tropical flowers. On a day like this there was nothing more refreshing than a swim. Tomorrow, Chris decided, she would go to the Evrion offices and begin working again. Today would be the last day of her holiday, and she would spend it at the lagoon.

Chris took a picnic basket of French bread, cold chicken, white wine, and cheese with her. The pool was just as she remembered—green, brilliant, placid, and tranquil. She removed her clothes and climbed the high, rocky cliff that bordered the lagoon. The climb took nearly an hour, but the breathtaking view from the ledge was worth the trouble. She could see the entire eastern half of the island from these high rocks. Chris still remembered the first time she had beheld the sight. As a young girl her curiosity had overcome her reticence, and she had made the dangerous climb up the craggy cliff. It had taken forever, but at last, over two hundred feet above the lagoon, she reached the spot at which she now stood. The ocean stretched into infinity before her, outlined by the white beaches of St. Marin on one side and the blue horizon on the other. Chris watched in silent meditation for long moments. She smiled to herself, remembering the first time she had looked down from the ledge and the panic she had felt when she realized that the only practical way down was a very steep dive. It was second nature by now, but the first time she tried it, her heart had stopped beating until she safely breached the water.

Chris dragged her eyes away from the ocean's sparkling azure vista. Below her, the water of the lagoon was a deep, crystalline blue. Taking a deep breath, she sprang from the jutting rock ledge, arcing outward, sailing down into the pool below, barely disturbing its mirror-blue surface. Blissfully, she swam nude, the way she had as a child. She floated on her back, dove beneath the water, then broke the surface, blowing bubbles in the air. All her troubles seemed to wash away in the cool, invigorating waves. Fatigued, but refreshed, she left the water to sun on a grassy flower-covered hill near the bank.

She dozed lightly for a short time. Her hair dried in

sunny waves. The sound of a twig snapping in the distance awoke her. She looked up to see the tall muscular figure of Kade Renault standing a few feet away. He was in his pirate's garb of black breeches, boots, and linen shirt open to the waist. Chris was surprised—no one had ever found her here. She noticed that his face had lost its angry expression.

Kade Renault had watched as Christina climbed the rocks and stood on the ledge gazing at the ocean beyond the beach. He'd known the same overwhelming attraction he felt the first time he saw her, high above the lagoon.

That had been three years before, but she had remained in his mind—a lingering image that floated through his thoughts at odd moments during the day and night, until he had at last made up his mind to return to St. Marin to see if perhaps the whole vision had not been a figment of his imagination. Even after their paths crossed, he was still not sure that he had really seen her dive from that incredible height.

But today he knew his eyes had not played him false, and the maid in his memory did indeed exist.

Renault had watched Chris as she swam, playing in the lagoon like a mermaid from the legends the old sailors told. For him, she was indeed a magical creature—one who could touch his heart and enter his mind even as he willed it otherwise. The enchantment that floated about her enfolded him in its aura so that he was afraid to blink his eyes, half-believing she would disappear—like a fairy of old, leaving one forever curious to know what would have happened next if only the spell had remained.

He knew that she was willful, headstrong, exasperating, and foolish. He spent much of the time wavering between a desire to make love to her and an urge to bend her over his knee for the sound beating he thought she badly needed. So far, Renault had succumbed to the former and postponed the latter. It was just that she played all the time. She never seemed to stop. She was uplifting, and fun, and endearing too. She made him forget her indiscretions, and made his heart laugh, and he didn't want that feeling to stop.

Renault knew a strong desire to force her to return his attachment—to see in her eyes a need and a longing for him as deep as what he felt at this moment for her. Calmly, he vowed that one day, somehow, he would make her feel all these things and more . . . if it took a lifetime.

His eyes roamed over her youthful, rounded breasts, trim waist, and long, graceful legs. The intensity of his gaze made Chris regain her senses, and she moved across the few feet that separated them.

For the first time she wanted to make love to him. Half of her deeply regretted having made him suffer, and the other half was sorry her plan had failed, but she could no longer deny the attraction he held for her or the way she was drawn to him physically. Not when the steady azure gaze told her how much he wanted her, no matter what he might say to the contrary. The air around him seemed to vibrate with his need. A feral vitality radiated from him like the pull of a magnet and caused fantastic visions to dance in her head. Renault stood looking at her, a dark satyr with brooding eyes.

He reached out and drew her against him. Lowering his head, his mouth moved over hers, as if he sought to draw her heart through her lips. Christina melted against him, allowing his hands to mold and shape her to his hard form as he wished. For the first time she touched him with her hands—wanting and needing to give him pleasure. She allowed them to warmly stroke his back and shoulders, then tangled her fingers in the soft hair at the nape of his neck. Chris liked the feel of tempered strength in the muscles beneath her fingers. When she lowered her hands to the small of his back, kneading and fondling the corded tendons there, he sighed with pleasure and lifted her high in his arms, then lowered her to the warm grass.

She helped as he unbuttoned his breeches, stopping now and then to press soft nibbling kisses on his chest. Chris heard him groan when his bronzed body covered hers. She looked up at him and saw a gleam in his eyes that was tremulously close to love, but then it was gone, and she thought it was a trick of the lagoon's reflected light.

Ah, but how she reveled in the warm solid weight of his body against hers! She stretched and sighed beneath him and watched his eyes blaze as the soft warmth of her body enveloped and caressed him. She circled his neck with her arms and smiled warmly as she kissed his nose, his eyes, and the dimple in his chin. The heat from his body seared her like a furnace, but she sought to enflame him more by massaging his flanks with warm fingers as he covered her.

In the past she had fought his advances and resisted his hands. Now she was all soft and eager for him. She was yielding and warm and his to love. Kade pressed her closer, unable to believe her willingness. It was as if he couldn't get close enough to that pliant softness. His mouth left her lips to press warm, melting kisses on her breasts and throat. He sucked gently at the nipples, sending rivers of sensation flowing from her spine to her fingertips.

Unable to restrain the leaping fires that burned inside him, his hands cradled her hips as he joined their bodies. She shivered beneath him, and they moved as one. This time she did not fight the rising swell of warmth when it engulfed her body and made her cling to him in passion and surrender.

He reveled in her caress, stroking her with his hands as he bent his head to bury his lips against her shoulder, tightening his embrace to mold her to him, telling her softly of his pleasure.

Then she felt the raw power of his body strain within her as his forceful thrusts surged and increased—driving his seed deep inside. Not until this moment had she experienced the full strength of their joining or known the full measure of the pleasure it gave.

She lay in his arms, listening to the sound of birds and crickets—the fresh clean smell of the lagoon with its exotic blossoms permeating her consciousness.

"Christina," she heard him whisper, the husky inflexion of passion still heavy in his voice, "don't run away from me again."

It surprised her. After a moment she said, "You would care?"

"I'd care," he said simply. He kissed her—a long, soul-stirring caress, his tongue seeking to memorize her mouth. When he raised his head, Chris looked at him with curiosity. She lay against him, enfolded in his arms. One of his hands rested on her hip while the other stroked her breast. It was difficult to think clearly. His swarthy skin was vivid bronze in the hazy glow of the lagoon. She looked at his face. It was too handsome to be real, the classic lines perfectly etched in the golden light of late afternoon. Chris wondered what madness kept her from loving him.

"I wasn't running *away* from *you*, Kade. I was running . . . toward . . . something *else*."

Kade's voice was curious and soft as he probed for answers. "Toward whom?"

"Not a 'whom' . . . a 'what'. My father taught me all he knew of people and life. He made me want to know myself—who I really am and what my place is in the pattern of things. I must do that before I settle down and grow gray hair. It's important to me to travel and learn, to go out into the world and explore it."

His blue eyes were calm and knowing as they gazed at her quietly. It suddenly dawned on her that he understood. "You know what I'm trying to say."

"Of course," he replied. "I've felt that urge myself. That curiosity you have is part of the reason I find it difficult to stay away from you."

She'd never expected that anyone would ever understand this need in her. She was intrigued. "Tell me about your life . . . before you came to Bajora. I know very little about you."

"I was born in Scotland, little one. My father was a highland lord, Sir Angus MacVeagh Renault. He died several years ago—my older brother Jamie is head of the family now. He's a rock, that Jamie—solid granite. I've always been the rogue of the family. The elder MacVeagh pronounced me hopeless when I was fourteen years old. Women and gambling were my strongest subjects at the university. When I came home, after being expelled from Cambridge for the third time, my father gave me a small sum, a hard kick in the rear, and told me not to come back until I'd earned my fortune, since I'd obviously never amount to anything at home. I took his advice and the money and set sail for Boston. It wasn't long before I learned about the profits to be made in the shipping trade.

"I left for Mexico and stayed for a year with Juan. Wild, I may have been, but naive, never. It took me only a few weeks to increase my small bank account to sizable sum through gambling and . . . ah . . . other activities. When I had enough to buy a ship, I got a crew together and contracted a cargo of cotton goods and farm implements and set sail for Bajora. It wasn't long before the *Falcon* and I were a regular part of the Caribbean trade."

"Then you set up your base on Bajora," she offered.

"Yes. I've a fondness for that rugged, green island. It's a lot like me . . ."

"Unpredictable and dangerous," she said.

"Yes, but not with you, sweet," he said as he kissed her. Kade lifted his head and gazed at her with mischief. "At least, I'm not that way until I see you sharpening your claws on an unsuspecting male who hasn't the wit to see through you as I do."

She attempted to rise, but he laughed and rolled over with her, pinning her under him in the soft grass. His mouth covered hers, muffling the hot words with his lips as her protests died in her throat. Kade made love to her again, with a tender regard and warm affection she had not thought him capable of.

In the warm, drowsy aftermath of their coupling, Christina murmured, "I suppose I am selfish and thoughtless at times."

Renault smiled and pinched her bottom. She squealed indignantly and he grinned. Then his expression grew sober. "I've learned, tiger, that some people bring happiness and others bring pain, but those we care for always bring both."

After that day a new intimacy developed between them. She no longer felt so ill at ease in his company, and his presence at the Keyes seemed natural. She began to think of him as a valued friend rather than as an intruding stranger. A certain affinity of temperament existed between them. Theirs were two spirits of similar nature—indomitable, wild, and free.

CHAPTER TWENTY-THREE

It was spring, and St. Marin was afire with excitement. Carnival time had arrived—a festival introduced to the island half a century ago by the French Catholics, who favored a night of feasting before the strict fasting required during Lent. Over the years it had evolved into days of opulent, elaborate parties, with masks, rich clothing, lots of music, singing, and dancing—with the drums of the Rawani supplying a steady, rhythmic beat.

In the market and on the quay, hundreds of people thronged the streets and narrow roadways from early morning to very late at night with only a few hours sleep before they returned to cavort again. There were games of dice and chance. Women came down from the hills to tell fortunes and sell charms. Everywhere small wooden stalls filled with succulent dishes and delicious breads sprang up to feed the rowdy, happy, milling throng. It was a time of laughter, bawdy jests, revelrous dancing and sexual license—a sort of exorcism in preparation for the weeks of piety to follow. It was no accident that all costumes were complete with masks. The anonymity was protective and necessary.

The island's leading families eschewed the practice of joining the street revelers, but they did throw open their doors to all manner of friends, neighbors, visiting business associates, and relatives no matter how tenuous the connection. This year for the first time Christina would take charge of preparing Mimosa Keyes for Carnival, and she was very excited. Chris decided the festivities would begin Friday morning and continue until everyone dropped from exhaustion. There would be a grand buffet on the rolling lawn and a soirée of magnificent proportions the following day. She was delighted with the challenge and spent long afternoons planning the elaborate three-day menu with Madame Ouvre.

Renault remained aloof from the frenzy that swirled around him and regarded Christina's scurrying form with some amusement. He was busy with shipping business in Bajora and had spent several days traveling back and forth between Mimosa Keyes and Falcon Hall. He rose very early to depart for Lawrence at dawn, leaving Chris fast asleep after their prolonged sessions of lovemaking.

One morning, as Chris donned a sea-green silk dressing gown and hurriedly swallowed a croissant in two hasty bites, she was surprised to see Kade enter their bedroom. She rarely saw him during the day—it was unusual for him to appear fully clad, and she wondered what made him linger. He was looking exceptionally handsome, even for him.

"Good morning. I've waited three quarters of an hour for you to awaken, madame. Your rising habits are atrocious."

"Every night, *mon cher*, I lie beside you while you do your worst. If I sleep late from exhaustion, it is your fault and well you know it."

Kade raised a mocking black eyebrow and feigned an expression of surprise. "Why, Christina, from your uninhibited cries of delight, I had the distinct impression that I did rather well. But if that was a complaint, I would be only too happy to remain here with you and practice."

"So that you will get it right?"

Renault rewarded her with a smart slap on the derrière. With a squeak she quickly changed to another topic of conversation and put several feet between them.

"Pray, tell me—what keeps you here this morning?"

"Before your interesting digression I had it in mind to bid you a tender farewell. Much as I regret it, I have to go to Bajora for a few days—I'll miss the start of your Carnival."

He was sitting beside her now on their bed, and his eyes dropped casually to the neckline of the loosely tied silk robe which outlined much and covered little.

"Perhaps that is best. All of the confusion here will be much worse as the day draws near."

"I find the confusion fun, but these matters can't be put off. I'll be able to join you later though."

"*Bien*, we shall await your return with anticipation," she said lightly.

Renault looked deeply into her eyes for a moment and much of the teasing air left him. He picked up her hand and gently spread the fingers across his palm. "Will you, Chris?"

She nodded, a little surprised by the mercurial change in his mood.

"Are you then reconciled to this marriage at last?"

The memories that question stirred incensed her even now, but she had to admit that the past few weeks had not been so intolerable. He was leaving today . . . why provoke a quarrel? She looked into his handsome, earnest face, her own full of mischief.

"Reconciled? I will never be completely that, but I dislike it less than I thought. No, let us say rather that I like it more than I imagined."

Kade's dark blue eyes glowed brightly at her words, and he drew her slowly into his embrace. Holding her, he whispered deeply. " 'Tis your own fault for being so rash a maid. You asked for a husband, madame, and being an agreeable sort, I obliged."

Chris sighed in mock dismay. "Yes. My grandmama Michelle always said that fools and children ask for what they do not want . . . and get it."

She felt a chuckle ripple inside his muscular chest. "Perhaps, Christina, but I warn you that I have found that this arrangement suits me, and I have no intention of ending it." Kade took her face between his hands, turning it up to look into the turquoise eyes. "I want your love . . . as I have given you mine. And Chris . . . I'm not a patient man."

Chris dropped her eyes, unable to bear the intensity of his gaze.

"Look at me."

A little reluctantly, she complied. His face was lighter now. The familiar mocking gleam had returned to his eyes.

"It is only fair, madame. I have given you exactly what you asked."

"You have given me much more than I asked and that is the problem," she smiled.

Kade pushed her back into the coverlets, half pinning her beneath him, "I intend to keep giving much more than you asked."

She opened her mouth to protest, but Renault silenced her with his lips.

CHAPTER TWENTY-FOUR

The guests began to arrive at midmorning. Chris noted with amusement that a few of Renault's Corsairs looked quite red-eyed, the result no doubt of an early beginning to Carnival. She welcomed the Laniers and Robillards and over a hundred and fifty associates and friends, people familiar to her from childhood.

It was good to laugh again. They began the day with games and an open-air play while the guests enjoyed a sumptuous buffet. Chris noticed that Janie regarded Joshua Logan with great interest all morning, and the tall black Corsair grew an inch whenever he caught her eye. She watched Andrew Hardy attempt to best Guy Savant at cards and suppressed a smile. If Hardy won, it would be because Savant allowed it.

The music, laughter, dancing, and dining lasted the entire afternoon, through the twilight and into the night. When darkness fell, Christina ordered several stained-glass oil lamps to light the courtyard. The garden was flooded with twinkling, multicolored candlelight.

The voices and laughter were more subdued now, and Christina suddenly felt vaguely uneasy, as if something terrible were about to happen. She hoped Kade would return soon. She drifted through the courtyard and gardens, stopping to talk with this or that guest, bidding farewell to a few who had decided to leave early.

Stifling a yawn, she headed toward the inviting

greenness on the outer edge of the grounds. The Evrion gardens were bordered on three sides by lush tropical growth, and the cool sweet fragrance of the rain forest drew her to the wrought-iron love seat at its border. As she sat down and looked back toward the mansion, she saw Renault emerge from the courtyard, tall and effortlessly dashing in a gray waistcoat and trousers.

She smiled at him as he walked toward her, admiring his easy grace and the heart-melting grin on his handsome face. Watching him, she could almost forget the sense of evil foreboding that plagued her. Rising, she walked forward to meet him. Suddenly a loud noise came from the rain forest. A sharp pain near her temple made her stagger and nearly fall. Dazed, she felt her head. It was wet and sticky. She looked at her fingers and felt her stomach lurch as she saw them covered with her own blood. Dimly Chris heard Kade's frantic voice telling her to get down. She tried to respond, but her body would not obey her mind. It was as if everything was moving very slowly, as though time itself had slowed.

A movement in the bushes drew her gaze. Deep within the trees, Hilda Lesky stood triumphantly, a look of crazed loathing contorting her face as she held a gun pointed at Christina's head. In that instant Chris saw her life pass before her.

Suddenly she was knocked flat by the hard impact of a body slamming into her. She heard the discharge of a gun in the same second. There was a deep groan from someone beside her on the ground. People were shouting and running toward them. Hilda's thin white figure was seized by two angry men. She turned toward the man lying beside her. It was Kade. He was unconscious. A red stain spread rapidly over his white linen shirt.

She was dizzy and her head ached, but somehow she knew she had only a surface wound. Guy Savant and Logan Armor carefully lifted Kade from the ground and bore him rapidly toward the house. Jacques LaCroix bent to pick her up, but she insisted on walking and hurried as best as she could after the two men carrying Kade. They took him to an upstairs room and gently laid him on the bed. Even as he lay unconscious, his face contorted in pain. The bullet must have gone deep. She heard a voice beside her say, "Don't worry, ma'am. I've seen him survive worse." It was Logan Armor. He regarded her with kindly concern. With one outstretched hand he offered her a handkerchief. Chris had not realized until that moment that she was crying.

Someone had hurriedly summoned William Moore, a St. Marin physician, from the remaining guests. Moore bent anxiously over Renault, ripping the reddened shirt from his chest. He cleaned the wound and probed gingerly for the bullet. Kade moaned as the doctor found the small piece of lead embedded in his chest and drew it out.

"The wound is deep," said Moore, "but it missed the lung and collarbone. There is still danger, and he will probably develop a fever. He should be carefully watched, madame."

Christina refused to let them put her to bed. She allowed her head wound to be cleaned and dressed, but never left Kade's room and had her meals brought there. He seemed to alternate between fever and chills, his body often shivering uncontrollably. Chris felt a tenderness and concern for him she hadn't dreamed possible. This man had saved her from death twice. She wouldn't leave him now if her life depended on it.

Several times in his pain and dreams he called her name. During these ravings she came to the bed and cradled his head against her breast, murmuring softly that she was there, that she would take care of him. She stroked his temples and forehead with cool fingers and sometimes kissed him gently. He never awoke, but seemed greatly soothed by her actions. His breathing became regular and the ravings ceased. On the third day Kade's fever broke. Christina was exhausted from her sleepless vigil, but her sense of relief and happiness was so great that she found it impossible to go to bed. When he awoke and looked at her through clear, unclouded eyes, she ran to his bedside and held him in her arms.

"Christina, are you all right?" he said slowly, still dazed from the fever.

She laughed with merry relief. "Am *I* all right? That is what I should ask *you*! You have been unconscious for three days."

"What? Oh . . . I remember now. Hilda . . . fired at you again. You couldn't move . . . I had to get you out of the way . . ."

"And you did," she said as she kissed him. "Thank you for saving my life . . . a second time." She smiled at him. "I must be careful from now on. It is said in the Rawani religion that a person whose life is saved three times by another loses his spirit to the one who saved him. If I let you help me once more, my soul will be yours forever." The intensity of the look he gave her made her catch her breath. With his good arm he drew her against him.

"Be careful! Your shoulder will start to bleed again."

"Damn my shoulder," he said as he kissed her. That night he taught her a new way of making love that did not bother his wound at all.

CHAPTER TWENTY-FIVE

During the next two weeks Kade slept a great deal. He was still very weak from loss of blood. When he was awake Chris read to him from novels or books or poetry. She told him how the Evrion businesses were going—she spent most of her days with Andy in Lawrence. It gave her less time to think.

Ever since the nightmare in the garden, Christina had been irritable, restless, and short with everyone, except Kade. Her head was completely healed and the scar was not noticeable, but her spirit bore a larger wound. That madwoman had nearly succeeded in killing her. She was barely eighteen years old, and Hilda had wanted to kill her. Her stepmother. The last link with her father, her past. She suddenly felt an unbearable ache, a lonely emptiness that made her long for her real mother, Blaise.

She climbed the stairs to the third floor of Mimosa Keyes, to a room she had not visited since she was a little girl. It was a sort of attic and storage room with a row of windows overlooking the sea. Many years of Evrion–St. Claire memorabilia were stored here. All her mother's personal possessions were now in this room. Her eyes fell on a large wooden trunk in one corner. It had belonged to Blaise. Her mother had often taken the sea chest with her on voyages with Mac. Christina opened the trunk.

It was filled with lovely dresses in soft hues of pink, yellow, and blue trimmed with fine lace and velvet ribbons. There was a silver brush and comb, several

fans with handles made from mother-of-pearl, and one
or two softly scented lace handkerchiefs. Chris picked
up one dress and held it against her. "We were nearly
the same size," she mused. For some reason the
thought pleased her.

Something shiny in the chest caught her eye. She
picked up a small rectangular silver box and opened
it. Inside she saw a small, beautifully bound diary.
With wondering fingers she touched it. "Why, this
book contains my mother's private thoughts . . . her
own words."

She sat in the attic, reading for hours, page after
page. Blaise had been a vibrant woman, alive with
emotion and feeling—knowing the same hopes and
fears that Christina felt. She read Blaise's small, neat
writing with rapt fascination. Her mother wrote:

> Today Mac and I sailed aboard the Fleetwood
> from the southern half of St. Marin. It is such fun
> to be with him! He told me about the British
> Isles and how green and misty the land is there.
> How I wish I could see it! But he can never go
> back because of the duel he fought. Would that I
> could go myself—I have never been away from
> the shores of St. Marin and my entire world is
> bordered by this blue sea. It is a peaceful world,
> but a very small one. Now I fear it is too late to
> think of leaving . . . the child will come by
> spring. It is a pity. Before I met Mac, I was
> searching for something. I have not found it. Now
> I never will . . .

Chris read the passage again. In her heart she knew
her mother had wanted the same thing her own young

soul cried out for, but Blaise never left St. Marin. Christina's own birth prevented it. In that moment, without conscious thought, Christina decided what she was going to do. Her life had nearly ended before her twentieth birthday. She would not give fate another change. Resolutely, she closed the trunk and slipped her mother's diary into the folds of her dress.

As Chris sat brooding in the attic, Janie was awakened by a noise as she lay in her bedroom in the east wing of the mansion. She listened for a moment as she tried to determine the sound of the noise and then sat bolt upright when she heard Robin's soft moan in the darkness. She groped in the dark for a candle and went to peer anxiously over her little brother's bed. What she saw made her cry out in alarm. Robin was tossing feverishly, and his body was racked with periodic tremors. He lay staring up at her, his soft brown eyes bright and glazed.

In a panic, Janie ran to the nightstand and poured a pitcher of water into the washbowl that stood there. She wet three towels and returned to Robin's side, gently mopping the perspiration from his brow. When he seemed more at ease, she went to her chest to fetch the medicine Gideon had given her for Robin's sickness. The large purple glass bottle was less than one-quarter full, but that would be enough for tonight. She poured it into a cup and returned to Robin, coaxing the clear liquid into his mouth.

In a few hours Janie relaxed as Robin's tremors and fever subsided. She sighed. He could be fine for months and then the fever would return. Without Gideon's medicine the attacks would grow worse and more frequent. The bottle was nearly empty. Sighing, she made plans to go into the hills tomorrow to get more from the old healer.

The next morning, after her work was done, she asked Chris for a cart and horse to go into the hills to see the Baudiens. Chris was sorry to hear about Robin's relapse. It seemed the whole household was ill, and she told Janie to take as much time as she needed.

The little cart wound through the green St. Marin hills and reached its destination swiftly, as Janie was in a hurry to get more of the medicine. Robin's attacks were unpredictable and came without warning. She stopped the small cart in front of Gideon's cottage.

When she knocked on the door no one answered. The whole area was deserted. Not even Gideon's helpers, the young men who assisted him with his work, were in evidence.

She waited for two hours before a young boy walked by, clad in light brown pants cut off at the knee.

"Where can I find Gideon?" she asked anxiously. "I have to buy medicine from him."

The young man frowned. "Why, he's not here, miss. He went to France. By now he is at the university, in Paris."

"Oh, no! Please, I need medicine for my brother. Is there anyone who can make the cure Gideon uses for high fever?"

"No, mademoiselle. We help him, but only Gideon knows the secret of that brew—none of us have ever seen it made."

"Are you sure!? There is no one here who knows?"

"*Oui*, no one."

"Oh, *mon Dieu!*" Janie said softly. "What am I going

to do?" She began to cry. The young boy watched, helplessly.

By the time she reached Mimosa Keyes, Janie was distraught. She walked dejectedly into Robin's bedroom and looked at the little boy's innocent sleeping face. She was helpless now to prevent the illness from becoming worse and eventually claiming his life, as it had their parents. In her entire family only she was immune.

"Robin, you will die, too, and there is nothing I can do for you," she whispered. Janie sank onto the floor beside her little brother's bed and wept.

Christina's malaise grew more pronounced after reading her mother's words. Only the thought of Kade's recovery seemed to lift her spirits. He was out of danger, and his wound was rapidly healing.

One morning as she emerged from his room, Madame Ouvre came to tell her that she had a visitor, Jacques LaCroix.

Chris was delighted to see Jacques. For days she had wanted to go into Lawrence for a long conference with Andy, but Kade's convalescence had prevented it. Jacques, however, could provide her with news of their affairs.

They talked for an hour about the shipping line, Hardy's progress with the new design, and Kade's affairs at Falcon Hall.

"Ah, Jacques, I can't tell you how good it is to talk to you about these things."

"*Oui*, Christine, I know. But tell me, how is our captain?"

"Much better. He should be with you again in two weeks."

"And you *chérie*—are you happy?" he asked.

"Yes," she lied. There was no point in burdening him with her discontent.

"*Bien*. I am happy that Renault's plans have worked out so well."

Chris cocked an ear. "What plans?"

Jacques laughed his merry, carefree laugh. "I had misgivings at first when he said he would have you at any cost. You were so young and so wild—I did not think your happiness was possible. But I was wrong. It is fortunate that Renault decided to wed you after your father died."

She regarded him quizzically. "What do you mean, Jacques?"

"When he heard that you needed a husband, Christine, he went to great lengths to offer his services."

She sighed. "Yes, he did, but Jacques, I will tell you a secret—I had hoped to wed and then take my leave of him. He was a prisoner of the Spanish, and I had no idea they would release him."

Jacques laughed. "No one could hold him for long, Christine. He planned the capture himself—to draw DeVilla from his palace."

She stared at Jacques for a moment. "You are saying that he planned his own imprisonment? That there was never a chance of his going to the gallows?"

"*Certainement*,"

"I had no idea that he had that much power," she said softly. "Then . . . why did he consent to the marriage? Why allow himself to be tied in so permanent a fashion?"

"Because he wished it."

Chris shook her head. "I don't understand why he

married me, knowing that I thought he would be executed."

"I think he knows you well, Christine," Jacques smiled. "He felt, correctly I suspect, that you would not give yourself to him otherwise. You did not wish a husband, did you—even though you needed to marry?"

"Jacques, are you saying he plotted the whole thing? That is inconceivable . . . it's just not possible."

"All things are possible where Kade is concerned," Jacques laughed. "Yes, I think he allowed you to pursue him, long enough for him to capture you. Christine, you may find it incredible—but you, of course, did not see the captain's eyes glow when Logan and I told him of the wood nymph we saw running through the forest in St. Marin. That sprite was you, was it not?"

She blinked and stared hard at LaCroix before she exclaimed, "So that is where I have seen you! Your face has always seemed strangely familiar to me."

LaCroix laughed.

Christina's mind raced. If what Jacques said was true, then Renault's deception had been even greater than her own. The memory of his deep, drawling voice drifted back to her: "After all, my dear, this marriage was your idea . . . I have only given you what you asked . . . now you must fulfill our pact by giving me what I want . . . and need . . ."

What he needed, indeed! *Mon Dieu*, what a trick he had played! How he must have enjoyed the jest. The man was . . . well . . . he was even worse than she herself, and he deserved a good reckoning.

Christina's angry thoughts were interrupted by the

sound of racking sobs in the *jardinière*. Jacques, too, cocked an attentive ear. Chris recognized that noise.

"Janie, is that you?"

After a moment the girl appeared, her eyes flaming red from hours of weeping and her face visibly swollen.

"What on earth is wrong?"

"Oh Mis' Chris, it's Robin. I'm worried about his illness coming back." She broke down again, and Chris put a comforting arm around her young friend's shoulder.

"Isn't there something we can do?"

"Y . . . yes. I gave him Gideon's medicine—he is all right for now, but Mis' Chris, you know the fever will return and I have so little of the bottle left and . . . Gideon, he has . . ."

"He has what?"

"He has gone to France! He is not coming back! And no one can make more of his medicine. My brother will die. My parents . . . I watched them with the fever. The attacks came more and more often, and my mother and father just grew weaker until . . ." She found it impossible to continue.

"*La malaria*," Jacques whispered.

Janie began to cry.

Chris was thinking. Robin caught the fever two years ago, but his health had improved with regular doses of Gideon's medicine. Everyone thought he would be fine. Now it seemed they had been wrong. She knew she couldn't let the little boy die.

"Janie, don't worry. I will send you to Paris to find Gideon."

"But I cannot leave Robin. I am all he has now, and he is so sick. Without me I know he will not live."

"But he will die anyway without Gideon's cure," Chris said.

Janie began to wail.

"Wait . . . no, do not cry. I cannot stand it. I'll go to Paris and find Gideon. He will tell me how he makes this distillation, and I will send the information back to you on the fastest ship. Can Robin . . . will he remain as he is for a few weeks until I can get word back to you?"

Janie nodded. "I think so . . . the fever is slow . . . but the attacks increase when the medicine is not used. He will be all right for a while. It is just that it is dangerous to wait."

"Don't worry. I will send word in time."

Jacques cleared his throat. "Christina, perhaps it is too soon for Kade to travel. One of my men could go in your stead."

Chris shook her head. "I could not take that chance with Robin's life. Gideon is a strange man, and he is known to be wary of strangers. At least I know what he looks like, and I think I can persuade him to tell me the secret of the cure."

"You will tell Renault that you are leaving?"

"No. He might want to come and he is too weak—or perhaps he would ask me to wait until he is well. That might cost Robin's life. I will tell him where I have gone and why, once I am safely at sea. Kade is healing very fast and will be well in a few weeks, but Robin has no chance without Gideon's help."

Jacques looked nonplussed, opened his mouth to object, saw the wisdom in her reasoning, and then shook his head in resignation.

In the morning she went to Lawrence. This time she arranged for passage to France herself, without telling

Andy. She made sure that the *Arbitor* was not one of Kade's newly purchased ships. She immediately dispatched a letter to the Maurieres giving them her expected date of arrival. Chris decided to take another maid, Cecile, with her. She was a petite brunette with big round brown eyes. Cecile's parents had come to St. Marin as identured servants from the province of Alsace-Lorraine in France. Cecile had never been to the country of her parents birth and wanted very much to come.

In the days before her departure, Christina knew many moments of indecision. She was very fond of Kade. She no longer resented the way his sardonic blue gaze lingered over her curves. At those times she came to him willingly and did not protest when he drew her against him with his good arm and joined their bodies in a loving embrace. But to stay in St. Marin meant to wonder forever what might have happened if she had followed her heart—just as her mother had always wondered. And that she was not prepared to do.

In the end, her mind was made up. She would leave a letter for Andy on the day of her departure, empowering him to manage the Evrion interests during her absence, and another for Kade, explaining briefly why she had to go and releasing him from any obligation to her, real or imagined. This time everything would go as planned—she hoped.

It was fortunate that Kade's injury remained sensitive enough to prevent them from being too often in each other's company. In a short while his shoulder would be completely well, but by that time she would be gone.

It turned out to be surprisingly easy. On the eve of

her departure she coaxed Kade into drinking several glasses of champagne, amusing him by saying, "The best time to celebrate is *before* something wonderful happens because then you can celebrate after as well." They laughed and teased each other and talked of silly things. She kissed him, blew in his ear, and played with him like an exuberant child. Kade suspected nothing and went to sleep with her arms around him, his head resting against her breast. He looked like Apollo. The strong perfect line of his jaw softened in slumber to an almost vulnerable innocence. It tugged at her conscience as well as her heart. But, hard as it was to leave him, she realized that if she didn't do it now, she never would. Quietly, she got up, allowing his dark head to descend to the pillow. Christina brushed Kade's lips softly with hers and left.

Cecile was ready and waiting as Chris gathered a few small things she couldn't leave behind. She took her mother's diary from its silver case and carefully slipped it into her small beaded purse. Once inside their carriage she looked back at Mimosa Keyes and tried to memorize its graceful lines and rolling hills. The image would have to last a long time.

Aboard the *Arbitor* she was filled with an excitement she had never known before. Her cousins—Paris! Finally she would go there. The adventure of experiencing another world soon outweighed all her apprehensions, and Cecile's boundless enthusiasm made Chris impatient for the day when the boat would dock on French shores. If the captain of the *Arbitor* thought it strange that two young women would travel alone, the handsome sum he'd received for their passage and an awe of the Evrion name commanded his utmost courtesy. The man was nearly doting. All in all, it was highly satisfactory and pleasurable voyage.

As Christina and her companion journeyed across the ocean, Charles Mauriere, Marquis de Lasqueront, sat in his study worriedly sipping a glass of fine wine. Dominique was often the cause of these solitary meditations. His wild, handsome young son was a source of great displeasure to his father. The lad had not yet reached his twenty-fifth year, and already he had sired several illegitimate offspring. Some of the girls were from respectable bourgeois families and the cost of avoiding scandal was becoming a burden.

Dominique Mauriere possessed an almost fatal attraction for women. He was handsome to the point of near feminine beauty, his features formed with such aristocratic perfection that the great artists of Paris had bid among themselves for the honor of doing his family portrait. He looked like an angel, with blond hair that curled gracefully over his collar and deep emerald-green eyes that surveyed the world with an air of serene superiority. He could be charming to a fault—but only to gain his ends.

His father, when generous, decided his son was not deliberately cruel. He was not evil, the marquis mused, merely thoughtless, self-indulgent, and cold. Nothing seemed to move him from his pedestal of untouchable perfection. The loveliest women in Paris failed to stir his heart.

The latest scandal was so serious that not even the marquis could overlook it. A young girl of decent family had informed his rake of a son of his impending fatherhood. He had it from a very good source that Dominique's reaction was a bored yawn and the reply, "*Chérie*, how tiresome. Just when I was beginning to enjoy you." He had assured the girl that marriage was out of the question.

The marquis agreed with his decision but deplored the tactless manner of delivery. The girl had slashed her wrists and died the next day. It was one thing to court opera stars, ballerinas, and the like in such a fashion, but a sheltered girl of seventeen was no sophisticate. Dominique should have known better. To make matters worse, Charles could not even tell himself that this was Dominique's worst exploit. For last year there had been a duel over a similar circumstance—a young girl, her honor ruined, a brother irate and demanding blood. Dominique had killed him. It was a fair duel, but Dominique was clearly wrong. If only the boy would be more selective. Or more discreet. Or both.

Charles Mauriere sighed heavily. It was his fault. Dominique was his son, hewn in his image. And yet, the young man possessed a wild disregard for life that the Marquis had never had, even as a youth. The marquis blamed it on the fact that Dominique was his only son, and that he had come to him and his wife after two girls, both of whom had died in infancy. Their joy at having an heir at last had been overwhelming—a son and such a charming and beautiful child at that. They had never disciplined him properly or curbed his headstrong spirit while it was still malleable. Now it was too late. Dominique never wanted anything he did not get, by fair means or foul. He had yet to encounter a will that was stronger than his own.

The interview after dinner had been painful. The marquis sternly and sincerely warned his son that if these escapades continued, his financial support would be reduced to nothing so that life as he now enjoyed it would be impossible. Dominique's emerald eyes had grown icy and hard. Then he smiled charmingly at his father and agreed to try harder to be discreet, thanking the marquis for his understanding and being so sincere that the old gentleman had not chastised him further. But the marquis was hardly fooled by his son's easy compliance. He was sure that within the month Dominique would find yet another escapade in which to embroil himself.

When Therese Mauriere walked into the study, her husband was lost in thought. His face was creased in the worried frown he always wore when he comtemplated his son.

"Have you forgotten our dinner engagement with the Defassants, *mon cher?*"

The Marquis looked up at his wife and smiled. "I'm afraid I had. As usual, the evening is never long enough."

"You were thinking of Dominique."

"I can never hide anything from you, can I, Therese?"

"Not often," she replied lightly. Then her face grew serious. "Give him time. He is young. He will outgrow his wildness."

"At times, I wonder. His grandfather . . ." the marquis's voice trailed off. "You are probably right. I hope so for his sake."

"Maman! Maman, please hurry. The carriage is waiting."

The Maurieres youngest daughter, Arielle, came floating into the study. She was a pretty girl of fifteen with soft auburn curls and large brown eyes. "Bibi has been ready for a half hour. She is waiting downstairs."

Elise Mauriere, their oldest daughter, had been called Bibi since birth. She was a worldly young sophisticate with rare beauty. Bibi resembled her father, with the same dark brown hair and hazel-green eyes. But unlike the marquis's hair, which was fine and light, Bibi's tresses fell to her waist in a dark, rich profusion of silken strands. Her eyes were fringed with seductive dark lashes and their shape was provocatively almond.

"*Eh bien*, darling, we are ready," said her mother.

When their ship arrived, Christina found a liveried carriage waiting to take her to the marquis's residence outside Paris. She caught her breath at the bays drawing the carriage. They were magnificent, and the elegance of the interior was altogether overwhelming. The two young women quietly accepted the assistance of the marquis's secretary as he escorted them to the carriage—completely in awe of what lay before them.

They rode in silence through the countryside as Chris noted the wooded forest, green and fresh with beech, oak, elm, and pine. She reveled in the lovely vales that overlooked the peaceful villages. The forest was sprinkled with chalk knolls, surrounded by spruce and chestnut. The knolls themselves were covered with broom and heather.

When the carriage skirted Paris and drew within sight of the marquis's chateau at last, Christina could barely believe what her eyes beheld. The marquis's home was breathtaking. The chateau was pentagon-shaped with a high slate roof dominated by tall chimneys. Two courts graced the front of its stately edifice, and a huge formal garden, meticulously manicured with trees cut in fanciful shapes, surrounded the whole of the main building.

As the secretary led them through the immense entrance hall, the elder Maurieres greeted Christina at the door of the great oval drawing room. It was a richly appointed salon, two stories high, occupying the rotunda of the chateau whose dome rose sixty feet above ground level. The room was so majestic that Christina felt dwarfed, and every conceivable space was filled with finely carved porcelain, jeweled statuary, intricately woven tapestry and graceful furniture. The marquis asked about Mac, his well-liked cousin. With a lump in her throat, Christina told him that there had been no further news of the ship on which Mac had been lost. Mac's body had never been recovered, but it was thought that there were no survivors.

"Still, there is always hope . . ." she finished.

"Of course. And faith is often rewarded," offered the marquis.

Therese tactfully changed the subject. "Come and meet your younger cousins, Christina."

The marquise led her into a small salon done in rose brocade and furnished with extraordinarily beautiful *objets d'art*. It was called "the Muse Room" because of the delicately painted ceiling overhead, an allusion to the classical interests of the Marquises de Lasqueront.

Chris saw a pretty girl with auburn hair reading a novel and a striking beauty with dark hair bending over a large frame of needlepoint.

"Arielle, Bibi—this is your cousin from America—Christina Evrion." Christina had not told the Maurieres of her marriage, deciding that it would only stimulate embarrassing questions about her husband's whereabouts. The two young women rose to kiss her cheek. *"Bonjour,* Christina. *Enchantée,"* said Arielle.

She received a measuring look from Bibi. Apparently meeting her approval, the dark-haired young woman said in a soft, pleasing voice, "Welcome, Christina."

"*Enchantée, cousines*," she replied.

"Our son is away, but you will meet him tonight at the party we have planned for you," said Therese.

Arielle's eyes lit up. "A party, did you hear, Bibi? What fun!"

"Yes," the young woman replied, again giving Chris another cool gaze of appraisal. "It should prove quite interesting."

"I would be delighted to attend." She turned to the marquise. "Madame, may I have a word with you and the marquis? There is a matter of some urgency I would like to discuss."

"Of course, child. Come with me."

The marquis led Christina to the library. Chris was stunned by the number of shelved volumes, well over two thousand. Never had she seen so many in one place before. Chris promised herself to read as many as possible during her stay. Realizing then that they were waiting for her to speak, she cleared her throat and began, "Sir . . ."

"You may call me Charles, Christina."

"*Non*, I could not . . ." she said in surprise. She was much too in awe of him and respectful of the differences in their ages to do that.

"Very well," he smiled. "Would 'uncle' feel more appropriate?"

"*Oui*," she agreed. "Uncle Charles, there is a favor I must ask of you."

The marquis raised one eyebrow.

"I have a dear friend whose younger brother is gravely ill with a malady of which most people die. A man in St. Marin concocted a potion which, taken regularly, preserves the health and life of the victim. I have reason to believe that this man, Gideon, is somewhere in Paris, engaged in the study of medicine. No one on the island has been able to duplicate Gideon's draught. Without it, my friend's brother will certainly die. Would you please help me to find him, Uncle Charles?"

"Yes, of course—but it will not be easy without knowing more about this . . . Gideon. What is his surname?"

"Baudien," she said firmly. Christina had gone again to the attic rooms on the day of her departure and read her mother's diary. She had discovered her mother had once been close to the mysterious healer.

"He is very eccentric. When he was a young man, he retreated to the hills of St. Marin to become a recluse."

"Interesting . . . but why did he do that?"

"It was because . . ." she began, reluctant to tell the marquis of her mother's involvement, "it was due to an unfortunate *affaire du coeur*."

Her elder cousin nodded sagely. Anything was possible when the heart was involved. "Of course, Christina, we shall help you locate this man. Now, tell us more about him so that we can decide where we might begin the search."

As Christina talked with her cousins in France, thousands of miles away in St. Marin, Mimosa Keyes was in a state of virtual chaos. When Renault discovered her absence and learned of her successful departure, his fury made the Carribbean hurricanes seem mild in comparison. The explanation Jacques gave him did little to diminish the force of his wrath and

LaCroix quickly left him alone. Gradually his rage turned to cold anger as he read again her short, cryptic note.

> I have to do this. I am sorry, but I am not sure when I can return. Andrew Hardy will help you with your business endeavors in my absence.
> If you wish to get a divorce, I will do nothing to hinder you. I wish you well.

> Christina

Damn the bitch! Damn her cold, unloving heart to hell! If he could get his hands around her throat once more, he'd end this torment forever.

A week passed. The Corsairs were worried. The captain was not behaving in a normal manner. He was rational enough, but his eyes were so cold . . . deadly. It gave them chills. Jacques and Guy did not quite know what to do.

"I've never seen him like this," Guy said to Jacques one day in the courtyard. "Not even after Juan, when DeVilla had done his worst. Christina is only a woman, after all, and hardly more than a child, at that. There are others. He could have anyone he wished. Tomorrow we'll leave for Bajora and fetch Maria Del Vega. Her singing always warms Renault's blood."

Jacques sighed. "I do not think it would work this time, *mon ami*. Christina is in his head now, and he will not forget her. *La petite* is a spirit untamed. The captain is a soul of great strength and power—he finds her challenge one he cannot resist. They are alike, and perhaps meant to be one, but she will not yield to

him, and he cannot let her go. They are like two
strong sea winds blowing against one another—very
destructive."

Guy shrugged. "He will forget her in time."

Jacques looked at him levelly. "No, have you not
seen his eyes? The pain there? It is like a wound that
ripens and festers. I don't like it at all . . . too much
strong emotion can destroy a man. And there is nothing stronger than love."

Logan Armor burst into the courtyard with a look
of intense concentration on his face. "Where is Renault? I have news that cannot wait," he said.

"Of Christina?" asked Savant.

"No. It is news from the highlands."

"Scotland?" asked Jacques.

"Yes. Where is he?"

"The library. Come."

The curtains of the Evrion library were tightly
closed. The room was dimly lit by one oil lamp. Renault sat at a large carved mahogany desk in the middle of the room, gazing fixedly at some shipping accounts. Jacques wondered idly if he'd turned a page
all morning. Logan walked toward him with care.

"Captain, I have some news for you. It is not pleasant."

Renault's eyes lifted swiftly to the Corsair's face.
Armor thought briefly that he had never been pierced
by a gaze so intense or so full of dread in his life.
Renault sat motionless, his eyes nearly daring Armor
to continue. He said slowly, "Christina?"

Logan swallowed and said, "No, Captain. It's your
brother—Jamie. He's . . . dead."

Disbelief, mingled with something oddly like
pained relief, flashed in the azure eyes. Then they

clouded with confusion. "What? Jamie? No . . . I don't believe it."

Armor looked disraught. "It's true, Captain. 'Twas a hunting party in the high country. Your brother's horse took a bad jump and fell. Jamie . . . his neck , . . he didn't survive the fall."

Renault turned his head and stared at the open space across the room. Logan Armor said softly, "I'm afraid, Captain, that your status has changed somewhat. Jamie's death makes you the new earl. Sir Kincaid Renault, Earl of Brenkirk—by grace of fate." As the Corsairs looked from one to the other, a pregnant silence filled the air.

Kade turned toward the tall Corsair and said in a deep voice resonant with calm resignation, "Prepare the *Falcon*, Logan. We set sail for Scotland with the morning tide, one week hence."

CHAPTER TWENTY-SIX

Christina sat with her two cousins in the girls' private sitting room on the second floor of the marquis's Paris residence as they finished a light meal. The marquis's apartments were on the second floor of the chateau. Bibi, Arielle, and Dominique had apartments in the east wing, overlooking the manicured greenery encircling their home. The winding paths of the garden courtyard, done in the popular Versailles style, threaded through a perfectly symmetrical pattern of circular spaces, borders, and lawns graced with statues and carefully shaped crystalline pools—a balanced harmony of art, order, and subtle taste.

Bibi and Christina could eat nothing more, laced tightly as they were into their corsets. Arielle sighed and said, "I wish I could come tonight."

Her sister smiled. "You know you are too young. You haven't even made your debut."

"I know, I know. But it is *très difficile,* this waiting to grow up," Arielle complained.

Chris laughed. "It won't be long, Arielle. Why, before you know it, you will be all grown up and married." I should know, she thought to herself.

Arielle's only reply was a long-suffering sigh and a charming pout.

Bibi turned her hazel gaze to Chris. "That gown is very becoming, cousin. Did you have it made here?"

Chris laughed. "Oh, no, but Madame Defaux would be ecstatic to hear you ask that. She is from Paris and her designs are very imaginative." She was wearing a diaphanous gold gown with skirts that floated from the bodice like morning mist. The cut was modest, but her young bosom rose gracefully from the neckline. She wore a single diamond teardrop on a golden chain and tiny diamond earrings that sparkled like small stars. Very reluctantly she had allowed Cecile to pin her dark gold hair in a fashionable Parisian style. The total effect was lovely, her turquoise eyes and creamy skin glowing radiantly against the soft gold backdrop of the gown.

Bibi looked serenely mysterious in a pastel blue gown that emphasized the dark beauty of her hair and the fair, fragile quality of her skin. Her strange eyes were particularly striking—greenish gold flecked with little dots of blue.

Arielle sighed again with petulant impatience. "By the time I am old enough to come with you, all the eligible men will be gone."

Bibi laughed. "No, *chou-chou*. There will be many for you, wait and see."

It was time to go to the *salon jaune* where the ball was being held. The opulent ballroom took Christina's breath away. It was lined with mirrors framed in solid gold, and huge white marble pillars decorated the room. The young guests waltzed in a blur of multicolored satin and brocade. There were so many beautiful women that it took Christina's breath away, and the men seemed so polished that the air was redolent with their elegance and poise. Chris noticed a tall young man who viewed the room with an air of bored insouciance. He was so unbelievably good-looking that she couldn't help staring. She was not the only one who noticed. Half of the young women in the room looked with longing at the broad shoulders, the firm athletic build, the deep green eyes like fine emeralds and the fair blond curls that fell softly about his neck. His face was classical perfection, but the expression in his eyes was cold and disinterested. He seemed indifferent to the stir he caused among the beautiful girls in the room.

Three lovely young woman simpered about him and giggled beneath their fans. Chris thought their behavior was silly and odd for the sophisticated French. With a graceful wave of his hand, he dismissed them and walked away, rather rudely Chris thought. He joined a group of young men playing cards in a small salon adjoining the ballroom. The young women looked disappointed, but not surprised. Whispering together, they left to join other friends in the ballroom.

There was something about his eyes that disturbed her. They were arresting, almost beautiful, but they lacked any trace of human warmth. He was like a young savage—transported from a more primitive time, and none too happy with the world about him.

The three young women who had surrounded the man left their friends and walked toward Christina and Bibi. They stopped nearby and Christina could hear their conversation.

"Isn't he divine, Clothilde?" said a short brunette.

"*Ah, oui,* I have never seen such a man," answered her friend. "But they say he is so wicked, Gabrielle. *Très dangereux.* I heard that he has already fought four duels."

"*Mais non,* not four! He is too young!" said Gabrielle de Vezy.

"*Oui,* four! And poor Athenée killed herself when

she heard she was with child and he refused to wed her," Clothilde Theroux replied.

"*Quel scandale*! Isn't it exciting?"

"Gabrielle, *tu es incorrigible*," laughed her friend. "I tell you the man is evil and you are all the more determined to have him!"

"But he is such a beautiful evil—how can one resist?" she asked. "It would be worth any pain he would bring to be held for a moment in his arms."

Christina looked toward the richly furnished salon where the card game was in progress. The young man was sitting down now, playing his hand with an intense concentration that seemed ominous. His green eyes were opaque and unreadable above the cards. An attractive red-haired youth sitting across the table from him looked nervous, as if he was losing a great sum. The young man watched him coolly with a smile that was casual and faintly sadistic. She found herself feeling sorry for the other player. One of the guests behind her whispered, "Dominique is winning, as usual."

She turned to Bibi and said softly, "Have you ever heard of a young man called Dominique?"

Bibi regarded her rather strangely. "Yes, I have heard of him," she replied. "He is my brother—your cousin, Christina. If you like, I will introduce you to him this evening."

"No," replied Chris. "It can wait."

A small crowd gathered in the *petit salon* to watch the outcome of the game. Lucien Brevard, the red-haired youth, had just wagered an incredible sum against Dominique Mauriere, in hopes of bluffing him. But everyone knew Dominique was not bluffable. If someone did not prevail upon Lucien's adversary for mercy, the young man would lose the major portion of his inheritance.

Arnaud Rochefort stepped forward on Lucien's behalf to whisper in Dominique's ear. "He has barely enough to cover the bet, Dominique. If you allow him to lose this sum, it will break him."

"If he could not afford to wager, he should not be sitting here," Dominique replied. The tall blond man regarded him coolly.

"He is very young, Dominique. Only a year out of the schoolroom and too innocent to be ruined. For once, *mon ami*, have compassion."

"He is a gentleman and a gentleman always pays his debts. You forget, Rochefort, that I could lose also. As for compassion, I have none."

Arnaud considered making a second appeal to Dominique's better nature, but a brief glance at the closed, unyielding face told him his efforts would be futile. Arnaud stepped back and folded his arms, resigning himself to the scene before him.

With a shaking hand, young Brevard turned over his card. "A ten of clubs," he announced loudly, relief written plainly on his clear, unlined face.

Slowly, deliberately, Dominique's artistic fingers curved over the remaining card. He turned it delicately until it lay face up on the table.

"King of diamonds," he said with calm indifference. "You lose, Brevard."

The young man stared stupidly at the card. His mouth quivered—then, appallingly, he began to sob. With a look of disgust, Dominique rose from the table. "Remove him. The sight offends me." Turning, he walked carelessly from the room. Over his shoulder he said, "My secretary will accept your draft in the morning." With that, he left the ball.

Christina watched the tall young man leave. The room seemed charged by his presence as his friends parted automatically to let him pass, watching as he walked by.

"What an unusual young man," she thought to herself, a little sorry to see him go.

The next day the marquis asked Christina to meet him in the library after the light morning meal. Once inside, a smile crossed his aristocratic features, and he informed her that Gideon had been found.

"Oh, where? Uncle Charles, that is wonderful news!" she exclaimed, delighted.

"It seems that he is widely known to the scholars of botany at the University of Paris and has visited with them many times over the years. If you would like, there is a carriage waiting to take you to the university where this Gideon may be found."

Chris gave the marquis an impetuous hug of gratitude. "*Oh, merci, mon oncle*, I am so happy! I will get ready at once."

The carriage arrived at the Rue de la Sorbonne in a short time. They trotted past the large open courtyard and the impressive Church of the Sorbonne as the carriage turned into one of the narrow side streets and rolled to a stop in front of a small museum. The coachman led Christina to a remote corner of the building and stopped before a door at the end of one long corridor. He rapped discreetly. There was a long pause before a low voice said in a surprised, though well-modulated tone, "Come in?"

She asked the footman to wait at the door and, with

an indrawn breath, entered Gideon's private sanctuary.

Inside, she was quite unprepared for the array of bottles, glassware, and botanical specimens she saw. The walls were covered with diagrams of plants and strange figures she couldn't understand. Strewn about on tables already crowded with glassware were essays and pamphlets by Voltaire and Jean Jacques Rousseau. She looked at the long tables and workbenches of Gideon's laboratory in awe.

Christina suddenly realized the extent of the man's dedication to his art and the enigma that surrounded him faded in the cool light air of the Paris morning. This was the real Gideon, the man behind the mystery, superstition, and legend. The books, the glass vials of multicolored liquid, the pages of script that lay scattered about the room—Christina began to see him as he really was, a man devoted to the pursuit of philosophy, botany, and medicine.

She saw around her many of the plants of St. Marin, both living and carefully dried, neatly labeled as specimens to be filed or set aside for further study.

"He must have been collecting things and bringing them to the university for years," she thought to herself.

Christina turned her attention to Gideon, who had been studying her as intently as she studied his laboratory. She saw a tall, gaunt man with the thin face of a hawk and skin the color of polished walnut, as tough and resilient as tanned leather, weathered by years of age and toil.

Gideon's alert gray eyes studied her face as if he were seeing a ghost. "It is not possible . . . and yet, I feel as if I am seeing her again. Who are you?"

"Christina Evrion."

The tall, thin scholar closed his eyes and sat down with his hand across his brow. After a moment he looked up. "That explains it. You, mademoiselle, are the daughter of Blaise St. Claire, are you not?"

"*Oui*, monsieur."

He stared again for a brief second that stretched across Christina's taut nerves into eternity. Then to her relief, his face broke into a smile.

"I shall always count it one of life's good fortunes to have met you. I once loved your mother very much."

"Yes, monsieur, I know."

He nodded. "Why have you sought me out? What brings you to France?"

"I am here as the guest of my cousin, the Marquis de Lasqueront. But truly I came to find you. Do you remember a young boy called Robin Tresgros?"

Gideon's face was blank.

"You treated him in St. Marin for the high fever. His sister Janie brought him to your retreat in the hills. Their parents died of the fever years ago. Janie has never been afflicted, but her little brother developed the chills and the trembling some years after their parents died. Your cure, Gideon, has kept him well."

"I remember now. Does Janie not have the potion I gave her?"

"It is nearly gone. When there is none left we are afraid Robin will die. Nothing else has worked."

"The potion I gave Janie is distilled from the bark of the cinchona tree. Here it is called quinine, and the malaria can be controlled with regular doses. He will indeed need more, if his attacks of the fever continue. You were right to come."

She nodded. "No one on the island could duplicate your medicine."

He shook his head. "I have not finished refining the process of distillation—I was reluctant to teach anyone else. But you have come at a good time. My work here has ended and all that I can do has been completed. My days of learning at this institution are done, and I know as much now as I shall need." Gideon smiled. "So you see, I am ready and impatient to return to my island."

Chris sighed with relief. It was going to be all right. Robin would live.

"Well, then, I think we should get back to St. Marin as soon as possible, don't you?" Gideon suggested.

"Oh, no, Gideon, I am not going back yet!"

"I heard of your marriage. Your husband has come with you then?"

Chris reddened. "No . . . he is . . . he stayed in St. Marin."

Gideon regarded her cryptically. "I cannot imagine that he would willingly allow you to come to Paris without him."

Mon Dieu, but the man was astute! "Well, no . . . I . . . didn't tell him of this journey until after I departed." She shifted her weight uneasily and felt very much like a small child caught in a bad act.

Gideon looked at her pointedly. "I'll wager you have long wanted to come here."

Christina was surprised. "Why, yes, how did you know?"

He shook his head. "You are more like your mother than you know."

She regarded him warily. The man's perception was uncanny.

He looked thoughtful as he picked up one of his vials, idly studying it as he spoke. "The ancient Greeks had a word, Christina—*sophrosone*. Roughly translated, it meant 'moderation and balance in all things', finding a focus in life, an equilibrium to guide you, a reason for being. This you have yet to find, and until you do, happiness will elude you. Your search has brought you here, but I do not think that you will find what you are looking for in this city."

"You cannot know that of a certainty," she breathed, startled again by his perception.

"One knows nothing of a certainty, but I feel that your journey has taken you far afield of that which you seek." He paused and added, "Neither can what you wish be found alone. Perhaps you should not have left him, Christina."

"Gideon . . ." she began, wanting to deny his words. It occurred to her suddenly that he did not know the circumstances of her marriage. Of course, his assumptions were no more than logic. Not wanting to explain the whole of the tale, she merely said, "Perhaps there is some truth in what you have said. I promise you, I shall consider well what you have told me and its meaning."

He nodded, seeming satisfied with her reply. "How very like your mother you are. It is almost as if she were here in this room." He sighed with fatigue and closed his eyes. "Go now. I am tired. As soon as possible, I will make arrangements to go back to the island."

Christina stared at him. His eyes remained shut. It was obvious the interview had concluded. "Thank you, Gideon," she murmured. "Farewell."

The next day the marquise and Bibi took Christina

shopping. The city was so beautiful that Chris did not know where to look first. The tree-lined streets, the old graceful avenues, the river Seine—all found an immediate place in her heart. Their carriage made its way slowly through the ville toward the fashionable dressmakers near the marquis's Paris residence. Inside the shop of Renée Rouvaise, Christina caught her breath a dozen times. She had never seen such luxuriantly rich velvets or wool so fine and soft to the touch. The lace was exquisite—like snowflake crystals and butterfly wings. And the silk! Even the tropical flowers of St. Marin did not grow in such vibrant colors. She ordered several gowns in shimmering fabrics trimmed with ruching, velvet, and bows.

She picked out several dress patterns for the opera and the ballet, to be done in lace and velvet, as well as one or two riding habits. Bibi informed her that the Baron de Rochefort planned a masque ball in a few weeks that would be great fun—so she should decide now on a costume. Christina decided it would be a great lark to go dressed as a young courtier, complete with rapier and waistcoat. After a great deal of persuasion, the marquise agreed, albeit reluctantly. "I'll be wearing a mask and a hat. No one will recognize me," Chris reassured her.

There was so much to see and do. The marquise took the two young women to the home of a relative whose first love was collecting art. Christina was awed by the portraits. They looked so real—she expected the person to step from the canvas and speak. The landscapes were so peaceful and green that she longed to step into each of the paintings. For the first time she saw mountains that were white and treeless, covered with snow. The porcelain was so delicate that

it was translucent. Chris put her hand behind one exquisite plate. She could see through it and count her
fingers on the other side.

Ah, and the food! She had never tasted such delicate, finely herbed cheeses or such deliciously smooth
and delightful wines. The array of hor d'oeuvres made
her head spin. There was a delicious spiced *rillettes
de porc, tartes du poisson, petites truites sautées, pi-
geons à la vigneronne, chartreuse,* and so many other
dishes she forgot their names. For dessert, the *crème
caramel* and *tartelette chaude aux pommes* were un-
forgettable. If she continued eating like this, none of
the dresses she had ordered would fit. Still, when she
was full she enjoyed just *looking* at the succulent,
splendidly displayed dishes.

The ballet was wonderful. She found the idea of
balancing *en pointe* intriguing, and she could hardly
wait to try it secretly when she got back to the marquis's town house. The ballerinas looked like flowers
blowing in a spring breeze. It was all like a very
lovely dream. The music was soft and melodic, like
the voice of a young girl. Oddly, it made her think of
St. Marin. She shook herself mentally. It was too early
to be homesick.

The opera, too, was enchanting. There were no
voices on St. Marin that could reach such high, ear-
piercing notes. It was rather remarkable, she thought,
that the people in those small seats in the back could
hear the singer as well as she. The performers moved
with a studied majesty. It was a very moving and regal sight. Her mother would have loved the opera and
the ballet. As she watched the brilliant lead baritone
take a well-deserved bow, her eyes filled with tears.

* * *

Carlotta DeCorba's marriage to James Marston was less than three months old, but already she was bored. It had taken careful planning to nurture his initial attraction into something more permanent, but with patience and guile she had succeeded. Now that the euphoria of capturing the well-born architect had passed and the first blushes of romance had faded, she was beginning to itch for something more exciting—a new challenge. Marston's gentle attention and tender advances were beginning to bore her.

Then she heard that Christina Evrion Renault had left for France—without the handsome captain. Carlotta thought Christina was a fool, and she intended to take full advantage of her carelessness. Another rumor had it that Captain Renault would soon leave for Scotland. If that was true, it meant there wasn't much time. And Carlotta was not one to pass up a good opportunity.

Fortunately, James spent long hours in town with surveyors, planning the new pattern of streets and buildings for Lawrence's growing commercial center. One morning after she bid him good-bye, Carlotta dressed in her most attractive riding outfit, a well-cut blue habit with an unusually tight bodice, and rode directly to Mimosa Keyes.

The butler opened the door. Captain Renault was in the courtyard; would she please wait in the library while she was announced? She chose a seat near the window on her right so that the sunlight would surround her in a halo of gold. Kade Renault looked surprised and faintly annoyed as he walked through the door.

What a magnificent man he is, she thought as her eyes roved sensuously over the hard, muscular planes of his body, now casually dressed in beige pantaloons, a brown linen shirt, and kid boots. It was difficult to maintain an air of nonchalance when she saw the raven-black hair and deep blue eyes.

"Why have you come, Carlotta?" a deep resonant voice asked her.

She let her eyes answer him. He saw desire and yearning smoulder passionately in their depths. Kade watched silently, then a smile played at his lips. "I seem to remember having this discussion before," he said.

"Kade, *mi corazón,* do not refuse me this time. I know that she left you. You are lonely. I, too, have need of someone. We can find solace together."

"Carlotta, I've told you . . ."

She did not let him finish. Her pride would not take another refusal. She would have him today—no matter what it took.

"What kind of man are you? She is gone. I am here. I want you. Apparently, she does not. My love, I would never treat you as she has."

Kade's eyes were like stone as he said quietly, "Oh? Will you treat me as kindly as you are now treating your husband?"

He had a wretched way of putting things, she decided. "James has found someone else," she lied. "I loved him very much at first, but he betrayed me. Must I allow myself to be used and cast aside, merely because I am a woman? I am alive and I have much to give. To you, Kade, if you let me. Or perhaps you would prefer to play the fool for your butter-haired bride?"

Renault looked at the snapping, green feline eyes and the hard line of the pouting pink lips and doubted every word of her tale. He had seen the way James Marston looked at Carlotta. The man was smitten. It was highly unlikely that he had taken another woman so soon, but it was easy to imagine Carlotta becoming bored with his adoration.

She was attractive. Moreover, she was here and, as she said, willing. Christina, the bitch, was thousands of miles away somewhere in France. God only knew when he would see her again. And he might just kill her when he did. It would be a pleasant sight to see those turquoise eyes bulging as his hands tightened on her creamy throat, those soft, provocative lips pleading with him for mercy. In the meantime Carlotta was close at hand—voluptuously beautiful and very eager.

Carlotta held her breath as she watched his deep blue eyes darken with desire. He moved forward and pulled her into his arms so roughly that it hurt. His mouth ground into hers with bruising force, so hard that her lips grated over her teeth and she tasted blood. She strained against him, seeking the painful tightness of his embrace, wanting to be consumed by the fire of his lust. "Harder, kiss me harder, my love," she whispered.

He raised his head and looked into her half-closed eyes, now liquid and glowing with desire. He smiled grimly. "You like being hurt, don't you, Carlotta?"

She moved against him sensuously. "Sometimes pleasure is concealed in pain," she said huskily, her hands moving over his back, raking him with her nails. "And pleasure is what makes life . . . enjoyable."

He looked down at her, his eyes black and unreadable for long moments. Twice before in his life he had known women who could find fulfillment in the act only if it was accompanied by intense pain. Carlotta appeared to the one of those strange beings.

At last he said, "Then let's see how much . . . pleasure . . . we can give you."

He ripped away the tight bodice of the riding habit and gripped her breast with crushing force as his mouth covered hers again.

She writhed in agony mixed with bliss as his fingers bruised the tender skin of her bosom. Abruptly he tore his mouth away from hers and pushed her roughly to the floor. In minutes her gown was in tattered shreds around her.

He continued to squeeze her breasts in that painful grip as he entered her. He rammed completely into her in one stroke, making her cry out with the force of it. He battered her mercilessly. She balled her fists and beat against his chest and back, writhing beneath him, alone with her torment, but she never asked him to stop, nor did she tell him that he was hurting her.

He rose briefly and turned her beneath him. This time she screamed aloud as he resumed his motion. "Stop, stop! That's not . . . it's too deep . . ." She turned her head to look at him. He gave no sign of having heard her. His surging motion increased, growing more rapid. She moaned. A swell of pleasure rose within her. Her body rose to meet his thrusts. She felt him grow rigid and tense inside her. Then he relaxed, and she knew it was over. Her whole body ached, but she sat up and touched the blue-black marks on her breasts with mingled wonder and delight.

Renault looked down at her as he fastened his trousers, his face unmoved and expressionless. "Someone will bring you a dress to wear home. If you'll excuse me, I have work to do. I would prefer it if you were not here when I come back. Good day, Carlotta."

Well, let him enjoy his airs, she thought. Carlotta stretched like a contented cat. Her body was sore, but she had a wonderfully warm and tingly feeling. She had never known such satisfaction. What a stallion he is, she thought. Yes, Captain Renault was definitely quite a man.

Therese Mauriere knocked gently at the door of her daughter's room. "Bibi, Christina . . . are you ready girls? It is time to leave," she said as she entered their room. Bibi was petite and lovely in a foam-green gown of voile and silk. She was dressed as a water sprite and carried a tiny green starfish with small sparkling jewels. The green domino she wore did little to conceal her identity. Anyone who knew her could tell from the large hazel eyes and flowing dark hair that it was Bibi.

Christina, however, was virtually unrecognizable. Despite Therese's subtle attempt at dissuasion, she stood firm by her decision to attend the ball dressed as a young courtier. Aside from the fact that she made an unusually beautiful and fragile-looking young man, the effect was totally convincing. She wore an immaculately tailored black-velvet waistcoat with a rich cream brocade vest. A snowy cravat rose above her impeccable white shirt, set up pertly by a glittering diamond stickpin. Her hair was hidden beneath a wig tied with a velvet ribbon at the nape, and a silver rapier was strapped to her side. The large domino she wore hid most of her face. A good thing, Therese thought, as she looked at the caramel pantaloons, beige stockings, and silver-buckled shoes Christina wore. Those well-shaped legs would draw admiring glances from the young women at the ball, and it was better for everyone if no one realized the extent of the deception.

Therese told the girls that she and her husband would leave for the ball later, following a small formal dinner with several of the marquis's old friends. Bibi and Christina kissed her and left for the ball in one of the marquis's silver and garnet liveried carriages. It was just as well that they were leaving early. The provincial palace of the Baron de Rochefort was many miles away, and the road was long and full of many winding curves and rough passages.

The marquise sighed after the girls had gone. She was worried about Dominique. Her errant son had not been home in two weeks. Although it was not unusual for him to be absent for even longer periods, it was rather strange that they had not received even the slightest bit of news regarding his whereabouts. None of his habitual friends had seen him. That was strange, even for Dominique.

As the marquise worried about him in Paris, Dominique Mauriere sat in an inn near the chateau of his friend, Paul Anvireau. He was bored to the point of distraction. He'd spent the past two weeks as Paul's secret guest in utter seclusion with his latest mistress, a striking young opera star with the voice of a nightingale and the face of an angel. But after a few days her company had grown very tedious, so much so that he'd left her one night as she slept to join Anvireau and some friends on a hunt in the country. But that too had palled rapidly. Now he sat here drinking alone, an expression of complete and utter boredom marring his perfect features.

It had been quite a while since he'd felt this way. He knew of only one thing diverting enough to lift the cloak of depression when it settled over him: he disguised himself as a highwayman and rode the postways in search of a coach to rob. That, he decided, was definitely what he needed to do tonight. Tossing the innkeeper several gold coins, he drained his mug and went to his horse. A few miles away he found a likely spot for an ambush on a secluded curve on a moderately traveled road. The dark brown clothing he wore was covered with a huge riding cape. He was hidden in the darkness.

Dominique did not have to wait long. In the distance he saw a carriage drawing closer, conveniently equipped with only two guards and a driver. With a start he recognized his father's garnet and silver livery. He saw his sister Bibi with an unknown young man. What luck, he thought to himself. How amusing it would be to rob Bibi, his own sister, and revel in the sheer knavery of thoroughly embarrassing that foppish-looking young gallant at her side. Dominique donned a dark cowl that completely covered his face and hair. Only his deep green eyes were visible through two holes in the mask.

He rode toward the carriage, taking dead aim at one outrider with his pistol. A shot rang out and the hapless man grabbed his arm, teetered precariously, and fell from his horse. Before his companion could collect his wits, Dominque fired again with the second gun he carried. He watched as the man grabbed his leg and moaned. In less than a moment, he toppled.

Confidently, Dominique rode up to the carriage.

The driver was an ancient and wizened little man, long past the lure of youthful heroics. Inside the carriage Chris tried to revive Bibi, who had fainted after the second man screamed. She was about to abandon slapping her wrists in favor of her cheeks when a man's voice from behind her said, "*Écoutez*, monsieur, get out of the carriage—now!" She turned to stare at a hooded apparition with frighteningly cold green eyes. The figure held a large dueling pistol aimed at her head. Carefully she opened the door of the carriage and stepped out.

Dominique noted with amusement that Bibi's escort appeared even weaker at close range. This prim young lad would cause him little trouble. Disguising his voice, he said, "Tell the mademoiselle to come out."

Chris lowered her own voice to a husky rasp. "She cannot. She has fainted."

It was just like Bibi to spoil his fun, Dominique thought with mild annoyance. Well, he would have to make do with her effete escort. He eyed the young man casually, then pointed nonchalantly to the courtier's neckcloth with his gun. "I admire your pin, monsieur. I have a great fondness for diamonds. Hand it over, if you please."

Chris was frightened, but she was even more angry than she was scared. The man's swaggering disregard for human life disgusted her. She ached to show him what pain was like and give him a taste of his own brew. Besides, the diamond pin was a Mauriere family heirloom. She could not relinquish it lightly. Christina replied coldly, "I don't please and if you were not a coward, you would lay down your pistol and fight me on equal terms."

Dominique's eyebrows shot up beneath the cowl. This was going to be more fun than he had hoped. "You challenge me, monsieur?" he asked with diabolical amusement. "You are not armed."

"I have a sword," she replied levelly. Then she looked at his waist. "So do you. Will you fight me fairly or continue to hide behind that canon?"

The little rodent had courage, Dominique admitted to himself. He said coolly, "I agree to fight you on your terms, but it will hardly be an equal match."

Chris gritted her teeth and strove for calm. The first thing Mac had taught her about fencing was that the battle was lost as soon as one fought in anger. Keeping her eyes on him, she removed her waistcoat and vest, thankful that she'd had the forethought to disguise her bosom with tight binding.

A brave fool, thought Dominique, looking at the frail, slim figure of the young man who appeared to have less than a third of his own strength.

But what Chris lacked in power she made up in pure speed. From the moment their swords clashed she was a small blur of movement, skillfully parrying Dominique's powerful thrusts and countering his attacks with well-aimed cuts of her own. Mauriere silently cursed. The damned little monkey was such a small target. He darted a lightning-quick blow toward her arm, but she anticipated his move and turned her body agilely so that his sword just knicked her shoulder ripping through the black velvet cloth to lightly scratch the skin below. She speared him quickly in an unexpected counterattack that sent her sword solidly into the large muscle of his left arm. He gaped at her in the moonlight.

Dominique stifled a roar of pain and rage. The bastard! He had planned to be lenient, costing the young imp only a few cups of blood, but now he was truly angry, and his handsome face turned murderous beneath the cowl.

Chris sensed the change in his mood and adjusted her movements to give him wide berth, but the man's bloodlust was excessive. Cunningly, he fought her until her arm began to tire. Seeing her fatigue, he backed her into the woods along the roadside. Her foot caught in a branch and she fell heavily on the leaf-covered ground. She caught herself with her hands as she fell, releasing the sword momentarily. Her heart sank as she watched it roll away from her—too far to be quickly retrieved. His laugh chilled her blood.

"So, my fine young cock," he said, "we are not so confident now, are we? Before I give you a very painful souvenir of this battle, I'd like to see the face of my adversary."

He carelessly cut the string of her domino with the tip of his rapier. The mask fell to reveal the strikingly beautiful face of an excited and flushed young woman, with flashing turquoise eyes and a provacative pink mouth. Dominique's mind refused to believe what his eyes beheld. He said in a strangely tight voice, "You're an uncommonly pretty youth . . ." Suspicion overwhelmed him and he whisked off her wig with his rapier. Waves of dark honey and wheat tresses fell over her shoulders and caressed her temples as the wig flew into the leaves behind her.

She heard a sharp intake of breath from the man as the wavy mane confirmed what he would rather not have known. Taking advantage of his momentary immobility, she rolled quickly out of his sword reach and grabbed her own rapier from where it had fallen. She leaped to her feet, but when she turned, all she saw was his retreating back.

"Coward, come back!" she shouted as she ran after him. When she got to the road, he was already on horseback.

"*Excusez-moi,* mademoiselle, but I do not fight women," he called over his shoulder as he galloped away.

Pig, she thought to herself. Not fight women! He had been fighting a woman for the last half hour. Chris looked at the two men in the road, who were barely conscious and bleeding. The little driver seemed very happy to see her alive. She smiled and told him to help her get the two men inside the coach. Bibi wouldn't mind being a little cramped. She was still unconscious.

CHAPTER TWENTY-SEVEN

Dominique Mauriere, the adored and pampered son of the Marquis de Lasqueront, was in a remarkably foul mood. He sat in a wing chair in the corner of the bedroom he had occupied at Chateau D'Anvireau for a week. That insolent chit had actually had the temerity to engage him in a fight. *Sacrebleu!* He still could not believe it. She was little more than a girl! A small voice inside him added, "And a very beautiful girl, at that." Little hellion. Who was she? Where did she come from? She was traveling with Bibi. *Mon Dieu,* that she-devil was with his sister!

Dominique drained a goblet of cognac. There was only one thing to do. He would go to Paris and force his sister to reveal the identity of this mysterious young tigress and more important, where he could find her. Dominique downed a second goblet of cognac.

The marquis and marquise were horrified by what had befallen Bibi and Christina. Charles Mauriere and several other noblemen commissioned a thorough search of the countryside to capture the highwayman who had the temerity to waylay the carriage of a nobleman. Daily reports were given to the marquis on the progress of the search. So far there had been no trace of the tall, hooded figure Christina described.

Bibi recovered, feeling very chagrined at having fainted in the middle of the excitement. The old coachman told everyone that Chris had challenged the highwayman and in the little man's words, "saved them all." Indeed, Christina achieved a certain fame from the escapade. People from the countryside often invented some pretext to visit the marquis in hopes of catching a glimpse of the unusual young woman who fought so well with a sword. The young women who heard the tale were scandalized. Ah, but they were so curious! Bibi was beset by visits from her friends. Many of them stared at Chris with mingled admiration and disbelief. With all of this activity, the marquis's Paris residence fairly overflowed with guests.

Into the middle of this confusion walked Dominique, calmly reserved and serenely aloof. Impeccably dressed in a pearl-gray waistcoat, pale champagne pantaloons, and shining black boots, he looked as if he had done nothing more strenuous in a month than hold a deck of cards. The marquis was so preoccupied with the search for the highwayman that he barely acknowledged his son's return. Dominique smiled briefly in amusement. Usually after one of his extended disappearances, his father lectured him sternly for more than an hour.

Dominique left his father in the state salon and went to his mother's apartments on the second floor. He found her instructing a new maid on her daily duties. "Good morning, maman," he said and kissed her on the cheek.

"Dominique, *tu es méchante!* Must you disappear for weeks without telling us? We worry about you! There is a dangerous highwayman in the area who had been terrorizing the countryside. For all we know he could have waylaid you and we would never know if you—"

"Enough," he laughed. Dominique seldom laughed with anyone except his mother. "I am fine, as you can see."

Therese relented. Dom was quite charming when he made the effort, although he didn't often exert himself. But today his smile was especially warm, and it was very good to have him home again. "Tell me, maman, is Bibi here?" he asked.

"*Oui*," his mother answered. "She is entertaining friends in her apartments. Oh, your cousin from America is visiting us. Do go in and meet her."

Dominique frowned. Another rustic relative to be bored by. The last female cousin who stayed with them was a plump, freckled mouse from Bretagne. She had developed an instant crush on him, and he had suffered her adoring calflike gaze for four months.

He walked through several richly appointed hallways until he came to Bibi's apartments. He found her with Gabrielle de Vezy, Clothilde Theroux, and three other young women of her age group. Dominique leaned nonchalantly against the doorway as he surveyed the room.

A movement in the room caught Gabrielle de Vezy's eye, and she looked up to find Dominique posed carelessly against the door. As always, her heart turned over at the sight of his fair blond curls and emerald-green eyes. He looked so perfect standing there in the pearl-gray waistcoat. His presence always seemed to command attention and a kind of reverent awe—how could anyone ignore perfection?

Gabrielle was not the only woman in the room who was affected by Dominique's presence. All five of Bibi's companions were now staring in open admiration at her older brother. As usual, he failed to notice. He was watching his sister with amusement as she played the spinet, struggling with the chords of an exceptionally difficult piece. Bibi heard a sigh begind her, and she looked at Gabrielle's infatuated countenance. Only one thing brought that look into Gabrielle's eyes. Bibi turned toward the doorway.

"Dom! When did you get back?" she said.

"Just now, *chérie*," he said easily as he walked into the room, ignoring the nervous fluttering around him. "And how is my little sister?" he asked as he stood beside the spinet.

"Oh, Dom! The most dreadful thing happened . . ." she began.

"Yes, I heard. I trust you were not harmed?"

"No, no. But I was so lucky to have been with Christina."

"Christina?" His expression was bright with interest.

"*Oui*. She was *fantastique*. So brave. Oh, I forgot. You have been away and have not yet met her. Christina! Come out here. There is someone you should meet!"

Christina was in a small room adjoining Bibi's salon, taking a nap. Since the night of their "accident"—that is how she always thought of it—the beauty of Paris had palled somewhat. The country now seemed as wild and dangerous as Bajora. At any rate, she napped in the quiet of the afternoon now, trying to restore peace to her disquieted spirit. The effects of the fight had not worn off. She felt nervous and edgy at odd moments.

Chris rose from the couch and stood up. For a moment she did not know what had awakened her. She wore a pale blue gown trimmed with white lace and deep blue velvet ribbons. It looked very soft and fragile.

"Christina!" Bibi called again.

She drifted dreamily into the salon.

Dominique stared in open astonishment at the young woman who entered the room. Her long, dark gold hair fell in riotous waves about her head and shoulders, and down her back. Her eyes were half-closed, and she looked like a small golden kitten that had just been rudely pulled from sleep. He had never seen a softer-looking female than this small, blue-gowned sprite before him. Dominique nearly laughed aloud. How could he have mistaken that lovely curved figure for the body of a lad? Could this soft bundle of fluff have wielded the rapier that had scarred his arm for life? If so, he owed her much in the way of retribution, and he would make sure that she got it.

"Dom," Bibi said with a smile "This is our cousin Christina from St. Marin."

Dominique walked slowly toward Christina and took her hand. The emerald eyes seemed to pierce her very soul, and Chris felt oddly chilled by their glittering intensity. Dominique raised her hand to his lips and kissed it lingeringly. *"Enchanté, cousin,"* he said.

She looked at him. He was even more handsome than the first night she saw him. It should have been a pleasure to be near him, but she felt only the nervous edginess that had plagued her since the accident—only now it was more intense.

"I'm being silly," she thought to herself. "This will pass in a few days." Mentally she gave herself a shake and looked more closely at her blond cousin. No wonder the young women in the room looked as though Adonis himself had materialized. Dominique Mauriere was a devastatingly handsome young man.

He had not released her hand.

"Bibi tells me that you saved her life. I must thank you, cousin, for protecting my sister," he said.

"It was nothing. The highwayman was clumsy. He could not have been on the road long." She thought his hand tightened over hers, but the sensation was so brief that later she dismissed it as her imagination. The green eyes seemed to burn, and she wondered what he was thinking.

He released her hand and smiled. "It is awful that you were accosted on the road. I shudder to think how you must feel about our country after such rough treatment. How frightened you must have been."

"Actually, I rather enjoyed it. I assure you, Dominique, it was not difficult to scare him off. He did not have much courage and was really very inept." Christina thought his face looked strange, and she asked him politely if he was ill.

Dominique wondered idly how he would put this arrogant chit in her place. Now, looking at the provocative soft pink lips and the lovely planes of her face, an appropriate revenge came to mind immediately. The task would be an enjoyable one.

"Cousin Christina is a very remarkable girl, Dom," Bibi chimed in with enthusiasm.

"Yes, very," he agreed. His voice held a slight edge.

Sarcasm? Chris wondered to herself. Was it her imagination or did her handsome cousin seem . . . covertly hostile? Christina looked piercingly into Dominique's deep green eyes. She saw amusement lightly tinged with malice. Jake's ribs! What brought that queer mixture to his eyes?

Perplexed, she turned from him and took a seat near Gabrielle, who was now green with envy at the way

Dominique's gaze followed Christina. He never looked at her that way. In fact, she doubted he had ever noticed her at all. In that instant, Christina made an enemy.

Dominique turned to his sister. "There is a special performance at the opera tonight that I am sure you will like. The new tenor has the voice of one of the lord's angels. In view of your ordeal I think you should come with me. It will help you to forget what you have been through."

"Why, Dom, I'd love to. You have never taken me to the opera. It will be a very special occasion." She smiled at her brother.

Casually Dominique added, "And I'm sure our cousin would enjoy it, as well."

"*Mais, oui,*" Bibi agreed. "Christina, we will all go together, *n'est-ce pas?*"

Chris was not happy about spending an evening in Dom's company, but she did love the opera very much, so she said, "That would be very nice, cousin." She thought she saw a barely perceptible glint of triumph in Dom's eyes, but dismissed it as a trick of the light.

"We shall leave at eight. Do not be late, *chérie,*" he said to his sister. He nodded in Christina's direction, and with only the briefest glance at the other young women in the room, he left.

The garnet and silver carriage of the Marquis de Lasqueront was waiting promptly at a quarter of the hour. Christina had chosen a mauve velvet gown trimmed with rich brown sable. Bibi was wearing her favorite dress, a mist-green silk trimmed with ivory lace. They descended the long staircase together to join Dominique in the *grand salon.* He met them at the foot of the stairs, his eyes passing briefly over his sister and then settling for a disturbingly long time on Christina. He kept his face expressionless as he took in the gold hair and aquamarine eyes. Her figure is superb, he thought to himself as his eyes dipped for the briefest instant to the young curves visible above the fashionably low neckline of her gown.

"I shall be the most envied man at the opera," he said to Bibi. Then his eyes shifted to Christina's and communicated an altogether different meaning to the words.

Once in the carriage, Bibi chattered cheerfully of small things while Chris remained quiet, drinking in the heart-rendingly beautiful sight of Paris at night. She looked up when she felt Dominique's gaze on her.

"How did you come by your unusual skill with the rapier, cousin?" he asked.

"My father was very determined that I learn as much as possible. Much more than is generally deemed necessary for young girls. He taught me the use of the rapier and to sail and shoot as well."

"What an unusual education for a girl."

"My father was a very unusual man. He thought his daughter should be as well equipped as a lad in her ability to cope with whatever life had to offer."

"He was very successful in that respect, cousin," he said.

Dom was very charming, when he wished to be, she thought.

"What did you do with your time on the island?" he asked.

"Oh, the usual. I learned to play the spinet and to embroider. There were many young people in St.

Marin near my age. I have several . . . close friends there. After Mac . . . died," her voice caught, "I took over the Evrion interests in the shipbuilding and rum trade. My father's former legal adviser is now a partner, and we run Evrion Enterprises together." Christina delivered the last piece of information with no particular emphasis. It was an accepted part of her life now, one that she all but took for granted. Yet to Dominique, for whom leisure pursuits were a full-time occupation, her statements were incredible.

"Are you telling me that you actually work?" he asked, his perfectly arched eyebrows rising with surprise.

Chris smiled. "Yes. Actually. I work. I enjoy it. To me, it's more fun than embroidery or the spinet."

The concept of this striking beauty bending over the blueprints of a ship struck Dom as uproariously funny, certainly nothing to be taken seriously. He threw back his head and laughed loudly.

Christina bristled. In spite of his ridiculously handsome face, she felt she could easily come to dislike Dom intensely.

"Excuse me, cousin," he said between chuckles, "but the idea of a *jeune fille* like yourself running a shipping business is ludicrous. I could not help the laughter."

Christina said nothing. She merely watched his chuckling form silently.

The opera was crowded with the Parisian elite. Evidently the new tenor and soprano were a resounding success. She felt eyes turn toward them as Dominique led them to their box. "You see," he said as he took her cape, "it is as I said. There is not a man here who does not wish to be in my place at this moment."

The soprano was arrestingly lovely. Her hands punctuated the sweetness of her song in a manner that was wholly charming. Their box was very near the stage, and Christina could not help noticing how the young woman's face turned often toward Dominique, or the way in which her hands seemed to reach out to him.

Dominique quietly acknowledged a particularly well-done aria with a slight inclination of his blond head. The singer's joy was obvious. They know each other well, Christina thought and wondered idly how long the girl had been his mistress. She looked at Bibi. Her cousin was as enchanted as she with the soprano's song.

During the intermission several of Bibi's friends visited the Mauriere box to greet them. The young men seemed quite taken with Chris and made little attempt to disguise their admiration.

She flirted with several, enjoying the game. She was surprised when she turned briefly toward Dominique and found his eyes dark with displeasure, a scowl marring his perfect features. Wondering at the quick change in his mood, she raised a quizzical eyebrow at him. His face was instantly smooth. A strange one without question, Chris thought and turned her attention once more to the opera.

Behind her, she heard one of Dominique's friends say, "*L'Étoile* is in rare form tonight, isn't she? She seems to be singing just for you, Dominique."

He murmured something unintelligible in reply.

"I heard she was very upset when you vanished into thin air for two weeks. If you are tired of her, *mon ami*, I will gladly relieve you of your burden," his friend whispered.

Dominique's bored reply was barely audible. "She is yours, if you want her."

Christina couldn't resist glancing at his face. The handsome features were molded in an expression of cold indifference. She felt a stab of pity for the lovely young woman who looked up at him adoringly from the stage as she sang.

After the performance Dominique, Bibi, Christina, and their party stood for a moment in the box, chatting idly about the night's performance. Suddenly a young man who had not been sitting with them hurried up to Dominique and said urgently, "Dom, you should leave at once. I've just come from *L'Étoile*, and she is not rational. If you remain here, she'll . . ."

The young man stopped abruptly as a melodic but imperious voice cut the air sharply.

"Dominique!"

Christina watched in fascination as her cousin turned slowly to face the angry soprano with an air of lordly superiority. He did not answer her. He merely cocked one brown eyebrow.

"Dominique! Do not think I will stand for this!" she said with malice.

"I beg your pardon, mademoiselle. For what won't you stand?" he asked coolly.

"Do not play the simpleton with me, Dominique! I know where you have been and with whom! You would drop me with no word? Nothing!? You are more of a monster than they say. I will not be treated this way! Do you hear me?" she screamed.

"It is difficult not to hear you, *chérie*. You have an operatic voice. As for your treatment, it has been my experience that women like yourself receive the treatment they request, knowingly or unknowingly." His voice was ice.

"*Cochon!* I will have you shot. You will not do this, you will not! I . . ." The young woman raved on and on. Christina's cheeks were burning. She glanced at Bibi, who was blushing even more furiously. Dominique's scowl grew more and more menacing. Chris wondered at the woman's courage.

Dominique took the opera star's arm firmly and led her into a tiny closet on one side of the box and closed the door. His friends tactfully began to lead Bibi and Chris out of the theater. As they walked away, Chris could still hear the muffled sound of the young woman's voice. Suddenly she heard a sharp noise, like the sound of someone being slapped. As they left the theater, she heard the doleful sound of a woman's sobs.

"Oh, that Dominique!" Bibi cried in exasperation. "He always does this. As soon as he sees a more beautiful face, he discards his old paramour like a pair of old boots! *C'est terrible!*"

"Please, Bibi," pleaded Arnaud Rochefort, "you are too young to even know of such things, let alone discuss them."

"How can I not know with such a brother! He has been doing this since he was fourteen!"

Arnaud sighed. "*Oui, c'est vrai.* Our dear Dominique is sadly lacking in prudence, I'm afraid."

Christina considered that a serious understatement.

CHAPTER TWENTY-EIGHT

Dominique was absent from the marquis's Paris residence for a week following the heated quarrel at the opera. The search for the highwayman seemed all but hopeless and everyone began to believe that the thief had escaped. Chris deeply regretted the loss of the marquis's diamond stickpin, which had been lost in the battle.

Bibi had been very upset by their evening at the opera. "He is unbelievable. You cannot imagine the things he has done to the women who have loved him. They adore him because he is handsome, but as soon as they care, he discards them without a thought. Be careful, Christina. I have seen the way he looks at you. Dominique wants you, but for your own sake, stay away from him."

Chris had looked at her with something like astonishment. "Bibi, we're cousins!"

"That will not make any difference to my brother, Christina. Believe me, I know." Her eyes were sad and distant. Chris reached out and put her arm around her cousin. Words were not necessary.

That had been more than a week ago. It was easier to forget about Dominique than to ponder the complexities of his dark soul.

One night Chris had a hard time falling asleep. Her thoughts were troubled. The nervous edginess that had begun with the coach accident persisted. It was particularly strong tonight. She was also curious about how the Evrion interests were faring on St. Marin and, although she would not admit it to herself, she wanted news of Renault. In the privacy of her bedroom she wrote a letter to Andy Hardy, inquiring about the shipyard and bringing him up to date on her whereabouts.

The letter had a calming effect on her, but she was still too restless to go to sleep. Perhaps reading will make me drowsy, she thought. She donned a long scarlet robe of soft velvet trimmed with dark fur and tied in loosely at the waist. She left her bedroom and tiptoed quietly into the library. It was dark inside save for the dim light from the hall. She lit a candle, walked inside, and closed the large carved wooden doors behind her.

Its Gothic stillness was solemn and awe-inspiring in the flickering golden light of the candle. A wall filled with leather-bound volumes drew her attention. Carefully she poured over the literary collection in the large Lasqueront library. She chose a classical selection, knowing that it would soon put her to sleep, and began to read.

She had been at it for several minutes when she heard the doors creak open on their heavy hinges. Chris turned and saw the black outline of a man standing in the doorway, silhouetted against the light from the hall. The figure drew the library doors shut behind him and stepped toward her.

"Dominique," she whispered.

"The same, *chérie*," he said with a smile.

She was annoyed at him for frightening her. "You are supposed to be at the Chateau d'Anvireau. You might have said something sooner instead of standing in the doorway like a ghost and frightening me to death. Do you always stalk about so quietly?"

"First, I am not 'supposed to be' anywhere. And in answer to your second question, yes I do 'stalk about quietly' when it is late and the household is asleep. As for frightening you, I have never known a woman less given to fear."

"How would you know?" she asked drily.

"Ah, but I know a great deal about you, *chérie*. A very great deal."

Christina regarded him warily. The residual feelings of post-battle nerves were never more intense than when he was near.

Dominique laughed softly as he drew closer. Chris took a step backward. He stopped. "Surely you are not really frightened of me, Christina," he said silkily. "I mean you no harm. You know that, don't you?"

"Perhaps," she said.

"Perhaps? You are not sure?"

"Nothing is certain in this world, Dominique."

"A philosopher as well as a swordswoman, *chérie*. Your accomplishments never cease to amaze me." He moved casually to a richly upholstered wing chair and sat down. "Be at ease, cousin. I only wish to talk. It seems neither of us is able to sleep tonight. Perhaps together we can discover why."

Dominique looked formidable in the stately chair. He was wearing a severely cut blue waistcoat and dark gray pantaloons. His impeccably polished boots held and reflected the sparse light. Without consciously thinking of what she did, Christina lit another candle. She felt more secure when she could see him clearly.

"Are you afraid of the dark, cousin?"

"It's not the dark I fear. It is what hides in it that worries me."

The emerald-green eyes scrutinized her. "What are you running from, Christina?"

Christina drew in her breath. "I'm not running from anything. Perhaps I am searching for something. But I am not running away . . . from anything. On the contrary, I am running to it."

"You mean to someone?"

"No, I don't believe it is a person."

"Then what is it you seek?"

"I'm not sure yet."

"How will you know when you've found it?"

"I . . . don't know exactly . . . but I do feel that once I've found it, I will know."

"You speak in riddles."

"You ask questions that are not easily answered."

"Your behavior makes me wonder about you. You are different from most young women your age. Tell me about your life—where you have been, where you come from."

"I grew up on St. Marin, as you know. Beyond that, everything is very simple. What you see before you is basically all there is to see."

"I like what I see—very much."

Uncomfortable with the direction their conversation was taking, she turned away from him and went back to the wall covered with books. "It is late. Bibi and I are leaving early tomorrow to visit Gabrielle de Vezy."

When she turned again, she stifled a gasp. He was directly in front of her, his emerald-green eyes intense and dark. Dominique took advantage of her temporary immobility to pull her into his arms. When her lips parted to object, his mouth closed over hers, and he felt her body go stiff with stunned surprise.

Christina couldn't grasp what was happening. I'm asleep, she thought wildly. In the morning this will be no more than a bad dream. But a calm voice in the back of her head told her that this was as real as the sea in St. Marin. A small detached part of her subconscious instinctively compared this kiss to the ones she had known before. This one was scorching—forceful to the point of pain. Dominique's hard lips nearly bruised her mouth with the intensity of his passion. There was no gentleness in his need. It was detached, aloof, and impersonal—for all its fire. The hard body that held her tightly failed to bring the warm swell of sensation she had known so often with—why did she think of him in this moment? But he filled her thoughts. She realized that the long-ago sensations she remembered were those she'd known in the embrace of Kade Renault.

Then Dominique's arms tightened about her so painfully that a gasp of protest escaped her throat, and she struggled with him until she succeeded in freeing her arm. Christina struck him with all the force she could muster. He backed away, his arms relaxing their painful hold on her.

"Well done, Christina," he said in a voice deep with passion. "For a first kiss, *chérie*, that was more than satisfactory." But his handsome smile had lost all charm for her.

She was angry. Yet her voice was steady as she said, "It was also the last kiss. If you touch me again, you will find yourself minus both your hands."

He angered her further by bowing with exaggerated grace. "I acknowledge the challenge. And accept it, Christina . . . with pleasure."

Warily, she stepped around him and paused in the

door to add as she left, "I meant what I said, Dominique."

When she had gone, Dominique smiled to himself and said softly, "So did I, *chérie*. So did I."

CHAPTER TWENTY-NINE

In Scotland, Kade Renault listened as his brother Bryce recounted what had transpired in Brenkirk during the ten years he was away. As he sat in the great hall of MacVeagh Castle listening to his younger brother, it was still hard for him to accept the quirk of fate that placed the title on his shoulders. He was indeed Sir Kincaid Renault, Eighth Earl of Brenkirk and Lord of Castle MacVeagh, yet inside, his soul was as restless and independent as ever it had been on the high seas aboard the *Falcon.*

Renault remembered the constriction in his throat on the day he had returned to Brenkirk as his eyes fell on Castle MacVeagh, rising above the green hills like a tall gray mountain, its high towers and spired turrets clearly visible through the highland mist. He led the Corsairs in a solemn procession to his ancestral home.

Now, in the huge main hall of the castle, he sat listening to Bryce, the red-haired younger brother who had idolized him as a child.

Brenkirk had fared well in his absence. The crops from the farms had been bountiful and the livestock healthy and thriving. Hunting was good, and the land prospered greatly. Therein lay the source of the crisis they faced. The prosperity of Brenkirk had not gone unnoticed by their unscrupulous northern neighbor, the Earl of Morwell. During the past year, raiding parties had been sent to Brenkirk to steal sheep and livestock and terrorize the small towns and farmers. It was clear that Garrick of Morwell wanted a pretext for a full-scale war which he hoped to win, gaining Brenkirk and its castle in the process.

In the coming weeks the new lord of Brenkirk organized a small, specially trained army of well-chosen men, led by the Corsairs and his brothers, Bryce and Barry.

Kade's twin brothers were younger by four years, but they possessed all the strength, courage, and cunning that had characterized the Renault clan for generations. Kade's memory of his mother was dim. She had died of pneumonia shortly after his seventh birthday, and the old earl had not remarried.

Renault planned to surprise Lord Morwell in his hunting lodge near the border and deal with him before the wily earl had a chance to provoke a clan war. With Jacques LaCroix and Logan Armor leading the advance parties, the plan had a good chance of succeeding. Guy Savant would not be going with them. Renault had another job for him.

One day when the Corsairs were in the earl's private rooms discussing the details of the attack, Renault drew Savant aside and said, "I have a special task for you, Guy."

Savant looked at Renault with curiosity. "You have but to name it," he replied.

"The young hellion I married is in France. This war prevents me from retrieving her and giving her the reward she deserves from me. Though there are matters I must attend to here, it is my intention to leave for France as soon as this business is done. I want you to locate her exact whereabouts and send word back to me. When this matter is settled, Jacques and I will join you. Until then, keep an eye on her and see that she stays out of trouble."

Savant smiled. The reunion between those two would make a war seem tame in comparison. "Consider it done, my friend. A holiday in France is just what I need." Guy chuckled softly to himself as he left Renault. My God, he thought, the man cannot forget her even with the threat of war hanging over our heads. I would wager a monkey that the next time he finds her, she will never get away from him again.

Two months later, at the Paris residence of the Marquis de Lasqueront, Bibi and Christina prepared to attend a party at the home of the Baron de Vezy, Gabrielle's father. Bibi was very excited about this soirée. She was quite taken with a young protégé of the baron's, a lieutenant named René Duvall. Chris watched her change the gown she would wear four times and rearrange her entire hairdo twice.

At the baron's residence Bibi lost no time in catching René's eyes. She exerted all her charm to hold the interest of the tall, attractive officer, and the effect was considerable. Christina watched with amusement as the young man lost his heart. Her attention wandered after several minutes of observing their game, and she began to survey the room, taking note of the guests. The salon was small, richly appointed, and filled with beautiful young men and women infused with the excitement and *joie de vivre* of the Parisian spring. Everywhere she looked she saw young couples falling in love. Even the chaperones seemed moved by the season as they leniently looked the other way. She turned her attention again to Bibi. Her cousin looked sublimely happy, gazing up adoringly at young Duvall. For the moment Bibi had her heart's desire.

A ripple of excitement seemed to pass through the room. Christina sensed a change in the atmosphere and looked around to find its source. As she watched, Dominique Mauriere, tall and blond, strode into the room with his accustomed air of perversely compelling insouciance. He never fails to cause a stir, she thought as she watched Gabrielle de Vezy's eyes follow him like magnets. Christina noted the determination in Gabrielle's gaze and thought wryly that the arrogant Mauriere would notice Mademoiselle de Vezy tonight or else.

The room was growing stuffy. Christina felt the need for air. She walked through the double glass doors that led to the courtyard and walked into the gardens outside. It was a warm spring night, and she thought she could hear a nightingale singing in the distance. A voice behind her said, "Well, Christina, I might have known I'd find you in a garden." Chris turned around and stared as if she were seeing a ghost.

Guy Savant laughed aloud at the expression on her face. "What's the matter, madame? Has my nose suddenly developed a wart?"

"Guy!" she exclaimed. "What are you doing here?"

"Enjoying the baron's soirée," he replied.

Christina shook herself mentally. "The last time I saw you, you were in St. Marin with . . ."

"Your husband?" He grinned devilishly.

She swallowed. "Yes, with . . ." she couldn't bring herself to say "my husband" . . . "with Renault. Is he . . . he's not . . . with you . . . is he?"

"No," Guy replied.

Chris suppressed a sigh of relief. She braced herself and asked, "Where is he?"

"In Scotland." Christina's stomach rolled with apprehension. Scotland was far too close! "He is attend-

ing to some . . . family matters. Forgive my bold-
ness, my dear, but if you had to make this journey,
wouldn't it have been better to do it with him along?"

She shook her head. "It was something I had to do
alone, Guy."

Savant looked at her. After a moment he said, "I
suppose you have your reasons."

"I do. I can't explain why, but the time I've spent
here, all of it, has been very important to me."

Savant nodded, thinking that Renault certainly had
his hands full with this one. But if he had to make a
wager and choose between them, he would put his
money on Renault. Guy looked toward the salon
where the strains of a waltz had just begun. "Madame,
would you honor me with this dance?" he asked with
a courtly bow.

Unwilling to let her mind dwell on Renault's disturbing proximity to Paris, Christina accepted with
enthusiasm.

Savant was an excellent dancer, and his witty conversation kept Christina in smiles and giggles for most
of the evening.

Dominique Mauriere watched his beautiful cousin
and the tall elegant courtier with growing displeasure.
He had not seen her laugh or smile so freely and with
such abandon since the day he had met her. Much to
his annoyance he realized he was jealous. And the irritating girl at his side was growing extremely tiresome.

Gabrielle de Vezy felt a happiness she had never
known before. She had managed to catch Dominique's
eye and he had asked her to dance. How often had
she dreamed of that! She conversed with him in a
voice she barely recognized as her own. When he

asked her to dance a second time, she knew she was close to heaven.

She looked up at him now as he stood next to her. As always, she found his handsome, bored face irresistible—the noble square chin, the clear green eyes, the finely chiseled lines of his face, carved so delicately that the effect of its beauty was nearly feminine in its calm perfection. The stern, brooding expression he wore now made her want to watch him forever.

Dominique did not notice the adoring girl beside him. His thoughts were of Christina; he was trying to imagine a way to exorcise the girl from his blood. She circled the room in a waltz, swirling in pale green silk and voile, a cloud of hair floating behind her as the courtier turned her in the steps of the dance. Dominique was always amazed when he remembered that he had actually dueled with that whimsical, provocative creature—held her at sword point and nearly run her through. It was difficult to imagine how those soft-looking arms had been strong enough to wield a rapier with such authority. She had actually possessed the speed and agility to elude his guard long enough to pierce his shoulder with her sword. He still owed her for that. The ache in his loins was a constant reminder of the retribution he planned to exact.

Dominique heard a soft voice address him. He looked down at Gabrielle. She was suggesting that they retire to the courtyard for a breath of fresh air. Grateful for the opportunity to put his disturbing cousin out of his mind, Dom favored her with a smile that made her heart obediently roll over like a small, happy puppy. Gabrielle was sure this was the happiest night of her life.

When he returned to the ball he saw Christina and Bibi preparing to leave. The tall courtier was bending attentively over his cousin, smiling at her and whispering something in her ear that made her laugh deliciously. Dominique knew a stab of jealousy so intense that he began to walk toward the man menacingly, with half-formed thoughts of issuing a challenge, but he stopped himself midway across the room. A more fitting—and far more pleasant—revenge occurred to him.

Christina and Bibi rode home in their carriage, animatedly discussing the De Vezy ball. Suddenly Chris heard three shots ring out and the sound of heavy objects hitting the ground, quickly followed by the moans of wounded men. There was a moment of tense silence and then the door to their carriage was ripped open by a powerful man. A tall, hooded figure regarded them silently. Christina recognized the notorious highwayman immediately and cursed under her breath. She was unarmed, and their attendants lay wounded in the road. They were totally vulnerable. Bibi began to cry. The highwayman produced a length of rope and bound Christina's hands behind her back. Her heart sank as he took a cloth from his cape and tied a thick blindfold over her eyes.

She felt herself lifted bodily from the carriage and carried some distance away. The brush of pine needles against her skin and the snapping twigs beneath the man's feet told her that he was taking her into the woods.

Never in her life had she felt so helpless or so angry at her own weakness. The highwayman laid her down on the forest floor, and when she attempted to get away, she found herself locked inside a powerful embrace. Warm hands delved into the low neckline of her gown, fondling her breasts as two hot insistent lips parted her own. She arched indignantly, pressing away from him, but his hard form followed her movements, and he tightened his hold as she struggled to evade him. She felt him shift his weight and cover her completely with his lean, hard body. The highwayman's hand worked through her multi-layered skirts and tore her lace pantelettes in two. She heard him catch his breath and release it slowly as he looked at her, spreading her legs wide apart despite her considerable efforts to prevent it. Anger welled red inside her as she felt an unwelcome hand caressing her womanhood, his relentless fingers stroking and squeezing, then invading the very center of her being. She began to scream, but found her cries quickly muffled by his hungry mouth.

In the distance, a faint noise like galloping horses pierced her consciousness. It sounded like—yes, it was—another coach! The highwayman seemed oblivious to the sound. She forced her body to go pliant. The man relaxed his grip somewhat. The coach was getting near—Christina could hear it clearly. Suddenly she wrenched her mouth away from his and screamed at the top of her lungs.

The driver had already slowed the coach to inspect the bloody scene in the road. Her cry brought the running footsteps of two burly coach guards crashing into the woods. The highwayman cursed and stood up quickly. He hesitated for an instant as he watched Christina sit up and adjust her clothing as best she could with her hands bound. Then, not wanting to take on two men in the confining wooded space, he turned and sprinted with amazing speed for his waiting horse.

By the time the guards reached her, Chris was cursing out loud. They untied her hands and removed her blindfold, freeing her to readjust her bodice, and then helped her back to the carriage. By now the highwayman was long gone.

When news reached Scotland that Guy had located Christina in Paris, Kade Renault was concluding a victorious raid on Garrick of Morwell. The new earl forced Morwell to sign a treaty that declared his own lands forfeit should he cross the northern borders of Brenkirk with armed men. The raid had been very successful. Few casualties were sustained by the Earl of Brenkirk's men.

Renault was particularly proud of the way Bryce had led a flank attack on Morwell's hunting lodge. The timing had been perfect, even though the Corsair assigned to give the signal to begin the attack had been wounded prematurely and had been unable to alert his brother. Led by pure instinct, Bryce had sensed the right moment and led the charge in time.

Renault grew ever more impressed by his brother's good sense. They had been very close as children, before the elder MacVeagh ordered Renault away. Fate played strange tricks. Kade was never reared to be the earl. He grew up as wild and free as the wind. But Bryce, like Jamie, was a homebound man who needed the stability of Brenkirk and MacVeagh Castle. Renault had decided soon after becoming earl to share with Bryce the responsibility of running Castle MacVeagh and the kirk and set about grooming him for the position. He knew that the land and the family's ancestral home would be in good hands with Bryce when his travels took him elsewhere. Bryce would guard the land and maintain the castle with his last breath. Renault would have time to continue the revenue-making enterprises he had begun in the New World—and also to find the errant young beauty who filled his nights with dreams and, much to his chagrin, half his waking moments as well. Renault made plans to pay a visit to the Marquis de Lasqueront.

Christina grew increasingly wary of Dom. Since the night of the Baron de Vezy's soirée, his pursuit of her had grown more intense. He was subtle. Neither the marquis or marquise suspected what he was up to. Only Bibi seemed to sense Dominique's interest in their cousin. Both of the girls were very upset over the latest incident with the highwayman. Little Arielle, Bibi's younger sister, thought that the man was exciting, but the rest of the household was appalled. Everyone except Dominique, thought Christina. He had listened to the tale with his usual casual indifference. Yet his eyes followed her covertly from the moment she entered a room. When Christina looked at him he didn't bother to disguise the desire that burned in their emerald-green depths. Instead he often pursed his finely shaped mouth ever so slightly in the form of a kiss. It incensed Chris, and he knew it. It was too small a motion to attract the notice of others, but his meaning was more than plain to her.

One morning she awoke to find the air cool and fragrant and the sun dawning in a crystal-blue sky. It was going to be a glorious spring day, the kind the memory cherished in the dead of winter when the world was frozen and gray. A day like this was meant to be spent in the garden. Chris put on a soft, mint-green robe. It was too early for breakfast—the rest of the household was still asleep. Quietly, she tiptoed down the long staircase, into the courtyard and out to the garden beyond.

There were green hedges and flowers everywhere. She closed her eyes and breathed in the cool green scent, listening to the birds and their morning song. A sound behind her disturbed the tranquility of the moment. She was about to open her eyes when two hands grasped her shoulders and spun her abruptly around. She looked up into the passionate green gaze of Dominique. His face grew enormously large and swam before her, as he lowered his mouth to hers.

His arms were twin bands of iron as he held her pinned against him. Grimly she struggled, desperately seeking a way to break his hold. But Dominique countered her movements very effectively. He grasped her arms and twisted them behind her, shifting both her wrists to one hand. She felt him part the thin material of her robe and slowly pull down her shift, exposing one soft, rounded breast. His hand cupped it eagerly, closing and squeezing with none too gentle a grip. He teased the nipple to tautness with his fingers as she squirmed uncomfortably against him. Using all her strength, she managed to rip her mouth from his.

"Stop it, Dominique!" she whispered fiercely.

His arm tightened around her as he lifted his head to gaze into her stormy turquoise eyes. His hand continued to fondle her breast, grazing the nipple so often with his fingertips that it became sore and tender.

His eyes were half closed with desire, and his face was so close to hers that she could feel his warm breath against her skin. The heat of her body seared him as it burned through the material of his robe. Dimly he thanked the luck that had made him too restless to sleep and left him awake at the window when she came into the garden. She was a fever in his blood now. The feel of her with so little clothing between them was a heady balm for his tortured body. It made him realize that he needed her softness and warmth as much as food or water. He lowered his head again, ignoring Chris's angry words as his mouth took hers, molding her body to his.

The sound of stirrings beyond the courtyard made him reluctantly release her. Christina's face was a mask of cold anger, and he thought of the night he had ripped the black domino from her face as she lay before him on the forest floor. Her turquoise eyes had held the same cold fury than that they did now. It reminded him of a dangerous animal, ready to run, or to spring. He could not tell which.

This time Christina chose to run. It was no good trying to fight him here in her nightgown with the rest of the household about to awaken. There would be a better place and a better time to deal with this savage, she promised herself. For now, the wisest course was retreat.

Dominique watched her small green figure as she disappeared beyond the courtyard. He felt a stirring inside that was unfamiliar and strangely pleasant. Somehow the knowledge that she was nearby, that he would see her during the day, was a source of exhilaration and happiness. The feeling was alien to him. He followed her path through the gardens, brooding silently.

CHAPTER THIRTY

After that morning, Christina made sure she was not alone with Dominique. She avoided meeting his eyes when he was present, but she could feel his silent green gaze following her movements in a room.

She thought seriously of leaving. She had been in Paris almost a year, and it would always be part of her heart. She loved its beauty, its life. It was more than she had ever dreamed. Not for anything in the world would she have missed the opportunity of seeing first-hand the opera, the ballet, and the theater. But a growing restlessness inside her told her that it was time to move on. There were other places to see and people to meet. Blaise had missed much; she knew that now. But Christina was not going to miss a thing, not if she could help it.

She had begun to have a queer feeling about Dominique, a kind of *déjà vu*. It was as if he knew what she would do before she did it, as if he had known her in some other place and time, and that knowledge gave him an insight into her thoughts, her feelings, and the way she reacted to the world. That was impossible, of course, but she felt it just the same. She had never set eyes on him before that day in Bibi's apartments. Whatever the cause of these feelings, Chris knew she had to leave soon.

Bibi was the only one in the household who was aware of what was going on inside Chris. One day she said, "You will be going soon, won't you, Christina?"

Chris did not bother to lie. Bibi saw the situation

too clearly to dissemble with her. "Yes," she said simply.

"Is it Dominique?"

Christina nodded.

Bibi sighed. "I thought so. His eyes follow you everywhere. You are wise to go. He will not rest until he makes you his. Would that I had been able to leave as you will do."

Christina looked at her cousin silently, with understanding and sympathy. She did not speak; there was nothing to say.

The marquis received an invitation to attend a hunt at the country chateau of his close friend, the Baron d'Anvireau. Therese thought it would be lovely to bring Bibi and Christina as well. When she proposed the holiday the girls agreed readily. The marquise was surprised when her sophisticated son casually mentioned that he would also enjoy the opportunity to spend some time with his friend Paul Anvireau, the baron's son.

"But you have visited him five times in the past three months, my son, have you not?" Therese asked.

"One can never see good friends too often, maman. Do you object to my accompanying you?" he asked.

"Mais, non, I was only surprised," she replied, still wondering at his unprecedented behavior.

The marquis's party set off for Chateau d'Anvireau in the blue and gold of a bright spring day in April. The garnet and silver livery of the carriages made an impressive retinue against the sun-kissed green fields of the French countryside. Christina and Bibi had a carriage to themselves. Dominique chose to make most of the trip astride his blooded stallion, Saladin, but when they were a few miles from the chateau, he ordered their carriage to stop, tied his horse to the back, and got in beside Christina. There was only one banquette in the carriage, and with all three of them sitting there the fit was rather snug. Christina was wedged uncomfortably in the middle. Dominique turned his body toward her slightly, ostensibly to provide greater comfort. She noted with irritation that it brought her back in close proximity with his chest, and his head so near her own that when he turned to look out the opposite window, his lips brushed against her cheek. When Bibi's head was turned, he took the opportunity to press soft, nibbling kisses along the line of her jaw.

Once she turned to ask if he had no sense of propriety or shame at all, only to find that her lips and not her cheek became the subject of his unruly mouth. She drew away quickly, staring at him with shocked indignation. He smiled and whispered, "I know, I know. You are incensed with me for my lack of discretion. But see behind you, *chérie*. My sister is asleep."

It was true. Chris looked at Bibi. Her eyes were closed, and her breathing was deep and regular.

Christina prodded her awake without a second thought. "Are we there?" Bibi asked drowsily.

"No, darling," Chris replied. "But your neck will be sore if you continue to sleep in that position."

She thought she heard Dominique chuckle beside her, and she fervently wished he was under the wheels of the carriage rather than in it.

The Chateau d'Anvireau loomed into sight. It was a stunningly beautiful, massive brown stone structure with red-roofed turrets and several graceful towers. It stood out against the surrounding farm land like a proud old courtier guarding his domain. The tranquil, pastoral beauty of the peaceful hamlet at the base of the chateau tugged at her heartstrings. The ancient building itself was flanked by water on three sides. Graceful bridges connected the grounds of the chateau with the surrounding countryside.

When they stepped from their carriages within the grounds of the estate, a liveried servant escorted them into the chateau. Paul Anvireau greeted them jovially and invited them into a large salon where the Baron d'Anvireau was receiving his guests. While the marquis and the baron stepped aside to greet each other and briefly discuss old times, Christina surveyed the guests. Paul and Dominique stood in one corner of the room laughing with Arnaud Rochefort and several other young men that she didn't recognize. The Baron de Vezy was here with his baroness and their daughter, Gabrielle, who was casting subtle looks in Dominique's direction. Bibi had begged the marquis to arrange an invitation for her beloved René Duvall. Christina saw Duvall chatting with another young lieutenant near their age. Clothilde Theroux and her family, the Marquis and Marquise d'Orlaise, arrived minutes later. All in all, Christina decided, the week might prove to be diverting.

The guests retired to their rooms to repair and dress for dinner. Chris found herself in the rose wing with Bibi, Clothilde, and Gabrielle.

Bibi was happy that René was so near. "Isn't it wonderful, Christina?" she exclaimed. "I'll see him every day for a whole week."

Gabrielle de Vezy had similar feelings about the proximity of Bibi's brother. She had been encouraged by the attention he had shown at her father's soirée.

Now was the perfect time to encourage the dalliance to blossom into something more. Mentally she dismissed the possibility of waiting any longer. Although she was not a bold young woman or even a very brave one, the love she felt for Dominique made her want to discard caution and bare her feelings. He was so aloof and distant, there really was no other way. She decided that somehow she would contrive to speak with him at dinner and let him know just how deeply she cared. Long ago she had made up her mind to become his wife and eventually the future Marquise de Lasqueront.

Gabrielle donned a pastel pink gown of cloudlike voile that went well with her chestnut-colored hair and brown eyes. She pinched her cheeks for color and made Clothilde choose a hair style for her. She could never decide the small details and was at heart a shy, nice, plain girl. Everyone liked her and thought of her as a little sister.

An elegant dinner awaited the Baron d'Anvireau's guests. Paul Anvireau escorted Christina into the majestic dining area of the chateau. Owing to the formality of the occasion, Christina had allowed Cecile to pin up her long, dark gold mane in one of the fashionable Parisian styles. Bibi walked dreamily on the arm of René Duvall, who seemed very content to have her there. Only Dominique was discontent with the dining arrangements, although he hid it well. As he walked at Gabrielle's side, only those who knew him intimately could discern the brooding intensity beneath his reserved, aloof demeanor.

Dinner was superb and Paul was very entertaining. He had a cutting wit and an intriguing turn of phrase that kept Chris amused the entire evening. She did not even notice Dominique's steady green gaze or the faint scowl that clouded his keen features.

When Christina left Paul to join Bibi, Dominique pulled his friend aside and said quietly, "You seem intrigued with my cousin, *mon ami.*"

Paul smiled at him. "She is very beautiful, is she not? I find her *très charmante.*"

Dominique's eyes narrowed imperceptibly. "*Écoutez bien*, she is not for you."

Paul looked surprised. "But Dominique, as your friend and peer, I could not be objectionable . . ."

"Where she is concerned, everyone is objectionable to me, understand?"

Paul regarded him silently for a moment before he said, "Perfectly, Dominique."

"Dominique?" a voice behind him said softly. It was Gabrielle.

"Yes?" he said vaguely, preoccupied with other thoughts. Paul Anvireau bid them good evening and departed.

"I . . . there is an important matter . . . that I would like to discuss with you. It . . . it is too urgent to wait until morning, and we must talk alone. Could you . . . meet me in the courtyard near the marble statue under the grape arbor . . . at eleven?"

Dominique regarded this shy young woman with a mixture of amusement and frustration. She was so young and inexperienced—the invitation was so obvious—that it barely escaped being gauche. Here was a little brown wren saying, "Take me, please," when what he really wanted was the exotic golden creature that eluded capture at every turn. Still, the week would be long without a woman, and this one was

clearly available and as good as any he was likely to
find at a local inn. He had never been one to worry
over a girl's station in life. If she awakened desire in
him, he took her. It was as simple as that.

"With pleasure, *chérie*," he answered and raised her
hand briefly to his lips.

Gabrielle felt as if the floor had risen beneath her
feet and the room was suddenly ascending into the
clouds. She smiled at him radiantly and blushed as
she turned to walk quickly up the stairs. Dominique
watched her go, wishing for all the world that she had
tawny gold hair and sea-blue eyes.

It took some maneuvering for Gabrielle to elude
Clothilde and the chaperones in the women's quarters
of the chateau, but she managed. She would have
managed anything to meet Dominique tonight. She
wore a dark cloak that covered her hair and face. Indeed, it was impossible to tell she was a woman. Even
so, she narrowly missed being discovered by a footman who surprised her as he turned a corner, apparently to deliver cognac to the room of one of the barons. She ducked into a doorway and emerged only
when she heard him close the door.

Once in the garden, she walked swiftly toward the
pale outline of the marble statue of Zeus beneath the
grape arbor in a secluded section of trees. As she drew
nearer she could see Dominique's tall outline in the
dark, his face calm and knowing.

He was so handsome standing there beside the
statue of a god that in her mind he surpassed that divine being, and for a moment she was unable to find
her voice. He watched her, his eyes faintly amused,
vaguely bored.

"Dominique . . . I," she began, but he interrupted her.

"Don't talk," he said as he drew her into his arms.

Gabrielle's world reeled as she felt his mouth cover hers. How many nights had she imagined his kiss, longed for the feel of his lips on hers? If this was a dream, she prayed she would never rise again.

Dominique's hands moved quickly to remove the voluminous black cloak. They were concealed by the thick leaves of the grape arbor and the darkness. But Gabrielle would not have cared if all Paris was watching. Tonight she was in the arms of her love, and the rest of the world ceased to exist.

She felt his hand searching, exploring, and discovering the forbidden curves of her body as she pressed closer against him, wishing she could move entirely inside him, become part of him and never leave him again, ever. The cool night air washed over her neck and shoulders. Her nightgown dropped below her waist, released by some magic he worked with his hands.

As he touched her she wished she could see him. Only the top of his blond head was visible as he bent to kiss her. Timidly she touched the fair curls. In her most abandoned moments of imagination, she had never envisioned a pleasure like this, so intense, so engulfing, and so wonderfully, soaringly private.

She didn't know exactly how it happened, but somehow they were lying in the grass at the base of the marble statue. The sea god seemed to leer down at her, and she grew suddenly afraid. Her gown disappeared completely, and the drew-covered grass was cold and wet against her back.

Dominique lay over her, and she felt something rock hard and searing press against her tender softness. "Dominique . . . ," she said haltingly. "Dominique . . . I don't . . . no . . . I didn't mean to . . ."

"Quiet," he said sharply. His voice was hard and unfeeling, like that of a stranger. She recoiled inwardly and made a feeble attempt to push him away.

He growled. Grasping her by the shoulders, he shook her until she thought her neck would snap. "What do you take me for?" he said harshly. "A callow youth? A schoolboy you can tease and leave at will?" He released her shoulders and grasped her wrists, drawing her arms above her head and securing them with one hand. "You asked me to come here and you have wanted this for a long time. Well . . . now you will have what you sought. But spare me your pious airs. I cannot abide hypocrisy."

His words stung, and she whimpered as she felt him again pressing into her. Then he lunged deeply. She was not ready for him, and he hurt her badly. Involuntarily, she started to scream. His hand struck her across the cheek. "Be quiet! Do you want them to find you under me?" He covered her mouth with his free hand, and she moaned as he tore into her, in and out, tearing and bruising her reluctant body. He was huge, quite too large for her really, and the agony was so great that she nearly fainted. She felt his movements grow more rapid as he shuddered and rammed into her several times. Her mind went completely blank against the white shocks of pain that exploded inside her. Then, mercifully, she felt him relax, and it was over.

When the pain began to subside, and she was capable of limited rational thought, she reached up to tentatively touch his face. He stirred and sat up, leaving her feeling empty and alone. His face was expressionless, and he seemed to pause to get his bearings. Now that the pain was gone, she wanted to talk, to tell him that she loved him in spite of the hurt and to hear him say that he cared. She wanted to know when they could marry.

"Dominique, I love you," she said softly, waiting quietly for his answer. Silence greeted her declaration. She held her breath, but his face remained stony and unmoving. She wondered what was wrong. Finally she ventured, "Did you hear, *mon cher*? I don't care what they say about you. You are not what they think. I have loved you since the first day we met. I knew even then that someday we would be together, just as we are now. Oh, Dominique, I don't want to wait! Tell me how soon we can be married. Could we do it quickly? Oh, do say yes. I don't think I can bear to be near you and not be able to do this, to love you."

A muffled laugh greeted her pleadings. Startled, she stared at him, unable to comprehend the source of his mirth.

"What kind of fool do you take me for? I have no intention of marrying you. Or acknowledging in any other way that we've been together. Is that clear?"

"You mean . . . you . . . don't intend to marry me?"

"My dear innocent, I could not possibly marry every virgin I have taken."

"But don't you care for me?"

"Of course. Having you has been very pleasant. Perhaps one day we will do this again."

"But I love you!"

He made a movement of annoyance. "Grow up, Gabrielle," he said. Then he added reasonably, "This has been an enjoyable interlude, *chérie*, and I am grateful, but I never said I loved you." Tired and anxious to be away from her, he spoke more bluntly. "You mean nothing to me. Now get dressed and go back to your bed, as I intend to do. Good night."

How long Gabrielle lay in the chill grass, she couldn't tell. She only knew her legs refused to walk and she felt numb and abused. Yet the pain that caused streams of hot tears to flow down her cheeks came not from her body but from her heart.

CHAPTER THIRTY-ONE

The morning's hunt had gone particularly well. The Marquis de Lasqueront and the Baron d'Anvireau were in excellent spirits as they rode back to the chateau. Christina rode beside them this morning. She was wearing a blue velvet riding habit that made Paul Anvireau compare her to Diana, goddess of the hunt. She was troubled by her musings as she rode, but she kept one ear trained to their conversation.

"Ah, I see my last guest has arrived," said the baron as he viewed the black and gold liveried carriage standing in the courtyard of the chateau. "You have not met him yet, Charles," he said to the marquis. "A most unusual man and a very wealthy one, thanks to some very shrewd investments in the New World. I hope to interest him in a joint venture with me. He recently inherited a title of his own in Scotland."

"Who is he, Etienne?" the Marquis de Lasqueront asked.

"Sir Kincaid Renault, the eighth Earl of Brenkirk," said the baron.

Christina could hardly believe her ears. She couldn't have heard him correctly. With an effort she calmed down and tried to reassure herself. There must be many Renaults in Scotland. Perhaps this was a different man. At least she hoped so.

As their horses drew near the carriage, she saw that its occupant had just alighted. With an ominous rumbling in the pit of her stomach, Christina followed the two noblemen as their horses rounded the carriage.

The man was speaking to his groom, his back turned toward them. But even from behind, Christina recognized the tall broad shoulders and curly black head of Kade Renault.

Her first impulse was to ride quickly away and explain later, but Renault turned as he heard the sound of their horses, and as if by instinct, gazed straight at Christina. Blue eyes met turquoise as he looked at her for a long moment. Her face was a mixture of incredulity, consternation, and faint hope that by some grace of God he would not reveal their true relationship to one another. But as she looked into his azure eyes, she found neither sympathy nor compassion. And in truth, she had not expected to.

The tanned face that regarded her was as handsome and sardonic as ever. If anything, time had improved the clean, chiseled perfection of his even features and the strong square line of his jaw. He was wearing deep brown traveling clothes, impeccably cut and tailored. The great riding cape he wore emphasized his height and the powerful breadth of his chest and shoulders.

"*Bonjour,* Renault," she managed. Her voice was barely audible.

"Hello, Christina," Kade said in the deep voice she remembered well. "We meet again," he added drily.

The Marquis de Lasqueront and the Baron d'Anvireau watched this interchange with interest. From the moment the Earl of Brenkirk had caught sight of Christina his gaze had not wavered from her face, and the intensity of his regard was most intriguing. He had not acknowledged the presence of the two distinguished noblemen with even a glance. Charles Mauriere cleared his throat tactfully.

"I see that you have met our cousin," he said politely.

Christina cringed inwardly. She tensed, waiting for Kade's reply. Was he going to reveal everything or by some miracle be mercifully silent? She searched his eyes intently and found no softness whatsoever in them. Instead there was only a thin smile of pleasure at having her totally in his power.

Kade turned to the Marquis de Lasqueront and favored him with the dazzling smile that was famous on two continents. "Christina and I are old. *amis*, Charles," he replied. "Your young cousin is also a relative of mine—in a manner of speaking. You see, we have been married, secretly, for two years. You have the dubious honor of witnessing a long overdue reunion with my dear prodigal wife."

Christina had never really fainted before, but this seemed like the perfect time to begin. The courtyard whirled, and she felt herself begin to slip from her mount. Renault was beside her in seconds. To her chagrin, she could not prevent herself from slipping lanquidly into his arms. The last thing she saw was Kade's handsome countenance peering down at her as he observed, "You are such a coward, my dear."

Much later, when Christina opened her eyes, she didn't recognize the room she was in. She lay on a huge bed. The furnishings of the room were typical of the chateau, but this room appeared more masculine. The chairs and desk were of massive polished wood, not like the delicate chaise and pastel curtains of her own accommodations at D'Anvireau. She heard a voice say, "Welcome back. Isn't it a pity we can't make our problems disappear by just falling asleep?"

Christina looked up at the impassive face of Kade

Renault. "Why did they put me in here with you?" she asked sourly.

"Because they are intelligent men and know that there is no reason for me to lie about our marriage."

"I could swear to them that you lied."

"That would be very unwise. In my present state of mind I need very little excuse to beat you senseless. If I were you, sweet, I would not entertain the notion of denying anything—and if anyone asks, you will confirm the truth."

"No."

Kade's eyes frosted to a glacial blue. She watched in immobile disbelief as he calmly raised his hand and slapped her—hard. Christina raised her hand to cool her burning right cheek. She couldn't believe he had actually struck her. When he spoke, his voice was smooth and deliberate.

"You haven't been listening. Pay attention this time. As I said, I would cheerfully break your neck for the price of a thimble. I advise you not to provoke a man who has already been tempted to strangle you for being a conniving, unfeeling bitch. Did you hear me, Christina?"

She nodded mutely.

"Good. I see we understand each other." He smiled drily. "It's the first time." He stood up to remove his great cape. "Your things will be moved in here. This will be our room for the rest of our stay at the chateau." Her stomach sank at his casual use of the word "our" and her feelings were reflected in her eyes. He smiled wryly. "Anxiety, *chérie*? Well, let me not keep you in suspense. We will indeed be sharing a bed. I have every intention of resuming our . . . intimacy. You have been remiss in maintaining your end of our agreement, and we will have to make up for lost time."

Her hand was still rubbing her cheek as she looked up at him. He stood gazing down at her for a moment. She thought she saw a glimmer of regret flit briefly across his face. He grasped her hand with his own, stilling its motion, and opened his mouth as if to speak, but the door burst open, causing the words to die in his throat.

Dominique Mauriere stood in the doorway, green eyes blazing as he took in the intimate scene. He looked directly at Kade as he said in a voice filled with icy rage, "I demand to know the meaning of this!"

Renault turned a questioning look toward Christina. Without waiting for him to speak, she answered, "He is my cousin Dominique."

Dominique looked outraged. "You explain *me* to him!?"

Kade looked at Dominique calmly. He was over a head taller than the fair-haired young man. "I'm afraid she had no choice. You see, your cousin is my wife."

The smooth planes of Dominique's face went blank, then tightened in cold rage. He blinked and cast an archly questioning look at Christina. Kade waited with an air of sardonic interest. She contemplated lying, but her cheek still burned and even a man of Renault's sophistication could be pushed too far, as he had shown her in no uncertain terms. After a moment's hesitation she said quietly, "He's telling the truth, Dominique. We're married."

She hadn't thought it possible for Dominique's eyes to grow colder, but colder they did become. But he was far too proud to create a scene. He said smoothly, "Your pardon. I intrude." And with that he left.

Renault walked to the edge of her bed and smiled thinly. "You tell the truth rather well, *petite,* for one who has had so little practice."

"Oh, stop baiting me," she said irritably. She wondered how he had found her. Then she suddenly knew.

"Guy certainly didn't waste any time in telling you where I was."

"No, he didn't. A good man, Guy," Renault said.

She was silent for a time and then said pensively, "You know, I've done some thinking, and I've come to a conclusion. It occurs to me that the reason I keep running away is because I don't want to be married. I don't suppose you would consider some sort of separation? Not a divorce, but a compromise agreeable to us both?"

The azure eyes flashed dangerously, and she wondered if he would strike her again. Unconsciously she recoiled. Her expression mirrored her fears, and he smiled grimly at her reaction.

"You know, Christina," he said evenly, "you are either very stupid or very brave. Or perhaps, a bit of both."

He took her by the shoulders and drew her near. "Listen to me carefully because I will not repeat this, although why I must say it at all is beyond me—it seems so very obvious. What I have to say is this—you will remain my wife for as long as I see fit. This marriage will end when *I* tire of *you* and for *no* other reason. You have no control over its duration or its terms. Is that clear?"

She nodded slowly. It was frightening when he was angry and his eyes glowed in that strange, smouldering manner. She had given him more than enough cause. It seemed prudent to go along with him. There was nothing to be gained by disagreeing further so she said, "All right, I understand."

"I hope so, for your sake," he said drily and released her. She watched him as he moved about the room, her eyes following him, but her mind lost in deep thought. After a few moments she focused on his actions. He had donned a pearl-gray satin waistcoat with pale champagne trousers.

"Where are you going?" she asked.

"To the musical recital Baron d'Anvireau has planned for tonight."

"Oh, yes, I had forgotten."

"Well, now that your memory is back, I suggest you get dressed."

Chris sighed and resolutely decided to wear a powder-blue silk gown. Kade had been here less than a day and already he was ordering her about. It was very annoying.

Dominique Mauriere swept into the library of his father, the marquis. Charles Mauriere was leisurely perusing several volumes of Latin prose. The marquis was known to be a scholar well versed in ancient history.

"Father, I have just come from the upper chambers of the chateau where I found our cousin lying on a bed with a formidable-looking man gazing at her in a way no gentleman looks at a young lady under the protection of her family. When I questioned his presence, the minx calmly informed me that he was her husband. *Sacrebleu!* What in the name of heaven is going on?"

Charles Mauriere, being well past the age of youthful indignation and folly, had already adjusted to the new-found status of his favorite cousin's daughter.

"Be at peace, Dominique. There is nothing you can do. What Christina told you is true. I have had a long talk with the Earl of Brenkirk, and I am satisfied that all is as he says. Our cousin is in fact Lady Christina Renault, Countess of Brenkirk." The look on his son's face startled the marquis. It was clear that for some reason Dominique had developed a rapid dislike for the earl, and Charles Mauriere decided further explanation might avoid a conflict. "Apparently," he began slowly, "Christina has had some difficulty in adjusting to marriage. The earl is confident that with patient handling she will become an exceptional wife and mother. He thinks that she is only going through a restless phase and will in time come to fully accept her role as his countess. My son, are you ill?" The marquis stopped upon noticing the flushed appearance of the young lord.

"No, father. It is only the excitement of the hunt and our cousin's little surprise. *Pardonnez-moi,* I shall retire to dress for the recital."

Gabrielle de Vezy had been miserable since that night in the garden. Her mind could not accept Dominique's harsh rejection. He *had* to care for her. What other explanation could there be for the way he had held her, the energy she had felt radiating from him when she was in his arms? If she could only speak to him once more, she was sure there would be an explanation. She had to find him.

As casually as she could, she strolled through the chateau, hoping to catch a glimpse of him or hear his voice. But he seemed to have vanished into smoke. She left the chateau to wander through the gardens. Then, over the tops of the low shrubs and flowers, she caught sight of his blond head and broad shoulders as he sat on a bench with his back to her, gazing over the green countryside. As always her heart rose to her throat at the sight of him. As she drew nearer she saw that a deep scowl marred his perfect features.

Dominique's mind was boiling with emotions he hadn't known he possessed. Uppermost among his turbulent feelings was jealousy—and a kind of murderous rage. He wanted to smash and break things and look with satisfaction on the havoc he created. He wanted to wound and hurt someone as he had been hurt. Christina was unreachable for the moment. But Gabrielle was here . . . waiting.

Slowly he smiled at her. It was a cold smile that did not reach his emerald eyes, but Gabrielle was too smitten to notice the calculating gleam that glowed in them. She could not believe her good fortune when he extended his hand and motioned her beside him. She knew then that no matter what he did or said she would follow him anywhere. He was her life.

Dominique led her to a secluded portion of the garden, hidden from view by dense, flowering shrubs. He took her with little preparation, intent on venting the raw emotions of the day in sexual release. Gabrielle, too inexperienced to know the difference between lust and love, writhed beneath him in a state of total ecstasy.

When it was over he looked at the trembling girl under him with mild disgust. The bitch had certainly enjoyed it. Even now her hips were moving, and he wasn't even in her. Well, he would use her as often as necessary to fight this damnable feeling of frustrated hunger—until he found a way to trap the game that would truly fill his need.

Dominique walked to the stables and withdrew a long black cape and hood from a box hidden in a chest with a false bottom. That night two young nobles were seriously wounded and the notorious highwayman escaped with several thousand francs in jewels and gold.

The Marquis de Lasqueront had planned a grand affair to celebrate the end of the hunt. The recital featured the most gifted musical talent of Paris, and he had sent invitations to all of the noble families within a radius of seventy miles. He smiled as he imagined the most beautiful people in France gathered in his salon.

Christina had chosen a rich gown of peach brocade trimmed with ermine and velvet. A delicate, finely wrought necklace of gold and topaz nestled between the swelling curves of her full young breasts. The dark gold of her hair caught and held the glowing candlelight, and the seductive shape of her mouth was emphasized by the rebellious feelings and growing sulk she struggled to control. The entire effect was arrestingly provocative. No man in the same room with her could resist the raw allure she projected.

She pretended a calm she did not feel as Kade Renault watched her move about the room. As always, his presence had an unsettling effect on her that was not in her power to control. He sat in a massive wing chair in the corner of the large bedroom with his feet propped up before him, calmly smoking a pipe as his eyes lazily caressed the more intimate parts of her body. A sudden thought struck her like a thunderbolt, something that the surprise of seeing him again had prevented from fully registering on her mind. She stood bolt upright and looked at him, perplexed.

"Kade, how did you become the Earl of Brenkirk?"

He smiled. "I was wondering when you'd ask." He told her of Jamie's accidental death and the highland war he had waged with Garrick of Morwell. He took his time in describing the beauty of Brenkirk, and when he finished she saw it through his eyes—misty, green, and majestic. When he stopped talking she looked at him.

Ruefully, she realized that time had done nothing to diminish his attraction for her. He was still more handsome than any mortal man had a right to be. Her eyes traveled from the firm, thickly muscled calves, over the long granite thighs, and trim, boyish hips, across the neat hard waist to his powerful chest and shoulders, stopping briefly there, only to roam again to the disconcertingly handsome face, her turquoise eyes locking with his deep blue ones.

He seemed terribly amused as well as pleased by her sweeping regard of his person. "Well, is everything still intact?" he asked, barely able to keep the laughter from his voice.

She couldn't keep the color from spreading across her cheeks, but she refused to look away from his eyes, and her voice was steady as she said. "I never said that I didn't find you attractive."

His smile broadened. "No, tiger. That is one thing about which neither of us has any illusions. Come here, little one."

Somewhat warily she walked to him and stood looking down into his eyes. He reached out and pulled her into his lap, gazing down at her for a moment. "You deserve far worse from me than you have yet received today, but the rest will have to wait." His mouth covered hers with a stirring hunger that quickened the depths of her soul. In all their months apart she had been sublimely unaware of how much she had actually missed him. But the strength of his arms around her, the familiar feel of her breasts melting against his granite-hard chest brought the deprivation of her celibacy home with shattering force. She responded, opening to him like a flower, putting her arms around his neck and returning his kiss with a loving passion that surprised them both.

When at last their lips parted he looked down at her with an expression that made her hold her breath. His face quickly changed, falling into the familiar sardonic mask.

"Minx," he said. "If you think that womanly kisses will relax the leash I intend to place on you, you are quite mistaken. As a matter of fact, they will have the opposite effect. Do you feign ardor to relax my guard, *petite*?" His voice was playful, but she sensed more than lighthearted teasing.

After looking at him for a moment she snuggled against him mischievously and said with a smile, "Not entirely." She felt his hand beneath her chin as he lifted her face and probed her eyes with his. He lowered his head and once again his lips moved over hers with coaxing pressure until she opened her mouth and allowed him his way. His arms drew her closer, molding her to him, and he drank in her softness, luxuriating in the sweet and brief compliance he had found.

When she felt his hand slowly begin to lower the brocade that covered her shoulder, she drew away until she could murmur against his lips, "The recital will be starting soon."

He raised his head slowly and said with a smile that curved down at one corner, "Time has failed to soften that stone in your breast. It must be uncomfortable, carrying a rock where most women have hearts." He watched her bristle and smiled with wry amusement as she struggled to hold her tongue. Grinning, he blew in her ear and added, "We will have to work on that."

From the reluctant way he released her, she concluded that he was impatient to begin. "With instruction from such a master, perhaps I will improve," she said.

"Let's hope so," he agreed with little modesty. "However, I am not too displeased that your education has not progressed since we parted. It augurs well for your chastity."

"I am not promiscuous. And you have often pointed out that I am much less attractive to men than I think, so why this talk of fidelity?"

He said nothing in reply, and a smile played at his lips. Chris turned away and walked to the mirror. As she adjusted her gown she heard him ask, "Was it here, little one?"

She turned to face him. "Was what here?"

"The thing you have been searching for that prevents you from being at peace with yourself . . . and me."

She faced the mirror again, feeling oddly transparent and vulnerable. At length she said, "No. It wasn't here. I haven't found it yet."

He might have sighed, but she wasn't sure. "I didn't

think you had. Nor that it would be here, waiting for you. Do you know that sometimes one looks in faraway places for something that is very near? We often fail to recognize what we are looking for, if it is very close at hand."

Quizzically, she turned to gaze at him. Christina searched his face, trying to find a clue to what he was really saying, but his expression was smooth and unreadable. "What do you mean?" she asked.

"Think about it, Chris," he replied. And despite her questions, he would say nothing more on the matter.

CHAPTER THIRTY-TWO

The Baron d'Anvireau was pleased with the distinguished gathering at his recital. The most beautiful members of the French nobility graced his salon tonight. It was a splendid occasion and he was more than satisfied as he surveyed the crowd seated before him. His son Paul mixed dutifully with their guests and cast surreptitious glances in the direction of his current fancy, Clothilde Theroux.

The Baron d'Anvireau noted that Dominique Mauriere was in a particularly foul humor tonight, despite the adoring attention of Baron de Vezy's lovely daughter, Gabrielle. He wondered why the young man scowled so darkly. After all, the recital was going well, and the music was exceptional. Ah, the vicissitudes of the young heart were beyond comprehension, even with the accumulated wisdom of his advanced years.

Dominique's miserable mood notwithstanding, Gabrielle found it hard to fend off the attentions of other young women as she sat possessively at Dominique's side. They found excuses to walk past his chair, "accidentally" dropping a handkerchief or stopping to exclaim how nice it was to see him after so long a time. He was easily the handsomest man in the room. Even if his prowess as a lover had not been a legend, he would still have been the center of attention on the basis of looks alone. Over the hum of the pre-concert excitement, a voice announced the arrival of yet another of the marquis's guests.

"The Earl and Countess of Brenkirk!"

Chris walked in on Renault's arm and was surprised by the hush that fell over the room. She had not known what a striking couple they were together. And she had totally forgotten the charm Kade Renault held for the feminine gender.

She could feel heads turn to follow them as he led her though the crowd. Renault moved with the easy grace of a lean panther. There was an air of danger and excitement in his bearing that caused a softly audible feminine sigh from the young women in the room as they glanced surreptitiously at Christina with undisguised envy. Renault, walking through the room with casual disregard of the stir he generated, headed for the Marquis de Lasqueront, who was talking with Dominique and Gabrielle.

Christina was only half aware of the pleasantries Kade was exchanging with the marquis. The other part of her mind was on the nearly tangible air of aroused interest as the guests continued to regard the new earl with curiosity. Unconsciously, Chris compared Dominique to Renault as they stood facing each other. Dominique was attractively dressed in a pale blue waistcoat and pantaloons. He looked as aloof and coolly handsome as ever. Yet beside Renault, her cousin seemed insignificant and fragile. Kade towered over Dominique by several inches. The tanned perfection of his well-carved features and the rakish charm of his sardonic grin titillated and enchanted in a way that her cousin's austerely attractive countenance did not. The warm blue of Renault's eyes made women want to lose themselves in his azure glance while Dominique's critical appraisal made them feel inadequate and somehow lacking.

Renault was joking with the marquis about a business matter. Chris looked at Dominique and was startled to find him scowling at her. With an embarrassed blush she realized that she had been staring at her husband. I wonder why, she thought. I should be used to Kade's looks by now. But tonight she noticed him just as every other woman in the room did and liked what she saw—very much.

She remained disturbingly aware of his presence throughout the evening. He sat at her side, arms folded loosely over his broad chest, a faintly contemplative expression on his handsome face. She found herself noticing his hand as it rested on his arm, so near her that the knuckles lightly grazed her breast. The fingers were long and tapering, well manicured. It was a sensitive hand. She found herself remembering a gentle caress in the darkness, a warm stroking that called her from a deep sleep.

Chris shook herself back to the present. She couldn't remember ever having been this distracted by his physical presence. Her eyes stole glances at his perfect profile. Chris couldn't keep her eyes from straying to his muscular thighs, well formed and hard as steel. With a great effort she dragged her mind back to the recital, where the violins were softly ending their solo, finishing the evening's concert.

After the entertainment ended she stood by Renault's side, strangely quiet and subdued by the new surge of attraction his nearness had spun around her like a web. She was too preoccupied with Kade to notice Dominique's intent regard as he stood across the room with Gabrielle in tow.

Dominique did not like what he saw. He hated the affectionately possessive way Kade looked at Chris when her eyes were turned elsewhere. When Renault's arm circled her waist, drawing her near as they stood talking with Baron de Vezy after the concert, Dominique knew a strong urge to kill. He realized then that something had been born inside him that was unlike anything he had ever known. Christina was as much a part of his being as his head or his heart, and he couldn't stand to see another man touch her.

Unaware of Dominique's thoughts, Chris felt Renault take her arm as they bid good night to their host. The elegant assemblage watched them leave—the men regarding Renault with respect, and the young women staring openly at Christina with envy.

When they arrived at their private apartments at the marquis's Paris residence, Christina felt suddenly shy and awkward, like a *jeune fille*. In their bedroom she watched Kade remove his pearl-gray waistcoat and vest, but averted her eyes when he began to remove his trousers. I haven't been this way since the first night he—no, even then I wasn't this aware of him, she thought.

She started to call for Cecile, but Kade stopped her, unlacing the gown himself. His hands grazed her back warm and strong, as he undid the complicated fastenings. Her breathing became shallow; it was difficult to draw in enough air. When he finished and the gown lay in a small mountain of satin and velvet at her feet, she felt his hands grasp her bare shoulders and turn her slowly to face him. She looked into his dark blue eyes, experiencing a new and tingling excitement because of the warm fingers on her skin and the close proximity of his tall, hard body.

He was gazing at her with an intent concentration that seemed to plunge into the depths of her soul—

forcing her secrets, exploring the remote, hidden corners of her heart. She returned his gaze steadily, without hesitation.

Christina's eyes wandered over the smooth planes of his face, the carved high cheekbones, the strong square jaw—firm and unyielding. A hint of a smile played at his mouth. Chris thought that any minute he would break into the mocking grin she had come to know and expect.

But he didn't. The expression on his face grew softer. His eyes looked vulnerable, open—silently asking for something he wanted but would not voice, for his own reasons. A surge of warm feeling for him swelled up in her—a flood of tenderness and caring and desire, all mixed with the growing sense of attachment she felt. Somehow, without her knowledge, this man had entered her mind and the heart he claimed she didn't have. She knew that from now on, no matter what she did or where she was, a portion of her thoughts would be of him. She would always wonder about him . . . and miss him.

Kade was still standing before her, his hands on her shoulders, with that soft, questioning expression on his face. Her eyes did not waver as the rush of feeling blossomed inside her. She watched as his querying look gave way to a heart-rending smile. He found what he wanted to see in her face, and it made him happy. She held her breath as his arms drew her closer and melted against him, not wanting to fight anymore. Kade's mouth fused with hers, and his lips were more tender than demanding, more gentle than hungry. This was a new Renault—she was used to searing passion from him. When he raised his head she looked at him curiously.

Again he smiled the intimate smile she had not seen before tonight. It was disarming. She warmed to it and to him. Christina raised her hand and softly traced the outline of his mouth with her fingers. He took her hand in his and pressed his lips into the palm. "Kade . . . ," she whispered, then wondered why she spoke his name. There wasn't a thought in her head, really, yet he looked at her as though he understood what she meant. Something passed between them, and this time it was Christina who smiled.

Taking her in his arms, he crossed the room and placed her on the bed, removing his clothes with remarkable speed. Nothing in Christina's past could compare with the wonder she felt, lying there in his arms as his lips moved caressingly on hers. His hands stroked her lovingly, before his mouth descended to her breasts, causing hot rivers of sensation to flow through her veins. A sigh of surrender escaped her lips, and she covered his shoulder with kisses, allowing her hands to roam over his neck, down the strong, hard muscles of his back, to his buttocks, which she gripped and kneaded, grazing the solid flesh lightly with her nails. A low sound of pleasure came from deep inside him as she pressed closer, feeling her body melt into his, merging with the strength and power of his manhood.

Kade's breath was hot and rapid against her cheek. In a faraway corner of her mind she felt the deep, steady beat of his heart, like the Night Festival drums. Time and space receded, and for Christina it was St. Marin and they were at Mimosa Keyes with the sea breeze blowing over them. He was like the ocean—ebbing, surging within her, the forceful thrusts opening and exposing her to his passion and his love. She felt welded to him, sealed for eternity, by the strange fate that brought them together and bound them more securely than chains. She put her arms around his neck when she felt his body strain within her, creating the closest possible contact, the fullest possible joining.

"Darling . . . ," he whispered as he felt her respond, enveloping him in the warm velvet walls of her body. He knew that she felt as he did and rejoiced in her efforts to match his ardor. "Christina . . . sweetheart," he murmured, "I love you . . . so much." A white-hot flash of sensation burst inside them, as Kade, holding her crushed to him, brought them both to joy.

It was a long time before either spoke. Kade traced the delicate line of her cheek with his lips, then moved softly to her mouth, gently letting her explore him. He kissed her passionately—causing small flutters in the pit of her stomach and prickles along the base of her spine. He was still strong inside her and the weight of him bore down heavily there. She moved against him, unable to remain still while they were joined. She heard him moan with pleasure, and again they shared the new happiness they had found. Afterward she slept, nestled securely in his arms. He might be the new Earl of Brenkirk, but to her he would always be Kade, the unpredictable but irresistible sea captain who took her at will and dared her to get away.

When morning light filtered through the white curtains of Maison Lasqueront, Christina awoke to find him beside her, resembling, as he always did in slumber, a handsome, innocent youth. His lashes lay in dark crescents on his cheeks and his mouth curved in a faint smile. Unable to resist, she pressed a kiss on his lips.

Kade stretched his lean, powerful body and opened his eyes. "Good morning," she said.

"Good morning," he smiled, pulling her down to him for another kiss. It was slow and unhurried, a satin eternity of soft lips and sweet essence. Chris wanted it to go on forever. God, she thought, I'm falling in love with him! She stiffened reflexively and drew back as the full impact of her discovery hit her, along with the realization of what it would do to her life.

"What's the matter, sweet?" he said, as his tongue pressed soft, caressing circles along the sensitive nape of her neck. She shivered and put her hands on his chest to push him from her.

"Christina?" he said, as his eyes questioned the change in her.

She couldn't explain. She didn't know exactly what had come over her. She only looked at him, agonizing over the indecision and conflict she felt. She watched in helpless dismay as his face went from puzzled confusion to cold anger. He flung her from him and rose furiously from the bed.

"What kind of heartless, teasing bitch are you? Can you turn love off and on at will, like a candle you light and snuff as it suits your fancy?"

Christina looked at him, expressionless and silent. Indeed, there was no answer she could give him. He grabbed a handful of her long hair and yanked it painfully, bringing her face level with his.

"I've had all I can stand of your lying, selfish disregard for the feelings of others and your thoughtless, childish actions. Do you have any idea, my fine little witch, how much you hurt people who care for you by doing anything you damn well please? I'm sick and tired of wondering if you're alive and well or dead on a dark road with a knife in your gullet!"

Her pride got the better of her. If he didn't like her behavior, he didn't have to stay. "If you dislike me so much, then leave," she said carelessly. His blue eyes flared dangerously. He released her hair and shook her by the shoulders until her head ached.

"I'm *not* leaving!" he yelled at the top of his deep baritone voice. "Grow up, damn you!!"

He released her shoulders, and she slid dizzily to her knees on the bed.

"Stop jeopardizing our happiness for some godforsaken ghost or thing you wouldn't recognize if it walked up and hit you. You don't know where to begin to look for it. You don't know what it is! Did it ever occur to you to look beyond your nose? What you seek might be staring you in the face, but you're so wild and impulsive that the slightest flicker from a firefly sends you running into the darkness!"

Christina held her head in her hands, trying to calm the pounding in her brain. The pain made her irritable when prudence was definitely the wiser course. She lashed back at him with fervor.

"Don't be a hypocrite! You enjoy my behavior well enough when it suits your needs!"

His mouth thinned. "I admit your wildness is seductive. It's as seductive as anything I've ever encountered in a woman. But hear me well, Christina. I will not tolerate another desertion. I'm not sure what I would do to you if I found out beforehand. I'm . . ." he searched for words, "you're the one thing in my life

I'm not completely rational about . . . and I'm afraid I might . . ."

He looked at her with haggard eyes, frustrated that he was not able to express himself. "Oh, damn it!" he swore with feeling. "No—damn you!"

She shrank from the emotion in his voice. It was the first time she had really feared anyone or anything. Her aqua eyes were wild and wide. Renault sensed her fear, and it triggered a raw, primitive reaction in him.

"If you don't believe me and you won't heed me," he shouted, "then I will have to show you, won't I?!"

He dragged her across his lap and beat her with the flat of his hand until her bottom was red and swollen. The pain was considerable, but the humiliation hurt more than the smarting blows. She heard him mutter, "You've needed this for years . . ."

When he finished she was crying, mostly from anger and acute embarrassment. He looked at her, unmoved by the watery display and noisy sobs. Kade turned his back and dressed, his mouth a grim line as her tears subsided.

When he finished he walked to the bed and said, "Quiet, that's quite enough."

She wanted to yell at him, but something in his face checked the tantrum, and it died in her throat. Instead she said soggily, "I will not be treated like a child!"

"You will be until you stop acting like one," he commented drily. "I am going to Scotland to attend to some matters I left pending in Brenkirk. When I return we'll leave for St. Marin and make arrangements for our affairs there to be run from our home in Scotland." His eyes were as dark as midnight as he said, "I will not tolerate any further caprice on your part. To be blunt, if you try any of your old tricks, I'll make you sorry you were ever born. When I come back," he said, taking her by the shoulders and pulling her against him, "I expect to find you ready and willing to act the lady when the occasion calls for it. And the rest of the time, tiger, be prepared to be a woman—*my* woman!" He crushed her against him in an embrace that took her wind. His mouth was insatiably hungry, as if he wanted to draw her soul between her lips and into his body. Then his mouth grew gentle, and she felt his hand cover her breast, softly caressing the coral-tipped aureole. Kade released her suddenly with a groan. Snatching his rapier and pistol, he left the room.

Christina was trembling as she lay on the bed. She could hardly believe that the passionate man who just left was the same sardonic young captain she had met that day at Mimosa Keyes. How dare he handle her in that brutal fashion! How dare he spank her, the presumptuous bastard! Husband or not, he had no right, the arrogant, overbearing scoundrel! It was so unexpected. Why, Renault never lost his temper. He was always in control of . . . well, everything. Who would have expected such explosive emotion from the man? It was overwhelming.

But a small voice inside whispered accusingly, "You know you liked it." Well, she had to admit he was exciting like that. It was like being lifted and carried aloft by a hurricane. She sighed. She couldn't wait for him to return. Humming, she rang for Cecile to help her dress.

CHAPTER THIRTY-THREE

Renault left for Scotland that morning. Christina watched his handsome, polished gold and black liveried carriage from the balcony of Maison Lasqueront. His eyes held hers for a brief moment before he entered the carriage. Something flowed between them, as if they sealed a pact with their eyes.

From a small secluded garden in the courtyard, Dominique Mauriere watched the momentary interlude between Christina and Renault. A muscle ticked in his patrician jaw, and his green eyes grew bright with grim determination. He strode through the flowered park and into Maison Lasqueront, concentrating on his plans. He was sure Christina was the only woman he had ever loved. In Dominique's mind it was clear that they were meant to be together, with no one between them. It was only a matter of time before he convinced Christina.

A butler addressed him timidly as he entered the foyer. "Yes?" he snapped, "I cannot stand here all day—what is it?" The butler blinked but did not flinch. The younger Mauriere was always curt with the servants. It mattered little whether he was pleased or indifferent with their work. His manner was unpleasant, and it never varied.

"Mademoiselle de Vezy is here, sir, in the *petit salon jaune*. She wishes to speak with you."

Dominique raised his brow in annoyance. It was ten o'clock, an early hour of the morning for a visitor to call, and somewhat compromising if Gabrielle had chosen to come alone. She was becoming an encumbrance, this de Vezy. He abhorred a clinging woman. And to make matters worse, he had noticed a decidedly possessive streak in her at the recital. No woman owned Dominique Mauriere, heir of Lasqueront—least of all a silly *jeune fille* like Gabrielle, too innocent to know better than to lose her heart.

With an oath of impatience he turned and headed for the *petit salon jaune*. It was a beautifully appointed yellow sitting room with fine porcelain figurines, artfully displayed in highly polished and gracefully carved cabinets. Gabrielle looked as fresh and innocent as a morning flower in her gown of lilac watered silk, but Dominique was too incensed to see. Nor did he notice the worried anxiety on her lovely young face. Impatiently, he removed his leather gloves and threw them with unnecessary force on the table. "Gabrielle, this visit is in extremely poor taste. Your behavior is becoming intolerable."

Gabrielle's lower lip trembled ominously. She whispered in a small, broken voice, "I had to see you, Dominique."

"Do you realize how you have compromised yourself by coming here as you did, unchaperoned, in broad daylight? *Mon Dieu!* How did you ever get away from Maison de Vezy?"

"I . . . I managed. A bribe or two . . . some extra persuasion. I had to come to you and tell you. Dominique . . . I . . . I'm pregnant."

Dominique's irritated expression froze. Then his face became a blank mask of indifference. "How delightful for you, *ma chère.* When is the blessed event?" he asked smoothly.

"Please, Dominique. Don't jest . . . I . . . can't stand it. When my father finds out, he will disown me! I don't know what to do."

"Well," Dominique said shortly as he turned away from her, "the solution is obvious, *enfant*. You must marry, and quickly."

Gabrielle gave a small gasp of happiness and ran to him. "Oh, my love, that is what I hoped you would say." She threw her arms around him and pressed quick, happy kisses on his chin and neck.

Slowly, Dominique unwound her arms and held her away from him. "You misunderstand, *chérie*. You should marry, *oui*, but not with me. I have no intention of making you my wife."

Gabrielle's throat constricted painfully. For several moments she was speechless. Then she said in a dazed voice, "Not . . . to . . . you? You will not marry me . . . and acknowledge our child?"

"My dear girl, marriage to you is the last thing in the world I desire. I have already explained." With an impatient gesture he said, "You are a very foolish young woman, Gabrielle. Now you will have to solve your problem as best you can. But take heart, *chérie*, there are many young men who will be willing to marry you because of your fortune and other charms. It should not take your father long to arrange a suitable liaison for you, but remember, I am not interested, and if I were you, I would not force the issue. It will make a most undignified and embarrassing scandal, *n'est-ce pas?*"

He turned to go with an air of disdain, but as he reached the door, her anguished cry stopped him. "Dominique! Tell me—is it your cousin?"

He turned and regarded her critically.

"Please . . . I beg you. Oh, Dominique, I love you so!"

He sighed, bored. His eyes held a contempt that wrenched the heart from her breast as he replied, "That, *chérie*, is a very great pity."

Dominique left the *salon jaune* and crossed the wide marble foyer to the grand staircase. At the top he heard the gay sound of young laughter, and he watched as Bibi, Christina, and Arielle descended the stairs, giggling. They were dressed for the morning's ride. He made a courtly bow as they approached, and his eyes lingered on his smiling cousin.

"Good morning, *mon frère*," Arielle said pleasantly. His youngest sister was always cheerful, still far too innocent to be affected by the troubles of the world.

"*Bonjour, petite*," Dominique replied, dropping a kiss on her forehead.

"Will you ride with us, Dominique? We will wait for you to change," said Bibi.

Dominique was about to accept the offer when Gabrielle suddenly ran weeping from the *salon jaune*. She paused at the doorway to look back at Dominique and the three startled young women at his side. Her eyes were red and swollen and her face horribly tear-stained. There was a look of utter desperation on her face that was disturbing. It seemed . . . not quite rational. With a huge hiccupping sob she ran through the open door, past the astonished butler and into the liveried carriage in the courtyard outside.

Bibi looked incredulously at Dominique. "That was Gabrielle, was it not?"

"I'm afraid it was," he replied with appropriate

sympathy. "She was very distraught over . . . a personal problem."

The girls regarded each other and discreetly refrained from inquiring further. Only Christina was bold enough to comment. "Yes. Life is so complicated—and problems are so easily contracted," she said acidly.

"How astute, cousin. That is very true," he replied without batting an eye. As they bid him farewell and walked away for their ride, he said softly to himself, "We all have our problems, *chère* Christine—and mine is you." Casually, he continued up the stairs, pausing at a window overlooking the courtyard to watch them mount. He added softly, "But not for long."

In the fashionable park bordering Maison Lasquer-ont, the girls rode in companionable silence for a time before Arielle's inquisitive nature got the better of her. "What do you think was bothering poor Gabby, Bibi?" she asked.

"I can answer in two words, Ari: your brother."

"Why would Dom make Gabby cry?" she said, surprised at Bibi's revelation.

"You are too young to know, Ari."

"Too young, always. Do I have to go through the rest of my life with people keeping secrets from me because I am too young?" She pouted prettily. "Even Christina did not say that she was married. And to such an exciting man!"

Bibi laughed and agreed. "Yes, Christina. You are a countess and you didn't tell us. Your husband is so handsome. If I had captured the heart of the Earl of Brenkirk, I would shout it to the world. How could you keep it a secret?"

There was really nothing Christina could say to explain. She hadn't known herself about the title until the day that Renault stepped from his carriage. She hoped someday to forget the little scene that had come after. "It came as something of a surprise to me also. He inherited the title while I was away, and I really didn't know until . . ."

Bibi laughingly interrupted, "Don't worry, cousin. We understand. You wanted it to be a surprise, no? And she fooled us well, didn't she, Ari?"

Arielle nodded. "When I grow up I hope I marry a man just as tall and beautiful as the earl, and I will *never* keep it a secret from *anyone!*"

Bibi corrected her. "Men are not beautiful, *chérie,* they are handsome."

Ari stood her ground. *"Mais non,* the *earl* is *beautiful."*

Christina laughed. "I think Kade has acquired yet another admirer."

Dinner was a subdued affair that night at Maison Lasqueront. There were no parties to attend that evening, and the marquis decided to escort his wife to the ballet. An elegant but simple *roti de veau,* accompanied by a savory chicken fricassee and shrimp *nantua* were served as the main course. Christina and her cousins chatted pleasantly with the marquis and Therese as the dinner proceeded.

Dominique was relatively silent, not joining in the dinner repartee, though no one seemed to notice. His brooding green eyes rested often on Christina, missing no detail of the soft velvet gown she wore or the way its mellowed gold color brought an enchanting glow to her skin. He could not drag his eyes from the round curve of her bosom, and he allowed his gaze to rest there when his mother and the marquis were occupied in conversation.

At last his father bid the family *adieu* and, taking Therese's arm, left for the ballet. Ari and Bibi went to their apartments to begin the night's embroidery and spinet lessons. As Christina rose to follow them, Dominique called her name softly. She turned to find him offering her a small cordial of after-dinner liqueur. She hesitated and he smiled. "You will like it, cousin. It is made from a distillation of banana rum at a nearby monastery and is very rare. It should remind you of your island."

Christina accepted the small glass. It did remind her of spice, St. Marin's favorite beverage. She drank it all quickly, thanked him, and went to Bibi's apartments upstairs. She didn't like being alone with Dominique for very long if she could help it.

Chris spent a half hour talking with Ari and Bibi. Ari was full of questions about Renault, and Chris found it amusing to indulge Ari's obvious infatuation. Presently she bid them good night and made her way to the room she used now that her true status was known. It was a large apartment some distance away from her cousins, with a lovely drawing room adjoining the enormous bedroom. It had become her habit to sit reading her mother's diary for a time before retiring for the night. Cecile helped her into a filmy apricot gown, held together by two satin clasps at the shoulders. It was loose and flowing, like a Grecian robe. She loved sleeping in it. It always felt so free, like sleeping with nothing on, which she actually preferred.

Tonight, as she sat on the couch before the small

fireplace in the drawing room, reading Blaise's words, her eyelids felt so heavy, that she could barely keep them open. A wave of dizziness assaulted her, and the page became blurred. She grew alarmed and cried out, but her voice sounded far away and strange to her own ears. She knew that her cry had been little more than a hoarse whisper.

From somewhere in the room she heard the deep sound of a man's chuckle. With great effort she turned her head in the direction of the sound just in time to see a bookcase swing backward into a secret passage. Dominique Mauriere stepped soundlessly into her room. She watched helplessly as he lifted her in his arms, his mouth descending on hers, possessively claiming it as his own. He walked through the opening as it closed behind them, plunging them into near total darkness.

He needed no light to make his way. Cold hard shocks of alarm coursed up and down Chris's spine. She couldn't speak, and her body would not move as she willed. She was kicking her legs with all her strength. Though she should have been thrashing about wildly, her movements were agonizingly slow. They certainly had no effect on him.

As her eyes adjusted to the dim light of the passageway, she looked at Dominique. There was no sympathy or compassion on his coldly patrician face. The curling blond hair and emerald-green eyes that caused so many maids to lose their hearts filled her with apprehension and a rising panic. She could feel his hand caressing her breast as he carried her, and she squirmed to evade his grasp. Her vision cleared slightly and her tongue felt less furred, but her limbs behaved as though they were wrapped in yards of thick cotton, dull and unresponsive to her will.

Dominique paused in the passageway to kiss her again. He smiled to himself as he recognized the taste of the drug from the banana cordial he had given her. The drink had taken effect quickly. She was as weak as a newborn. He pressed her closer, ravaging the soft recesses of her mouth. After an eternity, he raised his head and walked a few steps to a large lever, kicking it upward with his foot.

He stepped inside a large, ornate, masculine room. She recognized some of the clothes and possessions as his. Blast him, she thought furiously, I'll kill him for this. He was watching the play of expressions on her face with satisfaction. Slowly, almost lazily, he crossed the room and laid her on his massive antique bed.

A glimmer from a nearby nightstand caught her eye. She glanced in its direction and found herself staring at a large diamond stickpin—the pin she had worn the night of the "accident." It was the Mauriere family heirloom the highwayman had stolen from her, not seen again until now.

"How . . ." she began as she turned back to him.

"How did I get the pin? Is that what you want to know? *C'est simple, chérie.* It was I who took it from you."

"You? You're . . . the . . ." She formed the words with difficulty.

"The highwayman," he finished. "The man whose shoulder you pierced with that wicked little rapier of yours. I have waited a long time to repay you for that. Tonight, beloved cousin, our battle will be of a different nature and certainly more enjoyable than the first.

This time, Christina, it is your heart, not a piece of jewelry, that I wish to steal."

She watched in growing panic as he removed his green velvet robe. Dominique's body was hard and slender. Christina turned in an effort to roll from the bed, but he casually caught the skirt of her gown, easily stopping her by holding the material in his hand. Viciously, he ripped the garment in two.

Christina shivered, not so much from the cool night air that blew over her skin as from the blazing intensity of his eyes as they raked the now exposed curves of her body.

"I've wanted to see you this way since the night we fought in the forest. Your husband doesn't know you as I do! You've never shown him the side you've shown me, have you? The violent being inside you that will strike when angry and kill when threatened." He knelt on the bed, bending over her, his face inches away, his eyes gleaming wildly with desire. "I know you. You and I are alike, willing to kill for what we want because it suits us . . . even for amusement, if that is our whim."

"No," she said slowly, "I'm not like that . . . you are!"

She felt him lower himself on her. She jumped from the contact—his body was like a hot iron. Dominique lowered his head, but Christina turned to avoid his kiss. His mouth traced the line of her jaw to the unprotected hollow of her neck, then down her breast which he sucked hungrily. Her body convulsed, rejecting the contact and him.

"I'm not like you!" she whispered furiously. "I don't . . . kill and maim for pleasure."

He lifted his blond head lazily and smiled demonically into her eyes. "No, *chérie*? I suppose I believe you well enough. But you do wound. Especially men. Look at me. Hardened as I am, you managed to rend the heart from my body and dine on it."

"I . . . don't want it . . ."

"But it is too late, my love. You have it. It is yours . . ." she felt him part her legs, "just as I have you, tonight, and you are mine. That is very fair, don't you think?"

Desperate and frightened, she summoned every ounce of her diminishing strength and reared, but the motion was not sufficient to throw him from her, and Dominique used her movement to position himself as he wished.

With loathing, Christina looked up into the mesmerizing greenness of his gaze. He was like a malevolent cobra, inexorably charming his prey into submission. "I hate you, Dominique," she rasped. "One day I'll kill you for this."

"Hate and love are much alike, Christina. You cannot feel one without feeling a little of the other."

He entered very slowly, forcing her mind to dwell on his movement and the realization of her helplessness. When she felt the hot probing staff of his manhood fully lodged within her, tears streamed down her cheeks in wet angry rivers.

"You're mine now, *petite*," he whispered as he tightened his arms around her, tracing the tears with a kiss.

"I wish I had killed you that night on the highway."

"You may soon be glad you did not," he said, burying his lips in hers.

His body moved over hers with relentless strength until she thought she would rip in two from the sheer power of his thrusts. When it was over she turned her head aside and wept bitterly. He refused to let her go and lay above her, propped on his elbows, softly stroking the downy curls at her temples until there were no more tears left for her to cry. She looked up at him with such hatred and resentment that he sighed to himself, cursing the fates that had delivered him a woman he could truly love in so impossibly unattainable a manner.

In his dark heart he was as certain as Christina that evil would come from this night. But if later he must pay, then tonight he would enjoy his prize—for who knew when, if ever, this time would came again? Dominique gathered her in his arms and crushed her to his hard, lean body.

"Not again, Dominique! No!"

"Yes, again," he sighed. And again and again—until she sank into a dark liquid well from which even he could not rouse her.

CHAPTER THIRTY-FOUR

Christina awoke in her own room the next morning. Tired and dizzy, she focused her eyes with difficulty in the sunny brightness of the Parisian morning. Maybe it was only a nightmare, she thought dully, wondering if she had not imagined the whole thing. But much as she wanted to discount the night, her body told her that it had been real. Her handsome cousin was indeed the highwayman, and even more unbelievable was the fact that last night he had been her lover.

All this time, seeing him, dining with him and I never knew. It was too much to absorb at once. Wearily she closed her eyes.

That evening Dominique left Maison Lasqueront in high spirits. At last he had mastered the infuriating young witch. He could barely contain his good humor. Perhaps in time he could teach her to come to him willingly. The servants looked at him in surprise when he was pleasant and almost jovial with them. Why, the perverse creature even left the house whistling.

Dominique rode to Anvireau, with the pleasant intention of spending the night there with his friend Paul at their favorite inn. They laughed and wined away the golden afternoon until twilight fell with the soft cover of darkness. Paul Anvireau was coaxing a pretty brunette in his lap out of her blouse when a messenger entered their private room asking for Dominique.

"Here," Dominique replied. The messenger delivered an envelope, waited for his gold coin and left. Dominique opened the letter and read:

> I must speak with you. Please meet me at the Pont d'Avireau as soon as possible. I'll be waiting.
>
> Christina

It was more than he had dared hope for. When he left her he was certain she would never wish to see him again. At best it would take weeks of concentrated assault on her defenses to manipulate her again into his grasp. But the thought of her following him to Anvireau, making inquiries concerning his whereabouts, and going to the trouble of sending a messenger, made his pulse race. What would he find when he met her? An angry antagonist with rapier drawn and ready for combat? A woman whose heart had warmed to him, who now desired his love as much as he did hers?

The prospect of the latter made him shift with anticipation as he sat in his chair. "Saddle my mount!" he called to the groom as he went quickly upstairs to adjust his attire and splash cold water on his face.

When he returned, his horse was saddled and ready. The bay was as fast as the wind, and Dominique wasted no time on the road. When he reached Pont d'Avireau, he could barely make out the shadowy figure of Christina in the moonlight. She stood gazing at the river with her back to him. She wore a voluminous cape and hood. He could barely discern the desirable feminity beneath the garment.

"Christina," he whispered softly, walking toward her. "Christina, I have come, as you asked."

The cloaked figure turned to face him. Dominique stopped dead in his tracks as he stared into the barrel of the large gray metal pistol she held in her hand. "Christina, *chérie*, wait . . . " he began. He heard the pistol cock and felt a cold sweat beading on his forehead.

She removed the hood that hid her face.

"My God!" Dominique exclaimed. "Gabrielle!"

"How ironic, Dominique, that the last word to pass your lips in this life shall have been my name," said Gabrielle, her brown eyes glowing with the insanity of her pain. The gun roared once in the cool, still night. Dominique fell to the ground, a bullet lodged firmly between his surprised green eyes.

She watched his lifeless form for several minutes. Then she heard the sound of running footsteps and distant voices. Silently, she walked to the side of the bridge and looked down into the rushing dark water. As the footsteps drew closer, she climbed without hesitation over the bridge railing and jumped into the black swirling liquid. Gabrielle de Vezy had never learned to swim.

Dominique's funeral took place the following day. Paul Anvireau told the authorities that his friend had been slain by the notorious highwayman of Anvireau. An intensive search to find the criminal was organized, and they scoured the countryside for weeks. Christina knew the search was futile. She wondered how much of the truth Paul knew as well.

Gabrielle de Vezy was missing for more than three weeks before they found her nearly unrecognizable body several miles downriver. Her feelings for Dominique were well known. People whispered that she had thrown herself into the river rather than face life without him. Christina thought it unlikely that any of them would learn the truth in this lifetime.

The drugged night she had spent with her cousin grew dim in her memory. In time it would all but fade from her mind.

In the dark days of mourning at Maison Lasqueront, Christina had much time to herself. In her solitude she often turned to Blaise's diary for comfort and company. Her mother had been an extraordinary woman. Warm and passionate, yet gentle and well-read, she wrote of life with her husband and daughter in such glowing terms that Chris felt as if she were there with her mother, reliving those precious early days in St. Marin.

One night, after the household was asleep, as she read alone in her bed by candlelight, she came across a passage she read again and again:

> I have spent the entire day at the beach with Mac and little Christina. She loved the ocean so. Someday she well go to sea, that one. Mac is as always—loving, kind, and tender. I thank the fates that allowed our paths to cross.
>
> Once I wanted to leave the island. Something seemed to draw me away, calling me until I could not rest or sleep. My one consuming passion was to find out what it was, to locate and tame it and prove that I was stronger so my restless soul could find peace. But I didn't know what I was looking for.

I think now that I do. I look at my daughter and my husband and the sunny island that we call home and I know I have not missed the best that life has to give—the true essence of its joy. I have love, I give love. I am needed in this world. What greater thing can any of us find than that place . . . the special somewhere . . . where we are needed . . . where we are loved . . . where we are happy and where we may trust. That thing I wanted . . . needed to find . . . was my home. The restlessness that plagued me came from a lack of knowing myself and where I belonged in this world.

Home is never a place you see with your eyes. It is a place you feel with your heart, a spot on the earth where the soul is at peace with itself. Each of us must search for it and find it on her own . . . .

Christina stared into space for a long while. Of course, she was looking for that also, but she had never been able to put it into words as Blaise had. Was home a place that one found or a place that one made?

Renault returned from Scotland in the aftermath of the tragedy to find Maison Lasqueront virtually unrecognizable. What had once been a gay and lively household was now a dark and gloomy mausoleum.

It was difficult to recognize the dimly lit rooms as the elegantly appointed interiors he had known. He disliked the change in Christina. She was quiet and withdrawn, as somber as the black dresses she wore. He hated her in black. Her fiery nature belonged in bright colors. Both now seemed to be missing. She was distracted, distant, and more like a phantom than the flesh and blood woman he had left.

The first person Renault spoke with was the marquis. Christina wondered what they found to discuss in the library for four hours. When they emerged the marquis was smiling. Chris had not seen him do that for two months. She pulled Renault aside and whispered, "What did you say to him?"

Kade grinned at her as his blue eyes danced mischievously and replied, "I told him that his Therese was a fine-looking woman and too young to mourn the rest of her days. I pointed out that if he wanted another son, all he had to do was get busy, and he had better be quick about it before some eager young buck beat him to the ship."

"You said that to the marquis," she said incredulously, "at a time like this?"

"There was never a better time to say it, tiger," he replied.

When she thought about it, she knew he was right.

CHAPTER THIRTY-FIVE

Kade wanted to leave for St. Marin immediately. Although the spirits of the marquis and his family had lifted greatly since his return from Scotland, there was still something in the atmosphere of Maison Lasqueront that seemed to trouble Christina.

Chris herself was glad when he suggested an early departure. The day he had returned she had been happier to see him than she cared to admit, to herself or him. One sunny morning the shining gold and black carriage with its Arabian horses had appeared in the courtyard of Maison Lasqueront, and her heart had soared when he leapt from the carriage. The sun on his black hair made it shine like fine velvet, and his azure eyes sparkled with some inner amusement.

She had felt a tightening in the pit of her stomach, the familiar feeling she always fought unsuccessfully. But one look at the powerful shoulders and tapering waist made her melt. Those granite-hard loins held a dangerous fascination for her.

Chris was standing on the rear balcony as he approached. Walking toward Maison Lasqueront, he suddenly looked up, as if he felt her gaze. Their eyes locked briefly. Drat his charm, she thought with annoyance. He grinned and rakishly threw a kiss before he bounded quickly up the stairs.

The weeks had flown by and today they were sailing for St. Marin. Renault's affairs in Brenkirk were sufficiently settled to allow them to return. She wondered how he would view the island now that he had inherited the title. They shared the same bedroom, but he seemed to sense how much the heaviness in the air had affected her spirits, and he did little more than lingeringly kiss her good night and hold her until sleep overtook them. It was strange that he knew, but he did.

Jacques LaCroix and Logan Armor were already preparing the *Falcon* for the voyage. How much she had grown in these two short years! She had left St. Marin a wild young girl eager to see the fantasy city of her childhood. Now she would return a worldy young woman, wiser and more knowledgeable. But at home on her island could she be sure that the old cravings might not seize her again, pushing her headlong into danger and an uncertain future?

Her brush with Dominique had made her view Renault in a totally new light. She had appreciated him before, of course, but from a limited perspective. She had given him a certain objective admiration for his astonishing good looks and rakish charm, but she had never really appreciated *him* before—his gentleness, his understanding, his willingness to extend himself to people. After Dominique's selfish excesses and thoughtless cruelty, it would have been difficult not to notice these qualites in her husband.

Chris found herself being drawn by little things about him that had never affected her before—like the dimple in his chin; the way his eyes danced when he smiled; his hair when one unruly lock settled on his forehead; the sardonic grin she'd always thought so insolently mocking (now she knew he mocked himself, as well, with that grin); the way he had of folding his arms across his chest as he leaned against a post or gate; the soft, tender look she found on his face if she turned around quickly. When she surprised him that way, sometimes his face would mold itself into an unrevealing mask, but more and more often these days his expression did not change and the loving look remained. When he looked at her in that manner it seemed only natural to fold her arms about his neck and pull his head down for a long, languid kiss—an action so effective that in a matter of days he stopped hiding the look altogether.

Once when it happened she was in the courtyard, mentally memorizing the lovely shrubs and flowers so that she could carry the picture in her head always. She wore a dress of fine yellow lawn trimmed with white lace. Her hair hung long and heavy and blew gently in the spring breeze. A feeling that she was not alone made her turn around, and she saw Renault watching her with that soft expression in his blue eyes, the firm mouth vulnerable and smiling slightly.

Without thinking much about it, she walked up to him and put her arms around his neck, kissing him fully, withholding nothing, and gradually melting in his embrace. She heard him sigh deeply as his arms tightened around her, lifting her from the ground until their young bodies were as thoroughly welded as their lips. The moments when they put aside their antagonisms seemed to bring him immense pleasure. These days she often felt his eyes following her, a small dimple playing in his cheek.

The *Falcon* sailed for St. Marin in April. Chris found it a pleasure to watch Renault captain the ship. The easy camaraderie of the Corsairs and their confidence in him and the *Falcon* gave her a sense of security and well-being. These men had lived, fought, and loved together for many years. Their close relationship with Renault was obvious, and their allegiance to him seemed unshakable. Yet Renault accepted their respect and admiration without conceit or inordinate pride, characterstically taking it all in stride. He was such a complex man. It would take a hundred years to learn all of the subtle workings of his mind.

Chris's greatest pleasure during the long months at sea came from the easy minutes she spent watching her husband behind the great wheel of the *Falcon*, guiding the ship along its course. Standing there with the breeze ruffling his black locks, the white lawn shirt unbuttoned, revealing a broad, vee-shaped expanse of brown, well-muscled chest, his legs astride and braced against the swaying motion of the ship, she felt a rush of emotion that made her feel inexplicably warm and happy inside.

The intimacy between them grew. It became his habit to dine with her in the captain's cabin before attending to the night duties. He talked to her about the day's sailing, the problems with repairs or changes in the wind, and his plans for their business affairs in St. Marin. They agreed that she would continue to manage their local rum and shipping interests while he would expand their island sea line to include Scottish ports and the China trade, in addition to their American ports of call.

It pleased her that he accepted her role in their enterprises and did not expect her to remain cloistered in seclusion. She offered advice when she could and gave him an opinion on everything from the position of the sails to the conservation of the water supply. He seemed to enjoy the evening interludes and was never in a hurry to do the day's long entry or leave her company for long.

Their lovemaking deepened in meaning as well. Chris was surprised at the anticipation she felt as she watched the door to the cabin, waiting for it to open and reveal that wide, engaging grin. Thus the months at sea passed in the warmth of their new-found attachment for each other, and she felt the bond between them strengthen each day. She almost regretted the morning the *Falcon* docked in St. Marin Bay, but she was anxious to talk to Janie to find out how Robin had fared.

At Mimosa Keyes her friend was waiting , and from the smile on her face, Chris knew that all was well.

"Janie!" Chris cried as she ran toward the stair where she stood. "Tell me about Robin!"

"He's fine! Gideon came in time!" Janie beamed. She looked exceptionally pretty today. She was wearing a light blue linen dress with a white fichu and shawl. Her heavy black hair was loose, the twin braids cast aside. Chris suspected that all of this finery was for Joshua Boman's benefit. "I left Robin with Gideon in the hills. He is learning to make the quinine himself, so that he will not be in danger again."

Renault mounted the stairs behind them, smiling.

"Welcome back, Captain," Janie greeted him.

"Thank you, Janie."

"Captain, is Joshua . . ."

"Yes, he's back as well. I imagine if you are quick and run to the stables where the horses are being unhitched, you will just catch him."

Janie was gone before Chris could blink and she laughed.

Kade drew Christina aside and stood smiling down at her as he enfolded her in a gentle embrace. "You look happy to be home, madame," he said, nuzzling her neck.

"I am. This island will always be in my heart."

Kade smiled enigmatically and lowered his head, kissing her in a long, leisurely fashion. When he ended the kiss, his dark blue eyes were serious. "But you know that we will leave soon. Once our affairs are in order and we arrange adequately for the management of the shipping interests here, we will go to my estate in Scotland. Now that I am the earl, we must make our home there and not here."

"Yes, I know that our time here is not long, but I want to enjoy every minute we have left."

He nodded, knowing that the memories would have to last for a very long time.

In the morning Chris made arrangements to visit Gideon in the hills. She wanted to thank him, although she knew it wasn't necessary, and she had an inexplicable urge to see him once more before they left the island.

As the cart rolled to a stop in front of his cottage, she looked about her and reflected that little had changed. She could understand now why the flowers here were enormous and why the fauna grew to three times its normal size. Magic, perhaps, but a magic that Gideon could call forth and recreate at will with his bottles and liquids, not with the hexes and charms of his mother.

The front door was open, and she walked in. He was sitting with his back to her, bent low over a large vat filled with something green, stirring the mixture as it simmered over a flame.

"*Bonjour*, Christina."

"*Bonjour*, Gideon. How did you know it was me?"

He didn't answer, but merely turned from his work and smiled. "It is good to see you again. How was your voyage?"

"A smooth crossing. I came to thank you for saving Robin."

Gideon made a gesture of some impatience. Gratitude embarrassed him.

"He is well?"

"Very much so and constantly in my way. I sent him into the woods to gather plants so that I could steal a few hours' peace."

She laughed at that, remembering Robin's nonstop energy when he was well.

"And you, Christina?"

She smiled. "I too am well, Gideon."

"Ah, then you did find what you sought in France?"

Chris became uncomfortable. "Well . . . *non* . . . Paris was all that I expected . . . I mean . . . it was as beautiful as I had imagined, but . . . I did not resolve anything there."

"I did not think you would. Sit down, Christina. I am going to tell you something, and I hope that you will listen."

He waited while she did as he asked.

"Happiness comes to us when we find something to do that we love. It comes with learning to care for someone important—trusting, giving, being vulnerable, and eventually starting a family with the one you have chosen. It comes with striving to change the things in the world that bother you and always seeking a personal excellence in all things, a standard you set for youself—the balance of which we spoke in Paris."

"But, Gideon . . ."

"Do not interrupt. At some point in your life you will need to trust someone other than yourself. You will acknowledge that need and come to terms with it by depending on resources other than your own. At some time or other, Christina, you will have to face love, despite that fact that it frightens you."

She sat silently, wondering if he had finished. When he made no attempt to speak, she said, "But Gideon, how can you tell me that? You, who have lived a life of sacrifice and devotion to duty? Have you not spent your entire life alone here, with your work? I see no wife at your side. You are the most solitary creature I have ever known. You do not seem to need this thing of which you speak, and see how much you have helped us here—look at all the good you have wrought. I have nothing but admiration for what you have accomplished. Gideon, you must be happy with this life or you would not have continued with it—so why do you not tell me instead to live as you have lived?"

There was a pause before he answered her. "Because I am not happy. Yes, I do have my work, and as you see, I work alone. But I am alone because the love that was mine to give I gave to your mother, and she chose otherwise. After she married it was not there to give again, and I turned to healing and philosophy, provinces of the mind. I see the same ability in you, Christina, but I feel that such an escape for you would be a mistake, and that what you fear losing by allowing yourself to care is not as precious as you believe. You have your life before you, and I would not see you discard something of value to chase rainbows and butterflies."

"You mean my marriage."

"Yes."

She made a small gesture of impatience. "You do not know the circumstances that constrained me when I met my husband, Gideon. Ours was a marriage of convenience."

"But I can see that it has helped you grow, and the change has been good. That it was an *affaire de convenance* is no reason to discard it on whim."

"I am not so frivolous as that."

"No, I know you are not, but you are apt to chain yourself to the Evrion ship lines, given half an opportunity—to submerge yourself in that, just as I have done here with my work. It would be a mistake, child, not to work also at this marriage. I have made inquiries regarding Renault, and you should consider yourself a fortunate woman. I would like to go to my grave with the knowledge that a happy end lies in store for Blaise's daughter."

She did not query him on that cryptic statement. Instead she said, "These feelings you wish upon me are things I do not yet feel. I am not sure that I want to feel them. What you are saying makes me afraid, though I do not know why. I think it is because—there is something I must find before I come to know this peace of which you speak."

Gideon nodded and sighed. "I know what you seek. This answer that you believe you need, what would you do, Christina, if you found it? Do you think you would then be happy?" He shook his head. "If you are to be master of your world, Christina, you must first be the master of your own impulses, your own desires—and that you have not yet done. Whim rules you now. And the answer you seek is beyond you and always will be. Life is an end in itself. You will never find a higher meaning in this incarnation; existing as we do in this form, comprehension of the infinite is beyond our capability. As we now are, life is in itself an end, not merely a conduit to something greater."

"You cannot truly believe that, Gideon."

"I believe, Christina, that you are wasting something of value to find something of questionable worth." The old man's eyes suddenly looked tired, as if he had fought a long battle and had yet another to face. "But it does not all have to be resolved in a day. Part of living is struggling with worry and doubt. You must have your share, I suppose."

"Thank you," she said drily, and they both laughed.

She left him then, feeling a gnawing uneasiness, and thinking hard of the things he had said.

The news of Chris and Renault's arrival quickly reached the ears of Carlotta DeCorba. Since her marriage to James Marston, Carlotta had been unfaithful to him dozens of times, but only Renault had given her real satisfaction. He burned like a flame in her blood, and that brief interlude had scarred her heart forever. Now that he was back on the island, she had to have him again, and the sooner the better.

According to her sources, Renault had been in St. Marin a week, long enough to have settled in. Mimosa Keyes was not far from Willowbreak, the home Marston had built for them before their wedding. Since we are neighbors, no one will question the appropriateness of a welcome-home party in his honor, she thought to herself. It meant that she would have to invite Christina also, but that little fool lacked the good sense to appreciate what she had and would pose no threat to the fond reunion Carlotta planned for Renault. No, the only real problem would be Kade himself. He required expert persuasion, she recalled. Still, she was confident that she would win in the end, for if nothing else, she considered herself an expert at "persuading." Carlotta sang a little tune to herself as she went about making plans for a very special evening.

James Marston came home to find the household in a flurry of activity. The maids were scouring every corner to a high gloss and making the furniture shine like glass. He walked into the grand bedroom to find Carlotta instructing their housekeeper on a special menu for the party. Marston knew from the familiar glint in her eyes that she was hatching one of her damnable schemes and that someone would be hurt.

"Whose downfall are you planning now, Carlotta?"

She turned to regard him coolly. "I think that is a most unnecessary question, James. I am plotting to do no one harm." She smiled unpleasantly. "Why? Do you fear for yourself?"

"I fear the outcome of your efforts, if that's what you mean. You have proved to me often enough that I matter little to you. Tell me, what new lover has your eye this time?" Marston's face was a grim mask of pain.

"None," she said. It was the truth actually; Renault would not be a new lover.

"You'll pardon me if I don't believe you," he snorted. James had gained his knowledge from first-hand experience. When he was still in the first blush of romantic fervor for his darkly beautiful young wife, he had decided to surprise her with a gift of some very rare pink pearls set in three long strands. He left her while she was still sleeping softly by his side early one morning to make arrangements with the jeweller to deliver the necklace on her birthday. It was his habit to leave in the morning and return by late evening, but that day his excited anticipation of the happiness he would see in her eyes when she received the gift made him return several hours earlier than usual.

How well he remembered calling her name as he opened the door and ran up the long staircase to their room. He could still see the guilty look on her face as he watched a nearly nude youth disappear through an open window into the branches of a nearby tree and down to the ground below.

James left in shock and disappeared for several weeks. Carlotta thought she had seen the last of him. But he came back—a cynical, critical roué who drank heavily and regarded her with accusing eyes.

"You are a lying, deceiving bitch, my dear. You always have been, and you always will be. But don't try to lie to me. It won't do you any good and if I choose, it may do a great deal of harm. So, for whose benefit are we having this charming little soirée?"

She raised her sable-brown eyebrows in disdain. "Really, James, you don't think I'd actually tell you? Why can't you allow us some dignity? I don't question your life. Must you pry into mine?"

"I beg your pardon, madame," he said with mock regret. "I thought we were married."

"Please. It's unpleasant to be constantly reminded of my mistake." Carlotta turned away, in disgust.

She walked to the door and was about to leave when James said, "One of these days, Carlotta, you're going to go too far. And then I'll . . ."

"You'll go to Hades," she said calmly as she closed the door. James was a weak man. Carlotta knew that despite his constant threats, he would never leave her.

Christina received Carlotta's invitation with wry amusement. It was odd to remember how she had thrown Kade and Carlotta together—with her blessing. Now Carlotta was busily planning a very cordial and elaborate welcome-home party. There was no doubt in Christina's mind as to whom she was welcoming. Still, it would be fun to attend a soirée. There were so many people she wanted to see—people she had not seen in two years. And Carlotta could mobilize an elegant evening long before she herself would be able to prepare one—they were still in the very early stages of unpacking. She quickly penned a short acceptance to Carlotta's invitation and sent it to Willowbreak by messenger.

Renault was in Lawrence with Andrew Hardy. Chris had learned shortly after arriving on the island that Kade had moved all his business interests from Bajora to St. Marin. That had come as no surprise, and she was anxious to get involved in Evrion Enterprises again now that she was home. She had a carriage readied and quickly donned a cheerful, blue sprigged muslin morning gown. She would go to Lawrence today.

When she arrived at the Evrion offices she found Renault and Hardy discussing plans for a new rum refinery. Renault's agents had seen to it that a portion of his funds were invested in the lucrative rum business. Judging from the enthusiastic look on Kade's face, he was quite happy with the way things were progressing.

"You two look awfully pleased with yourselves," she said as she walked in.

Andy Hardy looked up and beamed at her. "Christina, child. It's good to have you back. And you've grown so stylish. I hardly recognize you."

She smiled. "It must have been all that shopping in Paris. The marquise knew every dressmaker in the city. I couldn't resist the urge to indulge myself."

Kade grinned. "Your weakness was our gain, kitten. Come and see what we've planned for the new facility." Renault spread out several blueprints on a wide table. She looked over the architect's plans and voiced her approval, but she was actually more interested in the new clipper. When they finished discussing the refinery, she asked, "What of the new mast, Andy? How did our lady like her new spine?"

"She took to the sea like a mermaid, child. There's none to compete with her in the Caribbean. Now that she's had three years to get used to the taste of sea salt, I'd say she was the finest ship the Evrion yards have produced in ten years."

"Then let's build more of her," said Renault.

"My sentiments exactly," Chris added. "But we'll need to meet with Van Auchs first to . . ."

"To see if we can cut down on the required sail. She's still too heavy," Kade offered.

Chris continued. "And that slows us down. You can never . . ."

"Have too much speed in a good ship." Renault finished.

Andy Hardy listened to this rapid exchange with a bemused expression.

"John's grave, but you two are beginning to think alike!" he said, shaking his head.

Christina and Kade looked at each other and began to laugh. It was true. There was nothing either could say to deny it.

When their laughter subsided, Chris looked at her husband and found that soft half smile on his handsome face. If Andy had not been beside them grinning broadly, she would have circled his neck with her arms and drawn him close for a kiss. Her thoughts were reflected in her eyes, and Kade's dark blue gaze became smokey with restrained passion.

Andy was no fool. Any male could read the meaning in Christina's glance, and Hardy could not fault Kade for his immediate reaction to the invitation. Andy cleared his throat and tactfully pointed out that he was expected at the shipyard for an inspection that would last the remainder of the day. He cheerfully bid them a pleasant afternoon, not that they would need any assistance, he thought.

Kade listened to the sound of Hardy's retreating footsteps and turned back to Chris. "It seems that Andy has left me with the formidable task of keeping you out of mischief this afternoon."

She looked up at him from beneath the thick fringe of her lashes. "I thought you had learned by now that it is not within your power to do that."

He turned and locked the door. Christina felt a twinge of anxiety even at this late date. She reminded herself that she no longer feared him. Hadn't he saved her life not once, but twice? He grinned at her rakishly. "I think that in the past my methods have been too subtle. I have learned that with you the direct approach is more effective." He reached for her but she neatly sidestepped his grasp.

"The problem with such a method," she said with a seriousness that mocked him, "is that it is easily seen." She carefully began to walk around him toward the door, watching him, anticipating another attempt to catch her. He feigned an attempt to her left, and, as she moved to the right to avoid him, he changed directions with agile ease and she suddenly found herself locked in his embrace, firmly pressed against his hard chest. Kade kissed her long and thoroughly. She felt herself being carried to a nearby table, which was hard and somewhat uncomfortable beneath her. When he lifted his head she looked at him with indignant sea-blue eyes.

"I didn't give you leave to . . ." she began.

"I do not need your permission, kitten, nor do I ever intend to ask." He grinned into her eyes in a manner that was almost indecent before his mouth covered hers. Perversely, she struggled with him, half-resenting the way he'd imposed his will even though only a few minutes before she had openly invited his caress with her eyes. She continued to fight even though her efforts were clearly useless. He quickly removed her pantelettes and spread her voluminous skirts as he opened his trousers and pressed close to her. When her resistance continued she heard his deep voice whisper, "Christina . . ."

She looked at him, and the need she saw in his eyes distracted her long enough for him to join their bodies. She sighed when she felt him inside her. He had won again. He always did. She put her arms around his neck and did nothing to stop the reflexive gripping motion of his muscles as he surged within her. Whenever she caressed him in that manner his handsome features took on an expression of transported concentration—as if he was momentarily lost in a world of pleasure and savored the visions the experience brought him. She felt his arms tighten, as though he were trying to draw her inside his skin, and she couldn't stifle a soft moan from the nearly painful pressure. His embrace relaxed enough to allow her breath, and his mouth covered her own with so many kisses that it became difficult to breathe again—for far more pleasant reasons.

Something magical entered her spirit like a gift from the man who held her. It was as if he imbedded a part of his identity within her, much as he implanted his seed. A voice inside her said, This is Renault, who saved your life and took you for his own. Accept your need of him and what he has to give. Fighting yourself and him will not change the fact that you are his, that you belong to him. Accept what has happened and find out what it is to be a woman who loves . . .

She relaxed. Her misgivings faded, and all her consciousness seemed to gather in the dark place where he was joined with her in the warm rhythym of love's timeless bond. Her hand caressed his back and the hard muscles of his buttocks. She bit his neck softly and her small tongue explored his ear. She heard him whisper soft, unintelligible words as he kissed her neck and gripped her hips with his hands to bring her closer. A deep, ragged sigh escaped him as she arched her back to meet his thrust. The sun burst inside them and they clung to each other, wrapped in a warm blanket of caring and need. A tangle of strong feelings rushed through their souls—not the least of which was surprise and a kind of grateful wonder.

In the carriage on the way back to Mimosa Keyes, Christina was quiet. Kade drew her companionably back against him, burying his lips in her hair, enjoying its fresh scent. She was thankful that he didn't tease her or attempt to draw her into conversation.

Her feelings were jumbled, and she sat in intense concentration, resting against him, trying to make sense of the closeness that was an almost tangible thing between them now.

At the Keyes, over dinner, she told him of Carlotta's invitation and her desire to go, explaining that it would be fun to renew the old ties with Marie and Veronique and all of the St. Marin crowd. His eyes were veiled as he suggested that it might be better to wait until Mimosa Keyes was ready for entertaining and then to give an affair of their own. Chris smiled but was firm in saying that she saw no reason to delay as long as Carlotta's preparations were so far in advance of any they could make for some time to come. He regarded her levelly for a few seconds and then capitulated. "All right, Chris, tell Carlotta we'll come."

In the days that followed, Chris spent long, happy hours attending to the myriad details of reopening Mimosa Keyes. Madame Ouvre was re-engaged, and soon Chris felt as if they had never left the island. Oddly, Jacques LaCroix and Guy Savant were conspicuously absent from the stream of Corsairs who regularly visited the Keyes. When she mentioned this to Renault he winked and grinned, telling her that the scuttlebutt was that Guy and Jacques had made it their business to be sure her two friends Marie and Veronique were never lonely.

As life went on at the Keyes, Carlotta continued the preparations for her *tour de force* at Willowbreak. She invited everyone, especially Marie and Veronique. She couldn't abide the two silly women, but they were Christina's closest chums, and the more preoccupied she was, the better.

Carlotta hadn't seen James in four days. She smiled to herself. He was probably licking his wounds in some brothel. It would keep him out of her hair, and as far as she was concerned, he could stay as long as he liked. She thought him a fool to care for her when she was obviously indifferent to him.

But he did care. James Marston sat in the taproom of the Alviron Hotel in Lawrence, consuming the better part of a bottle of dark St. Marin rum. He loathed the way she flirted openly with every attractive man within reach. But the worse part of living with Carlotta was the fact that, in spite of it all, he loved her. He had loved her since the night she came to his house and made it plain in terms that no man could misunderstand that she desired him. And it had been good—better than he had ever known it could be. He had wanted more. She insisted on marriage. When he thought about it the price seemed small. That had been over two years ago.

Now, even on a good day they talked to each other like polite strangers or maintained a civil silence when they found themselves in the same room. Yet, he still wanted her. No, it was more than that. Whatever she did or was, there was one fact he couldn't change—he loved her.

Marston bolted another glass of rum and swallowed hard as it burned its way down his throat. He'd had enough. He thought he couldn't live without her, but he was sure he couldn't live with her—not like this. Marston finished the bottle and dropped several gold coins on the table. They would have it out, he and his beautiful bitch of a wife, once and for all.

At Willowbreak the large open terrace was prepared and ready. The guests had already begun to arrive.

Marie Robillard was laughing with Jacques LaCroix, while her friend Veronique Lanier was regarding Guy Savant with rapt attention. Carlotta observed them with detached interest. She certainly could not fault their taste. The two tall Corsairs were very attractive. But she had set her cap for bigger game; for Carlotta, nothing less than their captain would do. And she wouldn't stop until she got him.

Carlotta had taken great pains to enhance her already considerable charms. Her gown was a deep, vivid coral that made her olive skin glow with warm lights. A topaz necklace of magnificent stones drew attention to her full, overflowing bodice. She looked enticing and she knew it.

Yet when she saw Christina walk into the ballroom on Kade's arm, she knew she would have a very difficult time seducing him from her side. Christina wore a dress that was so filmy and light that it seemed to be made of foam and sea mist. Its color exactly matched her aquamarine eyes. Her hair tumbled in rich profusion over her shoulders and down her back, where the long curls just brushed her tiny waist. The lovely face was aglow with the excitement of seeing old friends again, and the fine high cheekbones were flushed a rosy peach. She could hardly stand still at her husband's side, and she bobbed about like an agitated puppy. He smiled at her with an adoring look that wrenched Carlotta's stomach. She could barely restrain a frustrated grimace when Renault's hand gently caressed Christina's shoulder, and he bent his head to whisper soothingly in her ear.

Carlotta squared her shoulders and walked forward to greet them. She felt a rising surge of pleasure well up inside her as she approached Renault. He was such a handsome man. His broad, powerful shoulders were encased in a slate-blue waistcoat whose severe cut only heightened the reckless grace of his tall, well-muscled body. His pearl-gray trousers were impeccably cut, and Carlotta could see her reflection in the shine on his black boots. Tactfully she spoke first to Chris. "Ah, Christina," she purred. "So nice to have you back. I hope you enjoyed your stay abroad?"

"Yes, it was more than I'd dreamed really. I see you've fared well also," Chris said as she glanced over the elaborate decorations and richly appointed furnishings in the Willowbreak ballroom.

"We do manage," Carlotta replied easily. She turned to Renault. "And how have you been, Captain?"

"Very well, madame," he replied. The coolness in his eyes nettled her. "A few problems here and there, but nothing insurmountable."

Carlotta allowed her long lashes to flutter provocatively. "I'm sure you could handle almost anything." The double entendre was not lost on Renault, and he looked at her levelly. She turned again to Chris. "Come, let me take you to Marie and Veronique. They have been waiting."

She led them across the room to the laughing foursome. Marie and Veronique hugged Christina, while Jacques and Guy teased them with good humor. Carlotta endured their conversation for a half hour. Her attention strayed several times to the chiseled perfection of Renault's profile and the irresistible charm of his dazzling white grin. She was nettled that he seemed all but unaware of her, despite the pains she'd taken with her gown and jewels.

Out of the corner of her eye, Carlotta noticed the belated entrance of her husband. His blond hair was tousled and his cravat was askew, though that was imperceptible to all but the discerning eye. His brown eyes looked haunted, almost pained. Carlotta decided cynically that wherever he had spent the night must have proved very disagreeable indeed.

It was time to execute her plan. She maneuvered Renault slightly apart from the group with subtle positionings of her body until she could whisper out of range of the others' hearing. "I must speak with you alone," she said. "It concerns Christina's welfare. Meet me in the garden in a quarter of an hour.'" Her words had been spoken so quickly and so softly that she was half afraid he hadn't heard. But the inquiring expression on his face told her that he had. She smiled inwardly and excused herself from the group, relieved. She could never abide the chatter of Veronique Lanier for more than five minutes without contracting an acute headache.

Carlotta crossed the room to greet her husband. "Well, James, you decided to come after all," she said drily.

He looked at her through tortured gray eyes for a long moment before he said, "Carlotta, it's time we really talked, you and I."

She raised her eyebrows. "And what have we to say to one another that has not already been made plain?"

"Many things." His expression seemed almost tender. "There is really a lot that I want you to know. I think we can make things . . . better . . . between us."

"Do you, indeed?" she said drily. Then she laughed a small, brittle laugh. "You always were a dreamer,

James. You never see things as they really are. You're afraid to face them, to face me or yourself, and you're afraid to face life."

He took a deep breath. "That may have been true before tonight, but not any more. I have to talk to you. Come away where we can be private."

"Are you mad? We're entertaining guests, in case you haven't noticed. Now stop being ridiculous and be a good host. Nothing you have to say could possibly make the slightest difference between us anyway."

James watched her retreating back with a futile, melancholy expression on his face. She didn't care for him, and in that moment Marston resigned himself to the fact that she never would. As soon as he could he would leave Willowbreak with its bitter memories and, God willing, make a new life for himself.

Poor James was becoming worse and worse, Carlotta decided as she slowly made her way to the garden through the milling throng of guests. But he was right about the two of them. Things could not continue as they were for much longer.

She could make out a tall, shadowy form beside a white marble statue in the garden. Her heart began to beat rapidly. Renault had come. As she closed the distance between them she saw that his azure eyes were cool and unfriendly. He spoke first.

"All right, Carlotta. What is so urgent?"

Instead of answering him, she reached up and wound her arms around his neck, drawing his head close to hers and kissing him deeply.

In the ballroom Chris had grown suspicious when from the corner of her eye, she saw Carlotta whispering with Kade. She had felt a sharp pang of jealousy when Renault lowered his head to catch Carlotta's soft words. Damn it, she thought to herself. I was never jealous before. What's wrong with me now? She tried to reason her way out of the feeling, but when Carlotta disappeared and Renault left shortly after, her imagination gave her no peace.

She followed Carlotta with her eyes, and when she left James to go into the garden, Chris excused herself from the laughing group to follow the coral-gowned figure. She told herself that she was being quite silly. Chris was about to turn back when she saw Carlotta stop in the garden, and as her eyes adjusted to the darkness, she recognized Kade Renault's tall silhouette. Angry resentment and irrational jealousy welled inside her and clouded her vision like a red veil.

Quietly she walked up behind the woman, who was passionately kissing her husband. She stood for one second behind them. Then something in her snapped, and she gave a choke of pure rage. Kade's eyes flew open with surprise. Carlotta was too engrossed in the sensations of the moment to hear or notice that he had suddenly stiffened in her arms.

Christina reached out and entangled her fingers in Carlotta's brown hair and gave a powerful yank. Carlotta's head wrenched abruptly away from Renault's as she squealed with surprise and fear. As she turned to stare into Christina's wild eyes, she caught her breath in dismay. For a second she stood paralyzed by shock and surprise.

Christina still held a glass of champagne in her hand. Her blood boiled at the guilty expression she saw in Carlotta's eyes, and without thinking about it, she dashed the wine in the woman's face. Carlotta's hand flew to her eyes with a cry of rage as she desperately rubbed to clear her vision. But Christina wasn't finished. With both hands she grabbed the bodice of Carlotta's coral gown and pulled with all her strength. The fabric ripped away with a loud tearing noise, and when Carlotta's vision cleared, the first thing she saw was her own chemise, the coral gown gaping away from her body like a loose house robe.

"You had better go inside through the back and change your gown, Carlotta," Christina said with cold anger, "before I think of a more fitting way to repay your hospitality." Carlotta looked to Renault for aid, but he was smiling at them both in a infuriating way, and she could tell from the gleam of amusement in his eye that he was enjoying the scene immensely. She would get no sympathy from him.

Anger and bile rose in her throat. She stood facing Chris, her bosom heaving with rising indignation, gathering her strength as she prepared to charge. But just as Carlotta was about to lunge at her assailant, Christina smashed her champagne glass against the marble statue and held the jagged remnant inches away from Carlotta's face. Her voice sent chills up Carlotta's spine as she said, "If you don't leave, I'll cut your treacherous face to ribbons. Get out of here, Carlotta—now. Or no man will ever want to look at you again."

Carlotta hesitated for one brief moment, wondering if Chris would really carry out her threat. But the deadly calm in the turquoise eyes was more menacing than the fiery rage of a moment before. Defeated, Carlotta turned with a sob and ran to a secluded entrance on the far side of Willowbreak.

Christina lowered the hand that held the broken glass. She felt drained and shaky and suddenly cold. Then she heard a deep voice beside her saying, "Madame, you are full of surprises." She looked at Renault and felt a sudden wave of embarrassment. She almost laughed aloud when she thought of how incongruous it was to feel shy and embarrassed now of all times, after she'd nearly maimed poor Carlotta for life.

Kade was watching her with an expression on his face that was a mixture of undisguised amusement and smug pleasure.

"Well, you needn't look so pleased about what happened!"

"And why not, since I enjoyed it thoroughly?"

"You are incorrigible."

"Completely, but tonight I hardly think you are in a favorable position to sit in judgment of my behavior. I am of a mind to get you home as quickly as possible before your temper does real harm."

"Damn you, Kade. This is your fault! Before I met you, life was simple, and now look at me! What an innocent I was not to run away the first time I saw you."

"Innocent?" he inquired with one brow cocked.

"I was! Until you happened into my life and did your worst!"

Kade rubbed his chin with mock ruefulness. "You have hinted as much before. Actually, judging by your response, I've been under the impression that I've been doing rather well, but I'm willing to try again if you feel dissatisfied with our encounters so far."

Christina glared at him for a long moment and then smiled frostily. "Hoping you'll improve?" she asked.

Kade regarded her with an expression of utter sweetness and said, "No, my dear. I am hoping you will."

Chris bit her lip in silent frustration. There was no getting the better of him in the jocular mood he was in. She itched to beat her fists against his chest and scream at him in anger, but even in her state of agitation she realized that most of the frustration she felt was really directed at herself for having played the jealous wife. She turned and walked with as much calm as she could muster through the gardens toward their waiting carriage.

She was quiet during the long ride back to Mimosa Keyes. Her thoughts were wildly jumbled. There was no escaping the fact that she had been insanely, irrationally jealous. She had actually wanted to kill Carlotta, for heaven's sake! The woman had only kissed Renault, and she had wanted to slit her throat!

Upstairs in their bedroom she sat before her dressing table, lost in thought, brushing her hair. Christina took a long, hard look at herself. She had seen Paris, gone to the ballet, experienced the opera, known the admiring gaze of barons and earls, but none of that had made her one whit happier than she had been the day she left St. Marin. All her wanderings had brought her no closer to the spiritual home her mother spoke of, nor the peace and balance of Gideon's world. With a mixture of melancholy and chagrin, she realized that many of her happiest moments occurred when she was with her husband.

Kade walked in wearing a long robe of ruby velvet. He watched her for long moments as she sat brushing her hair, her eyes absently focused on the blue bay beneath their window. He crossed the room slowly and lifted her in his arms. She had not spoken a word since the tableau in the garden. He gazed into her serious eyes and lowered his head, fusing their mouths in a deep kiss.

Crossing the room, he laid her gently on the bed without breaking their contact. After a long moment he raised his head and said softly, "What are you thinking?"

Renault held his breath. There was an expression in her eyes that he had never seen before, and his heart refused to slow to a regular beat.

She sighed wearily. Even if she did love him, after what she had seen tonight she would never be able to trust him. She felt exposed and totally vulnerable— and inexplicably sad.

"Nothing. It is just the excitement. I'm still very tense."

For a moment she thought a flicker of disappointment crossed his face, but then it was gone.

He grinned sardonically, "Then let us see what we can do to help you relax."

Much later, Christina lay staring at the ceiling, unable to find the easy slumber that enveloped Kade.

CHAPTER THIRTY-SIX

At breakfast Renault told Christina that Guy Savant and Jacques LaCroix would come with him to Scotland. He needed two good men to help him with the lands there, which were considerably more extensive than either of their estates in St. Marin or Bajora. After a moment's thought, Christina concurred and suggested that Mimosa Keyes be left under Andrew Hardy's care, along with the St. Marin ship line.

Kade agreed that Hardy was a perfect choice, adding that Logan Armor would assume the management of the Bajoran quays and Falcon Hall, with Joshua Boman acting as the liaison between the two islands, as well as running a duty-free shop in St. Marin. With that settled, Renault wolfed down the enormous breakfast before him, kissed her good-bye, and left for Lawrence.

Christina left the dining room soon after, walking thoughtfully through the long foyer to the terrace, intending to spend an hour in the garden near her mother's grave, knowing that she would soon be leaving her childhood home.

When she reached the front entrance she was surprised to find Janie climbing down from a small carriage and beaming at her. Joshua Boman held the reins with quiet assurance, a hint of a smile on his face.

For two days Chris had been wondering where Janie was, and after the initial relief of seeing her, she noticed that the girl was wearing a gown that was entirely white—a fichu and cameo clasped demurely over her young shoulders and bosom.

"Janie, what are you up to . . ." Chris began, a sneaking suspicion dawning.

"Mis' Chris! Joshua and I eloped!" Janie grinned.

Chris smiled back and ruefully shook her head. "Joshua, you sly devil, stealing her from me. I should be angry, but I'm delighted for you both."

"I'll take good care of her, ma'am," Joshua said in his low, distinctly full tones.

"Come in, both of you. We must drink a toast to the happiness of the bride and groom," she said.

The weeks that followed at Mimosa Keyes were filled with activity. Renault wanted to make sure that everything could be run smoothly and efficiently from their new home. The lines of communication would have to be as fast and effective as possible. Chris spent hours with Hardy in Lawrence. She was not looking forward to leaving the Evrion line behind, but she admitted to herself that she was curious about the life that lay ahead of them, and her sense of adventure was stirred.

For several days she noticed that Guy Savant was a frequent visitor to the Robillard mansion and that Jacques LaCroix was seen with equal frequency at Veronique Lanier's home. Chris sensed something afoot. The two young women had been conspicuously absent as visitors to the Keyes, an unusual occurrence. Even more strange was the difficulty she had in reaching them. It was odd she thought, considering how close the three of them were.

Then one evening, Renault entered the *petit salon jaune*, tall and formidable, looking much like the cat who emptied the lily pond of goldfish. Christina had just finished supervising the packing of several crates of fine bone china. "It seems your two friends are about to make honest men of the two most determined rogues in the Caribbean, my love."

"What?"

"Jacques and Guy have decided that the bachelor life no longer suits them. It seems the charms of your two friends proved an irresistible lure."

"Veronique and Marie?"

"Exactly."

"*Mon Dieu!* So much excitement—it is overwhelming."

"But fun, too," he said, drawing her into his arms for a kiss. "And aren't you glad that they will be coming with us?"

She was.

The two weddings were lovely. Marie looked pale and beautiful in a white silk polonaise gown, panniered and ruched with insets of Belgian lace, while Guy stood by, quite the solemn groom and more serious than Christina had ever seen him.

Jacques and Veronique, however, beamed at each other in a most undignified manner as Veronique marched down the aisle on her father's arm.

Preparations for the journey progressed rapidly after the weddings. In the scant few days remaining before their voyage, Christina said farewell to Andrew Hardy, Janie, and Josh—and wished Logan good luck, although the man would scarcely need it. He was as solid and sensible as granite. Kade had chosen an excellent manager for his Bajoran interests.

Christina went to visit Gideon, but no one was in the large cabin in the mountains when she arrived.

She left a beautifully bound volume of *Paradise Lost* by Milton from the Evrion library as a parting gift.

On the day of their departure she stood on the steps of the Keyes, looking down at Lawrence Bay, blue and sparkling in the tropical sun. The *Falcon* was anchored there, waiting for them to board. Renault stood a short distance away, watching her, looking handsome and formidable in a severely cut waistcoat that accented the breadth of his shoulders. His blue eyes took on a rakish gleam, and there was a note of adventure in his voice as he said, "Ready, Madame Renault?"

Chris smiled back at him. "Yes."

"Then let's away."

He took her arm and led her to the waiting carriage.

CHAPTER THIRTY-SEVEN

In spite of the *Falcon*'s immense size and numerous decks, Chris felt cramped on the voyage. Kade and the Corsairs had the run of the ship, while Christina and the other women stayed in rather close quarters, although Renault made certain that they were allowed to use the forecastle for exercise and a stroll once a day. She developed a bad case of cabin fever, notwithstanding her love of the sea, and she was glad when they reached the English Channel. The *Falcon* sailed into the Firth of Tay and weighed anchor near Dundee, where Renault assembled their considerable retinue in horse-drawn vehicles and set out overland for Brenkirk and Castle MacVeagh.

The sky was a clear azure blue and the morning sun shone high above the ambling green hills, which were covered with purple heather and thickets of blue pine. Here and there, the trees parted to reveal a distant glimpse of the ocean.

Renault's band passed mile after mile of meadow, loch, and moor. Chris saw ruined abbeys, gray, peaceful flocks of sheep feeding in secluded glades, and small farm cottages with slate roofs, studded with short, squat chimneys of red and brown brick. An invigorating freshness filled the air once they were free of the town. Chris was chilly in the double-panniered riding habit she wore; even the cut-off velvet waistcoat did not keep her warm. She regretted not unpacking the fur-lined mantle Renault had purchased in Dundee and resolved to don it as soon as they stopped for food.

While they traveled Renault amused himself by telling her tales of the days when the Scottish borders were a fighting district, existing in part on plunder taken from English farms over the hills. Even though the wearing of the kilt had been banned for a time following the political upheaval that swept the country, the fighting spirit still lingered in the rugged green hills like a quiet shadow.

As they neared Brenkirk, Kade told her the history of the castle. Sir Gavin MacVeagh had built the fortress in the sixteenth century for the purpose of defense. Over the years it had proved indispensable as a bulwark against invaders of all sorts.

Castle MacVeagh was deeply rooted in the neighborhood, its inhabitants living abundantly but not ostentatiously on food grown on its own lands and dispensing generous but unpatronizing hospitality to local people of every kind. Kade's earldom was an estate of many hundreds of acres and numerous farms. MacVeagh Castle was a community of more than a hundred people—living, working, intriguing, and gossiping together. Moreover, the community extended beyond the household to a number of people who, in some way or other, were connected with the land and the Renaults—various relatives who came to stay whenever they could and the bailiffs, shepherds, herdsmen, and farmworkers who ran or worked the farms themselves. All of these were constantly coming and going; many were regularly fed at MacVeagh even if they did not sleep there.

Christina's first sight of MacVeagh came abruptly as they rounded a glade. It was massive and vertical—

nestled in a forest of ancient oaks and blue pines, surmounted by a complicated skyline of clustered turrets and gray lichened stone. She stared in silence for a moment; the structure commanded a certain respectful awe. Yet the overall appearance was friendly—MacVeagh was surrounded by a bower of lush woods and parkland, and bordered by purple, heather-covered moors.

The procession made its way up the pebble-strewn road to the castle itself. Despite the extensively groomed greenery surrounding MacVeagh, once inside, Chris could not dispel the feeling of being in a hunting lodge. A stag's head and antlers were mounted over every door she had thus far seen. Renault led them through the west entrance of the north wing, the oldest part of the castle. It led to the armory, where the family weapons and arms were stored.

"These are just antiques," Kade explained casually as Chris's eyes roamed the walls, covered inch for inch with mounted shields, swords, guns, and armor. "Relics of forgotten battles. The working weapons are stored on a floor below us."

Chris shivered a bit as she looked at a ball of spiked iron bound to a leather grip by a heavy chain. Kade caught the small gesture and shrugged, adding with a smile that despite the calm, green appearance of the land, all was not always peaceful.

An understatement, Chris thought to herself.

Christina asked Kade why his surname was not the same as that of the castle. He obligingly explained that one of his ancestors had been French, the younger son of a well-placed family in Normandy. His great-grandmother, Eileen MacVeagh, was the only surviving child of Raeburn, the fourth earl of Bren-kirk. The plague had claimed Raeburn's wife and he was himself dying of it when he gave his young daughter to Alan Renault of Normandy in marriage. It was an alliance made for her protection, and part of the nuptial contract called for a large number of men and arms to be brought from France for the fortifica-tion of MacVeagh. To this day the titled earl re-mained the recognized leader of Brenkirk's men, a civil and military authority responsible for the organi-zation of hundreds of soldiers ready to pick up arms if danger threatened.

Chris was amazed as she watched Renault inside his ancestral home. He seemed to fill MacVeagh with his presence. It was obvious that this was his ele-ment—the place from which he'd sprung and the source of his strength. Here Kade was at ease and very much in control. Renault was both autocratic and stern—his authority was absolutely beyond question. Christina was nonplussed—the transformation was un-settling. She soon decided, however, that it was not a transformation of all. This was merely Renault in his true guise, the part of him that had been hidden be-neath the glib, charming surface.

As they left the armory they passed into a superb sequence of reception rooms running through the east wing—a music room, two drawing rooms, an enormous dining hall, a sculpture gallery filled with statuary, an orangery—and near the end of the southern passage, a little theater, complete with a beautifully painted stage.

Kade paused at a latticed window to point out the great bridge in the west garden and the stables to the left of it. Springs on the moors above MacVeagh supplied it with ample water for ponds and cascades. Guests could drive through the wooded park, wander about the gardens and return to the theater for a play or concert, followed by a candlelight dinner in the main hall.

As Renault continued they entered the library, a long vaulted gallery lined with a seemingly infinite number of bound volumes. A balcony ran the length of the room to allow a reader access to the otherwise inaccessible shelves near the ceiling. Christina saw two young men rise from a pair of leather wing chairs near the fireplace. Spying their identical grins and glinting sherry-colored eyes, Chris realized that they were twins.

"Well, Kincaid," a jovial voice boomed, "you took your time about getting here."

"What did you expect?" the other young man said, laughing. "Have you ever known your brother to think of the convenience of anyone save himself?"

"I'll thank you two young jackanapes to keep civil tongues in your heads," Kade retorted.

"Ho, ho! Listen to that, will you now. Our brother's already beginning to sound like old Jemmie, God rest his soul."

Chris looked from one to the other and found it impossible to tell them apart. Renault took her hand and said, "These two worthless fellows are my brothers, Bryce and Barry. Lads, my bride Christina."

As they bent over her hand in turn, she murmured, "I am very pleased to meet you . . . Bryce . . . Barry."

A guffaw followed her greeting, and she realized with embarrassment that she had reversed their names. Kade laughed.

"Don't despair, love. It takes time to separate these ruffians." He turned to Bryce and said, "Are Guy and Jacques settled in?"

"Aye, we took them to their apartments, and they seemed well satisfied."

Kade had given his two lieutenants grants of one hundred acres of land from the MacVeagh estate, as well as a monetary sum sufficient for each to build a country manor if he wished. Until their homes were complete, however, they would reside at MacVeagh—which suited Renault because much remained to be settled.

Christina tried unsuccessfully to stifle a yawn.

"Have you no eyes to see that your wife is tired, brother?" said Barry.

Kade glanced quickly at Chris and smiled. "It has been a long day. There will be plenty of time later to become acquainted. Come, I'll take you to our apartments."

Renault led the way to the north wing of MacVeagh, the area where he casually mentioned most of their time would be spent. She found herself in a bedroom whose formality was unexpected. The room was dominated by an ornate, enormous bed—replete with a canopy and high spitalfields of blue brocade adorning carved mahogany posts. Renault was amused by the expression in her eyes, and he explained that the bedroom was used for christenings and other occasions of state, which explained the numerous chairs and couches in the room as well as the elaborate bed.

He left her then, with a casual remark that they would dine soon and that a maid would be in shortly to help her. With a light kiss, Kade disappeared.

After a moment she heard a knock at the door.

"Who is it?"

"It's me, mum. Your maid, Betsy."

"Come in, please."

A young girl dressed in a gray muslin dress and starched white apron entered.

"Did you say it was Betsy?"

The girl nodded and smiled.

"Well, I am happy to meet you." Christina noticed that Betsy was staring. "Is there something wrong?"

"Oh no! It's just that . . . well, mum, you are even more beautiful than they said."

The girl blushed. "I dinna mean it that way! It is only that we have all been so curious, you see, about the one who laid his lairdship low. He were never the sort to settle down—not him."

Chris was suddenly interested. "Tell me about him, Betsy."

"Oh, mum, he was the biggest rakehell in these lands—by far the wildest of the brothers. Sir Jamie, rest his soul, despaired of Kincaid ever living to see his old age, and whenever he came back to Brenkirk the lassies were nae safe. Not that they wanted to be— he was their favorite, was your Kincaid, mum," she concluded with a smile.

"He hasn't changed much."

Betsy grinned. "Well, something must have happened, for none of the mothers in Brenkirk could coax him to the altar and 'twas nae for lack of trying. There was one fair maid who took the news of his marriage much amiss."

"And who would that be?"

"Lady Gwendolyn Ellesmere, mum. A widow—and lovely she is. She was ever finding a reason to be about

when the earl's younger brother returned for a visit."
Betsy suddenly remembered the time. "My goodness!
Dinner will be served, and you'll nae be ready. Here,
mum, let me help you with your gown."

It took a few minutes to change from her riding
habit into a frothy *chemise à l'anglaise*, a daring new
style that flowed over the figure without the voluminous petticoats worn beneath panniered gowns. It was
made of gauzelike lingerie fabric and cut away at the
loose skirt to reveal a contrasting under-fabric of pale
green watered silk. It was very late and dinner had
been served long ago, but Kade had ordered a light
supper prepared for them before they retired.

Renault appeared once the table and settings were
in place. He looked marvelously handsome in a vest of
soft blue velvet, white lawn shirt, and cream breeches.

His blue gaze swept her appreciatively as he
crossed the room to stand before her. "What do you
think of MacVeagh thus far, Chris?" he asked as his
hands dropped lightly over her shoulders.

"It's . . . overwhelming. Kade, I had no idea that it
was so large."

"Yes," he smiled, pulling out her chair, "it is a bit
much at first, but you will become accustomed to it in
time."

As they ate, Renault amused her with stories of his
childhood. Chris listened with interest, laughing at the
mischief Kade and his brothers had fallen into when
they were young. She became so absorbed in his anecdotes that she scarcely noticed how much warmer the
sensuous expression in his blue eyes grew as the evening waned. Presently, Christina sat toying with her
second glass of wine. Renault endured her dawdling

until it became apparent that she had no intention of finishing. He looked at her significantly and rose.

Taking her hand, he led her to the canopied bed. A breeze played with the skirts of her thin gown, and she shivered as he drew her down beside him on the bed.

He muzzled the soft spot where her shoulder joined her neck, murmuring in his deep voice, "It is as green here as your island."

She laughed with real amusement. "Yes, but your castle is cold at night."

The blue eyes smiled at her in the darkness. "You'll soon be warmer," he said as he began to untie the ribbons at her waist. "As will I."

She felt herself melting beneath the probing tenderness of his kiss. He made love to her slowly, unhurriedly, as though he savored the occasion of their first joining at MacVeagh. His caresses were gentle and stirring. As she lay in Kade's arms, the solid presence of his warmth beside her was infinitely reassuring. She relaxed and allowed him his way.

Her entire body became liquid and flowing, surrounding him with a heat and warmth that was reflected from him back to her, a reciprocal warmth that kindled them both. She felt filled to bursting by the solid thrusting hardness that surged within her. Christina was seized by a paroxysm of pleasure that stole her breath as he rose like a well-tempered sword into the core of her being. Kade's steely warmth worked like a drug on her senses, and she felt herself melting, merging smoothly with him in an unspoken bond of love.

He lay over her—his weight still upon her—as if he wanted to stay, not to leave her. Chris wound her arms about Kade's neck, holding him close, knowing in that moment the full force of the love she felt for the man who cradled her so warmly in his embrace. Listening to the deep sound of his breath, resting against his solid shoulder, she drifted quietly off to sleep.

In the morning Betsy was in a jovial mood as Chris quickly donned a pink and white striped satin gown with a white satin stomacher, tiny peplum, lingerie ruffles, and lace ruching. She hurried down to breakfast. Kade had risen long ago, and she strongly suspected that the household rose at an earlier hour than she was accustomed.

Chris greeted Marie and Veronique with a fond hug and smiled at Kade, who stood talking with Jacques and Guy a short distance away. As Chris turned her attention to the long mahogany dining table, her eyes widened in surprise.

Never had she seen so much food at this hour of the morning. She turned to Kade and said, "Such an early hour for a banquet. Is it a jest?"

He laughed. "No, it's breakfast. Have some," he said, popping a raisin-studded scone into her mouth.

The larder before them groaned under the weight of a dozen silver chafing dishes brimming with buttered, farm-fresh eggs and broiled mushrooms, tomatoes, thick English bacon and savory Scottish porridge, kedgeree and kidneys, poached finnan haddie in milk, thick slices of cold, undercooked roast beef, lamb chops, hot rolls, kippers, scones, and several mouth-watering marmalades and honeys.

Christina looked at the table for a moment before she observed with some disappointment, "There are no croissants here."

Renault guffawed. When he regained his composure he said with a smile, "No, there are no croissants—you'll have to make do, I'm afraid."

She tried everything and found it all delicious, but she could not help thinking to herself, Curious . . . all this and not one small croissant.

Bryce and Barry walked into the dining room, full of rowdy good spirits and morning cheer.

"Good morning! Had your breakfast, I see," Bryce piped cheerfully.

"Yes," Renault replied, "and you two would do well to finish yours quickly, in view of your late start."

"We were only waiting for you to rise, brother," Bryce grinned.

"Yes, we thought you might like an extra hour this morning. I know I would have," Barry said, casting a sidelong glance at Chris.

Renault raised a brow, silently warning them to curb their tongues. "What news have you of these months past?"

"Well," Bryce answered, "if you wish, we can tell you now or mayhap you would prefer to wait until there are no ladies present."

Christina shot Kade an arch look that he found hard to ignore. "Tell us now," he replied.

"Morwell still has an eye for the crops and livestock here. He had a bountiful harvest and prospered, but two of the farms on Morwell's land failed completely. He could ill afford it. You know about the raiding parties he sent into Brenkirk last year. In the past few months his raids have become more frequent. Half of the sheep and livestock on MacLaren's farm have been stolen. It cannot go on forever. The farmers along the border will not go into their own fields for fear their animals will not be there when they return."

Renault's eyes became a glacial blue, which Chris thought boded ill for Morwell. He looked down at her and said, "Why don't you take your friends into the garden for tea? Bryce and I have a small matter to discuss this morning, but I will join you this afternoon for a ride."

She started to protest—she wanted to hear more, but there was no arguing with the quiet note of command in his voice. She acquiesced with a sigh.

"What do you think Kade will do, Christina?" Veronique asked as she nibbled a piece of Dundee cake.

Chris watched while Renault and the men left the dining hall, walking toward the library. She turned to her friend.

"To be honest, Veronique, I have no idea. Come, there is no point in remaining here."

Marie and Veronique followed her into the garden, where tea was waiting on a lace-covered table.

Marie Savant sighed heavily. "The Earl of Morwell is very cunning. Guy told me that after Renault defeated him in last year's battle, Morwell agreed to respect the northern borders. In return, Renault allowed him to retain his own lands. But less than a year has passed, and Morwell has rearmed his men—and already raided several Brenkirk farms."

"This is the first I have heard of this Morwell," Veronique exclaimed in exasperation. "Jacques never tells me anything. Just wait until we are alone tonight," she fumed.

"He did not wish to frighten you, I'm sure," Marie said placatingly.

"I suppose not," Vernoque sighed. "There is so

much to think about now that I despair of keeping track of it all. Our new home is uppermost in my thoughts."

Marie smiled. "Mine also. I love MacVeagh, Christina, but I am consumed with impatience, waiting for our own home to be built."

Chris murmured a sympathetic response, but she was barely listening to the conversation. In truth, she would have given a chest of gold to be in the library with Renault and his men—the suspense was terrible.

CHAPTER THIRTY-EIGHT

In the library Kade Renault was lost in thought as he stared into the fire. He sat in a huge morocco-leather wing chair, absently drinking port as he listened to Barry argue with his brother.

"Blast it, Barry, you're slow enough at times to grow moss on your pate. If you had your way, that devil Garrick would have had the whole of Brenkirk for his own by now!" Bryce swore passionately.

But Barry shook his head. "You were ever a hot-head, brother. I know better than you what Morwell has done. But I'll not say yes to a war that would harm the land and make paupers of those who trust us."

Kade looked up at Guy Savant, who stood leaning nonchalantly against the fireplace.

"You've been very silent, Guy."

Savant looked at Kade. "For once I agree with Bryce. Morwell's last raid leveled three farms, and the prize livestock he's stolen will be difficult to replace. He has to be stopped, or he will take our inaction for acquiescence."

Renault silently concurred. He felt more strongly about Morwell than any of them, and it galled him that he'd been lenient with his malevolent neighbor during the first attacks. Like Barry, he'd hoped to avoid the ravages of a major border war. But the farms which Morwell had raided were among the best in Brenkirk—it was time to recover the losses as well as put an end to his perfidy.

Kade turned to Barry with a charming, but implacable smile. "I share your reluctance to engage Morwell in yet another battle at the border, Barry, but ignoring him is not an acceptable alternative in this case. We *will* pay him a visit—and one that he will not soon forget."

"Can we obtain aid from the king?" Barry asked.

Renault shook his head.

"We do not need it, and the king is preoccupied with our Spanish neighbors, as you well know. It would only delay matters to contact him and constrain ourselves to wait months for his reply."

"It seems we have no choice in the matter," Barry muttered.

"I think not, but do not worry. I have a plan that will cost us little and gain much in the way of advantage over our esteemed neighbor."

The better part of an hour elapsed before they emerged from the library. A light mist fell on the evergreens and shrubs of MacVeagh. The air was cool, scented with pine, heather, and fresh earth. Guy left to begin preparations for the coming mission, and Barry headed for the stables. Bryce joined him, with the intention of paying a call on his latest love, Alison McWilliam, daughter of Ian of Aberfoyle.

As he left the paneled elegance of MacVeagh library, the eighth Earl of Brenkirk was in a thoughtful mood. He strode through the garden, letting its tranquil quiet calm his heated thoughts. His booted feet fell noiselessly on the grass. Turning a corner, he spotted Christina strolling along a secluded path with Marie Savant beside her. He was hidden from view by the tall shrubs, and he stood there silently, drinking in his wife's beauty until they disappeared behind a curtain of tall knotted spruce.

Renault sat down on a marble bench, his blue eyes trained on the bubbling fountain before him, fixed and unseeing. More than anything else he wanted Christina's love. Her wild young body came alive beneath his touch, and he reveled in the warm softness of her caress, but he wanted something deeper, needed something more lasting, a feeling to rely on as a source of strength and caring. He wanted her love; somehow he would get it.

There were times when he felt very close to her, as if in an instant, if he neither drew breath nor moved too quickly, she would come to him and tell him what he longed to hear. He'd seen an expression on her face that was tremblingly close to love, but it invariably faded, and she became again the mocking, provocative pixie who dared him to play on her terms.

Kade sighed. He'd used all the tricks he knew, but nothing worked. She remained responsive beneath his touch, but stubbornly locked away when he tried to reach her in other ways. It was maddening, but now there was new hope. He had at last succeeded in bringing her to his domain—and here everything and everyone deferred to his will. Kade smiled as he contemplated the intriguing prospect of winning her at last. He began to plan.

With all of the confusing activity during the next few days, Chris would have been utterly lost had it not been for Kade's maiden aunt, Mara Renault. Chris liked her enormously. She was beyond her prime, but years hadn't lessened the twinkle in her brown eyes or the fire in her voice. From Mara, Chris learned quickly that having six guests in residence was called "having no one in the house." Meals were eaten in the upstairs dining hall in winter and the great hall in summer. Before his death Jamie had built a gallery adjoining the theater with soft, cushioned benches and carved oak paneling warming its length. She soon learned that politics was discussed in the library, business never. The Renaults, she surmised, were like no one else—yet they were very much like each other, lively, absent-minded, full of waggery, quick to anger and as quickly to forgiveness.

The new earl had been away for some time and was anxious to meet with old friends. He invited a small group to MacVeagh for a performance of Shakespeare's *A Midsummer Night's Dream* by the Brenkirk players. The list of invited guests was extensive—it included the family and several old friends.

During intermission Christina sat in the long gallery outside the little theater with Barry. She wore a *robe à la française* made of soft robin's-egg-blue taffeta edged with scalloped ruffles, bows, and velvet ribbons. The stomacher and collarette of the gown were frothed with delicate lace insets and tiny pearls. She sat idly watching the guests as Kade emerged from the theater. Their eyes met as she smiled at him. Kade started for the little alcove where they were seated, but took no more than two steps before a tall, statuesque redhead determinedly grasped his arm. Renault looked puzzled as he gazed down at her, then his face lit with recognition. The warm smile that spread across his handsome features caused a painful lurch in Christina's heart. The girl stood on tiptoe and whispered something in Kade's ear that made him throw back his head and laugh aloud.

Chris seethed inwardly as the young woman fairly glowed with satisfaction, the expression on her face caressing and seductive.

"Barry, who is that woman speaking with Kade?"

"Lady Gwendolyn Ellesmere."

The gown she wore left little to the imagination. It was cunningly wrought of thin green silk, so gauzelike that the décolletage of the bodice revealed almost as much as it covered. The jeweled stomacher and plunging neckline of the dress were outrageously bold, but the gown only served to heighten the young woman's already striking looks.

"Tell me about her," Chris said thoughtfully.

"She is the widow of Baron Lionel Ellesmere, who passed on five years ago. Gwendolyn finds the widowed life much to her liking, I think. There are dozens of men who would convince her otherwise, but she'll have none of it. Not even Bryce has found a place in her heart—and not many women are able to resist my brother. But then, there has never been any doubt which of the Renaults Gwen prefers."

"Yes, she does make that quite obvious."

"Jealous, Chris?"

When Chris failed to respond, Barry laughed lightly. "I always thought Kade was made of stone to be able to resist her," he said, looking wistfully at Gwendolyn's pretty, upturned face.

Chris looked at his ardent, open eyes with surprise.

"Why, Barry, I believe you're in love with her."

"Guilty," he admitted ruefully. "But that has never done me any good. She barely looks my way—and when she does, she calls me Bryce."

Chris swallowed the giggle that welled up inside her.

"I'm sorry. Perhaps someday it will work out for you."

Barry watched as Gwendolyn continued to gaze sensuously at the earl.

"Perhaps," he said, unconvinced.

Guy and Marie ambled across the gallery to join them in the little alcove as they sat waiting for the play to resume.

"Does tonight's entertainment meet with your approval, milady?" Guy asked.

Chris smiled and nodded an affirmative reply.

"The play is quite good, don't you think, *chéri?*" Marie said, turning to her new husband.

Guy grinned rakishly. "Yes, my love—but then everything seems better to me now that we are wed."

Marie favored him with a radiant smile, and Chris felt a twinge of envy at the accord that existed between them.

Veronique and Jacques stood a few feet away. Chris could hear them discussing the play. Veronique had not understood the performance, and she remarked now to Jacques that she found it confusing and scattered.

"No more scattered than your wits, my love," Jacques replied with a grin. Veronique tried to cuff him, but he laughingly put up a hand to ward off her blow.

Bryce entered the gallery with a striking young auburn-haired beauty on his arm. Barry told Chris that she was Alison McWilliam, the lovely maid Bryce had been courting attentively for many weeks. She wore a supremely fashionable *lévite* gown of soft pink silk with satin trimming and matching ribbons along the hem. Alison's hair hung in shining loose curls that framed the slender column of her neck like a fine painting. She was serene and quietly confident as she stood beside Bryce, her hand resting lightly on his arm.

Bryce, normally brash and full of mischief, was dignified and subdued as he escorted her to Christina's small circle. From the way his eyes caressed the girl, it was easy to see that he was in love. Christina smiled warmly and turned to Alison. "Bryce tells me that you come from a shire near Doune. That town is famous for its silver thistle cups and pistols, is it not?"

Alison nodded, her dark eyes twinkling. "It is indeed, ma'am. It has been said that the men of Doune cannot decide whether to shoot each other or toast one another's health."

They laughed and Chris thought wryly that Bryce was no fool. Alison was delightful and exactly what he needed.

The performance resumed, and Renault left Gwendolyn amid a crowd of admiring gentlemen to escort Chris to the family box. As the theater darkened and the actors took their places, Chris felt Kade's warm fingers cover her own as he briefly raised her hand to his lips. Ordinarily that action caused delightful tingles along her spine, but tonight she felt queasy and more than a little ill. The feeling had come and gone for several days. It was annoying, and she willed herself to ignore it.

Later, while their guests lingered over a late buffet, gradually drifting to their rooms, Renault again took her hand.

"Come, I have something to show you," he said.

They walked into the courtyard, gray and still in the moonlight. Kade followed a pathway leading to a narrow stone staircase, beyond which lay a parapet bridge and a very old tower.

"How enchanting," Chris said.

"Yes," Kade replied. "This part of the castle is very old and I have always loved it. My brothers and I played here as children. Jamie was the king and I his trusted first consul." He lit a lantern and drew her inside the tower. It held one huge room with several odd-looking contraptions that were unfamiliar to her.

"What is all this?"

"A few trifles that have filled my leisure."

Chris had seen enough of Gideon's paraphernalia to recognize a laboratory when she saw one. This room held shiny solid objects fashioned of various metals with strange-looking parts that moved. She looked at him inquiringly, and he laughed deeply.

"I have developed a great passion for the gadgets here, and when time permits I tinker with the things you see before you. One day I believe they will prove to be very important—for you and me, as well as everyone else."

She blinked, not quite understanding his words.

"The world is changing, Christina. Ideas are being born which alter the minds of men even as we stand here. Not even the Inquisition in Spain has been able to destroy them completely. Newton, Kepler, and Galileo—the teachings of these men and others like them have begun to change the way we look at the universe."

He motioned toward a far corner of the tower with his hand. "That odd-looking object on the platform is called a telescope. It was invented by a Dutchman named Lippershey in the last century."

Christina walked over to the table on which the

round, long tube lay. Kade followed and in a moment guided a small cylinder to her eye. Peering through the open stone casement at the dark night sky, Christina gasped as she viewed a star that appeared so near that she longed to reach out and touch it. She straightened and looked at him in wonder.

"Was that . . . ?"

"Yes," he answered. "That is what a star really looks like. Before Galileo was condemned to death by the Spanish Inquisition, he charted many heavenly bodies not previously seen. We are still in the process of learning more about them."

Renault picked up a large black cloth and began to cover the strange-looking instrument. Christina found this new side of him fascinating and was eager to know all about what he was doing. "Please do go on . . ."

When Kade finished cloaking the delicate telescope, he looked down at her.

Chris's blue eyes were sparkling with admiration and curiosity. Renault smiled and sat down in a nearby chair. He crossed his long booted legs casually in front of him and regarded her with a mischievous gleam in his eye. "Kiss me first," he said at length.

Christina looked away, annoyed by his mercurial change of mood. It was like him to bargain for a favor, now that her interest was aroused!

Kade chuckled to himself and waited.

She swallowed the hot retort she longed to fling at him. Dutifully, she crossed the room and kissed him lingeringly on the mouth. When she drew away at last, Renault's handsome face had grown serious, and he gathered her into his arms.

"I am going to add a few rooms here and begin some rather serious work. Eventually, much of my time will be spent in this room." He looked down at her, his blue eyes glowing as he gently took her hand. "I could add a suite for you also. Would you like that?"

She looked at him. His aristocratic features were softly illuminated in the lamp's dim light. In a tiny corner of her mind she conceded that he was without question the handsomest man she had ever known. The expression on his face now reminded her of someone, but whom? She lifted a hand and softly traced his features. Why, Barry, of course, as he sat watching Gwendolyn in the gallery.

Renault caught Christina's fingers and pressed his lips into the palm. He planted a warm kiss there that left no doubt regarding the direction of his thoughts, but Chris drew away.

"What is it?" he asked, feeling her withdrawal.

"I'm sorry, Kade. It is just that I do not feel well tonight."

"Why didn't you tell me earlier? Are you ill?"

"No, only a little tired I think. Perhaps it was the voyage that weakened me."

He nodded. Though disappointment was clearly written on his face, he stroked her hair gently and sighed. "Perhaps I had better take you back now."

Once outside her bedroom, she asked, "Will you retire also?"

He shook his head. "I'm going back to the tower to finish some of the work I began this morning. I'll come to say good night later—if you are still awake." He kissed her lightly and left.

Christina watched moodily from her window as Renault strode purposefully off to the tower, his tall form receding in the moonlight. Lately he seemed so accessible, so open. Could she be mistaken in believing that he could not be trusted? After all, it was as much her fault as his that he had wound up in Carlotta's arms. Perhaps it would not be a bad thing to admit that she loved him. It had taken a great effort to keep her feelings locked away inside, one that she had tired of quickly. It seemed pointless now to hide the love she longed to acknowledge.

Chris picked up a cloak to ward off the cool night air and followed the path to the tower, but soon she discovered that someone was walking ahead of her. She stopped in surprise as the female figure scaled the winding stairs and crossed the parapet to the lighted tower.

Christina listened as she heard a knock and Renault answered, pausing in the doorway. Lady Gwendolyn Ellesmere's red hair glimmered in the lamplight. The door closed behind them, and Chris waited, hoping to see Gwendolyn leave.

When the light in the tower flickered and died, Christina's heart sank. She felt a painful mixture of betrayal and remorse—and then as quickly, an uncontrollable anger. With a heartfelt curse, she whirled and walked off into the night.

In the tower above, Kade Renault was damning the draft from the door that had extinguished the room's only light. Several minutes passed before he succeeded in relighting the lamp.

"Now, Gwen, what is it?"

Lady Gwendolyn purred a response and in answer kissed him fully on the mouth.

"I suppose that means you are glad to see me," he said with a wry smile, when Gwendolyn pulled away.

"I would love to show you how much, dearest," she said, moving closer to his lean, inviting warmth. Again, she pressed a pair of eager lips to his mouth—and several seconds slipped by before she noticed his lack of response. She drew away and looked at him in the dim lamplight.

"You always enjoyed my kisses before."

Renault sighed. "Yes, Gwen, but that was some time ago."

"Well, what is wrong?" she asked, an edge spoiling the silky quality of her voice.

"Nothing, but therein lies our problem, sweet. Everything is very right."

"You are speaking in riddles that I do not understand, and if you are joking, Kincaid, I do not find it amusing. Surely you cannot intend to let this marriage change things between us?"

Renault's expression was unreadable in the shadows. "I'm sorry, Gwendolyn."

She stared at him, not believing her ears. No one ever refused her. Heated words rose in her throat, but she thought better of it and swallowed them discreetly. After all, this was Kincaid Renault—not just any recalcitrant lover.

"Don't be, my love. There is yet time to change your mind," she said, smiling seductively. Picking up her cloak, she kissed him a lingering good-bye and stepped lightly through the door, hoping that patience would be swiftly rewarded.

CHAPTER THIRTY-NINE

As summer waned, Renault and Savant selected an elite corps of men and trained them for the confrontation with Garrick. A plan was underfoot, Christina knew, but the exact date of the assault remained a secret. When questioned Kade would say only that there was no need to worry until next spring.

In the meantime it was late August and the hunting season had begun. The earl regularly took parties into the high, scrubby, mountainous plateaus to shoot grouse, pheasant, and partridge. Chris soon discovered, however, that stag hunting was his favorite sport. Kade used the MacVeagh deer stalkers, trained by his brother Jamie and the old earl. They were highly skilled, rugged men of great stamina who knew the moors and forests as well as they knew their own farms.

Christina thought it an exceptionally grueling sport, usually beginning with a long, fatiguing hike over damp, wooded land as the stalkers went over gulleys, along boulders, through dips, hollows, and wet bogs for interminable hours. Kade chided her for her lack of enthusiasm, pointing out that a good hunter needed the lungs of a gazelle, the stamina of a bull, and the eyes of an owl. Christina smiled and said that a man like that would make a very strange-looking animal, indeed.

She stared at him now as he stood in the courtyard, still unaccustomed to seeing him in highland dress. The kilt was returning to Brenkirk after being out of fashion (as well as illegal) for several years. Renault thought it instilled a sense of community and morale to wear it—consequently he donned it whenever he went into the forest to hunt stag. Renault stood before her now, resplendent in plumed bonnet, sporran, kilt, and tartan stockings. He bore a newly bagged pheasant in his hand, and from the pleased expression on his face she knew that there would be venison on the table at MacVeagh for several days.

The hunting party included Guy, Jacques, Kade's brothers, several close friends, and Gwendolyn, who enjoyed hunting as much as the men. Much to Chris's annoyance, Gwendolyn was an excellent shot. Chris left Renault to chat with Marie, who stood across the courtyard, eyeing Jacques's brace of pheasant dubiously.

When her gaze turned again to Renault she found that he was not alone. Lady Gwendolyn stood nearby—as close as convention allowed—with a caressing look in her eye that left no doubt regarding the drift of her thoughts. Chris watched the display for a full five minutes before she could stand it no longer. She crossed the court to intercede and favored Gwendolyn with a look of undiluted hostility. The young woman left with reluctance to join Barry and the other guests in the great hall.

Chris found herself alone with Kade. She was incensed, and the fact that he was looking at her with considerable amusement in his eyes did nothing to improve her disposition.

"Madame, you look piqued. Is something amiss?"

"Must you let that red-haired wench paw you continuously?" she blurted out, frustration getting the better of her control.

Renault grinned wickedly. "Why, my dear, I do believe you are jealous."

"I am not," Chris snapped. "I merely posed a question."

The look on his face showed plainly that he knew better, and she reddened with annoyance. Kade put his hand beneath her chin and gazed intently into her eyes.

"Tell me, have you yet asked yourself *why* you cannot tolerate the sight of Gwendolyn at my side?"

The question was so blunt that Christina was taken aback. She could not think of a plausible excuse. Nothing occurred—save the truth.

Kade could see the warring emotions plainly written on her face. Damn it, he knew she loved him—they both did! But she was too perversely stubborn to admit it. Why did she not simply say what lay in her heart? Did she think him a fool who could not tell when a woman loved him? He watched her as she stood there—beautiful, desirable, all that a man could want. Kade felt a sudden urge to grip her throat and wring from her the words he wanted to hear.

Angrily, he took hold of Christina's shoulders. "I have waited a long time, madame, for the day when you would see fit to unlock the love you guard so jealously in your heart. I have been patient—because for some unknown reason I valued that prize as highly as you and hoped that you might one day give that gift to me of your own free will. But there is a limit, Christina, even to my patience—and you have well exceeded it." Kade's hands left her shoulders, and his eyes were filled with bitter disappointment and anger.

"Be assured, my sweet, that from this day forth, you

have nothing to fear from me. I will not intrude on your privacy. Believe me, there are warmer hearts elsewhere."

He turned and strode toward the laughter and merriment of the hall, leaving Christina alone in the court. Stunned and chagrined at his reaction, she stared open-mouthed at his broad, retreating back. What she had said about Gwendolyn had not been that awful, surely! No, she thought, contemplating his angry words, those feelings have been building for a long time. My remarks merely released the hammer on the pistol.

Reluctantly, she followed him into the great hall, where the hunting party and guests had retired to sup and refresh themselves. The hall was a cavernous room with a vaulted ceiling, filled with long oaken tables and low benches. The rowdy good cheer contrasted sharply with Christina's gloom as she took a seat beside Barry and Veronique. A steward brought thistle cups of ale to ward off the morning chill, which the others emptied readily as they nibbled buttered oak cakes and currant-studded scones.

Christina barely touched the light repast, directing her attention instead to Renault, who stood laughing and drinking at the other end of the hall. Lady Gwendolyn stood nearby with a look of adoration on her pretty face. Christina turned away, finding the sight too upsetting to watch.

CHAPTER FORTY

The following morning Christina was more ill than she'd ever been before. She spent the night alone and upset, unable to erase the memory of Kade's caustic words. She got up, feeling wretched, but the thought of staying in bed seemed worse than the prospect of rising. Kade had not come to her room during the night or bid her good morning, as was his habit. It boded ill, and Chris had been miserably sick for over an hour.

Mara hailed her during breakfast. Chris had become accustomed to the enormous morning meal, which was set out at sunrise and kept warm through midmorning. Guests could drift in and partake at their leisure. Today the sight of food made her ill.

"Well, my dear, when are you going to give the earl an heir?"

Chris blinked in surprise. She'd told no one of her secret.

"How did you know, Mara?"

"I've seen enough pregnancies in my day to know what that green-around-the-gills look means at this time of morning, especially when it comes as regularly as it does with you. That and your close proximity to my nephew these months past can mean only one thing. When are you due, child?"

"It's very early yet," she replied, her voice heavy with fatigue.

"You have told him?"

Christina shook her head.

"Why on earth not?"

"I have wanted to tell him for weeks, but the time never seemed right. Now we have quarreled . . ."

"Ah, that explains why he has been stalking about the house in the devil's own temper. 'Twas more than a little quarrel that put him in the foul mood he's in, I think."

"Oh, Mara, things are in such a tangle between us that I am not sure they can ever be set aright."

"Well, whatever you do child, do not give up the trying. Think of the rest of us suffering along with you."

Chris managed a weak smile.

In the weeks that followed, however, Renault became even more distant and remote. When Chris announced the coming birth he reacted with formal pleasure and a lavish gift, but relations between them remained cold and strained. Not once did he come to Christina's apartments, nor was he present at MacVeagh in the evenings. Day by day, her depression grew.

Chris tried to keep her mind occupied with the reports of their shipping interests in the Caribbean. Andy, Logan, and Joshua were doing so well there that Renault planned to enlarge their existing fleet—but the new acquisitions would have to wait until the border conflict with Morwell was settled.

Janie wrote that Robin was spending most of his time studying with Gideon. The old man was pleased by the boy's progress and seemed as happy with him as a father. That was well, Chris thought, because Gideon had no children of his own. She remembered that he seemed very tired when she visited him in Paris. She wondered if he had been ill. Near the end of her letter Janie gleefully wrote that she was expecting a baby. Chris smiled, wondering which of them would be first to give birth.

CHAPTER FORTY-ONE

Spring brought the border conflict to a head. The Earl of Morwell's estate marched with the properties of two of Kade's peers, the Earl of Rotham and the Baron of Linsbury. Retaliation for Morwell's raids had been delayed until an assurance that these two parties would remain neutral was secured. Baron Linsbury had done them one better by enthusiastically volunteering men for the mission. It seemed that he too had been the victim of Morwell's greed and perfidy.

Kade and his men left on a chilly spring morning in April. Christina was two months from her time and heavy with child. For several weeks they had barely spoken save for polite and formal exchanges, but she felt a familiar tug at her heart as she bid him farewell. Now that she bore his child it was doubly important that he should return unharmed.

He sat carelessly astride his horse, a roguish smile on his face as he waved good-bye to her, looking as if he were off to do nothing more unusual than hunt stag. But Christina knew better. The size of the force and the number of arms the men carried indicated that the conflict would continue for weeks. She watched him ride away with the chilly realization that life would be empty and hollow once he was gone.

With a heavy heart she walked back to MacVeagh and found Marie looking equally dejected.

"It will be a very long spring, won't it, Christina?" Marie said softly.

"Yes," Chris agreed, watching the horses and their

riders as they galloped over the moors, growing smaller in the distance until they finally disappeared altogether. "A very long spring."

As her time drew nearer, Christina felt so enormous that she was certain something was wrong. Mara tried to reassure her, but Chris's anxiety remained. She could think of no one in her experience who had grown to her present size before a birth.

When her time came the whole of MacVeagh was alive with excitement. Mara was at her side, calm and reassuring, for Christina was in agony. The pains were so wrenching that it was all she could do to gasp for breath before another vicelike paroxysm gripped her. She was more frightened than she had ever been in her life. Mara's soothing voice floated above her, instructing, cajoling, while Marie mopped her brow with a blessedly cool cloth. Veronique visited the birthroom, but soon left, finding the ordeal too excruciating to watch.

Just when she thought she would die if she had to endure one more contraction, Christina heard the distant, wailing sound of an infant. From the bottom of a dark pit she heard Mara's delighted voice crying, "It's a lad! MacVeagh has an heir."

Christina opened her eyes. She found that Marie was smiling at her and that in her arms she held a tiny, perfect being with curly raven locks—crying loudly with a strong, lusty voice.

Chris drifted off to sleep and dozed for a short time. She was awakened by a drawing sensation deep within that signaled the beginning of yet another contraction. Mara was at her side, and the old woman was puzzled by the girl's continued discomfort until she realized that Christina was about to birth another babe. Two hours later the second child arrived, also a boy, with hair as dark and soft as the St. Marin night.

It took several weeks for news of the birth of his sons to reach Renault at the border. He was about to conclude a battle that had taken a heavy toll of men and arms, but Morwell was broken and little remained to be done save the formal terms of surrender, which Renault quickly assigned to Savant and La-Croix. Kade was nearly overcome with fatigue, but the happy news renewed his spirit and gave him strength. He ordered a squire to saddle his mount and left with a small party for MacVeagh.

When they reached Brenkirk, Kade went directly to the nursery and found Christina asleep. Mara beamed at him as she sat beside the twins' cradle. The two tiny lads were awake and playing. She smiled knowingly and left them alone.

Tenderly, Kade bent low to look at his sons, who instinctively favored him with a smile. One wee lad was the image of himself—dark blue eyes, black hair and the promise of swarthy good looks to come. The other more closely resembled his mother. Renault was amazed as he beheld his second son. Never in his life had he seen such strange and arresting eyes. They were like a tiger's—green and yet yellow—with fiery flecks of copper and gold near the dark centers.

This one will surely grow to be a warlock, he thought to himself.

Kade crossed the room to the bed and stood looking down at Chris. She looked fragile and lovely in a diaphanous white gown. Gently, he brushed her lips with his. As her eyelids fluttered open he whispered softly, "Madame, I have come to thank you for my sons."

She smiled at him dreamily. In that instant they shared a peaceful moment of happiness.

But as Christina opened her mouth to speak, Renault's face altered. It was as if he suddenly remembered the battle between them. A mask of polite courtesy veiled his handsome features. Kade kissed her hand formally, turned, and left the nursery—leaving Chris to stare in wonder and remorse at his retreating.

CHAPTER FORTY-TWO

Following the earl's return to MacVeagh, life fell into a predictable pattern. Christina spent most of her time in the nursery with the babes, who were christened Alan and James in the days that followed. Each morning Kade visited the nursery for an hour to play with his sons. Then he was off for the day's affairs, and Christina did not see him until the following morning.

It was both painful and frustrating. Especially galling was the fact that she could not dispel the feeling that the trouble between them was of her own doing. She spent the quiet minutes of the day, when the twins slept, wondering how to lessen the tension that lay between them like an invisible wall, but nothing came to mind. She was left with a feeling of depression and sadness.

Chris had all but given up hope when one morning a small crack was made in the ice that lay between them.

Renault stood above the exquisitely carved rosewood cradle as he rocked it gently with a booted foot, smiling at little Alan and Jamie while he tickled their chins. Chris watched the scene, feeling a glowing warmth inside and a sharp pang of regret that all was not well between them. He looked so handsome standing there. The morning sun filtered through the white curtains of the nursery and bathed the black curls on his head with pale gold light. The perfectly proportioned planes of his aristocratic features were relaxed in a gentle smile, and a dimple played at his mouth while he watched Jamie's amusingly futile attempt to catch his father's finger. Kade looked as fit and strong as ever—the battle had done little more than deepen the healthy tan of his skin.

This morning he wore a chamois leather vest and a shirt of fine lawn whose flowing sleeves ended in lace folds at the cuff and collar. His solidly muscled chest provided a disturbing treat for her eyes. Characteristically, he'd neglected to button the garment and the appealing view his open shirt and vest afforded did nothing to aid her composure. Christina sighed in frustration, trying in vain to prevent her gaze from straying to his ridiculously trim waist. The light blue breeches he wore clung to his powerfully muscled legs in a manner that left little to the imagination. She shifted uncomfortably in her chair and forced her attention back to the embroidery before her.

Renault looked up from the cradle and felt a frustration as acute as her own. She looked indecently lovely sitting there behind her embroidery frame, delectable and soft in a gown of pink taffeta trimmed with lace frills, with ruffled sleeves.

Her hair fell heavy and flowing over her shoulders, an errant lock playfully resting on her demure décolletage, teasing his eyes and inviting his touch. He had always been fascinated by the color of her hair, vivid honey shot with lighter strands of wheat. Renault had trouble dragging his eyes away from the gently rounded curve of her bodice as it rose and fell hypnotically with her breath.

Kade felt as defenseless as ever before the pull of Christina's charm. Her effect on him was inescapable and complete, an unswerving attraction that plagued his days and troubled his dreams, leaving him tense and drawn by fatigue with dawn's light. It was physically painful to resist the magnetism she exerted on him, but resist he would until she was prepared to come to terms with her feelings and face the responsibility of their union. Long ago he'd made up his mind that this time nothing less than her avowed love would satisfy him.

Ah, but the waiting was agony! Kade felt a drawing sensation in his loins that made him long for the warmth he knew he would find in her arms. But he would not relent now.

Christina felt his gaze and looked up, unaware that her own thoughts were naked and unmasked in her eyes. Renault caught his breath. Christina's gaze was open, direct, and alight with the fires that burned inside her. Renault felt as if he were seeing her for the first time, the inner being, without guile or subterfuge. It was like being drawn into a clear hidden pool, deep and knowing, disturbing and mysterious, but infinitely desirable. Kade gripped the edge of the cradle as he struggled for control.

As their eyes met, Chris felt the magnetism between them envelop her like a pair of warm arms. She was about to brush aside the embroidery and go to him as she had longed to do these past weeks, but Kade whirled abruptly and left the nursery. Chris remained immobile for long minutes, struggling with the emotions that warred inside her.

That night, Christina found sleep elusive. She listened as Renault prepared to retire in the room adjoining hers. It surprised her that he'd decided to retire early this evening. It had been his habit to leave MacVeagh these weeks past and not return until the wee hours of the morning. She listened until the silence in the next room convinced her that he was asleep.

Chris lay on her back, staring into the moonlit darkness of her bedroom. It was unbearable, knowing that Kade was so near and yet so far beyond her reach. She thought of all that had taken place—the adventure, the painful moments, and, yes, the life they had created between them—and felt that it could not end this way—with each of them wrapped in a cold, unresponsive shell of indifference. Not when she loved him, with all her heart.

Yes, she did love him. No matter what had gone before, she loved him as surely as he was the father of her sons. And she was lonely.

"I have not been willing to admit it, but I feel a terrible emptiness without him," she whispered into the night. "I cannot let this continue without trying—just once—to put aright what has gone amiss. Perhaps it is too late, but I cannot lie here without knowing, one way or the other."

Christina left her bed and pulled a soft blue velvet mantle over the diaphanous nightshift she wore. Quietly, she opened the heavy oak door that separated her bedroom from Kade's. He lay on the bed, breathing evenly in untroubled slumber. He seemed so approachable lying there, the handsome planes of his face relaxed in sleep, no longer remote and threatening.

Chris drew off her robe and sat down beside him, gently, so that he would not awaken. Kade lay on his back, the coverlet flung aside as if he'd turned restlessly in his sleep. Tentatively, almost shyly, Chris placed her hand lightly on the muscular surface of his stomach and drew it gently across his steel-hewn chest.

The soft caress brought no response from Renault. Emboldened by his inviting nearness and feeling more secure now that she knew he was deeply asleep, Chris lay down beside Kade and put an arm softly about him. She remained motionless for a time, content simply with being close after the long weeks of separation.

But she could not lie silently beside him for long. Raising up, she looked down at Kade's handsome face and gently traced his features with one finger. He stirred at her touch, absently brushing aside her hand, but instinctively turning toward the gentle warmth beside him. Christina put her arms about his neck and kissed him softly. Kade's eyes opened slowly. He blinked as he felt her inviting warmth beside him. Chris heard him whisper her name in a deep voice and found herself suddenly molded against him, enclosed in his strong, hard embrace as he pressed hot, urgent kisses over her face, neck, and shoulders.

"Kade, I . . ." she began, but Chris found herself silenced by a deep kiss that stole her breath as well as her thoughts. Kade pressed her into the covers, his heavy, muscular frame pinning her firmly. He kissed her slowly—infusing a rising heat that spread with a swiftness that was startling. Christina's heart soared with the wonderful warmth of their renewed closeness, but a nagging doubt in a small dark corner of her mind would allow her no peace.

It took several minutes and most of her strength to pull sufficiently away from him to whisper, "Kade, what of Gwendolyn Ellesmere?"

"Gwendolyn?" he said in a voice made lower by full-bodied passion. "What do you mean?"

His blue eyes searched her face in the darkness and comprehension lightened his handsome features. "She is little more than a childhood friend—what was between us died long ago."

Christina was in no mood to contradict him, and she accepted the simple explanation willingly. Yet she could not help adding, "And Carlotta?"

Kade brushed a soft lock of hair from her forehead and pressed his lips to her temple before he said with a serious note in his voice, "Had you but given me an indication that you cared, I would never have noticed her. You left me, little one—or have you forgotten that abominable habit of yours?"

She felt a sharp pang of regret for the pain she had caused him. If it were possible to live again the past months, she would have spared him the hurt he'd suffered at her hands. She kissed him in an unspoken apology. Kade watched her intently. She was looking at him with an expression more open and honest than any he had yet seen on her face.

"I'll never leave you again, Kade. I regret the pain I've caused you more than you know. Can we begin again?"

Kade grasped the beautiful face beneath him with his hands as if he wanted to peer into her soul. "Why?" he asked, a sharp edge in his voice. "Tell me! Tell me why you have come to me at last, and be honest this once for both our sakes."

When she replied, her voice was barely audible in the quiet of the room. "Because . . . I love you . . . and I want very much . . . to be with you tonight . . . and always."

Renault smiled at her in the moonlight.

"Tell me again, damn it—I've waited years to hear you say it."

"I love you. Kade . . . I need you. Please . . . won't you put aside what has come before and accept my heart . . . as I long to have yours?"

He looked at the sea-blue eyes, glowing with the warmth of her emotion, and said, "Gladly, my love." Renault pressed a kiss to her lips that held more tenderness than passion. He raised his head and grinned wickedly. "It has taken long enough, sweet, to realize that you are mine, but I vow that after tonight, you'll not again forget."

Kade removed the diaphanous nightgown she wore. She felt the solid, pulsing warmth of him as he pressed her close. His hand traveled down the smooth length of her belly, seeking and finding the softness of her . . . caressing sweetly . . . lingeringly . . . tenderly . . . her body responded with a will of its own. Chris caught her breath and exhaled in a long, shuddering sigh.

Renault fondled her breast with a gentle hand, teasing the nipple with his fingers before his mouth closed warmly on the soft bud. She quivered as she felt the gentle yet demanding pull of his lips and found her fingers entwined magically in his dark hair. She could feel the throbbing warmth of him urging against her, pressing close, slowly robbing her of thought. Kade joined their bodies, thrusting gently and deeply within her, molding her to him as he whispered his love, his breath soft and warm in her ear.

His hands caressed the slender curves and hollows of her body until the pleasure became unbearable. Kade's mouth left her lips and slid slowly to her breasts, making her cry out softly as he filled her with his solid thrusting presence. She could feel her body expanding to accommodate the pulsing hardness that surged inside her; a drawing paroxysm rippled through her as she lay penned beneath him. Her entire body became liquid and flowing—surrounding him with a heat and warmth that fused their souls in a bond as ancient and timeless as love itself.

Kade felt a joy greater than any he'd ever known. There were no walls between them now. As Christina lay trembling beneath him, he sensed that she was truly his at last. His arms tightened reflexively as he felt a boiling inside, as if his entire being were concentrated in the solid length buried deep within her. Kade felt an irresistible surge of love and knew an overwhelming desire to embrace her as closely as possible, to thrust his seed deep within her.

Christina watched as Kade's handsome face became taunt and fixed. His eyes seemed to focus on some point in the future. His body grew rigid and seemed to expand. She strained to meet his powerful thrusts as he filled her with his love.

Later . . . much later . . . she heard Kade's deep, resonant sigh of triumph as he reluctantly left her, and gathered her close in his arms. She could feel the ghost of his presence still and longed to cradle him again, but there was no hurry. A lifetime of love lay ahead of them.

Much later, when coherent thought was possible, Christina whispered softly in Kade's ear, "I've loved you for so long—but I couldn't bring myself to admit it. Do not ask me why. Kade, you won't leave now, will you?"

"I assure you, sweet, that I am possessed of none of

your bad habits. I expect your only complaint will be that you see far too much of me. Rest assured," he added with a smile, "that *I* intend to see a great deal of *you.*"

Chris laughed lightly as he kissed her. She felt a drowsy contentment envelop her as she lay in the warm confinement of his arms. When Kade raised his head at last, Christina curled against his side—warm, happy, and very much in love with the dark corsair who had stolen her heart.

EPILOGUE

In the days that followed Christina and Kade knew a happiness that neither had dreamt possible. The old hurts faded, leaving in their wake a sense of peace, contentment, and love. They drew strength from each other, and neither feared what the future might hold, for they knew they would face it together.

Some weeks later Christina received a letter from Janie telling her that Gideon had died—peacefully in his sleep. Chris sat alone in her bedroom while she read the words, pausing to gaze in silence through an open-latticed window at the purple, sun-brightened moors. She knew a sudden urge to be surrounded by growing things, and she left to find Kade, with the idea of coaxing him into a picnic on the heather with little Alan and Jamie.

A short time later, as she sat on the moor with Kade's head lying in her lap, the twins gurgling happily nearby on a blanket, she told him about Gideon.

"I'm sorry, darling."

"He was a very wise man, Kade. Gideon told me that the only answer I would find was already within me. He said I had only to search inside to find it. And he was right . . ." She related all of the things Gideon had told her.

"He knew you well, didn't he?"

"He loved my mother and said I was very like her."

"As I love you."

"And I love you, just as Gideon said I would. I could not help it in the end."

"Did you try awfully hard not to?"

"Of course," she replied, grinning mischievously at him. "But you were just too wonderful to resist."

"Come here, minx. 'Tis obvious you need kissing for that."

"Very obvious," she smiled.

The warmth of spring filled the air, and the wet earth was redolent with the scent of pine, fir, and spruce. A new day had begun. The world was peaceful at last, and Christina had found her home.

Dell Bestsellers